FRACTURED

The Stealth Stalker

C.S. Dodds

Cedar Hill Book Group

Contents

For my husband.
Thank you for your support and the encouragement
to follow my dream.

PROLOGUE

THE TWO WOMEN LOOKED at one another, knowing they only had two choices—get out now or die. FBI Special Agent Cameron Chadwick nodded at the young woman next to her, and with that, Lisa Allen raised a long leg, knee to chest, and rammed her foot into the cellar door. The old pinewood cracked and split. Shoulders to the dry, worn wood, they broke through the rest of the way and then fell onto the floor of the old house. The sound of the door breaking echoed through the emptiness. Dust rose, reflecting the faint early morning sun like glitter in a snow globe.

They examined each other with slight smiles of satisfaction that they were almost free. Cameron rested on all fours, weak from the four days of captivity and abuse in the dank, dark, cavernous cellar. Or was it five? Six? In the darkness, time was fluid.

Lisa pushed herself up, held out her hand to her new ally, and helped her stand. She had told Cameron she was a student at the University of Georgia and had been walking back to her off-campus apartment after an evening class when a man grabbed her and stuck a needle into her arm. Everything had faded to dark like she was passing out. When she'd awakened, she was lying on a dirt floor in front of Cameron. That was at least three days ago.

"It stinks in here." The girl frowned, catching her breath.

Cameron stood, panting from the exertion of breaking the door open. Under different circumstances—*normal* circumstances—the old door wouldn't have challenged her. She leaned against the cool wall of the deserted house for support, pressed her lips together, and quickly took a whiff of the air. "Mildew." The word blew out of her with a sputter of coughs. When the man in black had shoved her down the wooden stairs and into the dark abyss below, the stench of mold fumes had overpowered her. Her body had convulsed into a coughing fit as she lay in a drug-induced fog on the dirt floor. Over the last several days, as her strength deteriorated, the forceful spasms had turned into feeble wheezes.

They looked around the deserted farmhouse. The cellar door they had just emerged from was under a staircase and they now stood in a short hallway between the front of the house and a kitchen. Lisa rushed for the kitchen door, but it was locked from the outside. She ran from room to room, kitchen to dining room to living room, and ended up at the base of the stairs that led to the second floor. She'd gone in a circle. To her left stood Cameron still braced against the wall, a parlor in front of her and to her right, the front door. Lisa rushed toward it as Cameron limped behind. Eager to be free before their captor returned, they tugged at the door and turned locks but to no avail. The warped wooden door with its peeling paint, their only pathway to freedom, was nailed shut. It clung to its frame, unmoved, secured permanently into place, no matter how much they pushed and pulled and kicked at it.

Turning and leaning against the door, Cameron scanned the abandoned old house. Long planks nailed into the walls covered the windows, leaving only slits of light escaping between them that hinted at the sunrise on the other side. "Are the windows in the other rooms also boarded up?" she asked Lisa.

"Yes. What are we going to do?" Lisa replied in a shaky voice.

Desperation crept its way into Cameron's heart and mind. *We need to get out of here now.* She nodded at the picture window in the parlor. "Come on," she said. "We'll pry the boards loose and get the hell out of here."

Lisa nodded in agreement and followed Cameron to the nearest window. The two set out to work on the large, two-by-eight oak planks covering their escape route. Torture and starvation had left them in desperate shape, but their battered bodies felt no pain as they worked feverishly to loosen the lumber from the window frame. They pulled, pushed, and kicked, but the wooden boards wouldn't budge.

"We have to find another way. He'll be back soon," Lisa said as tears rimmed her eyes. She knew when the man in black finally came back he would kill her, because he'd told her so, and so did Cameron.

"We need something to shove between the wall and the board," Cameron said, breathing heavily. Her week had started with the promise of closing a case and catching a killer, before life had taken such a terrible turn. Exhausted, broken, and now with freedom so close, she had no choice but to save herself and her young friend. It was her fault he'd kidnapped Lisa. Had she only begged for her life the way he'd demanded her to…

Lisa said, "Look," and pointed to a fireplace in the next room, and on the floor, a gift from God—a black iron fire poker covered in cobwebs and dirt. She darted to it like a young gazelle leaping with ease, her bare feet leaving one-dimensional prints on the dusty pine parquet.

This was the first time Cameron had caught a good look at the woman abducted, tortured, and used as an instrument to break her. She observed with envy as the lithe, youthful body bounded across the room effortlessly. Her own body ached from just standing, watching. Lisa was taller than Cameron by a mere inch, athletic-looking and pale, too pale. She wore a University of Georgia Women's Soccer sweatshirt with "Allen" and the number twelve emblazoned across the back. The school's mascot bulldog scowled on the front, as if someone had stolen his favorite chew toy. A jagged tear in her jeans revealed a raw burn, like fresh meat, oozing with infection and caked with dirt and blood, courtesy of their kidnapper. Her dirty, long dark hair hung limp around her face and over her shoulders. Violet, green, and yellow splotches of puffy skin surrounded a swollen, split lip smeared with dry blood from where the man in black had hit her in the face with a loose brick. Her bright blue eyes were watery with fear but filled with determination.

Lisa gripped the poker tightly and jammed the tip against the wall to pry the board away, but she couldn't force the blunt, narrowed end under the wooden plank. Terrified and desperate, she screamed, "Fuck this!" She lifted the iron rod over her head and slammed it into the wall, causing chunks of old, yellowing plaster to fall to the floor.

Cameron croaked, "Do it again!"

Adrenaline perked in Lisa's veins. She smashed the rod repeatedly into the plaster, her muscles burning as her dehydrated body went into overdrive. With the joists exposed, she'd created enough space to jimmy the poker under the plank. She used the stud as leverage and pushed the poker with the full weight of her body, grunting at the effort she put into freeing the board from the wall behind.

"Hurry! Hurry!" Cameron urged.

Inch by inch, she separated the heavy oak from the window until her end fell to the ground, twisting the nails at the other end and loosening their grip on the wall.

Cameron gave the plank a good jerk, jumping back as it crashed to the floor. Both women froze at first because of the clatter resonating through the house, but then Cameron swatted at the air, choking as a plume of shiny dust particles filled her dry throat.

Through the gap, they could see outside. Dewy, high grass sparkled in the rising sun, a cardinal darted past in a red streak, and 200 yards away, a dirt road cut through the woods.

They tugged at the next board as if flames consumed the house. One more fell to the floor. One more, and they could break the window and run to the roadway. They pulled and strained, and wood splintered and pierced their fingertips, but the plank didn't budge. Lisa grabbed the poker again and swung hard, breaking chunks of chalky plaster from the wall and exposing the joists beneath. She once again forced the rod between the wooden barrier and the beam of the house, pushing until it loosened enough to pry free.

They were working frantically to loosen the other end when a noise from behind startled them. They spun around simultaneously. The man in black was standing in the doorway. The man Cameron had described as a serial killer. The man who had imprisoned them in a filthy cellar and tortured them. The man they would attack in a final fight for their lives.

"No," Lisa whispered as her body shook.

Cameron prayed the girl remembered her words from earlier that morning. *"If he gets back before we're gone,"* she'd cautioned when they were freeing themselves in the cellar, *"you have to fight. Punch or kick him in the throat and the groin. The soft parts. I know you're afraid, terrified, but you can't freeze. Remember to fight. It's your life on the line. Do you understand?"* She'd explained to the terrified college girl that she was FBI and the man in black was known as the J-Bird, a serial killer she'd been hunting. It had been difficult for her to speak at all after he'd choked her into unconsciousness, bruising her larynx and neck. She'd awakened to Lisa whimpering at her feet and begging the man for her life.

Now, as Lisa faced the man in black again, trembling and gripping the iron rod of the poker like a baseball bat, she stood frozen in fear. Tears welled and slipped over her bruised cheeks.

Cameron read the terror in Lisa's eyes and said in a low, even tone, "Lisa, you've got this. *We've* got this." She shifted her aching body into a fighter's stance as Lisa met her eyes. The FBI agent gave a nod to the strong, young woman next to her who nodded back. Cameron recognized the fear wash from Lisa's face as it morphed into rage and the will to live as if a switch had flipped in Lisa's brain.

Lisa let out a harrowing, guttural scream and lunged at the man in black with the fire poker hoisted overhead. It happened so quickly, she took the man by surprise. He dropped the bag in his hand and raised his arms in self-defense, but she didn't hit him with the iron rod at first. Using the strength of her long, muscular legs that had carried her to soccer championships throughout high school and college, she plunged her foot into his gut and knocked him to the ground. Then she stood over him, as he'd stood over her for three terrifying days, and used her position to her advantage. Lisa swung the iron poker, striking the back of his head. The impact of metal to flesh split his scalp open and a spray of bright red blood splattered the floor.

The J-Bird struggled to kneel, pressing a palm to the back of his head as she kicked him again. She pulled her foot back for a third blow, but as it came his way, he seized and twisted it, causing her to fall backward.

Cameron swept in, reaching for the poker laying on the floor next to Lisa. The beating heart in her own body was the only thing she could hear. Her heart pounded and the blood roared in her ears. *Whoosh, thump, whoosh, thump.* Her eyes never left the man in black as she deftly snatched the firestick from the floor and swung it like a golf club, catching him in the chin. The man in black screamed out. The two women attacked, kicking and hitting him until he lay barely conscious, curled in a fetal position, with a small pool of blood forming next to his head.

Cameron gripped her younger counterpart by the arm to stop her. "Let's go," she shouted, nodding at the window.

Lisa Allen took one last swipe at her kidnapper, grabbed the fire poker, and swung hard at the now exposed plate-glass, shattering it down to the lawn below. The twosome jumped out of the opening, onto the glass-spattered grass.

"Run, Cameron! Run!" Lisa shrieked as she seized Cameron by the arm, dragging her on the sharp, wet grass.

Cameron scrambled to her feet. The pair half-limped, half-ran, holding each other up as they headed toward the road and their freedom.

The man in black pulled himself up to his knees and screamed after them, "You should have killed me! I will hunt you forever...until I *kill* you! Do you hear me? Until. I. *Kill*. You! You will never be free of me. Not until you are both dead!"

The voice in Cameron's head agreed, *"He's right. You should have killed him."*

CHAPTER 1

The person branded by the police as the Stealth Stalker leaned against a US postal box and surveyed the surrounding area.

Taxis jockeyed for position on the road with the occasional blare of a horn. A garlicky breeze wafted from a nearby restaurant. Residents navigated around tourists who strolled slowly, relishing the last remaining warm summer nights in early September. The city was not a favorite place. Between the noise, the traffic, and the dead rat in the street, Stealth longed for home.

Everything seems to slow down this time of the year, Stealth mused as people wandered past. *No one wants to rush through the last beautiful days of summer.*

Across the street stood the Fairchild Nursing and Convalescent Home—the center of Stealth's attention. A multitude of windows lit from within gave the looming, red brick building an eerie glow. Even at the late hour, visitors still arrived and departed through the double front doors covered by a maroon awning stretching out to the sidewalk. Mostly they departed, some with happy demeanors, some grim.

A woman inside fit the description of a past adversary Stealth was determined to see as dead as the rat. Stealth waited patiently for the woman to appear while ruminating about their past. She was law enforcement and had tried to catch the killer in the past. When someone nearly murdered her a few months ago, Stealth came to life. If she would die, it would be at the hands of her old nemesis, not a psychopathic rapist. The promise, or threat, made over ten years ago was about to come to fruition. They had hunted one another with futility, and the game had grown tiresome. Neither could live any longer with the threat of the other hanging over their heads. They both needed their freedom from the impending danger of the other. One of them had to go.

In the dark of night, Stealth had made mistakes and the wrong woman had died. The hunt and the kill were still enjoyable, but a letdown. Tonight would be different. Stealth fingered the cold steel of a concealed hunting knife and surmised, *It was her fault those women died. If she hadn't moved to this city, they would all be just fine, living life as usual.*

Dressed in black jeans, a black collared shirt, and a lightweight black jacket with deep pockets, the camouflage of a night predator, Stealth watched the front entrance of the nursing home. As the name Stealth Stalker aptly implied, a little stalking brought some much-needed information, and Stealth had learned tonight's quarry visited the Fairchild twice a week at the same time.

The prey exited the nursing home. A tinge of excitement sparked within Stealth. She looked about the right age and height from a distance. Her shiny brown hair cut into a lob framed her fair face, swaying slightly as she descended the stairs. Washed out jeans touched the ground, making it hard to view the heel height of her shoes. A fitted, dark-colored, V-neck shirt, possibly navy or black, flaunted her lean, athletic build. A leather tote straddled her shoulder. She looked around, cautious like a fox exiting its den and surveying her kingdom, deciding which way to travel.

Stealth pretended to make a phone call while willing her along in thought. *Cross the street, sweetheart. Come on, cross the street.*

She turned to her right and walked in the opposite direction of Stealth. *Damn it! Now I have to play catch up.*

Stealth hurried down the street, pretending to look at the cellphone but keeping an eye focused on the target.

The woman took a right turn down the next street.

Stealth crossed the road while dodging a cab and a minivan, maneuvered around annoying pedestrians, and quickened the pace to close the gap.

A couple straggled arm in arm across the way before entering a small apartment building. The busy avenue with its restaurants, shops, and late-night ramblers disappeared as the woman's path took her into a residential neighborhood. Her perfume lingered in the air, an unfamiliar scent of citrus and roses. Her hair was styled a little shorter than ten years ago, but it made no difference. The feet were all that mattered...they would confirm her identity.

Right on her heels, Stealth relished the growing excitement, not quite able to control the urge to smile.

She glanced back at the stranger walking in stride with her.

Their eyes met.

She smiled. "Nice night, huh?" she asked, turning slightly.

"Beautiful."

"You look familiar. Have we met somewhere?"

"I don't think so. I spend a lot of time at Fairchild Nursing Home, and I don't get out much."

"Hey, I was just there," she said, seemingly happy they had something in common.

"Really? My mother is a resident there."

"My dad is recovering from a stroke there. Hopefully, he'll be coming home soon." She glanced at the stranger again. "You're not from around here, are you? I detect a southern accent."

"Aren't you clever? Georgia is my home."

Up ahead, an alley perfect for privacy came into view. Stealth surveyed the street, finding no one behind and no one across. Curling a hand around the knife, the killer grabbed the target's elbow with one hand, her waist with the other, and steered her into the darkness. "We can finish our conversation here."

"Hey, what are you doing? Stop! I don't like alleys. They scare me, especially at—"

The thrust of the blade was swift. She crumpled to her knees.

Stealth gripped her around the shoulders with a free hand and moved her to the ground. The sharp steel of the knife passed smoothly through her flesh and with little resistance from what was a navy-colored t-shirt. She looked up, her mouth moving as she tried to speak, and then nothing. Her eyelids drooped, and her breath stopped. Stealth pulled the knife free, cleaning it on the woman's leg.

"Now, let's see if you are who I hope you are." Stealth moved to her feet and removed her checkered Vans and socks. A small flashlight retrieved from a pocket shed light onto the soles of her feet.

Anger welled up at the sight of yet another failure. Stealth took the knife and slashed at her clothing, releasing fury with every cut.

Why, why, why couldn't she have been the one?

CHAPTER 2

RUNNING LATE, CAMERON COOPER couldn't find her shoes. She knelt next to the king-size bed and peered beneath, spotting their red leather soles along with a missing sweater and enough dust bunnies to start a colony. She grabbed the shoes, slipped them on, and checked her reflection in the oversized, wood-framed mirror clinging to the wall. A blonde tendril of hair jutted out of place. She fingered it back in line, smoothed her black pencil skirt, and did one last check over.

Cameron didn't want the detective to think she was sloppy. Sloppy clothes, sloppy work. It was important to be sharp the first day on the job.

She moved through her apartment, bedroom to living room to kitchen, searching for her bag. At the kitchen counter, she found it hanging like a giant black spider on the back of a counter stool. She slung it over her shoulder, took one last sip of coffee while being careful not to dribble on her white silk blouse, and placed the mug in the stainless-steel kitchen sink. Draping a black leather jacket over her shoulders, she headed for the door. As Cameron glanced around to make sure nothing was burning, she realized her apartment needed a good cleaning.

Perhaps tonight.

Anxiety grew as she pressed the elevator button and checked the time on her cell phone. *I'm going to be late. Shit!*

The elevator came after only a few seconds but crawled to a stop before opening to her. Cameron entered the small, wood-paneled box and pressed the L button, then leaned back as the floor numbers passed. The car stopped at six. Her neighbor, Mrs. Hutch, took her time entering.

Damn it! Hurry up.

In her arms, Mrs. Hutch carried her Yorkie, Lovey Howl. "Good morning." Mrs. Hutch nodded and then looked down at Lovey, who growled, showing off her tiny teeth to Cameron.

"Morning," Cameron said.

Lovey shot off one annoying bark, followed by another soft growl.

"Right back at you, Lovey."

"*Mrs. Howl* is only saying hello in her own way," Mrs. Hutch said as she patted the beast on the head.

Cameron had angered the old lady but didn't have time to care. The elevator doors separated, and instead of politely waiting for the two old bitches to get off, she moved past them. Over her shoulder, she tossed Mrs. Hutch an empty apology, explaining she was late for an appointment.

As Cam pushed through the door of the apartment building, she overheard Mrs. Hutch complaining to Lovey about her. Spotting the yellow cab she'd called waiting at the entrance, she slipped in, gave the driver the address, and as he pulled away, Mrs. Hutch and Lovey shuffled out the door. Cameron realized if she wasn't careful, she would be Mrs. Hutch carrying her own Lovey in forty years.

Her mind turned toward the morning agenda. She was meeting with Detective Hunter Finnegan to discuss an ongoing case. They had met a few months earlier when her former partner with the FBI, Jeff Alexander, recommended her to him. Cameron had been consulting at another police precinct when she mentioned to Jeff that she needed more work, so he'd set up the intro with Hunter Finnegan, his old college roommate. She remembered meeting the handsome detective and how he had appeared annoyed with her. Now he'd called her to consult on a possible serial killer.

Her last case as an FBI analyst had involved a serial killer. One serial killer too many. She'd quit the FBI, moved out of Georgia, and floated for ten years. She'd meant it to be a brief hiatus, but years sometimes passed without notice.

Tired of running, hiding, evading, she'd settled down in New York City, one measly piece of hay in a mountainous haystack. She'd had no clue what she would do for work, to occupy her time, to avoid going mad from boredom, but then she'd read in the newspaper about a serial-rapist destroying lives on the West Side. Confident she could help, she'd visited the police station and offered her services as a consultant. Investigating the rapist case exhilarated and terrified her, but she'd enjoyed getting back to work and facing the demons nipping at her heels.

NYPD Special Consultant Dr. Cameron Cooper interviewed the victims, heard their stories, saw their bruises. The tears, the heartache, and the pain in their eyes were hard to forget in the quiet of her home. The process left her exhausted, and many nights, she suffered from stress-induced migraines, but catching the son-of-a-bitch made the stress and headaches worthwhile. She felt proud of herself.

A serial killer challenged her on a different level. The last one she'd pursued had been a dark and twisted man, a man who had promised she would never be free of him. He'd left his mark on her, both physically and mentally. He haunted her dreams...his threat to hunt her until she was dead always loomed in the back of her mind.

She gazed out the window of the cab, observing the people busy in their own lives and caught up in their own thoughts, ignoring the people in front of them. They passed a young woman with her daughter walking down the sidewalk. The toddler held a stuffed toy puppy in one hand while the other hand gripped her mother's. She cradled the brown, fluffy puppy with love and kissed it on its head.

The kiss triggered Cameron's memory, taking her back to a warm February in Georgia when a little girl about this girl's age, Adeline Adair, had disappeared. They needed one break, an eyewitness or the sighting of a child out of place. Cameron recalled the excitement in the sheriff's voice when he'd called the team and told them to meet him at the Pridgen Farm on the Old Country Road. Adeline had been missing for 37 hours and time was running out.

That day, it had been an old coon hound named Ralph that had given them the break they needed. He'd howled as the teams of people jumped out of vehicles in front of him, and Mary Pridgen, the dog's owner, had looked shocked. She'd called the sheriff to evict a trespasser and didn't expect he needed an army to do it. Mary explained to them that Ralph kept howling all day, so she'd gone to investigate. Up ahead on the dirt trail that ran through their property sat six old slave shacks. The Pridgens had converted them into living quarters for the seasonal help that came their way in the spring and summer. No one should have been living in them, yet somebody was in the first of the six little cabins.

Cameron had braced herself for yet another grim discovery. She didn't want to go in. She didn't want to see the remains of a kid. A child dying in any circumstances was hard, but seeing a child die like that, at the hands of a psychopath, had become more than she could bear. She wished that, just once, they would arrive before it was too late.

Dread had run through Cameron when she entered the cabin. She'd turned to her left first, spotting a small, yellow sweater folded on a plastic chair. Her stomach clenched as her heart raced in her chest. To her right stood a closed door. She took a breath, turned the doorknob, and pushed it. In the darkened room, a torn and dirty mattress rested on the floor. On it lay Adeline, so very still. Cam would never forget how she'd felt at that moment. She didn't even know this child and yet her heart had ached, begging her to leave before she verified for sure Adeline was dead. She holstered her gun and knelt next to the child. A loud sigh escaped her as she stroked the little girl's hair. Then she'd trailed her fingers down her neck, searching for a pulse.

Adeline had moaned and her eyes fluttered. She sat up with a furrowed brow, asking Cameron who she was. Cameron had scooped Adeline up in her arms, squeezed her tight to her, and told her she was the happiest person on the planet because she'd been looking for her and found her! And she was okay. She was more than okay. She was untouched by her kidnapper. They had arrived in time. They had gotten the miracle that day. What she'd imagined would be another tragedy had turned out to have a happy ending. Cameron would never forget the relieved and grateful parents kneeling in the dirt, crying and hugging little Adeline Adair.

The taxi slammed to a stop at a red light, jolting Cameron out of her thoughts. The girl with her stuffed puppy was blocks away. The images in her mind of rural Georgia and the Adair family were erased by the towering brick and mortar buildings and the congested traffic of urban life. She was back in New York City, in a dirty cab, and at the cusp of the hunt for a serial killer.

Searching for a missing person was a different scenario than hunting for a maniac killer. Cameron hated serial killers. Most were quirky, with an extensive history of violence, abuse, and isolation. The lack of empathy coupled with an extraordinary amount of patience troubled her the most. Cameron was the opposite—overly empathetic and impatient.

She had done her research on the alleged serial killer the police called the Stealth Stalker. He was different from the last killer she had pursued, Jason Julius Jonette, aka the J-Bird. Different but the same. The two monsters were different in their methodology but the same in the end results: someone had died. Profiling a serial killer was a ticking time bomb puzzle. People's lives were on the line. From what she'd gathered from newspaper stories, there were three murders that could possibly be connected, but there could be more. There could always be more.

CHAPTER 3

The cab pulled up in front of the police station, an old brick building four stories high, painted a fading white and gray. It was time for Cameron to reacquaint herself with Detective Finnegan. Perhaps this time he'd be more interested in what she had to say. She paid the driver and hurried up the front steps. Engraved in gold numbers, the year 1881 gleamed on a marble marker over the double-wide doorway. She checked her phone. She'd made it at 8:59, with one minute to spare.

Since she'd been to this precinct a couple of months earlier when initially meeting with Detective Finnegan, she knew what the security procedures were once inside. She entered onto the main floor of the police building, which had a modern but dated aura. Yellowing, oversized marble tiles original to the building covered the expanse of the floor. The ceilings stretched high above her, creating an echo chamber. It seemed as if voices and sounds came at her from every direction. Front and center sat a high wooden desk and, behind it, a middle-aged officer with white temples, a pink face, and a pair of half readers perched at the tip of his nose. Directly behind him were wide staircases going up and down. Cameron passed through the security gate where two younger officers stood ready to pounce on anyone who caused the alarm to blare. She placed her bag on a conveyor belt where a short, plump female officer checked its contents on a screen. After clearing security, she presented the desk officer with her identification and explained that she was meeting with Detective Hunter Finnegan. The officer at the desk handed her a visitor's pass and gave her directions to the third floor.

The precinct swarmed with uniformed cops, department employees, prisoners in transport, people filing reports. She'd just become one more ant in a very active colony.

Cameron climbed the wooden stairs with a tight grip on the banister, her heels clicking with every step. Catching her transparent reflection in a window as she climbed, she checked herself. She walked through the doors on the third floor into a wide-open room with high ceilings, windows stretching almost from floor to ceiling, and hallways to her left and right. Four rows of gray metal desks ran ten deep. The place buzzed with phones ringing and voices talking, shouting, and laughing. A typical office, except most of the employees had guns. The officer downstairs had told her Detective Finnegan sat at the last desk on the left, next to the window.

Cameron walked toward the back of the room with only a glance from one or two people. Nobody seemed to mind a stranger in their midst.

Several officers were gathered around the last desk, listening intently to a broad-shouldered man, fortyish, sitting in a swivel chair and holding court. His light brown hair formed thick waves on top, tapering into a close crop, and his pale green eyes crinkled at the corners. He wore a dress shirt, no tie, and sleeves rolled up to his elbows. All at once, his audience burst out in laughter, and Cameron realized they weren't talking crime but listening to a story, a funny one at that. Hearing them laughing brought a smile to her lips, and when Detective Finnegan glanced up, he met with Cameron's smiling face.

His own smile faded as he said, "Can I help you, miss?"

Cameron's face warmed. "Yes, uh, hello. Detective Finnegan, I'm Dr. Cameron Cooper. We met a few months ago and spoke on the phone yesterday?"

The man behind the desk stood and stretched out a long arm toward her. "Yes, Dr. Cooper, I remember our meeting. Nice to see you again." His hand encased hers as if it were child-sized. Easily six-four, he towered over the other officers and herself. "Dr. Cooper," he said, giving Cameron the once over. "Let me introduce you to my team. This is Detective Vince

Barone." He pointed at a man with deep-set eyes no taller than herself. "This is Detective Bobby Murphy, Detective Glen Levine, and Detective Rhonda Saintil."

They shook hands with Cameron and stood sizing her up as she sized them up.

Murphy appeared the most casual in jeans and a T-shirt. He was of average height and build, but his smile struck her. He was genuinely happy to meet her. If he were a dog, his tail would have been swinging wildly behind him.

Levine appeared polished in a tailored navy suit and designer shoes. His bald head shone under the fluorescent lights in the room. Round, hazel eyes swept her from dark roots to her own designer shoes. His aura went beyond professional to superior. Not friendly, merely well-mannered. Cameron concluded he came from money or wanted people to think he did.

Rhonda Saintil wore long sleeves on a warm day and didn't make eye contact comfortably. Her glance was forced and fleeting, her hand-shake quick and light. Dark brown hair hung close to a face with a little too much concealer under the left eye. She concealed more about herself than a little make-up could hide. The arms she kept covered told the story. Cameron didn't think drugs, that would be too hard to hide from her coworkers. Maybe domestic abuse or something as simple as eczema.

Barone was friendly and loud. He enjoyed being heard, drawing atten-tion to himself. A tight-fitting shirt clung to his muscular body. A gym rat, and proud of it—proud of everything about himself. He squeezed Cam's hand to the point of pain in a childish power play. His black, curly hair was crisp with product, and Cam was sure he dyed his goatee to match as silver roots shone like tiny beacons nestled next to his skin.

Her attention went back to Finnegan. When their eyes locked again, he appeared amused.

"Dr. Cooper is here to consult on our alleged serial killer," Finnegan started. "She's an expert in criminal psychology and a former FBI analyst." His eyes narrowed as he studied her, and then, as if to dismiss whatever he was thinking, he shook his head and continued. "We will share everything we have so far with Dr. Cooper and keep her informed of any updates. I'll start now, so you guys...back to work." He made a shooing motion with his hand as the group dispersed, giving Cam the side-eye.

Detective Finnegan picked up a stack of folders from his desk and tapped them into a neat pile in his hands. "Let's go into the back office where we'll have more room to spread out the evidence," he said, nodding to a room ten feet behind his desk. "We can discuss the case without interruption or distraction in there."

She followed him into the small space housing another gray metal desk, three chairs with worn, black vinyl covers, and a window facing the squad room. The small quarters made Cameron claustrophobic.

He offered her a chair and took the one opposite of her, then tapped a finger on his lips before saying, "Dr. Cooper, I understand it's been a while since you've worked a case like this. True?"

"Yes, a little over ten years." Cameron grew more uncomfortable. "But for the last few months, I worked on a case involving a serial rapist in Chelsea, which just closed. The lead detective was Gina Rossi. I'm sure she'd provide a reference if you need one."

"I already spoke to Detective Rossi. She gave you an excellent review. However, Jeff Alexander told me your last case with him, also a serial killer, had complications and left you somewhat traumatized, leading to your decision to leave the FBI. He said you didn't want to engage with the horrific crimes your unit investigated anymore. I want to be upfront with you, Doctor. The murders are ugly. You need to understand what you're getting yourself into."

"I appreciate your concern and your honesty, Detective, and yes, I left the bureau because I'd had enough, but that was a long time ago. I've had a lot of time to process everything that happened and to heal. I want to help, and I'm confident I will. I assure you I'm fine and will be nothing but professional in my assessment of your case." *Is he trying to protect me, or is he a patronizing jerk? And what the hell did Jeff tell him?*

"Good to know, Dr. Cooper. Jeff's recommendation means a lot to me. He's the reason I called you, but I needed to ask for peace of mind. You understand, don't you?"

"Yes, of course. I would've done the same." *Maybe.*

"I guess if we solve this case working together, we'll never hear the end of it from Agent Alexander. He'll tell everyone he solved the case by introducing us." He smiled, revealing straight, even teeth and an elongated dimple on the right.

"Yeah, sounds like Jeff." Cameron forced a tight-lipped grin as a sign of accord and brushed a non-existent hair from her face. She noted the detective's posture was relaxed in his chair. He was self-confident in what he was doing and didn't feel a need to over-exercise his authority with her. It was a good sign.

"Let's start, okay?" Detective Finnegan moved to the seat next to Cameron and plopped a thick file on the desk. "First off, the chief of detectives assigned me to put together this special task force to catch this guy. I handpicked each one of those detectives. They are, in my opinion, the best of the best. The other precincts in the area have similar groups. The chief wants this guy stopped and has made the case our team's top priority."

Cameron nodded in understanding.

He turned the cover of the manila folder, taking photos and papers out and spreading them in front of her. The first picture was a headshot of a youthful woman. He held the image in his long fingers and studied it for a moment, then held the photo up for Cameron to see. "This is Jennie Saunders—a street cop at another station. Thirty-five and a mother of one. Divorced. Her kid took this picture a few days before she died." He handed her the photo.

Jennie had dark brown hair, blue eyes, and a beautiful smile with a deep dimple on either side. A beauty mark sat left to the corner of her mouth.

"How many victims are there?" Cam asked.

"Three," he said, not looking up. "Number one, Jennie Saunders." He nodded at the photo Cameron held. "Number two, Linda Birch." He held up a picture of a pretty, forty-something-year-old woman with light brown hair to her shoulders, pale blue eyes, and a smattering of freckles crossing her nose. Tossing the image in front of Cameron, he held up another photo. "And Number three, Amy Larsen." He placed the picture on top of the last one.

A slightly younger brunette, hazel eyes, her arms around the neck of a nice-looking man. She was in great shape, had an athletic build, a dazzling smile, and appeared so happy in the photo that Cam imagined she had a perfect life. Until she didn't. "What makes you think this is the same individual?" she asked.

Detective Finnegan arranged the photos next to one another. The women's physical similarities were striking. "All three victims are brunettes with blue, green, or hazel eyes. They're all about the same height and build. They look enough alike to be related. Their murders are identical. A knife in the gut, straight through the abdominal aorta."

As Cameron picked up the next photo, the door opened.

Rhonda Saintil glanced at Cameron and then directed her words at Finnegan. "We have another one." Her flat voice showed no emotion. She turned and walked away.

Finnegan jumped up, gathering the papers and folders. "Damn it! Come on, let's go. You're about to be thrown into the lion's den." He gave Cameron a quick nod as he straightened and closed each file, stacking them together and then tapping them lightly on the table as an extra measure of orderliness. He grasped the folders firmly as if they could suddenly implode and scatter themselves like confetti without his restraint and then hurried from the little office.

Cameron followed, observing as he yanked open one of the oversized, metal filing cabinets next to his desk and placed the folders carefully inside another folder labeled "Stealth Stalker Killer." The files were meticulous, each one color coded and labeled with perfect penmanship.

"Hey! Who put a green folder in with the blue?" he shouted over his shoulder and moved the offending file to its correct spot in the drawer. And then under his breath, "Is it really that hard to put the files back where they belong?" He closed and locked the drawer.

Cameron glanced around at the team as heads shook and shoulders shrugged. "Uh, Detective, I noticed your file says Stealth Stalker Killer. What does that mean?"

"We have a theory about this guy. The victims were all employees of the NYPD. We think he hides in plain sight and stalks our personnel to pick out his next victim. You know, Stealth Stalker."

She shook her head. "I'm afraid you lost me."

He laughed an easy laugh that embarrassed her.

Cameron, not sure why, suddenly felt foolish.

"Stealth Stalker comes from a popular video game. Murphy and his kid play it together. Stealth Stalker refers to how inconspicuous an assassin in the game remains in a public place. When we decided this guy was watching us in our own environment, Murphy used the term and it stuck," Detective Finnegan said before weaving his way through the room, past the other officers.

Cameron tailed him down the stairs and out of the building, trying her best to keep up with his long-legged stride, a feat not easily achieved in her high heels. *Stupid,* she thought. *I should've known better than to wear these shoes in the first place!*

"Come on. You can ride with us." He jumped into the front seat of a black SUV with shiny silver hubcaps that matched the trim and bumpers.

So much for chivalry. Cameron opened the back door and climbed in like a billy goat climbing a mountain. *Damn, I never realized how high up these things are.*

Glen Levine sat behind the wheel of what had to be his personal vehicle. The interior mirrored him—meticulous and well-dressed in soft, black leather, dark brown mahogany trim, and custom floor mats. The radio, volume low, played classical music.

Figures. We get it, Levine, you like the finer things in life.

"Buckle up," Levine said, looking at Cameron in the rearview mirror. "We don't want you getting tossed around back there." He threw his blue light on the dashboard and pulled out, smooth but fast.

The trip to the scene was quicker than Cameron had expected. The murder had happened within five minutes of their police station. *Brazen.*

Levine pulled up to the bright yellow police tape blocking an alleyway. Recognizing the car, the responding officers cleared the way. The two men hopped out with ease as a stocky police officer hurried over to them.

Cameron struggled to undo her seat belt as the detectives were briefed. Once free, she exited the car with caution out of fear she might break a leg. She hurried over to the detectives as the uniformed cops gave her the once over. Cam knew they wondered who the lady in the high heels was and what she was doing at their crime scene. She questioned the same thing herself.

The stocky cop was animated and visibly upset as he spoke to Finnegan and Levine. Cameron overheard him cursing between almost every other word. He was distraught, angry, confused, and more than a little scared. She wondered why a cop would react in such a way to a crime scene before it occurred to her that he knew the victim.

Finnegan gave Cameron a side glance when she reached him. He paused, meeting her eye to eye. She sensed he wanted to say something but was choosing his words before he spoke.

"This is Officer LaTesta. LaTesta, Dr. Cooper. She's consulting with us as a profiler on this case." They nodded hello—no time for polite handshakes. "Officer LaTesta just told us what they found here. It's grim. You sure you're up for this?"

"I wouldn't be here otherwise. Lead the way, Detective," Cameron said in a stern tone. The kid-glove treatment was getting old.

"LaTesta is...was friends with the woman. She's Property Officer Medina Montan, thirty-seven, married, two kids. Her husband reported her missing last night when she never returned home after visiting her father at

Fairchild Nursing Home," Finnegan said as they made their way into the alley. "Let's get to work." He handed her a pair of latex gloves and motioned for her to go ahead of him.

Cam's heart beat faster as she slipped the gloves on, her nerves pinching every part of her being. She walked past cops and medical personnel, into the unfamiliar alley that seemed all too familiar. A waft of pungent garbage filled her nostrils. A flash in her mind of the alley in the dark of night caught her by surprise. A memory? Her imagination? A small voice whispered in her ear, *"You shouldn't be here."* Chills ran through her, skipping down her spine and branching out through her body.

A light rain dampened the scene as the first responders draped the body with a yellow tarp, waiting for the crime scene examiner to arrive. Cameron assumed they also covered her out of respect since the killer had shredded her clothes and scattered the pieces on her partially naked body.

"Talk to me," Cameron said, looking up at Finnegan. "Where do you want me to start?"

"The cause of death is always a single stab wound to the abdomen, slicing the aorta open. The victim bleeds to death almost immediately. The women he selects are a distinctive type. They're between five-five and five-eight, brunette, with light eyes. They're never sexually assaulted. This is the first time he disturbed the clothes. Usually, it's just the shoes."

Officer LaTesta interjected, "Is it okay if I'm the one to tell her husband?"

Finnegan placed a hand on the shorter man's shoulder and gave a gentle squeeze. "Of course. I'm sorry, Tony, for your loss. Medina was more than a coworker. She was your friend. Tell him the whole department is praying for him and we won't rest until we find the animal that did this."

LaTesta's eyes moistened, and he managed a nod before hurrying off, head hanging.

Finnegan turned to Cam. "Do you understand how personal this is?"

Cameron wasn't sure if Finnegan wanted a response or if he was thinking out loud.

"This asshole is killing police department personnel in their own neigh-borhoods," he said, pointing back to the street. His other hand strangled a small notepad. "He has some set of brass on him, that's for sure."

Cameron stared down at the lifeless body of Officer Medina Montan, someone's wife and mom. Their world was about to implode with the ring of a doorbell. That night, her children would go to bed for the first time without a mom. The cruelty and senselessness of Medina's death made her want to hit something. Her own eyes filled with tears, and she tried to blink them away. *Breathe*. She then did something she would never have done in the FBI. Cam knelt next to Medina, took her hand, and said a silent prayer.

In the past, she would never have let her emotions show. She would have walked away until she composed herself. It had taken a long time, but she'd learned over the last several years it wasn't unprofessional to show her emotions. If she felt sad, she could show it. She should show it. If she vomited at an ugly scene, it didn't make her weak or unqualified. It made her human. Suppressing her emotions, stuffing them inside, was what had gotten her into trouble so many years ago. She wasn't about to bottle them up again to impress a cop she'd just met.

A tear ran down her cheek as she held Officer Montan's hand. When her composure returned, her heart and mind calm, she took a deep breath and rose. Pulling a tissue out of her pocket, she dried her face and wiped her nose.

She expected to find Finnegan disapproving of her weakness, her show of emotion. Instead, when she turned to him, it astounded her to see all the officers, Finnegan included, with their heads bowed. The group in mourning, showing their respect, was such a touching sight that she almost cried again.

Cameron walked back to Levine's car, making mental notes of the scene. She'd seen enough and needed to get to work. She had a profile to build.

CHAPTER 4

At the station, Finnegan acted distracted and on edge. The other detectives avoided his desk and all eye contact with him. He brooded with a finger pressed to his lips, eyes narrowed, his lanky body tilted back in his chair as he watched and listened to everything and everyone around him.

Cameron wondered if he was lost in thought about the killer or pissed at somebody. Seemed like both to her. She sat across from him, poised for him to say something. The longer he remained unmoved, the more uncomfortable she grew.

"Detective, you appear agitated. Want to talk about it?" *I am a psychologist, after all.*

His attention shifted to Cameron. He stared at her.

She focused on him, locked in his gaze. *Yikes, is it me? Did I do something wrong? Was it the crying thing? Is he angry because everyone took a moment at a crime scene?*

"Dr. Cooper, I'm beyond agitated. I. Am. Pissed." He leaned in, folding his arms on the desk. His stare became more intense the closer he moved. "My people are being killed practically in front of me, and I don't have a clue as to why or by whom. And you know what really has me pissed? What really concerns me?"

She shook her head as she sipped her coffee, so as not to interrupt.

He pressed even closer, so she did the same. Secret time. He said in a hushed voice, "I think this guy might be another cop. And I'm sitting here wondering if the son-of-a-bitch is walking around here feeling all smug because we're clueless. And that is *really* pissing me off."

He had a valid point. The thought had crossed Cameron's mind. She said, "I think another cop is a decent theory, Detective. I considered the same idea myself. But I think the killer is more likely someone who goes to the same bars and restaurants the cops frequent, someone who wants revenge on police officers for being arrested and imprisoned. Or someone abused by a mother who was a cop." Sensing he didn't want anyone to overhear their discussion, she added, "Why don't we go into the office to discuss this and finish going over the files?"

He nodded his agreement and then retrieved the folder from the cabinet while Cameron gathered her things.

Once again, they convened in the tiny, closed-off office, but this time, Cameron felt more comfortable. She was becoming familiar with this man and the way he processed information. Familiarity bred comfort.

Finnegan slapped the file on the desk, the words "Stealth Stalker Serial Killer" glaring back at them both. He collapsed onto the worn office chair, his broad body filling its frame, and ran his hands through his hair. "You know, after the first three killings and the women were all from area stations, I assumed coincidence. I was in blind denial. I didn't want to admit a maniac has targeted our department. I shouldn't have been so naïve." He nudged the file. "So, you think this guy is an ex-con?"

"Could be a possibility. I worked a half-dozen serial killer cases in my days with the FBI. In all of them, there was a method to their madness, as the saying goes. Nothing was random. We need to link these women beyond the physical similarities." She stared down at the Stalker file and reconsidered her statement. "Or maybe it is just physical. The killer is looking for someone specific but hasn't found her yet. For example, an arresting officer. He could've been in jail for such a long time that he doesn't remember exactly what she looks like anymore. Or now she's older, and he's attacking women who resemble her when he was sent away."

Finnegan ran his hands through his hair once again, this time clasping them behind his head as he mulled this over.

"Is there anything other than physical attributes that link the women together?" She pulled her chair closer to the desk and turned the file around so it was facing her.

"We've looked into everything we could think of, but here we are—empty-handed. The only links are the physical similarities and that they all work for NYPD. Nothing in their backgrounds matches up. Hell, there's no evidence these women even knew each other."

"Have you started mapping where the murders took place along with where the victims worked and lived?"

"Yeah, Levine can show you a map he created on his computer." He pushed himself up from the chair and stretched, his hands reaching toward the high ceiling. "I'm going for a cup of tea. I'll tell him to come in with his computer. Do you need a refill?"

"No, thanks. Is there a rolling bulletin board or a whiteboard I can use?"

"Yeah, I'll find you one. You want it in here?" Finnegan appeared a little confused.

"That would be great. Thanks," Cameron said with an assuring smile.

Levine came into the room first with his laptop in hand. He set the sleek black computer on the desk in front of Cameron and pulled a chair over next to her. "Some first day, huh? We put you right to work." He gave her the once over, not missing anything from her fingernails, short and polished in a natural pink, to her shoes, high heels, diamond stud earrings that were a gift and again probably not the right choice for police work.

"I've had worse." She gave him a slight smile. Nothing too eager. She gave him the once over as he'd sized her up. He also had manicured nails, a personal turnoff of hers. She liked a man to be clean and well-groomed but not beauty parlor fresh. He wore polished Italian leather shoes that showed no signs of the alley they had just spent hours in. *He must keep a shoe care kit in his car,* she mused. *And his suit fits him perfectly. If it wasn't custom made, then at least custom-fitted to him. Maybe he married money.*

"A worse first day than today, huh? You've got me curious, Doc. How could any day be worse than today? One of our own dead in the street like a stray?" He glared at Cameron as if he wanted to challenge her to a smack down.

She wanted to give it to him. *How about your day starts with three dead kids, all under the age of five, and a manhunt for their mother because she's your prime suspect?* She decided against provoking him. After all, people were dead and this wasn't a pissing contest. "You're right, Detective. I wasn't thinking. Today was awful. Let's make sure we don't face another day like today and get to work. Okay?" She studied him as he frowned at her, then motioned to the laptop. "Can you show me your map?"

As Detective Levine opened the computer file, Detective Finnegan rolled a whiteboard into the room that took up one full wall by itself. He produced a marker and magnets from a clear case attached to the frame.

"I assume you'll want this." Finnegan handed her a black marker. "We also have red and green right here on the ledge." He motioned with his hand like a game show model showing off a prize.

Levine smirked.

"Thank you, Detective," Cameron said as she took the felt-tip pen from his oversized paw.

"If there's anything else, please ask," he teased. He'd become more comfortable with her too. They had established a foundation for trust, which was necessary for them to succeed.

"I'll come *straight* to you with all *my* needs." She realized as the words stumbled from her mouth to their ears, what she'd meant had come out wrong. Was it a snappy come back, or a come on? Neither. She blushed with embarrassment.

Levine cleared his throat and turned the laptop in her direction. "Our first victim, Jennie Saunders. Divorced mom, one kid."

Cameron took notes. "How old is the child?"

Levine flipped through the papers as he searched for an age on the kid. "Ten, a boy. Goes to Queen of Peace Elementary School."

He's anticipating my questions. Excellent. So much easier on me for him to be so cooperative. "And the ex-husband, what's his story?"

Levine stared at Cameron with icy blue eyes. "He's a cop, and a damn good one. He's received medals of honor for bravery. He's the guy who runs into a burning house and saves a baby before anyone else arrives on the scene. In fact, that's how he earned his last medal."

She'd pissed him off, and his anger made his New York accent more prominent, but she understood he directed his anger at the circumstances, not at her.

"Detective Levine, I understand this is a stressful situation for everyone. These aren't strangers being targeted, but your friends, your family. But if we're going to be completely honest, anyone is capable of murder. Even a cop. We frequently hear about those kinds of cases in the news. A cop, or former cop whose wife disappears or is found murdered, and time reveals he's the murderer."

"Not Charlie Saunders. He's a friend. Yeah, he might not have had any love lost for Jennie, but she was his kid's mother, and he would never hurt her."

"Okay. I believe you. But when we examine these cases, we must remain professional and unbiased. It's not uncommon for someone to kill another person in the heat of the moment. Or they don't mean to kill someone, accidents happen, and out of fear, they deny any wrongdoing. Or perhaps they kill someone and, to cover up the crime as a one-time murder, they kill again and again in the same way to create the appearance of a serial killer. Only one murder is intentional, the rest random to throw us off the trail."

"We've considered that angle." Detective Finnegan pushed himself from the wall he'd been holding up. "And we investigated each murder as if it stood alone. You'll see as you read further into our case files. We *are* certain this is a serial killer, Dr. Cooper. We need to link these murders together." He sat back down in his chair and tapped his index finger to his lips again, studying her. "We aren't new at this, Dr. Cooper. We're experienced professionals who know what we're doing. Levine's been a detective for ten plus years. I've been doing this for seventeen years. Let me remind you, you aren't here to tell us how to do our job. You're here to make our job easier."

Now Finnegan was angry too. She needed to fix the mess she'd created before it blew up in her face. "I'm sorry, Detectives. I didn't intend to imply you're not qualified or doing an excellent job. I just want to make sure we cover all the bases. I have a great deal of respect for you, and I understand these murders are particularly sensitive because of who the victims are."

"Forget it. Let's focus on the map." Levine pressed a button on the laptop, and a map popped up. "A park employee found Jennie's body here, at a small park two blocks from the station where she worked. *Two* blocks," he said as he waved two finely manicured fingers in the air. "The red dot marks where they found her, and the blue dot marks the station building."

Cameron reached into her tote bag and pulled out a paper map of the area, a roll of tape, and a spool with five colors of string: red, blue, green, yellow, and purple. She unfolded the three by four map, found the same locations, and marked them number one with the colored markers.

"What are you doing? I have it right here for you," Levine said, indignant.

"You do, and it's very impressive, but I'm a little old school. I prefer things I can touch rather than a computer screen. This is the way I've always worked. I can't kick the habit. That's why I need the whiteboard. I need that visual. I need the material to be big and...touchable." Cameron shrugged.

Levine stared at her, dazed.

A smile tugged at the corners of Finnegan's mouth.

Cameron attached the sizeable map to the whiteboard with the magnets, then wrote #1 and attached Jennie Saunders's photo with another magnet. She cut lengths of the red string and taped an end to where they had found Jenny and the other end to the corner of her picture. She did the same with where she worked. Turning to Levine, she said, "Can you show me on this map where Jennie lived?"

"Doc, come on. It's already mapped out right here." Levine pointed at his computer screen.

"I know, I know. Please humor me. I work better this way."

Levine studied his map and then stood, grabbed the black marker, and put a dot on the map where Jennie Saunders had lived. Once again, Cameron cut a length of string and taped it to the paper map and Jennie's picture. Helped by Levine, she did this for each victim. They finished as Murphy stuck his head into the room.

"Hey, Hunter, the chief wants to see you pronto." He eyed Cameron's map and added, "Nice map. Much easier to see than looking at that little computer screen." He glanced at an agitated Levine and back to Cameron with a little wink.

Finnegan arose. "This can't be good. We'll continue here later."

CHAPTER 5

Hunter Finnegan stood in the dark at the corner window of his apartment with a scotch neat in hand. His view of the city became speckled with water droplets as a light rain fell. Even under dark storm clouds, wet and cold, the city thrived like a July night. Buildings showcased a million sparkling lights. Taillights and headlights of a thousand cars formed red and white snakes along the avenue, and people rushed along concealed under umbrellas.

He thought about Medina Montan. Out of all the victims, Medina troubled him the most, but he wasn't sure why. Something nagged at the back of his brain. When he'd examined the pictures of the victims side by side, they all looked similar yet different. What bothered him the most was that they all seemed familiar, like someone he knew but couldn't pinpoint.

His thoughts jumped around from the victims to his meeting with the chief earlier to the indigestion that burned his insides. With zero progress in the case and another body, Chief Michael Dwyer had laid into him, and Hunter couldn't blame him, but his stomach could.

His thoughts turned to Dr. Cameron Cooper. She had an old-fashioned approach to an investigation, similar to his own, which he liked. Her style gave them something in common. He'd been stunned and touched when she'd knelt next to Medina and held her hand. The simple gesture moved the veteran cop. That, he didn't like. Emotions made him vulnerable and compromised his objectivity, and even worse, made him feel out of control.

He'd served as a cop for over twenty-three years, and not since his first year had he ever become emotional at a scene. And that one time was understandable. The sense of vulnerability conjured up a ghost—his first partner, Officer Thomas Reilly, a lifer. Reilly had been closing in on retirement, but the older man never complained. He'd walked the streets with Hunter as if they were the same age. Extremely fit, Reilly took excellent care of his body. At sixty-one, he'd still run five miles every morning. "Not as fast as when I was twenty-five, but I get it done," he'd told Hunter more than once.

Hunter took a sip of his scotch and smiled a little at the memory of his mentor. He'd enjoyed walking the beat with the seasoned Reilly, who regaled him with stories of being a cop in the greatest city in the world. Real cop stories. "There isn't a crook out there who can outrun Thomas Reilly," he would tell the young Finnegan. Foot chases, car chases, murders, kidnappings—Thomas Reilly had witnessed it all. He'd shared life lessons with Hunter, which revolved around family and how to treat a lady. He was an old-fashioned gentleman. "Always open the door for a lady, and if you love her, treat her like you love her. If you treat a woman like shit, take her for granted, don't talk to her or share your life with her, she'll grow to hate you and you'll never know until it's too late." Hunter heard his voice as clearly as if Reilly were standing right next to him.

Thomas Reilly had been wounded three times in his forty years as a cop. The first time, he'd run into a burning building and saved an elderly woman from being consumed alive by the flames. He'd suffered second and third-degree burns on his legs and hands, which took months to recover from. His stint in rehab had been the only time in his life Reilly didn't rise at 5:30 a.m. to run.

The second time, he'd suffered a gunshot wound when he crashed a convenience store robbery. The bullet had landed in his shoulder but didn't stop him from tackling the shooter and "accidentally" breaking his nose when he arrested him.

The third time had embarrassed the proud Reilly. Ready to march in the annual St. Patrick's Day parade, a police horse got spooked, reared up, kicked him, and broke his arm. Missing the parade had made him angrier than the broken arm.

Hunter's thoughts led him to the day he didn't like to recall—the last time he and Thomas Reilly had walked the streets together. Reilly had talked about his newly purchased boat, the long-awaited trip to Ireland he and his wife would finally take, and his first grandchild due any day. He'd been a happy, happy man who loved his job but counted the days until he could start his "new life" spent with family and friends, fishing, traveling, and growing old. The two officers had been laughing when they turned the corner and walked right into a street fight between two rival gangs. They instinctively pulled their weapons and ducked for cover. Hunter never saw the kid crouched in a doorway with a gun pointed at him. Reilly spotted him, jumped in front of Hunter as the gun went off, and took the bullet in his chest—a testament to the cop, and the man, Thomas Reilly was. He'd fallen to the sidewalk in slow motion, the echo of the gunshot turning fuzzy and far away in his ears.

At the explosion of the pistol, the gang members had run in different directions. Hunter had looked down in shock at Reilly collapsed on the ground. Blood oozed through his blue shirt, his gun still in hand, and his own blue eyes shone with shock and disbelief at what had happened. Hunter sank to his knees next to his mentor, his friend, and called for help. He'd pressed one hand over the wound to slow the blood flow, and with the other arm, lifted Police Officer Thomas Reilly onto his lap and held him close.

Reilly had patted Hunter's hand, his voice weak. "The one thing I could never outrun, a bullet. Ha-ha..." And then, "Enjoy life, kid. That's the important thing. It's why we're here, to live and to love. Tell my Kate thanks for the best life any man dared ask for and I love her. Okay?" He'd smiled up at Hunter.

Hunter had nodded as the last breath escaped Thomas Reilly, then hugged him tighter as he sat on the sidewalk, covered in his friend's blood. Tears had run down his cheeks as a crowd gathered. He'd been twenty-four.

As the memories of his old friend's death filled his thoughts, Hunter's eyes moistened. He knocked back the rest of the scotch in his glass. Alone in the safety of his home was the only time Hunter thought about the tragedy, a life-defining moment for him. He'd had nightmares for months after Reilly's death, and for a while, he questioned whether he should be a cop. He decided he would take work one day at a time. Those "one days" had turned into twenty-three years before he knew it.

Hunter squeezed his eyes closed, inhaling sharply as his exhale fogged the window, dulling the shiny droplets clinging to the other side. *Think about something else, damn it!*

His thoughts turned back to Cameron Cooper. In his mind, he pictured her eyes, intense blue eyes fringed by black lashes that studied him and everyone and everything they came upon. Always in analyze mode, or did he imagine it? He smiled at the thought of her. He was attracted to the profiler, and she intrigued him on an intimate level. She was a woman with a rough coming up. A woman who almost brought him to tears within hours of joining his team. A woman embraced by the scent of vanilla and coconut. The soothing fragrance made her more desirable.

What word had Jeff Alexander used? Distressed? No...traumatized. What happened to her that was so traumatic? He decided to call Jeff Alexander in the morning for more information.

Meanwhile, in the darkness of night, he considered what he'd already learned. Not much. She'd received excellent recommendations from two people he trusted, Jeff Alexander and Gina Rossi. Jeff had mentioned she'd achieved an above-average success rate in her field. She was eager to work. He lay down on his bed and stared out the window as the rain turned to a downpour.

God, I hope I made the right decision bringing her on. I hope she can help us catch this bastard.

He drifted off to sleep, soon becoming entranced in a vivid dream. First, restless visions of Medina, which turned into calming images of Cameron. No more nightmares tonight. Tonight, his dreams turned to a beautiful woman. Thomas Reilly would have approved.

CHAPTER 6

THE SUN HAD SET, and a black, starless sky hung over the city. Channel 5 News at 11 played on the television. The anchor, Diane Downing, was beautiful. Her luxurious auburn hair gleamed under the studio lights. Her voice washed over her viewer like warm, melted caramel coating an apple. Her speech was impeccable, devoid of any regional accents, and her pronunciation meticulous. She was nothing like the bitch cop who had unwittingly become a target.

"Good Evening, I'm Diane Downing, and this is News 5 at 11. We start tonight with the tragic events of this morning when a passerby found Police Officer Medina Montan dead in an alley downtown. Officer Montan was the fourth victim in what police are calling the Stealth Stalker Killings. Police Chief Michael Dwyer held a press conference earlier today."

So, they've named me the Stealth Stalker. I like it.

The news feed switched to the video of Chief Dwyer. "Good morning and thank you for coming. I will only make a statement. I will not take questions. This morning at approximately 6:15 a.m., a passerby on the street saw what she thought was a woman passed out in an alley. She called 911, and police and paramedics responded. When responding officers arrived, they found the woman unresponsive and declared her dead at the scene. They identified the woman as Officer Medina Montan. Police blocked off the area to preserve the scene and forensic evidence. The medical examiner confirmed she died in the same fashion as three other police bureau employees, and we believe this is the work of a serial killer. We have no motive for these murders. The only link between the victims is that they were all NYPD personnel. Officer Montan worked at the Fourth Precinct for ten years as a property officer. I notified her family immediately and ask you to honor their request for privacy.

"This is a developing case and as we gather more information, we will disperse it to the public. We will find whoever committed these heinous crimes, and they will pay for their actions. We are working around the clock, searching for the sick individual who is responsible. I am personally involved in this case and will not rest until this killer is behind bars. I will make a more detailed statement and answer questions either later on today or tomorrow as I am briefed by detectives. For now, that is all. Thank you."

How anticlimactic. "I am personally involved in this case and will not rest until this killer is behind bars." Blah blah blah. That man couldn't catch me if I... Oh, Diane is back, let's see what she has to say.

"We have just listened to Police Chief Michael Dwyer vowing to find and bring to justice the person responsible for the heinous killings of four women in the past two months. He stated the police were treating this case as the work of a serial killer. The latest victim, identified as Police Officer Medina Montan, was found dead in an alley earlier today. Officer Montan was married with two children, aged ten and eight. After investigators brief Police Chief Dwyer, he will make a follow-up statement. Channel 5 News will follow this story and keep you up to date as more information becomes available. Another top story tonight involves the mysterious disappearance of a local..."

Stealth turned off the television. *So disappointing, Diane. No profile or sketches of the suspect. The cops do not understand who they're dealing with. They'll never find me, but I will find my cop and then I can move on. I'm sorry about Medina Montan. Sorry she wasn't my girl, but not sorry I ended her life. The hunt is always part of the fun and killing is part of hunting. I feel so...so powerful. Yes, that's an excellent word to describe the moment I drive my knife into the softness of someone's belly. Powerful. I am POWERFUL. I know when to stop for someone to live. I could leave them bleeding, merely wounded. But at that moment, the power is mine. I decide if they live or die. And that is what I do. To let them suffer would be inhumane.*

Stealth contemplated what the next move would be. More research would help.

Perhaps the first time I searched too soon. She had just moved here. Maybe the records weren't updated yet.

At times like this, Stealth wished for a better understanding of the computer. It would be so much more efficient to hack police records to find the information.

Perhaps the cops themselves have given the answer. According to the newspaper, a police source said they surmised the killer frequented the same bars and restaurants as the cops to pick the next victim. Hmm, not a bad idea. I'll watch them in their own environment, like going to a zoo and watching the monkeys.

Stealth rose with fresh hope for ending the hunt once and for all.

CHAPTER 7

Cameron had awoken earlier than usual, anxiety manifesting itself in restless sleep, and now she was apprehensive to begin her second day of work. She knew she had to prove herself to Detective Hunter Finnegan because of his comments the previous day. *"Jeff told me that your last case was complicated and left you somewhat traumatized.…It's grim. You sure you're up for this?"*

Nervous energy buzzed through her as she quickly showered and dressed. Something about the alley where they'd found Medina Montan bothered her. A sense of familiarity, like déjà vu but stronger, skipped around her mind. Cameron hadn't been able to shake the sensation all afternoon, and when she'd climbed into bed, she still couldn't escape the feeling. Yet, she'd never been there before. Thinking about the alley as she dozed off, it haunted her all night.

Later, I'll walk past again and see if I remember anything, she decided.

Hunter Finnegan also danced through her mind during the night. He'd contacted her, and yet she wasn't sure he trusted her. The detective would make her work for it. Fair enough. Something about him made her nervous. Her mother would have described him as rugged and handsome—an appealing combination. He also had an intensity to him and a commanding presence. His team respected him, a respect she wagered he earned daily.

Choosing her shoes with more thought than the previous day, she decided on a sturdy pair of loafers versus the ridiculous heels that had hampered her all day. Not the neatest person, her search for the shoes was like a treasure hunt. First, she checked under her bed—nothing. Not in the kitchen, not in the closet. She finally found them pushed under the couch, as well as some mail, her sneakers, and one glove. Jackpot!

Standing in front of the mirror, she gave herself the once-over. She'd pulled her long, blonde hair into a chignon. Her light blue blouse was neatly tucked into navy trousers, and her belt matched her shoes. As a psychologist, she understood the vital role appearance played, even though most people would never admit to judging someone by their looks. It was human nature to form opinions based on first impressions. She'd done it the day before.

Cameron grabbed her blazer and bag and headed out. The early hour ensured she didn't run into Mrs. Howl, her human, or any other neighbor. She hailed a cab and collected her thoughts during the stop-and-go ride in city traffic to the station. The news had nothing new on the killer.

Hopefully our serial killer took the night off.

Even at 7:00 a.m., the station buzzed with activity. Personnel had already started a new day as the night shift slowly petered out. Phones jingled, voices carried throughout the floor, and the smell of freshly brewed coffee lingered in the air. Cam made her way up the stairs and headed straight for the little office in the back corner, only to find the gray metal door locked. She turned around, startled to see Detective Saintil standing right behind her.

"Hello, Detective Saintil."

"Morning." She seemed less than thrilled at the sight of Cameron.

"I hoped for an early start. Would you have the key to this office?" Cameron sensed the detective's unfriendliness.

"No. But I can get it." Saintil walked away.

Detective Saintil returned a minute later with the key and unlocked the door for Cameron. She pushed it open and stepped aside for Cam to pass her.

Cameron put her things down on the small desk and realized Saintil still stood at the doorway.

"You need anything else?" Saintil stared at Cameron's shoes, which made Cam notice hers—plain, black Sketchers sticking out from below dark blue jeans.

"No, thanks, I'm fine."

Saintil nodded and returned to her desk.

Wow, she sure is hard to read.

The large whiteboard stood as Cameron had left it the night before. Still no discernible pattern, nothing overlapped. Right then, with everything she'd done so far, her work was nothing more than a multicolored random mess. She needed the files. She hadn't had the chance to go through each one yet, and the answer might be a page turn away.

Cameron sat at the table and jotted down questions she had for the detectives once they arrived. The aroma of coffee hit her, and a pang of hunger squeezed her stomach. She closed her book and headed for the break room, closing the office door behind her.

Levine and Murphy looked up from their corner table in the break room as Cam entered. Levine raised his cup to her in a greeting and Murphy smiled, then went back to sipping his coffee. As she poured herself some coffee, she spied an assortment of goodies on the table—muffins, bagels, donuts, and rolls.

"Help yourself, Doc," Murphy called out. "The deli next door brings us that stuff every morning. It's their way of saying thank you for all we do."

Not the healthiest choice, but her nervous energy needed fuel. And what better fuel than carbs? As she grabbed a vanilla-frosted donut, Murphy called to her again, "Doc! Come over here and join us."

Saintil had just joined them and shot Cam her usual look of hatred.

Maybe a scowl is her natural expression. Cameron smiled at her, lips closed, and nodded, the gesture more polite than friendly.

Saintil barely acknowledged her as she sat down next to Murphy, who was the exact opposite. He was all smiles. Eyes shining.

Cam thought he was about to hug her.

"Ready for day two?" His bright blue eyes locked on her own. There was nothing off-putting about this man who had the demeanor of a human golden retriever—always happy, ready to please and to help. A genuinely friendly guy.

Cameron relaxed, sitting with Bobby Murphy because of his calming influence on her. *What an eclectic group Detective Finnegan has here,* she thought. "Oh, yes, I can't wait to start. The sooner we stop this guy, the sooner we can all sleep better at night, right?" She directed the question to Saintil, but she just stared at her and sipped her coffee. *Hmm, not a morning person?* Cam turned her attention back to Murphy. "Detective Finnegan said you have a son. How old is he?"

"Which one?" Murphy laughed. "I have four. The wife kept trying for a girl, but she kept getting another boy. She's finally accepted that she's not meant to have a daughter. Anyway, the oldest is twelve, then ten, the next one is seven, and our four-year-old who, as my mother would say, has the gift of gab. The kid never shuts up. You'd think a four-year-old would have nothing to talk about. But this kid can go on and on."

"He gets it from his old man." Detective Hunter Finnegan, the man himself, cut Murphy off upon entering the break room.

Murphy and Levine both laughed, and Detective Saintil almost smiled with amusement.

Cameron turned her gaze to him. The sound of Hunter Finnegan's voice sent a vibration through her body.

"Morning, Dr. Cooper. Did you have a well-rested night after your first day with us?" Finnegan smiled, holding a cup with the tea tag hanging from the mug. He wore a crisp, white button-down shirt with the sleeves rolled up to his elbows and washed out blue jeans.

Turning to answer him quickly, she accidentally knocked her donut, icing side down, onto what appeared like brand new tan leather loafers. "Ohmygod! I am so sorry. Let me clean that for you!" Cameron grabbed napkins from the table, leaned over, seized the donut from Finnegan's shoe, and tried to wipe the icing remains from the soft leather. "I am so sorry. Oh no, it might stain."

Detective Finnegan stepped back and raised the front of his foot to assess the damage. "Don't worry about it, Dr. Cooper. The shoe will survive." He smiled at her and winked. Before Cam said anything else, he added, "I'll be at my desk when you're ready to start your second day." He glanced around the table at his team. "I assume you're all ready to start now."

Levine smirked as he swirled his coffee. "You two are too cute."

Hunter walked away shaking his head and grabbed a blueberry crumb muffin on his way out.

The detectives finished their pastries and refilled their coffee cups as Cameron sat self-conscious and, she was afraid, beet red. She was trying too hard to gain their acceptance and trust and felt like she was blowing it. As she reminded herself to breathe in through the nose, out through the mouth, Detective Murphy came over and placed a new donut with white icing in front of her.

He grinned. "He's had drunks throw up on his shoes. Don't sweat a little sugar." He gave Cam's shoulder a brief squeeze. "And don't let Levine bother you."

She thanked him for the thoughtful gesture. She liked Murphy and hoped to meet his family someday.

Murphy and Saintil filed out of the breakroom, leaving silence in their wake.

Carefully, she ate the donut and sipped her coffee, afraid she might end up with it all over her blouse. A police officer in his mid-twenties came in, noticed her sitting alone, and sat down at the table with her.

"Hi." He nodded at her. "I've never seen you here before. Are you a transfer?"

"No, I'm a consultant. Cameron Cooper." Cam stretched her hand out to him.

He gave her a hearty shake.

"Oh, right. My brother told me about you. I'm Tommy. Tommy Murphy." He smiled, and Cam saw the resemblance to his older brother. They shared the same smile, bright eyes, and friendliness. Tommy Murphy had a slighter build than his brother and had more hair, but he had the same aura as the older Murphy.

"Bobby just left. Your brother didn't mention he had a brother who was a cop."

He laughed. "He has three who are cops and a sister who's a detective at the 31st. And our old man is a captain across town."

"Wow! So is the whole Murphy clan in the serve and protect business?"

"No, not all of us. I have another brother who works in the DA's office. He's the black sheep of the family," he said with a laugh, and she caught on that it must be a running joke with the family. "And we have two more sisters. The baby is a student, away at the University of Notre Dame and the pride and joy of the family. My oldest sister is a trained chef. She runs the kitchen at our family restaurant."

"Your restaurant?"

"Bobby didn't tell you about the pub? My family only owns the best Irish pub in the entire city." Pure pride beamed from every ounce of his being.

"Let me guess—it's called 'Murphy's.' "

"Not a bad guess, but a wrong one. Pat O'Brien's. He was my great-grandfather, and the restaurant is celebrating its 100th anniversary next month! How cool is that?" He smiled a big, white-toothed, youth-infused grin. "Pat O'Brien was my mother's grandfather. Mom ran the place for years with her brother. And then my sister became a chef. She went to the Culinary School and everything. Katie brought that place into this century. There's still your pub burger and fries, but she's elevated Irish food into Irish cuisine. You'll come and be our guest. Promise, okay?"

"Yes, yes. I'd love to try some Irish cuisine." Cam smiled as widely as Tommy Murphy. His smile was contagious, and her nerves had calmed down.

"Much better," he said, examining her with narrowed green eyes. "When I first spotted you sitting here alone, you looked like you'd just lost your best friend. Now you're smiling, and you look much better. Nice talking to you, Doc, but I gotta run. My partner's a cranky old-timer who doesn't like it when I keep him waiting. Let me know when we'll see you at the pub."

"Okay, thanks, Officer Murphy. I will. Have a good day." Cam sat smiling to herself as she watched him hurry off. She realized how strange she must seem sitting alone, smiling, but it was better than looking like a wounded animal. She gathered her things together, took the last bite of what was a delicious donut, and started back to the little office where Detective Hunter Finnegan was waiting for her.

Finnegan met her halfway. He slipped his blazer on as he walked and nodded toward the door. "Come on," he said. "The chief is giving a press conference out front regarding our case. He wants everyone directly involved standing up next to him. That means you too."

He took her by the elbow and led her toward the stairs as countless officers and detectives did the same. The entire building emptied onto the front steps and sidewalk.

Of course, this case affects them all. This is personal, and they're all a part of it. They'll show the killer what he's up against just by their sheer numbers.

CHAPTER 8

WHEN CAMERON AND FINNEGAN arrived outside, they saw a podium erected at the bottom of the steps with multiple microphones attached to it. Reporters and camera crews were setting up on the sidewalk and into the street in front of the station. Cameron stood uneasy, absorbing the frenzied scene. She was a stranger among the group, but she believed she was just as dedicated as anyone else to catching the killer. And this wasn't her first press conference. She'd been to dozens with the FBI. Yet, something made her gut ache. A voice in her head warned her she shouldn't be in front of the camera.

Finnegan said something, but she didn't quite catch it as her thoughts consumed her.

"What?"

"Are you okay? You look pale." His hand rested on her shoulder, and his brows furrowed in concern.

"Yeah, I'm fine," she hedged.

The press secretary, Wendy Earhart, moved people around and arranged them to her liking. Before Cam could stop her, Wendy grabbed her by the arm and positioned her right next to the podium on the left, and Rhonda Saintil next to it on the right, mumbling something about attractive women could only help. Finnegan stood on her other side, and next to him were Vince Barone and Glen Levine. The rest of the detectives and officers united in a half-moon around the podium, leaving an aisle down the center for the chief to walk straight out of the building and down to the pedestal. There was ample room for his staff, lieutenant, and the mandatory politician or two.

Cam was leaning over to tell Finnegan she needed to go when the chief and his entourage made their way to the podium and he began his address to the waiting reporters.

Police Chief of Detectives Michael Dwyer had a deep baritone voice, and even though journalists had erected a slew of microphones in front of him, he didn't need them. Everyone could hear him loud and clear whenever he spoke. A burly man with a big voice, he seemed intimidating, but most people found him charming and warm. Detective Rossi's team had told Cameron stories, however, and she'd learned the chief had a temper. When he was angry, he lowered his voice to a menacing whisper. Most people were never on the receiving end of his whisper. He reserved it for those who had truly pissed him off.

Dwyer stepped up to the podium as Cam tried to swallow a sensation of uneasiness. She shouldn't have been standing with the officers as she surveyed the members of the press before her. It wasn't smart of her to appear on television. She'd spent the last decade trying to be invisible, and now she found herself front and center, tempting fate. The world spun around her, camera lights blinked on, and Dwyer's booming voice echoed in her head. She wasn't in control.

Cam took a deep breath and blew it out, hoping to calm herself down. A hand pressed on the small of her back as Finnegan steadied her. She glanced over her shoulder at him, and he mouthed the words, "Are you okay?" Ignoring the question, she grabbed her sunglasses from her blazer pocket and put them on, tilting her head down in disguise, hoping the cameras would stay zoomed in on Dwyer.

Chief Dwyer's statement was short and direct. He maintained his patience as reporters rephrased the same question repeatedly until he'd had enough. "Look, I've told you everything," he said, his voice discernibly lower and even-toned.

Cam cringed. This was his way of angry-whispering to the press.

"We believe we are dealing with one person who to date has killed four times. The victims...members of the New York Police Department family. We are working around the clock to find this individual and put a stop to these senseless crimes." He stopped as his expression intensified, with thick angry brows hovering over narrowed eyes and his jaw tight. His head lowered like a vulture as he glared into the camera and finished, the words slow and methodical, his voice beyond intimidating, "When we find him, and we will, the individual responsible for these crimes will suffer a swift and just punishment. And you will be informed first."

Cam recognized he was no longer speaking to the reporters but directly to the killer, sending a threat.

Chief Dwyer straightened himself up and finished the press conference by saying thank you and leaving. Not one reporter opened their mouth to ask a parting question. They knew better.

Cam wondered, *What was his definition of a "swift punishment?" A bullet to the back of the head?*

After the press conference ended, some officers and staff went back inside while others lingered on the sidewalk, speaking in hushed tones in small groups. Their faces were solemn and their anger palpable. Attacks on police officers and their comrades were the worst offense, right up there with harming a child. Finnegan touched Cam's hand, his fingers gentle to her skin. She tilted her head up at him to find his green eyes examining her. Her head throbbed and looking up to meet his eyes made her dizzy. She faltered, and he braced her with both hands. He gripped her shoulders and kept her from sinking to the ground.

"Whoa! I knew you weren't okay. Come here and sit down." He guided her to the steps, easing her down.

Cam's head throbbed as her budding migraine became more intense.

"What's wrong? What can I do to help you?"

Touched by his concern, she suddenly had the sensation that they had been friends forever. "It's just a headache. I'm prone to migraines. I should lie down somewhere dark and quiet and take my medicine," she said, rubbing her temples.

"Well, there's nowhere dark or quiet around here. You should go home." He motioned to a rookie cop as he spoke.

"No. I can take some aspirin, and I'll be okay." As she said this, she tried to stand and nearly fell right on top of him.

Finnegan caught her in one muscular arm and brought her back down to the step. "I insist. We don't need you falling down any stairs and suing us."

Cameron started to protest that she would never sue when he gave her a little wink. He was kidding. Within a minute, the same rookie pulled up right in front of them in a sporty dark gray Cadillac sedan. The young man ran around and opened the passenger door for her like a professional valet. She wondered how he even had the keys. Finnegan grabbed her by her arms and wrapped his other arm around her back, holding her hip and helping her to the car. A weakness ravished her body, and she conceded. She had to go home.

"Is this your car?" she asked as she sunk into the cushy front seat and closed her eyes.

"Yep. Made in America."

"Nice. Unexpected but nice."

"Hey, Levine isn't the only one with some class."

She relaxed as a familiar Garth Brooks song from her past played softly in surround sound.

Finnegan drove her right to her building. Cam didn't ask how he knew where she lived, assuming he'd checked her out as part of his job. He parked right at the front door and when the doorman tried to protest, he waved his badge.

Great, the doorman's going to think he found me drunk somewhere and brought me home. Or worse, I picked up a cop and we're having a quickie. But her head hurt too much to care about it right then.

Finnegan whisked Cam past the frowning doorman without acknowledgment. He brought her up to her apartment, which she reluctantly let him into, and he helped her to the couch.

"Where's your medicine?" Finnegan spoke in a hushed voice as he laid the blanket strewn on the sofa and floor over her.

She pointed to the breakfast bar. "The white bottle. Please get me some water with it."

He went into the kitchen and opened several cabinet doors before he found the one with the glasses. She heard the water running as he filled a glass. He gave her the bottle and sat down while she opened it and took two pills out. Then he handed her the glass and left the pill container on the coffee table. He walked back into the kitchen and searched the fridge.

Is he hungry? Should I offer him something? Oh, God, I think I might puke, but I can't. Not in front of him. Cam took deep breaths to quell the nausea.

Finnegan reappeared with a gel mask she kept in the freezer for easing migraines.

"Where did you find this?"

"My sister gets migraines too. She always keeps one of these in her freezer. I took a wild guess that you'd have one too."

"I guess that's why you're the lead detective."

He closed the curtains to the sliding glass doors, darkening the room.

Cameron lay back, resting her eyes just for a moment, and when she opened them again, it was three hours later. Finnegan was gone. She propped herself up on one elbow, checking the apartment. A note on the coffee table from Finnegan read:

You dozed off, so I left.

I'll call you with any updates.

Feel better.

–H

She sat up too fast, and her head throbbed. *Damn these headaches!* For the last several weeks, she'd been getting them, which she tolerated when she didn't have work. But now that she had a job consulting with the police department, she needed to get a handle on them. She wouldn't be much help if she had to keep leaving to lie down and take a nap.

Cam thought about calling Detective Finnegan for an update, but her head hurt too much and she didn't feel like talking to anyone. It took slow, deliberate movements to get up off the couch. She grabbed her bottle of pills and the glass of water, carrying them to the bedroom.

Not hungry as nausea crept back, she tried to do some research on her laptop in bed. She compared the current murders to past cases she'd worked on. She also had access to a national databank where she researched missing women with similar attributes to their victims.

Maybe he's new to the area but not to the crime.

The light from the computer screen proved too much for her as she struggled to concentrate. After about an hour, she closed it and gave up. Experience had taught her that not eating would make things worse, so she ordered soup for delivery and waited on the couch for it to arrive. Cam contemplated Stealth Stalker and the driving force behind someone killing police personnel as she waited.

He certainly has a death wish, she thought grimly, *because killing cops is a suicide mission.*

After she finished eating, she brushed her teeth and slipped out of her clothes, leaving them scattered on the bathroom floor. She popped two more pills and climbed into bed. The pounding in her head had a certain rhythm to it, and soon, Cameron drifted off.

CHAPTER 9

It was nearly eleven when Stealth sat down on the sleek leather couch to watch the newscast. Not tolerating the inane shows and commercials on television, Stealth waited for precisely 11:00 to turn the TV on. The news was the only show with appealing content, and it had the added perk of Diane Downing.

Perhaps after I'm done with the cop, I'll turn my attention to Diane. She won't come willingly at first, but in time, I'll convince her to stay with me.

Diane greeted her audience and had begun with the highlights of the day when a small picture of Police Chief Dwyer appeared in the corner over her left shoulder. She announced, "Police Chief Michael Dwyer held a press conference early this morning in front of the Sixth Precinct to address the Stealth Stalker killings. His top advisors surrounded him, along with what appeared to be every officer at the station. Let's go to Bill Klug on the street for the latest update. Bill?"

Oh, how I hate Bill Klug, Stealth mused. *He has a superior attitude, and he glances at his notes way too much. But if I want to watch the press conference and hear what they're saying about me, then I have no choice but to listen to his smug reporting.*

"Good evening, Diane. I am outside the Sixth Precinct where earlier today, as you said, Police Chief Michael Dwyer held a press conference to address the recent string of homicides targeting police personnel. Let's go to his statement now."

There he is—the big man of the hour. This guy loves a camera as much as he loves his food. He's not saying anything of value, just promising again to do the impossible—catch me. I suppose…Wait a second! What's that?

Stealth scrambled for the remote and paused the TV to take a better look at the picture.

It can't be! Could it be this easy? My girl is standing right next to Chief Big Mouth!

Stealth walked over to the television and drank her image in. She appeared older and her hair was shorter, but it was her. *It will be such a pleasure, after all these years, to have you in my hands. To look you in the eye and watch you fade away, knowing I caught you* first. *Now I have the information I need to end this. Your appearance now, and where you work, the Sixth Precinct. I get the bonus of humiliating "Chief Swift and Just Punishment." Wait until he realizes my intended victim was standing right next to him as he threatened me. So unprofessional.*

The next move would be to watch the station, wait for her to exit the building, and then follow her home.

It will all be over with soon, and I can get on with my life. My life. It will be mine once I eliminate her for good. I'll never have to worry about her dominating or trying to shut me away again.

CHAPTER 10

Hunter Finnegan had a hard time falling asleep. Guilt consumed him for leaving Cameron alone when she didn't feel well and not checking in later to see how she was doing. It concerned him that the job might have something to with her illness. Stress often caused his sister's migraines.

Helping her today, bringing her home, getting her a drink, and making her comfortable all seemed so...natural. The better he knew her, the more intrigued he became. Her beauty had attracted him to her from the moment their eyes met. Lying in bed, he stared at the ceiling, considering what about her struck him the most. Those beautiful blue eyes, deep in color unlike his own, which were pale green. It surprised him how, in just a couple of days, he'd become so infatuated with the beautiful doctor with the "traumatic" past. He checked the clock, 11:45. Too late to call now. If she didn't arrive at the station first thing in the morning, he would call her then.

He reminisced about the first time they met, last June when his buddy, Jeff Alexander, had contacted him about a friend looking for work. Jeff had given Cameron an excellent recommendation, said she was the best at what she did. Hunter had made no promises as far as a job but agreed to meet her. When Jeff told him her name was Dr. Cameron Cooper, Hunter's mind had painted a picture of an older, bespectacled woman, lips tightly pursed, who would study him as he worked—something he wasn't interested in enduring. When Cameron called him and asked if she could stop by the station, Hunter had said okay with little thought. He forgot to put it on his calendar, so when the beautiful blonde with deep blue eyes and a contagious smile walked up to his desk and asked if he was Detective Finnegan, he'd been unprepared. She'd taken his breath away. After a brief discussion about her background and experience, he'd said he would keep her in mind if they ever needed any consulting work and offered to walk her out. He'd been short with her out of his own feeling of inadequacy and embarrassment at not being ready to meet with her. When she'd lost her sandal on the way down the stairs, he couldn't take his eyes off her face and how she blushed when he handed her the shoe. After she left, he'd realized his hands were sweaty and his heart beat a little faster.

When she'd stood at his desk two days earlier, he'd played it cool and pretended to not recognize her—but he had. He couldn't forget her face. It was a permanent snapshot in his memory. He realized he was excited to have a reason to work with her and was looking forward to the morning and seeing her again.

Grisly murder scenes and a menacing laugh riddled his dreams. In a snap, the images turned to Cameron's eyes looking at him, smiling at him, and then crying eyes, screaming in fear. The more she screamed, the farther away he drifted. No matter how hard he tried, he couldn't help her.

Hunter awoke with a start, breathing hard, a slick sweat moistening his body. The illuminated clock read 3:38 a.m. Calming down, he recalled his dreams. Cameron was in trouble, and he tried to help her. Her screams were vivid as he moved in slow motion, his feet not moving the way he willed them. She drifted farther away as he grew more frantic. His heart picked up the pace again. Taking a deep breath, he decided to call his old college roommate and Cameron's former colleague, FBI Agent Jeff Alexander, first thing in the morning. Hunter didn't believe in psychic powers, but he trusted his gut. It never let him down.

When Hunter arrived at his desk in the morning, he looked up Jeff Alexander's number. As he dialed Jeff, he questioned his own motives. He was prying into Cameron's personal life, a place where he didn't belong. There was a possibility he would find something he wished he hadn't. Perhaps he should wait for Cameron to tell him about her past. The call went through, ringing on the other end. It wasn't too late to hang up. But he didn't.

Jeff Alexander answered the phone with, "Alexander here."

Hunter rolled his eyes. "You can't say hello like normal people?"

"Who's this?" Alexander demanded.

"Hunter Finnegan." He grinned at the pleasure of annoying his old friend.

"Hunter! How ya doing, man? Hey, how's my girl, Cameron? Are you taking care of her?" Jeff had a way of sounding like a frat boy even though decades had passed since he'd attended college.

"Dr. Cooper is fine. And she's the reason I'm calling you." Hunter tried to be patient.

"Oh? Perhaps not so fine?" Agent Alexander's deepening interest showed in his voice.

"Last time we spoke, you mentioned Dr. Cooper had suffered some kind of trauma. Can you elaborate on that for me?" Hunter asked.

"I suppose. What's this about, Hunter? Does this have something to do with your case, or are you just curious about Cameron's past? Because, for as much as you're my friend, so is she and I'm not willing to betray her trust." Agent Alexander liked to keep things casual but didn't want to be the source for gossip.

"I'm asking because I need assurance that she can handle this case. We're dealing with a serial killer who has chosen NYPD cops and employees as his targets. The other day she cried over a body at a crime scene, and yesterday I had to drive her home because she fell ill. I'm concerned." Hunter had no intention of mentioning that nearly everyone cried over Medina Montan's body. That was need to know only.

"So you think she's having a rough time?" Alexander said.

"Yes, she might be. What happened in her past? Was the situation similar to what we're dealing with now?"

"Okay, I'll tell you this much. Several years ago, we worked on a serial killer case on the outskirts of Atlanta. Cameron was the analyst, and she built a profile right on the money. Because of her, we were closing in on the guy when the worst thing possible happened." Alexander stopped and took a deep breath. "He nabbed her."

"What?" Hunter said, shocked by the words.

"You heard me—kidnapped. We figured the killer had read about Cameron working the case in the newspapers, and when he saw her on the TV news, she became his next victim. Only this time, he didn't hunt and kill. He grabbed her." Alexander paused for Hunter to process this and respond.

"He kidnapped her, and what? I mean, obviously you found her in time, or she wouldn't be here. What happened to her when he had her?" Hunter's stomach clenched as different scenarios raced through his mind. He'd been on the job for a long time and knew the sick tactics serial killers used to torture their victims. His subconscious mind jumped to the worst-case scenarios, but he resisted.

"It was bad," Alexander replied, seeming to not want to say the words aloud. "He tied her up and tortured her. He told her he'd kill her piece by piece. A toe here, an ear there...you get the idea. He wanted her to beg for his forgiveness, to beg for her life. He started with psychological warfare, and when that didn't break her, he moved on to physical torture. She hung in fairly well, but he realized she was tougher than he gave her credit for."

"So what happened? Did she escape?" Hunter grew angry and shocked. He didn't want to believe Cameron had gone through something so horrible.

"The guy grabbed another woman, Lisa Allen, a co-ed from a nearby college. This creep brought Lisa back to the old house where he'd imprisoned Cam and threw her at Cam's feet. He beat her, burned her, cut her, and told Cam he'd kill her right in front of her. This girl was only eighteen years old. This guy had done none of those things to his other victims. He barely left a mark on them. We found each one posed as if asleep. You can imagine how angry Cameron became. She started her own psychological war on him, called him a coward with mommy issues. She drilled into him. You should read the report. You'd have nightmares for a month!" Agent Alexander talked faster and sounded more excited as he recalled the details for Hunter. "That night, he left the two women shackled in the basement of the abandoned house out in the middle of nowhere. He beat them both into unconsciousness, and I guess he figured he'd finished them for the night. But Cameron came around. She realized he'd left them alone and went to work on getting out. God! I can't believe I'm telling you all this."

"Please, Jeff, don't stop now," Hunter urged.

"Okay, but I have to cut to the chase. The two of them worked for hours to break free. By the time they broke the door down, it was already dawn. The perp had boarded the house up from the inside. They pried some boards down from a picture window and were about to make a run for it when the guy came back. The two women attacked him with whatever they had—their fists, feet, anything lying around. They overtook him, knocked him to the ground, and beat him until he wasn't moving anymore. Cameron and Lisa did what they had to do to escape. Then they smashed the picture window, jumped to the ground outside, and ran for the road. Two guys on their way to a campground spotted them, stopped, and called for help. Cam told them what had happened. The two guys were hunters and had high-powered rifles with them. They staked out the house and protected the women until the local cops arrived. But our perp disappeared."

"What do you mean, he disappeared? You never caught him? Ever?"

"No. We never caught him. And he stopped killing after that," Alexander replied.

"Who was he?" Hunter asked.

"Jason Julius Jonette. He went by JJ. We called him J-Bird because he left a single blue bird's feather in his victim's hands." Agent Alexander sounded tired.

"How did you get a name?"

"Jonette was so confident Cam would die, he told her. When she woke up in the basement, he introduced himself! Turned out to be an alias. We ran the name every way possible and never found a Jason Julius Jonette."

"Can I read the files on this guy?" Hunter asked.

"No, not unless you come here. Why do you want to see them?"

"Do you think my serial killer could be your J-Bird? What if he's come back to finish what he started? He could be searching for Cameron and just hasn't found her." As soon as the words came out of his mouth, Hunter realized he was wrong. All the victims were brunettes, but Cameron was blonde.

"I guess anything is possible, but I doubt it. Your guy likes to use a knife and is going after women involved in the department. The J-Bird picked random women and preferred drugging and strangulation. He left few marks..." Jeff Alexander sounded lost in thought. "Listen, I've got to go. I hope Cameron is okay. If you want to read the files, call me."

"Jeff, one more thing. Don't tell Cameron I called, okay?"

"Sure, no problem. *Adios.*"

Hunter typed "Jason Julius Jonette" into his computer. A grainy photo of a white man, mid-thirties, brown hair, beard, and mustache popped up on his screen. Next to it was an artist's sketch of the man. Under status, the report read FUGITIVE, with no recent activity attributed to him.

Maybe the women maimed him when they were escaping, and he crawled off somewhere and died.

Hunter searched J-Bird near Atlanta, Georgia. Several newspaper articles popped up, and he opened the most recent. He skimmed it, coming across a reference to FBI Special Agent Dr. Cameron Chadwick. Hunter read through the article, which confirmed everything Agent Alexander told him except the part where Cameron's name was Chadwick, not Cooper. The

J-Bird drugged the women with a mild sedative, then sexually assaulted and strangled them. They were probably coherent enough to know what was happening, but sufficiently dazed so they couldn't fight back.

Hunter sat back in his chair and stared at the screen on his computer. He wished he'd done a background check on Cameron before he'd agreed to her coming on board with the investigation. Her involvement in another serial killer case had to be hard. He wondered if she'd married since then, or if she changed her name for another reason.

Of course, she changed her name to hide from Jonette. And what better place to hide than New York City?

Hunter checked his watch, seeing it was almost 8:00 a.m. His team would be at his desk any moment for the daily morning update. He'd started the meetings to make sure everyone was on the same page during their investigations. The Stealth Stalker case was their only assignment by order of the chief, who wanted them working on it 24/7. The three lead detectives and their captains from the other stations had a similar meeting each week at a central station. At the moment, no other case took precedence over this one.

He wanted to call Cameron to check on her. He also wanted her as far away from the case as possible if Jonette and Stealth were the same guy. She would never stand for it, of that he was positive. If Jonette had returned, she would dig in even harder, determined to catch the bastard herself. Hunter also wanted to tell her he'd spoken to Jeff Alexander.

Will she be angry? Or relieved?

As his team took their seats across from him and the meeting began, Hunter watched the clock, unable to concentrate fully. He needed to talk to Cameron, but he would have to wait until she arrived.

CHAPTER 11

Cameron Cooper's migraine attacks were better in the morning but worsened as the day went on. She decided the intensifying pain must be the stress of working on the case. Taking advantage of only having headache symptoms as compared to a full onset migraine, she set out to do some work. As she reached the police station's third floor, she immediately spotted Hunter at his desk, reading a file. Fluorescent tubes illuminated the little office behind him, and she clearly saw her chart. Uncomfortable with everyone able to view her work, she blushed. She didn't want anyone to think she was archaic in her methods.

Hunter glanced up, and their eyes met. He put down the file and leaned back in his chair. "Hello, Dr. Cooper," he said as she made her way toward him, past row after row of gray metal desks. "You look much better today. You even have a little color in your cheeks."

Yeah, the color of embarrassment. "Morning, Detective. I'm better today. Thank you again for all you did for me yesterday."

"No worries. I'm happy to help a colleague anytime," he said, smiling. "I'm sorry I left you the way I did yesterday, but I had some pressing business to take care of."

"No need to apologize, Detective. You didn't even have to drive me home or help me inside. You went above and beyond, as they say. I wouldn't have wanted you to stay and babysit me." Her cheeks warmed again at the memories of the day before.

"Okay, then. I hoped you'd be well enough to come in today. I'm eager to go through the victim's files with you. Hopefully something will jump out at you that the rest of us have overlooked."

"I'll grab some coffee, and we can start."

"I've already taken care of that," he said, standing. He extended his hand toward the office door, and she walked over to the doorway, peering into the confined space. "I always like to be prepared." On the desk were two coffee mugs, a pot of steaming coffee, and a donut with white icing on a plate.

Ugh, that donut will haunt me forever.

He grinned from ear to ear as she looked up at him.

She glimpsed at his shoe, the faint outline from her last donut permanently stained on the leather.

"I, uh, remember how much you like vanilla donuts, so I grabbed one before they disappeared," he said as he squeezed past her into the office. He pulled out a chair, and Cameron dutifully sat down.

She had to smile a little herself. He was having fun with her, and she liked the playfulness.

Finnegan poured the coffee and added the slightest splash of cream to hers.

"Wow, Detective, impressive," she said, taking a bite from the donut.

"What's impressive?" he asked as he sat on the chair next to her.

"That you know how I like my coffee."

"You'll learn, I'm *very* observant. Not too much gets by me." He had an aura of satisfaction about him. Detective Hunter Finnegan exuded confidence. "So, let's begin. I have here all the files on our victims. We'll start with number one and work our way up to this week. Okay?"

Her mouth full of donut, she simply nodded.

He continued, "Jennie Saunders. After work one night, she went out to dinner with friends. They parted company at the restaurant. Jennie had told them she would walk home because she lived nearby. That was at 11:40 p.m. on Friday, September 20."

"Where was her son?"

"Sleeping over at his father's house. It was his weekend with the child. His girlfriend was with them and has accounted for his presence the entire night. We checked with building video surveillance and found no evidence of him, or her, leaving the building until about noon the next day. Sanitation workers found Jennie at 10:15 a.m. on Saturday. She'd been dead for approximately ten hours, according to the autopsy." Finnegan studied her photo on the wall for a moment. She was pretty and far too young to be dead. He continued, "She was stabbed once in the abdomen, severing the abdominal aorta. She bled to death almost instantly. The workers found her lying on her back, arms folded over her body as if she were sleeping."

"Any sexual assault?" A standard question, but one Cameron always disliked asking.

"No. No sexual assault. Stabbed once and laid down to die with arms folded over the body. None of the victims had even a hair out of place, except for Linda Birch, who died in the pouring rain, and Medina Montan, whose clothes he tore." Finnegan's eyes searched the board, studying each photograph with a grim expression. "They found each woman in the same position with the same fatal wound. The shortest woman was five-five and a half, the tallest five-eight. They were all brunettes with light-colored eyes, but you know that already," he said as he leaned back in his chair and tapped one long index finger to his lips.

"Have you found anything about the women that is obviously different?"

"Only their marital status. They all had different jobs but with the department. Um, Dr. Cooper, there's something else, something I need to speak to you about. Yesterday, I made a—"

Detective Vince Barone stuck his head into the office. "Boss, I need to speak to you for a minute. I think we have our first break in the case. We found surveillance footage from the night Jenny Saunders died. There appears to be a guy with a beard trailing her. It's grainy, but it might be something. Levine has it on his laptop."

"Excuse me, Doctor," Finnegan said, rising from his seat.

Cameron picked up the file and skimmed the contents. On top were pictures of the crime scene, including several detailed photos of Jennie lying on the ground in a beautiful white dress desecrated by a massive red stain at its center. Her blue cardigan looked as if it had been straightened and buttoned at the collar. She flipped through picture after picture from every angle. Each one was unique, but they told the same story—a woman was dead.

She turned over the next photo and froze. Her hands shook, and the room swayed. Her vision blurred as she struggled to draw a breath. The voice of a child whispered, telling her to leave. *Where is she?* Her entire body trembled, and her head pounded like it might explode, or already had, and this was the aftershock. She fumbled for the trash can, and just as Hunter Finnegan walked back into the office, she vomited.

Hunter rushed to Cameron's side and held back a tendril of her hair. She stood up abruptly, with the garbage can held to her chest and her eyes fixated in front of her.

"Can I help you?" he asked.

"No, thank you. Please excuse me." Her voice was flat, and her posture seemed different to Hunter—straighter, not that she slouched.

He observed as Cameron marched stiffly past groups of detectives, the can of vomit held tight against her chest. He wasn't sure what to do or what to make of what had happened. He sat back in the chair she'd vacated and picked up the pictures she'd been viewing. They were the crime scene photos from Jennie Saunders's murder. Nothing unusual. Nothing that should elicit that kind of response from a seasoned professional. He put the images back inside the folder.

What the heck, he wondered as he stared up at the rainbow-colored web adorning the whiteboard. Dr. Cooper was methodical in her work and knew what she was doing. He wondered again if the stress was making her sick, especially now that he knew what had happened to her.

After ten minutes, Cameron came back to the little office, no garbage pail in sight. Hunter didn't want to embarrass her by asking her what she'd done with the can. He would ask the supply officer for a new one. He didn't want that one back anyway.

"There you are, Detective. I've been looking for you," Cameron said as she walked into the little office, placing her hands on her hips.

"I've been right here, waiting for you to come back. Are you feeling better?"

"What? I'm fine. I just had an idea. It's a beautiful day, so I'm going to take a walk and visit each crime scene. And, if you don't mind, I'd like to visit the stations where the victims worked, ask some questions...observe their work environment."

"You want to *walk* to each crime scene? That's a lot of walking, Doc."

"I walk every day. This little trek will help me reach my 10,000-step goal for the day," she said as she gathered her things and put them back into her bag.

"Are you sure about where you're going? You haven't lived here that long. I have time to come along for part of the day."

"Oh no, Detective, you have more important things to do than lead me around. I'll ask Detective Levine to print out the map he created and use that as my guide. He's at his desk right now," she said, nodding toward Levine. "Let me catch him before he leaves."

Hunter watched her walk away again and noted her posture once more. The stiffness was gone.

Detective Saintil approached Hunter as he stood watching Cameron with Levine. "What's up with her?"

"What do you mean?" Hunter replied, only half interested.

"I just saw her in the ladies' room, emptying a wastebasket of yuck into a toilet. Then she took the top off the ladies' room garbage can and shoved the wastebasket down inside. She washed her hands, splashed some water on her face, and rinsed her mouth out. I said, 'You okay?' and she ignored me. So, I repeated myself, 'Doc, you okay?' She acted like I wasn't there. She just stared at herself in the mirror as she dried her hands. And then things got weird."

Saintil had Hunter's full attention now. "What do you mean, *and then* things got weird?"

"I was concerned, so I touched her arm, you know, to grab her attention. Maybe she's deaf in the ear I was talking into, so I touched her. She recoiled from me and said, 'Excuse me. Please do *not* touch me.' Real stern like. And she walked out. Weird, right?"

"I'm sure she's embarrassed by taking ill here, in the station. She probably wants to forget it ever happened. Let's give her a pass today."

He could tell by her expression she was unconvinced.

"Back to work, Detective," Hunter said more as a suggestion than an order. He walked over to his desk and sat on the edge, waiting for Cameron and Levine to finish. He listened as Levine gave her tips for where to start and the routes she should take for efficiency.

When they finished, Cameron turned back to Hunter. "I'm sure this will take me at least the rest of the day, if not longer, so I'll see you tomorrow? I'll text you later how far I've gotten and what time I think I'll be in, okay?"

"Yeah, sounds good. Be careful, Doc."

"Will do."

Odd, Hunter thought as she disappeared down the stairs. *That was very odd.*

CHAPTER 12

Morning dawned and the sunlight burned through Cameron's skull and into her brain. Her head throbbed. Covering her eyes with one hand, she eased out of bed and drew the curtains closed, leaving enough light to move around. She headed for the bathroom, took two migraine pills, and splashed cool water on her face and neck, waking her up a little more. She wasn't well-rested. Her body felt sluggish and heavy.

Thinking it must be from the migraines, she decided a shower might help. She took her time as she stood under the water jets and let the warm water soothe her tired body. *Detective Finnegan must wonder what he has gotten himself into by bringing me into this case,* she mused as steam filled the room. *I hope he isn't too curious. If he discovers my past, he might not want me around. I probably should come clean about my history. My past does make me particularly well suited for this job. I have personal experience with a serial killer. How many people can say that?*

After she showered, she searched for something comfortable but professional to wear. Her feet hurt from the day before, so she decided on sneakers. She noticed yesterday's outfit dangling wrinkled on a hanger but was sure she'd left her clothes on the bathroom floor. *Maybe I've been sleep-cleaning, and that's why I'm not well-rested?* Her cell phone rang, and Hunter's name flashed across the screen.

"Hello, Detective Finnegan," she said, trying to sound cheerful. The effort hurt her head.

"Morning, Dr. Cooper. How are you?"

"Fine, thanks. I have one last crime scene to look at today, and then I'll head your way."

"All right. I figured I'd call since I didn't hear from you last night. I wanted to see how your 'trek' went yesterday. Did you find your way around okay?"

"Yes, no problems. I'll tell you about it later. I should be back around lunch time."

"Lunch time. Sounds good. I'll make sure I'm available when you get here. See you later."

"See you later."

After Cameron and Hunter made a plan to meet back at the precinct around lunch time, she disconnected the call. She hated being on the phone when she felt ill. She dressed slowly to avoid any sudden movements. Her medicine kicked in and she began to feel better. She sipped some tea and munched on some toast, hoping the food would stay down. The light meal sat well, and once she found her darkest sunglasses and threw a water bottle, notepad, and her cell phone into a lightweight canvas messenger bag, she was ready to head out to the last crime location on her map.

Cameron took her time walking to Jackson Park, where Amy Larsen had been found fatally stabbed. It was a bright, sunny day, not great for someone with migraines, but the warmth of the sun on Cam's face felt good. After she examined the area and took some pictures on her phone, she headed for the precinct where Amy had worked and poked around before starting back to the Sixth Precinct and Hunter Finnegan.

At mid-day, the noise in the building and the horrible lighting assaulted her senses, sparking a renewed dull ache in her head. When she came upstairs, she found Detective Levine busy at his computer. The rest of Finnegan's team, Detectives Murphy, Barone, and Saintil, were nowhere in sight. She found Finnegan in the little office, facing the whiteboard she'd covered in colored strings going in multiple directions.

He must think I'm outdated. With all the technology they have here, I'm playing with colored yarn!

"Detective Finnegan, I guess it's good *afternoon*?" she said, trying to smile even though her head throbbed.

"Hello, Dr. Cooper. How'd it go today?" he said, scrutinizing her.

"Fine." She put her bag on the table and sat in the chair next to Finnegan. Looking at the files he'd opened and spread out on the table, she asked, "What are you up to here?"

"I've been looking at your board and at these files, trying to see what jumps out at me. You know, this board really is old school. Levine did all this work on his computer, which we can project onto a large screen, and I think you may have hurt his feelings a little with all this. He loves doing this computer stuff—all the cross-matching and intersecting. They tell me it's called technology," he said it with a slight grin.

Cameron wasn't sure if he was making fun of himself, her, or both. She had to laugh at his remark. "I know, I know, the whole thing is old school. I guess I'm old school. I need something physical I can touch. It helps me process information. Besides, I can see this plain as day. If I had to use Levine's program, I wouldn't even be able to open it!"

"He can teach you. He's tried to teach me, but he says I'm purposely obtuse, so he has to do all the work. Now, do you think I would do a thing like that?" he said, smiling at her.

He had a beautiful smile. His entire face smiled, not just his lips. His eyes crinkled and dimples appeared in both cheeks. Cameron gazed at him too long without responding, making the moment uncomfortable. Flustered, her headache spiked, and she reflexively shut her eyes and rubbed her temples.

"Dr. Cooper, I think you may have pushed your recovery. Can I bring you something?"

"No, I'll be okay. No sudden movements, right?" She tried to smile but couldn't muster sincerity.

"I told you, my sister has migraines. You're not as well as you say you are. I'm okay if you want to go home and rest. In fact, I insist." He rose from his seat and took her by the arm. "I promise if there are any breaks in the case, I'll call you right away. Okay?"

"Sit back down, Detective. I'm not going home yet. Trust me, I can manage this. I'll go to the break room and eat my lunch that I bought at the food truck out front," she said, holding up a black plastic container and waiving it under Finnegan's nose. "And then I'll take my medicine. After that, we'll go over the notes I took yesterday and this morning on my expedition. Okay?"

"Smells delicious. What'd you buy?"

"A chicken pita. The chef assured me the chicken's not too spicy."

"I'm kind of hungry myself. I think I'll run down and grab something too."

"Meet you in the break room?"

"Okay. Be right back," he said as he grabbed his blazer from the back of his chair and slipped it on.

Cam followed him out of the office, cradling her lunch. They parted at the stairs as Hunter headed down and she veered off down the hallway.

The break room was crowded when Cameron walked in. She wasn't the only one who'd stopped at the food truck. She grabbed a table for two in the corner, placed her food container on the table, and hung her purse and coat on the back of the chrome-framed chair. She fixed a coffee for herself and a cup of tea for Finnegan at the beverage counter. Finnegan wasn't the only observant one.

Detective Finnegan walked through the door as she sat down. He sat across from her and took a sip of the hot tea. "Thank you for getting me tea."

"You're welcome, Detective."

"We aren't all that formal around here. I'd like it if you would call me Hunter, okay?"

"Sure, and you can call me Cameron. Or Doc. I like Doc." She couldn't help but smile at the new friendship they were forming. "What did you get from Gyro George?"

"A gyro. I feel safer sticking with what each truck does best." He took a big bite from the sandwich. "Wow! Best gyro I've had in ages," he said with a mouthful.

Cameron dug in as well, nodding in agreement as she enjoyed the first bite that her sandwich was also delicious. She asked, "Does George stop here every day?"

"Yeah. George is a regular, along with Dagwood's Sandwich Company and the Old Milk Truck."

"The Old Milk Truck?"

"Ice cream," Hunter said, wiping his mouth. "*Good* ice cream. They have some unique add-ins to mix into the ice cream, and the flavors change with the season."

"I love ice cream. I'll keep a watch for the Old Milk Truck."

Hunter nodded in agreement. "There are a lot of great food trucks in the city. Levine goes online and researches which ones have the highest ratings. Those are the ones we try first. If we like them, we go back. Other than that, I'm not much of an experimenter. I let someone else be the guinea pig."

"Unpleasant experience?"

"No, and I want to keep it that way." He smirked. "Besides, if the food is terrible, I don't want to waste my time or money." He examined her for a moment. "You look much better now that you're eating. The color's come back to your cheeks. My sister's migraines sometimes last for days. How about you?"

"It varies for me," she said, nodding. "The longest I've had a migraine was five days. But I've read studies where some patients had migraines that lasted for a month or longer. I can't imagine being in pain for so long. It's so debilitating. People like that can't hold down a regular nine-to-five job. And the public is judgmental toward them. They're accused of faking or being lazy. People don't understand there are different levels of migraine pain, and some individuals suffer for days and weeks as part of their condition." She stopped talking abruptly. *Keep boring him, Cam. He'll be asleep in no time.* "Sorry."

"For what?"

"The boring doctor talk about migraines. I'm sure you were hanging on every word," she said, shaking her head.

"Actually, I find the doctor talk interesting. Learning something new is never boring, especially when the teacher is so attractive."

Did he just compliment me? Her cheeks flushed.

Hunter asked, "Do you have patients you see?"

"No. I went from school to the Bureau. The only patients I ever had were the criminals we caught. I'd talk to them during interrogation, compelling them to confess, tell us where a missing person was, or how many bodies to search for. It was never therapy. It was about understanding the mind of a psychopath and getting leads."

"I wasn't aware analysts had such extensive education."

"I went into law enforcement after getting my doctorate in psychology. I double-majored in psychology and criminal justice. The two connected in my mind. It always interested me—the way the mind worked, what drove someone to behave a certain way. How most people were kind, but others were cruel and violent beyond imagination. But I was also interested in justice for the little guy, the person unable to protect themselves. I wanted to be the voice for them. I considered being a lawyer or a social worker."

"And what changed?" he asked with a genuine interest.

"There was a case I studied involving a little girl terrorized by her stepfather. He would lock her in a small closet and beat her mother into unconsciousness. The girl would press herself into the corner of the closet, wrap her mother's long coat around herself, and place her mother's tall leather boots in front of her to hide. She would squeeze her eyes closed and cover her face with her little hands. If she couldn't see the monster, then the monster couldn't see her either. Then she would sit in the dark, camouflaged as a lumpy coat, and pray, begging her Angel to protect her. When her mother stopped struggling, her stepfather would open the closet door and drag the girl out by whatever he grabbed first: a leg, her hair, her dress, her throat. He was a terrible drunk who became more and more violent as time passed."

"Was that one of your cases?" Hunter offered her a napkin.

She realized she'd teared up thinking about the child. "Sorry." She shook her head as she wiped her eyes with the napkin. "I get caught up when I think about some past victims. She was the reason I didn't become a lawyer. If I were a lawyer, I'd come in after the fact. I needed to be the rescuer, the one to stop or even prevent the violence from starting. That's why all the psychology."

"Whatever happened to the girl?"

"It has a happy ending, sort of. As the wife told it, her husband came home drunker and angrier than usual. Unhappy with dinner, he threw the plate at her. The wife stood up to him for the first time, told him she was leaving and taking her daughter and ran from the kitchen. He followed her, grabbed her by the throat, choked her until she lost consciousness. Left her on the living room floor and went for the child. He grabbed the kid by her arm, yanking it out of the socket. The wife said he was threatening her crying daughter when she came to and screamed. He turned to where she was kneeling on the floor. She'd stashed his gun under the sofa cushion. She pulled it out and shot him...five times...in the chest."

Cameron had reread the newspaper articles so many times, she recalled them from memory. "The neighbors heard the gunshots and called the police. When the cops got there, they were shocked by what they found. The woman was sitting with her daughter on the front lawn, rocking her back and forth, and her husband lay dead on the living room floor." She took in a deep breath and released it. "The court declared it self-defense, and mother and daughter were free of him and safe."

"Wow. That poor kid! I wonder where she is now. I imagine all of that had to be incredibly damaging to her."

Cameron nodded in agreement. "She didn't remember any of it when the police questioned her. She said, 'Angel rescued me,' over and over."

She studied Hunter for a moment. "Your turn. Tell me about yourself, Hunter."

He laughed, "Uh-oh, I feel like I'm being analyzed."

"Making fun of me? I'm not analyzing you." She rolled her eyes. "I want to learn a little more about the man I'm working with. For all I know, *you* are dangerous." She narrowed her eyes at him.

"Dangerous? I'm a cop. I protect and serve, remember?" He grinned.

There's that gorgeous smile again. "Come on, not all cops are 'good' cops." Cameron spoke in a hushed voice so no one nearby would hear and take offense. "Maybe I need to assure myself that you're not one of the bad guys." She sat back and folded her arms across the front of her in wait for his response.

"Okay, well...where should I begin? I grew up here in Manhattan, and my father was a cop, my mother, a teacher. I have one sister, Maggie. I attended Fordham, where I played football and majored in law. Fordham is also where I met my wife." He drew a deep breath. "The beautiful Elizabeth, with whom I fell in love at first sight."

Well, the good ones are usually taken. "A wife, huh? So do you have kids too?"

His lips formed a slight grin like he knew the joke, and she didn't. *What the hell?*

"No, no children. I'm a widower. But I like the way you seemed disappointed by the revelation that I had a wife."

Her cheeks warmed again. "Oh no, not at all. You don't wear a ring, so I was surprised when you said 'my wife.' Did she pass away recently?"

"No, it happened a long time ago. And that's a conversation for another day." He stood, gathered the empty food containers, and pushed them into the garbage can. "Ready to go back to work?"

"Yes. I'll finish my coffee and be along in a minute."

"Okay, meet you in the back office."

After Hunter disappeared from sight, Cam reached into her canvas bag and took out her bottle of pills. The break room had grown quieter. Only two other women still chatted over coffee. The fluorescent lighting and the noise had caused her headache to spike. She'd barely gotten her lunch down. She shook two pink capsules into her hand and threw them back with a swig from her mug, swallowing hard.

Leaning forward with her elbows on the table, she cradled her face in her hands, covering her eyes from the intrusive light. Deep breaths calmed the queasiness. After a few minutes, the medicine kicked in and she felt somewhat better. Determined to make it through the day, she gathered her belongings and headed for the little office and Hunter Finnegan.

CHAPTER 13

Hunter was right where he said he would be, in the back office. Sitting at the small metal desk, he stared up at Cameron's whiteboard and the mass of colored string connecting photographs to points on a map. Cam sat down at the table across from him and examined the board herself.

"My map is an organized mess," Cam said. "No discernible patterns, nothing special about dates, and nothing unusual about locations. We can deduce these were premeditated killings and not random because their work links all the women. They were all employees of the NYPD."

"Yeah, and they have similar characteristics," Hunter added.

"Was the victim profile disseminated internally? Anyone who has similar features to these women, tall, athletic build, brunette, light eyes, should be extra vigilant whenever they're out."

"Yes, after the third homicide, we sent out an internal memo stating employees who matched the description were potential targets. That was ten days ago, and things have been quiet since then."

Cameron thought about the number of days between each killing and said, "Even the time length between the killings appears to be random." She reached into her bag and pulled out a yellow pad containing her notes from each scene she'd visited, scribbled in blue ink. "I have to be honest, Hunter, as I visited each site, what struck me the most was nothing. Nothing struck me at all. Each scene was different. Different neighborhoods, different depths of exposure. Most were right out in the open where anyone could have happened upon the killer as he attacked. Only Medina Montan was found in an area offering any kind of cover."

"Yes, I agree. The attacks are swift. He moves in, strikes, and disappears. If anyone saw something, they wouldn't have realized what was happening. We have a few eyewitnesses who may have given us insight into how he gets close to the women. For example, the night Linda Birch died, it was pouring out. She went into the market and left her umbrella at the door. The checkout clerk, a kid named Robbie Diaz, said a man took Linda's umbrella and she chased after him. Approximately five to ten minutes later, Robbie found Linda with the umbrella on the ground next to her. Robbie didn't see the guy, but he'd heard Linda yell after him about taking her umbrella." Hunter shook his head as he studied the board again.

"Linda Birch was a street cop, right? It was her night off, and she ran into the market for a couple of items."

"Yes. Then there's Amy Larsen," Hunter continued.

"Ah, yes, Amy Larsen. The precinct 'sweetheart.' She was so well-liked someone thought to mention that even Chief Dwyer liked her."

Hunter smiled slightly. "I didn't know he liked anyone." He studied the photo of the attractive woman on the whiteboard, and his expression saddened. "Well, a jogger found Amy on the ground in front of a bench in Jackson Park. We have a witness's testimony stating she observed a woman, presumably Amy, approach a well-dressed man lying on the ground. The witness thought the woman was trying to help him, and she had her phone out. She was afraid to get involved and hoped Amy would help the man. Records show that Amy called 911 at the same time the witness spotted the woman helping the person on the ground. Amy told the 911 operator a white man with a black beard had stabbed her. We think this guy pretended to need help to lure Amy Larsen over to him, and when she knelt next to him, he struck."

"Did she go to the park regularly?"

"Every Tuesday and Thursday night, she took a yoga class. She took the shortcut from her house, four blocks away, through the park to the door of the yoga studio."

Cameron shook her head. "She was a popular lady. Her death left a hole in the ranks. When I went to the precincts where each woman worked, I talked to some of the people they worked with daily, including Jennie Saunders's partner, Officer Leo Gentile. They all said the same thing. They couldn't imagine anyone having a reason to hurt these women. They had no known enemies or threats against them. They were all described as the nicest, kindest, most professional. Not one negative comment about any of these ladies. It killed me to talk to Officer Gentile. His name befits him. He's still visibly upset by her death. He had a hard time talking about her, but he wants this guy caught more than he cares about his own pain."

They continued to go over her notes, trying to find small connections that hopefully would lead to a big break. They were deep into theories and motives when Hunter opened Jennie Saunders's file. Her photo topped the stack of paper in the folder. He flipped the picture over, revealing a crime scene snapshot of Jennie's body.

Cam's headache spiked. She reflexively rubbed her temples and closed her eyes.

"Leave."

She opened her eyes. *That voice again.* "What? Did you say something?" she asked Hunter.

"No, I didn't say a word. You look pale. You want some water or something?"

"No, I'm...I'm fine." She sat back and took a deep breath. "You know, on second thought, I'm gonna grab some coffee. Do you want some?"

"No, thanks."

Cameron stood slowly, unsteady from the pain attacking her brain like a sledgehammer pounding cement. She walked past the rows of desks, nausea creeping its way into her as she heard the whisper once more.

"Leave." It was the voice of a child, but there were no children in the room.

Cameron perspired as the migraine gained new momentum and strength. She hoped the caffeine in the coffee would reduce the pain as she made her way to the break room.

She poured the steaming hot liquid into a mug and inhaled the fragrant aroma. The break room was far too bright, and she stepped back into the hall where she spotted a dark office. She tried the doorknob, which was unlocked, and entered, closing the door behind her. A slit of light from the door's window dimly lit the room, and Cam could make out a wooden desk with a leather chair, two club chairs in front of it, and a small sofa along the far wall with a low table next to it. She sat down on the couch and sipped her coffee. Her headache spiked again and she dropped the coffee, wincing at the pain. Pressing her palms to her temples, she slumped back onto the couch and lost consciousness.

"Hello?" Adrianne Schechter gently nudged the woman lying on her couch in the dark. She touched her wrist for a pulse. It was rapid but not alarmingly so.

Dr. Schechter had no afternoon appointments and hadn't expected to find anyone in her office when she came back from a meeting down the hall. When she opened the door, she found spilled coffee and a woman she didn't recognize asleep on the couch. Concerned, Schechter tried to wake her.

"Hello." She nudged the woman again.

The woman moaned, and her eyes fluttered.

Dr. Schechter grabbed tissues and squatted down to clean up the spill and pick up the coffee cup. She turned on a desk light, giving the room a soft glow. Looking up at the woman again, she said, "I'm Dr. Schechter. Can I help you?"

The woman slowly sat up, straightened her wrinkled clothing, and brushed the hair from her face. "Hello." She glanced around at her surroundings. "Who did you say you were again?"

"Dr. Adrianne Schechter. This is my office. I just found you on the couch. Coffee spilled on the floor. Are you okay? Do you need help or someone to talk to? I head up the Employee Assistance Unit. I'm a psychologist, and whatever we discuss is strictly confidential," she said, her voice soft. "And you are?"

She stood up tall, smoothed the front of her pants with her hands, and said, "Embarrassed. If I caused the mess you found, I apologize." She turned to walk away.

"Is embarrassed your first name or your last?" Schechter smirked at the woman in front of her.

She stopped and turned toward the well-dressed doctor, considering a retort when she felt a vibration in her pant pocket. She retrieved a cell phone and checked the caller ID. "You must excuse me. I need to answer this." She walked out of the office and down the hall.

"Hey, wait a minute," Schechter called after her. "Who are you? What were you doing in my office? Do you work here?" She followed her out of the office just in time to see the woman give her a wave over her shoulder and turn the corner. "I'm reporting this," she shouted.

Dr. Schechter went back to her office and looked around. Everything appeared in order as she wondered what the hell the strange woman had been doing in her space.

From his viewpoint in the small office, behind his desk, Hunter caught a wild-eyed Cameron rush to the doors and forcibly push through them, nearly knocking down another officer, then disappear down the stairs. He grabbed her coat and messenger bag and followed her. When he arrived at the bottom, she'd vanished.

CHAPTER 14

HUNTER HAD A STACK of folders in front of him and a furrowed brow when Cameron arrived the next day. She knew sorting through the files wouldn't be easy for him, and sifting through paper wasn't her way of working. She needed a new angle that didn't involve reading folder after folder.

"Morning," she said as she entered the small office they were using as the work zone for this case.

"Good morning, indeed. Everything okay?"

"Yes, why do you ask?" Cam placed her sweater on the back of the chair and a black leather tote on the floor next to her.

"You left kind of abruptly yesterday. I thought you had an emergency."

Cam stared at him with a blank expression. "Did I? I didn't realize. Um, sorry."

"You didn't realize? When I chased you down the stairs to give you your bag and coat, you didn't realize you should've told me you were leaving? Or, at the very least, get your stuff before you left. I thought the building was on fire and you were the only one who knew."

What the hell? Did I leave suddenly? I don't remember. Cameron shook her head and smiled, "I'm so sorry, Hunter. That was kind of you to bring me my things. I had an urgent phone call, but everything's okay," she hedged.

"I didn't bring you your things. When I got to the bottom floor, you'd already disappeared. They're over there," he said, nodding to the corner where a chair sat with Cameron's coat and messenger bag perched on it.

Cameron's face warmed with embarrassment. She'd tried to bluff her way through the conversation and was now in an awkward position. "I had a sudden migraine attack and needed to get home. I don't remember leaving abruptly. Not unusual with these kinds of attacks," she bluffed again.

"Was it a headache or an urgent phone call?"

"What?" she asked, confused.

"The reason you left so abruptly. Was it a headache or an urgent phone call? First, you said it was a phone call, and then you said it was a headache."

Shit! What is going on? Change the subject and figure it out later. "Oh...both. I received a stressful phone call that caused my headache to spike. I apologize for my unprofessionalism. I'm here and ready to work, so let's get to it."

"Maybe you should make an appointment with Dr. Schechter."

"Dr. Schechter? Who's he?"

"She. Dr. Adrianne Schechter, the in-house psychologist who runs the Employee Assistance Unit. She helps officers and other employees deal with work-related stress and coping with serious issues, like the loss of a fellow officer. I thought the two of you'd met."

"Oh, I've met so many new people I have a hard time keeping the names straight. Why do you think I should make an appointment with her?"

"I'm concerned this case is causing your migraines. What do you think? Does it sound like a possibility?"

"I suppose anything is possible, but I have my headaches under control. I don't need an appointment with Dr. Schechter as I'm a doctor myself, right?"

Hunter held a finger to his lips as his eyes searched her face. "You know, I've always heard doctors make the worst patients. Don't be your own worst enemy, okay?"

"Yeah, okay. So, what are you looking at?"

"Case files. I'm still trying to find a connection."

"I want to take a fresh approach today. I'm aware your people have already interviewed the victims' families, but I'd like the opportunity to speak to them. Would you like to help me?"

Hunter ran his hand over the top file, contemplating the question. "Okay. I think you have a point. You might ask a question or notice something my team didn't. Fresh eyes, right?"

"Exactly. And it will make it easier for me to find a common thread between the victims if there is one. There might not be."

Hunter nodded in agreement. "I'll call the people we already spoke to and ask them if they wouldn't mind coming in for a follow-up. You can handle the interview, and I'll chime in when I think it's necessary. We can start with Charlie Saunders, Jennie's ex, ask if he's up for another interview. Her parents live out of state. We also interviewed the friends she ate with that night. They had little to add. They were all pretty shaken up. In shock, I'm sure."

"I'm sure," Cameron agreed absentmindedly.

Hunter opened a folder, retrieving a photograph. He examined the glossy page before holding it up for Cameron. "This is Linda Birch, another cop." He pointed to where her photo hung on the whiteboard behind him. "The one found by the grocery store with a small bag of mushrooms on the ground next to her." He stood and tapped the red magnet on the map marking the grocery store location, then ran his finger along the string back to a green magnet that marked her home. "She lived three blocks from the market," he said, shaking his head. "Turns out she was making dinner for her boyfriend. After they found her, two uniforms went to her house to investigate. The boyfriend was waiting for her. I'm sure he would come in any time."

Cameron pulled a notepad and a pen out of her bag. "Excellent. What's his name? And do you have his number? I can call him right now."

"Mark Ryerson. Here's his info," Hunter said, sliding a piece of paper across the table to Cameron. "I'll call Charlie Saunders at my desk while you call Ryerson."

Cameron nodded, examining the paper Hunter had slipped her. The fluorescent lights in the tiny office strained her eyes, and Hunter's comment concerned her. She hadn't met Adrianne Schechter. She would have remembered meeting a colleague. *What the hell? Could Hunter be mistaken?* She dialed Ryerson's number from the precinct phone.

"Hello?"

"Hello, Mr. Ryerson, my name is Dr. Cameron Cooper. I'm working with the NYPD on Linda Birch's case. Do you have a moment to speak?"

"Sure, I have a minute."

"First, I want to offer you my condolences. I'm very sorry this happened to Linda and to you. And I will do my best to help catch this guy."

"Thank you, I appreciate it."

"We believe Linda's murder links to two other deaths. I'm new to the case, and I'm following up with family and friends of the victims as a way of putting a fresh perspective on the situation. Would you have time to meet with me today or tomorrow? Or I'll meet you somewhere. I promise I won't take up a lot of your time."

"I have some free time this afternoon if you wouldn't mind meeting me near my office."

"Sure, no problem. You tell me where and when."

"How's 2:00 at Perks on 41st and Broadway?"

"Perfect. See you then." Cameron disconnected the call and glanced over her shoulder at Hunter, still holding the phone to his ear.

She gazed at him nodding and listening, not talking, except for the occasional "uh-huh" and "hmm." She walked over to his desk and sat across from him, watching him as he sat pensive, his oversized hand cradling the small cellphone. With his left hand, he scribbled notes onto a pad, underlining certain words with heavy strokes and exclamation marks. His broad shoulders tensed and strained the seams of his Oxford shirt. She enjoyed working with him. He was detailed, seasoned, and passionate about the work. She pondered if he was just as fervent in his personal life. A handsome man, but not vain. He seemed unaware of the way his female colleagues ogled him. She wondered if he had a girlfriend.

Hunter put his phone down, sat back in his chair, and rubbed his face. "That was more intense than I hoped it would be. Charlie Saunders may be the ex-husband, but he still cares for Jennie. She was a great mom, and his kid is distraught, which is making him distraught."

"Is he willing to sit through a few more questions?"

"Sure. He's a cop, remember?"

The conversation with Levine flashed in Cameron's memory. Charlie Saunders was one of the good guys. "Right. Charlie's the hero cop who rushed into a burning building and saved a baby."

"Correct. He's coming in during lunch. We can sit down with him and you ask him whatever you like. He's been searching for this guy every day and would love to be the one who nabs the bastard."

"I'll make some notes while I wait. I spoke to Mark Ryerson, and I'm meeting him at two near his office. Do you want to come with me or give me some follow-up questions?"

"Let's see how the day unfolds. How about Eric Larsen? The news of his wife's death left him stricken. Levine and I spoke to him initially. He had a tough time giving us the little information that he did. Hopefully now, he's in a better place to talk."

"I'll call him. I can lend a gentle touch to my approach," Cam said, standing to go back to what she now considered her office.

"What? You think I don't know how to be gentle? I can be gentle," Hunter teased, eyes wide and hands held out in front of him.

"I'm sure you're incredibly gentle, but I'll call him just the same," she said with a smile.

As she retreated into the office with the harsh fluorescent lighting, she stopped in the doorway and squinted up at the glaring fixtures. They were a known trigger for headaches. She hit the light switch to determine how dark the office was with them off. Sitting at the table with a pen and pad in hand, she decided she needed the lights on. As she stood to hit the switch again, she found Hunter smirking in the doorway.

"Um, what's up?" he asked.

"The lights," Cam said, pointing at them with one finger. "Fluorescent lights are awful for migraine sufferers. The glare from them can trigger headaches."

"I didn't know that," Hunter replied, studying the overhead lights. "It's too dark in here with them off. I have an idea. Give me a few minutes to see what I can find," he said with a wink and that little smirk, which gave Cam a happy feeling.

She sat back down and watched Hunter walk away. It was the perfect opportunity to sit in a somewhat dark and quiet room to rest her eyes and her head. She meditated for ten minutes, and when Hunter still hadn't come back, she took a walk to the break room for a coffee and a snack.

As she poured a cup of steaming coffee, a voice behind her said, "Well, look who it is. Sleeping Beauty."

Cameron turned to eye a stylishly-dressed woman, late forties, light brown hair that skimmed her shoulders, and the most striking, angry blue eyes she'd ever seen. "I beg your pardon? Were you speaking to me?"

"Getting some coffee? Plan on holding onto it today?"

"I'm not following. I think you may have confused me with someone else." Cam gave the stranger a slight smile and walked over to the table with the daily offerings from the deli. She grabbed a napkin and picked up a cruller. As she turned again, the stranger stood in front of her, arms crossed over her chest, and one eyebrow raised in what Cam interpreted as annoyance.

"We met yesterday, in my office. You were asleep on my couch and had spilled your coffee on the floor. Ring any bells?"

Cam was about to respond with a drawn-out "no" when she remembered what Hunter had said to her about meeting some doctor, the police psychologist. "Yes, yes...that's right. Dr. Shephard, right?"

"Sheck-ter. Doctor Adrianne Schechter."

"Sheck-ter. Right. I'm Dr. Cameron Cooper." Cam extended a hand.

Adrianne Schechter shook her hand with a firm grip and, Cam thought, a somewhat aggressive demeanor.

"I know who you are," Schechter said. "Detective Finnegan told me all about you."

"Did he? What did he have to say?"

"He said you were a consultant to the department regarding the suspected serial killer."

Cam replied, "Not suspected. Definitely a serial killer."

Schechter eyeballed her up and down. "Do you always crash other people's offices?"

"No, not at all. In fact, yesterday afternoon is a blur to me. I suffer from migraines. The lights in here"—Cam pointed to the ceiling—"are killers for people like me...those prone to headaches. Too long under these fluorescents, and I can't see straight. That's why I stopped in your office. I tried to escape the barrage of glare from the cheap light fixtures."

Adrianne Schechter appeared unmoved, her intense blue eyes remaining focused on Cameron. "So why did you run out without introducing yourself?"

Hunter stuck his head into the room. "There you are. I have a surprise for you. Come on. Hello, Dr. Schechter, how's it going?"

Before Adrianne Schechter answered, Cam replied, "Gotta go. So nice meeting you, Dr. Sheck-ter."

Cameron moved past Hunter in the doorway as he gave Schechter a nod and left her standing alone, fuming.

CHAPTER 15

Hunter led Cameron through the open space where gray desk after gray desk lined up. The office door was closed, and the room dark.

"What's going on? What's the surprise?"

"I think you'll like this," he said, opening the door to the tiny room. He motioned for Cam to go in, and she obliged. Hunter clapped his hands twice, and two floor lamps lit up.

Cam beamed at him. "Hunter, these are wonderful. You didn't just buy these, did you?"

"No. I went down to the basement, and there were a few of these lying around. I seem to recall someone else had a similar problem with the lighting here. The 'clap on, clap off' feature is an added bonus." He smiled broadly as he leaned against the door frame.

Cam touched his arm, laughing. "Well, I love them. They're perfect," she said, giving him a playful nudge.

"Glad you like them. I hope they'll help assuage those headaches."

"Yes. I think they'll definitely help. Thank you. I really appreciate your thoughtfulness," Cam said, still smiling up at him. She wanted to say more. She wanted to tell him how much she liked him, not just the lights. That he was also perfect. "And I guess now I have no excuses. Time to get back to work."

"Yeah, me too. Levine and I have a meeting with the chief in a few, but I should be back in time for Charlie Saunders. See you later," he said with a nod.

"See you later," Cam replied.

She watched as Hunter gathered his things, slipped on his blazer, and walked toward a waiting Glen Levine. *God! Look at him! He's so handsome. So thoughtful. And he's single, and he made sure I knew it. Maybe he feels the same way I do. Could be a lot of fun.*

She picked up her phone and dialed Alex Larsen, daydreaming about Hunter until the ringing was cut off by a man's voice.

"Mr. Larsen?"

"Yes. Who is this?"

"Mr. Larsen, my name is Dr. Cameron Cooper. I'm a consultant to the NYPD, and I'm calling to see if you can spare a few minutes to talk to me regarding your wife's case. But first, I want to extend my deepest condolences. I'm so sorry for everything you and your family have been through."

"Thank you, Dr. Cooper, for the condolences," Alex Larsen replied. "In what capacity are you working on the case?"

"I'm a former analyst for the FBI. I'm what some people call a pro-filer. Now I do consultant work with local law enforcement. Detective Finnegan, whom I'm sure you recall talking to, has brought me in on the case for my expertise. I've worked on cases involving serial killers in the past."

"So, it's official? Amy's death was at the hands of a serial killer?"

"Yes, I'm afraid so. I'm sure this must be very difficult for you, but do you have time to meet and answer some questions? You could come here, or I could come to you. Whatever's easiest for you."

There was silence for a few seconds, and Cam expected to hear an angry outburst.

"Yes." Alex Larsen's voice quivered. He took a deep breath and blew it out. "You can come here, but you have to leave by 3:30." His voice continued to shake. "My children will be home from school by then."

"Thank you, Mr. Larsen. I'll stop by this afternoon between 2:30 and 3:00. Is that okay?"

"Yes, Dr. Cooper, that's fine. Goodbye."

Cameron disconnected the call and placed her cell phone on the table in front of her. She'd heard the heartbreaking pain in Alex Larsen's voice. Interviewing the people closest to the victims was an unwelcome job but a necessary one for finding a connection between the women and their killer.

At 12:00 sharp, Charlie Saunders arrived on the third floor of the Sixth Precinct. He spotted Hunter and made his way to the back of the room. Hunter stood to greet him, and the two men shook hands and exchanged greetings.

"Thanks for coming in, Charlie. I want you to meet a colleague, Doctor Cameron Cooper." Hunter walked Charlie over to Cameron's door and gave a knock before entering.

"Cam, Charlie Saunders is here. Charlie, this is Dr. Cameron Cooper."

"Officer Saunders," Cameron said, standing and extending her hand to the man. "I'm so sorry for your loss."

Charlie gave her hand a brief shake. "Thank you, Doctor. Jennie's death is still shocking to me."

"Please, have a seat." Cameron motioned to the chair across from her. "And you can call me Cameron." She gave Charlie a warm smile. "Can we get you something? Water or coffee?"

"No, thanks. I'm good. Let's just get this over with."

"I understand. We'll try to be as brief as possible." Cameron met Hunter's eyes, and he gave her a nod. "I realize you've been over this already with Detectives Murphy and Barone, right after the shocking news of your ex-wife's death. I thought perhaps since then, you may have recalled something new. So now that you've had time to process everything that happened, can you think of anyone who would want to hurt Jennie? Someone she arrested, or someone in the neighborhood? Possibly a relative?"

Saunders shook his head as Cameron spoke. "No, no, and no. She didn't bust any dangerous criminals. She didn't have any beefs with neighbors, and if any relatives were giving her a hard time, she would've told me."

"How can you be so sure?" Hunter asked.

"We may have divorced, but we were still close friends. We were high school sweethearts. She got pregnant unexpectedly, so we got married. Marriage didn't work for us, but we remained best friends. If she had a problem with someone, she would've told me. She always put our son and his safety first. Besides, Jennie was a sweetheart. Everyone loved her."

"The park they found her in, did she go there often?" Cameron asked.

"Not that I'm aware of, but it's close to her apartment. She probably walked by there all the time. I don't think she ever went there to hang out or whatever. Hanging out in a park wasn't her style."

Hunter opened Jennie's file and slid two photos across the table to Saunders. "These are pictures from building surveillance cameras. Do you see the person behind her? He's a person of interest. We believe he was following her, and he fits the description another victim gave a 911 operator. Does he look familiar?"

Saunders examined the blurry black and white photos, then tossed them on the desk in front of Cameron. "No. I don't have the slightest possibility in mind of someone who looks like that. The only guy I know with a beard is my buddy, Sean, and that's not him."

"How can you be so sure?" Hunter asked.

"He's a ginger. Bright red. Fire engine red. I heard about the 911 call. The guy who attacked the lady in the park had a black beard."

Hunter turned to Cameron, anticipating another question.

She sat relaxed in her chair, staring at the pictures on the desk in front of her. She seemed mesmerized by them, her eyes fixated, and she was eerily still.

"Cam, do you have another question for Charlie?"

She remained fixated on the photos.

"Cam?" Hunter spoke again. When she still didn't answer, Saunders gave Hunter a concerned look. "*Cam*," he said, a little louder.

"Is she having a seizure?" Saunders asked.

Hunter stood, leaned over the desk, and slapped his hand down. "*Cam*."

She blinked once, and her eyes met his, then traveled over to Charlie Saunders. "Oh," she said, sitting straight up in the chair and squaring her shoulders. "This," she said as she picked up the two photos and held them for the men to examine, "is not a killer. This is some schmuck walking down the street." And then she tore the photos slowly in half, holding Hunter's gaze.

Hunter sat dumbfounded.

Cameron's eyes shifted to the open doorway where she noticed Adrianne Schechter across the room, studying them. She continued, "And there's the condescending woman I ran into, staring at me as we speak. So smug. You should've seen the way she looked at me. With pity in her eyes. Can you imagine someone like her having pity for me? And as for you, Officer Saunders, I surmise you wouldn't recognize a killer if one were sitting across from you."

Cameron stood, straightened, and smoothed her clothing, then raised a hand to the doorway like a game show model. "We're done here, gentlemen."

Hunter and Charlie Saunders looked at one another and back to Cameron. Hunter was astonished, Saunders pissed.

"Wha— Um, you have no more questions?" Hunter stammered.

"No."

He motioned to Charlie. "I'll walk you out."

Charlie stood glaring at Cameron. "Hunter? What the hell is going on here?"

"Uh...we have what we need for now. Come on, I'll go downstairs with you."

Cameron called after him, "Oh, Detective, tell Doctor Superior that staring is rude and she should move along if she knows what's good for her."

Hunter glanced over to where Adrianne Schechter loitered, watching them, and back to Cameron as his gut ached.

CHAPTER 16

Perks Café was a gourmet coffee and sandwich shop where business-people who had no time for a sit-down breakfast or lunch could grab something quick, yet it was just as good as any restaurant. The shop offered delicious breakfast sandwiches, fresh pastries, salads, and lunches to grab and go. For those who had time to sit, eat, and relish the wonderful aromas of the petite café, there was a small dining area with tables for two or four.

Cameron, escorted by Detective Glen Levine, arrived several minutes early for her meeting with Mark Ryerson, hoping to settle in before he got there, but when she walked through the door and spotted the man sitting alone in the corner, she realized he'd beaten her there.

"Mr. Ryerson?" Cameron approached him cautiously.

The man glanced up at her, the sadness in his eyes obvious. At forty-one, Mark Ryerson resembled a surfer boy with wavy blond hair, gray eyes, deep dimples, and a lean physique. "Yes," he said, standing and extending a hand.

"I'm Cameron Cooper. Thank you for meeting me. This is Detective Levine," she said, motioning to the tall, bald man next to her. Levine's presence annoyed Cameron, but Hunter insisted she take him with her to interview both Mark Ryerson and Alex Larsen.

The two men shook hands, Levine pulled another chair over to the table, and they all sat. "You have my condolences, Mr. Ryerson. I understand you and Linda were in a long-term relationship. I'm sure this must be extremely difficult for you, and I appreciate your meeting with us."

Ryerson nodded slightly. "Yes, Linda's death has left an enormous hole in my life. Sometimes when I wake up in the morning, for a moment, I think the memory was a nightmare, but then I realize it all really happened and my heart hurts all over again." He sat with his hands folded on the table in front of him, his pain apparent to Cameron and Levine.

Levine asked, "Can you tell us what happened the night Linda died? Did she go to the market every Friday night? Was that routine for her?"

"No, it wasn't routine for her. Linda had no routines. She lived her life spontaneously. She would go to the store when she needed to, work out when the mood struck, eat when she was hungry. The only thing routine in her life was her job, and even that varied. Every day presented different challenges, but the hours were standard."

"Do you have any idea why Linda went to the market that night?" Cam asked.

"I think so. When I got to her house, she wasn't there. Music was playing in the kitchen. She liked to listen to music when she cooked. Dinner was almost ready. She'd prepared all my favorites," Ryerson said with a slight smile, his dimples accenting his chiseled face. "There was a cake in the oven, crab cakes ready for frying on the stove, and veal. She was cooking veal marsala with roasted potatoes...my favorite dinner. She was a fantastic cook. She wanted to be a chef when she retired from the force." He stopped talking and stared at his coffee, the smile fading from his lips.

Cam reached over and touched his hand. "Can you go on, Mr. Ryerson?"

His eyes moist, he nodded. "She must've forgotten the mushrooms for the marsala. They were in the bag next to her on the—" He took a deep breath and a sip of his coffee. "She'd planned a romantic night. I'm sure she planned on asking me to move in with her, but I had my own surprise. I had a ring to propose. I was so nervous." Ryerson stopped again, lost in thought. And then he added in a dreamy tone, "Did you know she saved a man's life? Linda performed CPR until the paramedics arrived. And she helped deliver a baby. She was a great cop...loved her job...loved helping people."

"Did she ever mention anyone giving her any problems? Another officer? A neighbor? Or did she ever receive any threats?" Cameron asked.

Mark Ryerson shook his head. "No, she had a lot of friends in the neighborhood and was well-respected on the job. This should never have happened." He slammed his hand on the table, spilling his coffee and startling Cameron and Levine. He grew suddenly angry and revved up. "Linda shouldn't be dead, and we shouldn't be here talking about her this way. I hope when you find whoever did this, he gets the death penalty and suffers as much as she did."

Cameron didn't want to be the one to tell him New York had no death penalty, so she let the wish go. "What about someone who always seemed to be hanging around? Did she ever say anything like 'Oh, I ran into so and so again today?' "

"No."

"How about people who worked in her building? Anyone ever ask her out, flirt with her, or come on to her?"

"Before we started dating, I think she dated a cop or two. At least one, anyway. She didn't say much about it, only that the guy was a detective, not in her precinct, but somewhere close by. The subject only came up because she ran into him somewhere. She bragged her ex told her she looked gorgeous. She was kidding around with me, trying to make me jealous."

"Did she say anything about his features or a name?" Cameron asked.

"I don't remember. The conversation was brief. I'm not easily shaken. I didn't obsess over some guy she briefly dated."

Levine chimed in, "We have a person of interest. White guy with a black beard. Can you think of anyone who fits that description?"

"Sure, we're in the middle of 'Movember.' Half the guys I work with have dark beards. They like to take the movement beyond the mustache. But a beard doesn't exactly make them murderers, does it?"

"No," Cameron responded. "But did any of them ever have a problem with Linda?"

"No, these are respectful guys, not murderous umbrella-stealing creeps."

"Would it make sense to you that the reason her attacker got so close to her without alarming her was because she knew him?" Cameron asked.

The expression on Mark Ryerson's face changed at the realization his beautiful Linda may have known her killer. He reddened with anger as he leaned into the table. "If she knew the bastard who did this, he'll have to answer to me." He stood, swallowed the last of his coffee, and said, "I need to get back to work. Call me if you have any more questions. Any time, day or night, I'll be available until you catch this asshole...dead or alive."

Levine seamlessly weaved in and out of traffic on the way to Alex Larsen's house as Cameron gazed out the window, lost in thought. He said, "Any thoughts, Doc?"

Cameron shook her head as she continued to process the conversation they'd had with Mark Ryerson.

"Maybe after we speak to Alex Larsen, something will jump out at you."

"Hmm," she responded.

"Eventually, we will find a lead. These kinds of killers either make a mistake, or they try to taunt the police, which is another mistake."

"I agree," Cameron said, still staring out the window.

Levine pulled up in front of a beautiful, well-kept brownstone and squeezed his SUV between two parked cars. "We're here," he said, sighing. "Amy Larsen was a lovely lady. I wish we didn't have to do this."

Cameron and Levine exited the vehicle and stood on the sidewalk, taking in the incredible five-story home in front of them. They climbed the steep front steps side by side, and Levine tapped the door knocker three times.

A petite, middle-aged woman answered the door, inviting them in. "I'm Patricia. I manage the house for Alex and Amy." She shook her head and nervously wiped her hands on a kitchen towel draped over a shoulder as she led them into a posh parlor with the flair of a professional's touch off to the left of the entryway. "It's as if she'll be walking through the door any moment now. I don't think I'll ever get used to her not being here. Please have a seat. Can I bring you something? A drink?"

"No, thank you," Cameron answered.

"I'll tell Alex you're here," Patricia said. "Be gentle with him, please. He's quite vulnerable right now. I'm sure you can understand."

Cameron and Levine simultaneously nodded in understanding.

In front of two floor-to-ceiling windows were four club chairs circling a low, marble-topped coffee table. Cameron and Levine took a seat and waited less than a minute for Alex Larsen to appear in the double-wide doorway. He stood a lean six feet, with graying blond hair and pale hazel eyes that revealed his pain. They both stood as he walked into the room.

"Hello," Larsen said as he extended his hand. "I'm Alex Larsen."

He shook both their hands. "Please, sit."

"Mr. Larsen, thank you for meeting with us today, and on behalf of myself and Detective Levine, I want to say how deeply sorry we are for your loss," Cameron started.

Levine added, "Yes, our condolences. I knew Amy. Not very well, but she was a kind and caring person and incredibly well-liked in her precinct."

"Thank you."

"Alex, I understand your children are from another relationship?" Cameron asked.

"Yes. Lara and Christian. My first wife had problems with addiction. She fought her demons for years, but about six months after Christian's birth, she started using again. She suffered from postpartum depression, and the drugs were her only solace. I tried to help her, but the problem got to where she refused my help and she filed for divorce, said she didn't want a family anymore. She hasn't seen Christian since his first birthday. Neither child remembers her. Amy was their mother...the only real mother they ever had," Larsen said, gazing at a glossy black-and-white photo of Amy on a table next to Levine.

"When was the last time you saw your ex?" Cameron asked.

"Oh, several years ago. Right before Amy and I married, I tracked her down to tell her. I thought it was the right thing to do, you know? I also told her Amy would adopt the children. Jean, my ex, had signed away her parental rights when we divorced."

"How did she feel about the adoption?" Cameron asked, scribbling notes on a pad.

"Jean was fine with the idea. She congratulated me and wished me well. It broke my heart, though, when she didn't ask about the kids. Didn't even ask to see a picture of them. She was so disconnected from us. She was doing okay at that point, had a job, a one-room apartment, and was trying her best to stay clean. That was ten years ago, and I lost track of where she is now or even if she's still alive."

Levine shook his head. "What a rough situation. Addiction is one of the biggest problems we face every day."

"Yes, it's a terrible disease," Larsen commiserated.

"Did Jean have any problems with violence? Did she have a temper?" Cameron asked, hoping for a little more insight on the ex.

"Jean?" Larsen chuckled a little. "Not a violent bone in her body. Even when she was on a bender and out of her mind on drugs, she wasn't violent. You wouldn't be suggesting Jean had something to do with Amy's murder, would you?" His eyes darted back and forth between Cameron and Levine.

"We're just trying to exhaust all possibilities," Levine said.

"Alex," Cameron continued, "where was Amy going that night?"

"Home. Every Tuesday and Thursday night, she took a yoga class at a studio about four blocks from here. Class started at seven and ended at eight. She called 911 after eight, so she was definitely on her way home."

Cameron flipped through her notes and asked, "She called 911 at 8:47. Is it possible she stopped somewhere on her way home?"

"I doubt it. Amy was friends with most of the people in the class, and sometimes they would linger after class. The studio has a health bar for healthy snacks, juices, and smoothies. She brought one home once, a green frothy shake made from kale and other so-called healthy things. It was terrible," he said softly, chuckling at the memory. "Anyway, sometimes the group would have a quick snack and hang out for a little while after class. That's probably what she did that night."

"So, it was routine for her to walk through the park every Tuesday and Thursday?" Cameron asked.

"Yes. She enjoyed the park. Especially in the summer, when kids are still playing in the park at 8:00 and there are a lot more people around, but now that the days are shorter and the evenings colder, the park is pretty much empty at that time."

Deep in thought as she read her notes, Cameron said, "Except the night she called 911, someone else was there. An eyewitness said they observed a woman calling out to someone on the ground, asking if they were okay and kneeling down next to the person. The eyewitnesses account coincides with Amy's 911 call. I'm confident we can safely assume the woman the eyewitness encountered was Amy, but she kept moving and didn't watch what happened once Amy knelt down. But we can presume what happened because, at that point, Amy had already contacted the 911 operator and said a white man with a black beard had stabbed her in Jackson Park. When he struck, he struck quickly."

Levine nudged her arm, and when she looked up, Alex was holding his face in his hands and slowly rocking back and forth in his chair.

"Alex, I'm sorry. I didn't mean to go on like that. Are you okay? Can I get you something?"

He shook his head and wiped his wet face with his hands. "The facts are hard to hear, you know? The way Amy died. She spent her last moments on earth fighting for her life. Stabbed by someone she tried to help. She deserved so much better. She was so much better than that, that...*bastard* who did this to her." He stood and picked up Amy's photo. "Everyone loved Amy. I have no idea how I'm supposed to do this without her. Our children cry themselves to sleep every night. So do I. The situation is awful, just so *goddamn* awful."

"Alex, we're almost done. I wanted to ask about Amy's job," Cameron said. "She worked as an administrative assistant at her precinct, right? Did she ever mention someone threatening her? Hanging around, or someone who came onto her?"

"Yes, she loved her job. Working at the station gave her a sense of giving back to the community. But she never mentioned anyone harassing her. She was a positive person and always saw the best in people, so even if someone had ill intentions, she may not have been aware," Alex said as he traced Amy's image with his finger. He turned his attention to Cameron and Levine. "I can't imagine anyone hurting Amy. She was wonderful."

Levine stood and extended his hand to Larsen. "Thank you for your time, Alex. We'll be in touch, and again, we're so sorry for your loss."

Cameron followed, and she and Levine walked down the front steps as Patricia arrived with Lara and Christian. Alex lingered in the open door as the two children scampered up the steps and hugged their father fiercely. He gave a nod to Cameron and disappeared into the house with his children still clinging to him.

CHAPTER 17

Cameron and Levine joined Hunter in the little office that had been transformed into Stealth Stalker central. After they updated him on the interviews with Alex Larsen and Mark Ryerson, the conversation changed to motive.

Scanning the whiteboard behind where Hunter sat, Cam said, "I still think the guy works within the police department in some capacity and that he's had multiple romantic rejections."

"Or maybe he just likes killing female cops," Levine said.

"But not all the victims were cops. Amy Larsen was an administrative assistant. The resemblance between the women is striking. I think he has a type that he likes, and when they don't give him the attention he seeks or agree to go out with him, he loses control. His ego can't handle rejection, and he gets angry. Angry enough to commit murder," Cam said.

"None of the women reported anyone bothering them at work or behaving inappropriately. They didn't even mention anything like that to friends or partners," Levine said, still not convinced.

Hunter sat, tapping his finger to his lip and listening to Cameron and Levine go back and forth. He finally said, "It's possible you're both right. He's targeting women who work for the NYPD *and* he has a type. Perhaps he's looking for a particular person and simply hasn't found her yet." He flipped through his note pad and found the page he was searching for. "When we first discussed this case, Cam, you suggested the Stalker was possibly an ex-con seeking revenge on an arresting officer, but years passed, and the guy can't remember exactly what the officer looked like. His memory is fading. He's searching for her and, in the meantime, the wrong woman is killed."

"Wouldn't he realize he grabbed the wrong woman when he's face-to-face with her? Why kill if she's not the right one?" Levine asked.

"The guy is angry—insanely angry. What's he going to do? Grab a cop, drag her into an alley or park, and when he's able to take a good look and realize she's not the one he wants, say 'Oops, pardon me, you're not the person I want to kill,' and let her go?" Hunter replied.

"Wouldn't he know her name?" Levine asked.

"Hmm, excellent point. She got married or divorced, changed her name."

"Either theory is good," Cameron said. "While we haven't figured out the why, we do know the who: females associated with the NYPD who are approximately five-six to five-eight, thirty-five to forty-five years old, brunette, light-colored eyes, and athletic build. Their build is an important clue. These women were in shape and physically capable. When the killer strikes, it's without threat...it's immediate. The victims have no time to react or to fight back. He probably doesn't examine the face until after she's dead."

Hunter nodded in agreement. "I think we should set a trap for our *Stealth Stalker*. Unfortunately, we'll need bait for our trap. We need to assess all personnel who work within the ten-block radius of the killings and fit the description. We're going to put a plan in action to draw this bastard out. Glen, I need you to search the personnel database, find any woman who fits our description. Ask Barone, Murphy, and Saintil to help you. Can you create a composite of the three victims? Morph their faces together as one face?"

"Absolutely. I'll start now," Levine said and left the room.

"I see where you're going with this," Cameron said. "The plan is risky and could backfire. You may end up with another death."

"That's why we'll plot carefully before we implement our plan. And we must make sure we use the right person to be our bait."

"And if my theory is correct? The rejected suitor? You won't have the right bait if she's not somebody he's interested in dating. A random woman could walk around town naked, and he wouldn't pay attention."

"We'll start with the women whose appearances are similar to the three victims. We can interview them and see if any of them were approached by, dated, or rejected the same man. Hopefully, we'll get lucky and won't need to use any bait at all."

CHAPTER 18

RHONDA SAINTIL WATCHED AND waited for Hunter to finish up with Levine and the doctor as they worked in the small office behind Hunter's desk. She assumed the meeting had ended when Levine left, but Cameron and Hunter remained in the office, which irritated her.

Hunter had asked her to prepare a report and a cross-reference graph of the victims for Chief Dwyer, who wanted an update on the information obtained so far. It pleased Saintil that Detective Finnegan had assigned her the task. Asking her to create a report for the chief meant he trusted her, but the extra work also meant leaving the station house later than usual, which put her on edge. As the youngest and newest detective in her unit, she was always burdened with the tedious work—filling out reports, filing papers, and making follow-up phone calls. She would pay her dues and was okay with earning her way. Used to waiting for what she wanted, she put in the time and work necessary to achieve her goals but was very punctual at quitting time and worked overtime only in an emergency. It was getting late, and she needed to go home.

Upon finishing the report, when she'd searched for Hunter, she'd found him still in the office with the doctor. They had spent the last hour going over the case as she finished up for the day at her own desk, and the typically patient Rhonda Saintil was growing more impatient with every passing second.

Maybe I'll leave my report on his desk and go, she thought. *We can go over it in the morning. No, I want him to see it before I leave.*

She approached the open door and knocked, catching a bit of the conversation.

Hunter was saying to Cameron, "As soon as the season starts, I'm going to take you to your first Yankee game."

Rhonda became pissed almost instantly. *They're not even talking about the case!* "Sorry to interrupt," she said, poking her head into the office, "but I completed the report you wanted. The one for the chief."

"Whoa, is it after 5:00 already?" Hunter asked, checking his watch. "The afternoon flew. Didn't it?"

"It did," Cameron agreed.

"Let me look at what you've got," Hunter said, reaching out his hand for the report as he stood and stretched. "We can go over your synopsis at my desk."

Saintil turned from the doorway, walked over to Hunter's desk, and watched impatiently as he made his way over to her.

Hunter sat down in his chair and examined the report. She wished he would say something. She was about to ask if that was all when he put the papers down, folded his hands in front of him on the desk, and focused on her. He held his stare for a beat before he spoke. "Rhonda, this is excellent work. Take a seat for a minute," he said, nodding toward the chair across the desk from him.

Saintil stared at him and reluctantly obeyed. She sat up straight and kept her eye contact with him.

"I noticed you appear a little...pensive. Is there anything wrong?"

"No, sir," she said quickly.

Hunter's eyes narrowed as he searched for a way to engage her. She'd seen this expression before, but she remained resolute in not letting him in.

"Rhonda," he continued, "are you unhappy in this unit?"

"No, sir."

"Is everything okay at home?" he asked, trying a fresh approach.

"Yes, sir."

Hunter tapped his finger on his lips. "Rhonda, I want to make sure you understand that I'm not just your boss. I'm your friend. I'm concerned about you. When I see you, I feel as if you're carrying a burden, and as your boss or as your friend, I'm here to listen if you ever need to talk. Okay?"

"Yes. If I need to talk, I'll consider you. Is that all?"

"Yeah, I guess so. Rhonda, be aware of your surroundings. Remember there's a serial killer out there, and it occurs to me that you might fit Stealth Stalker's type. Tall, athletic build, brunette, fair-skinned, and hazel eyes. And a cop."

She nodded in agreement and turned to go to her desk.

"Hey, Rhonda," Hunter called after her. "Most of our personnel are pairing up coming and going from work. Is there anyone you can walk with?"

"No, I'm fine, Hunter. I promise to be careful and stay aware of my surroundings."

"Okay, stay safe."

"Goodnight, Hunter."

Detective Saintil collected her coat and hurried for the door. *I need to get home before there's trouble.*

Hunter heard Cameron behind him and turned just as she clapped her hands twice, turning off the floor lamps in the office.

"I love those lamps, Hunter," Cameron said, closing the door behind her. "It was so nice of you to bring them up for me. Thanks again."

"Happy to help. Before you go, I wanted to talk to you about what happened earlier with Charlie Saunders."

"What do you mean? What happened?" Cameron stood next to Hunter's desk with her coat and bag draped over her arm, ready to leave.

"To be blunt, you were rude to Charlie, who was here to help, and you ended our meeting abruptly. You appeared upset by Dr. Schechter. You said she was condescending. What did she say to you? Because I won't stand for anyone treating someone on my team unprofessionally."

"Oh, forget about it, Hunter. I've dealt with worse than her."

"No, seriously. Dr. Schechter can be a polarizing figure. People love her or hate her. I've had run-ins with her in the past. If she treated you unprofessionally, I'd like to hear about it."

"We took each other by surprise. I startled her. She startled me. We got off on the wrong foot."

"If that's the way you want to handle it, but if she gives you any trouble, I want you to come to me so I can address the situation before it gets out of control."

"Okay, will do. Are you leaving now?"

"Yes. I just need to put Rhonda's report on the chief's desk. I'm starving," Hunter said as he put the case files in the filing cabinet and locked it. "Barone demolished a giant meatball sub for lunch, and I've been craving Italian all afternoon."

"Sounds good. I'm hungry myself," Cameron said, checking the time.

"Do you want to join me? I know a great place a couple blocks from here," Hunter said as the two walked past the rows of desks.

Cameron pushed open the door to the stairwell and replied, "Sure, I love Italian."

"Great. I'll put this on the chief's desk, and we can go."

As they walked through the doorway, they came face-to-face with Adrianne Schechter.

"Going to dinner?" Schechter asked, glancing them over. "Tomorrow morning, I'll be speaking to the chief about you, *Doctor* Cooper. I don't think you should work here. I think you're unstable."

Hunter replied, "Why don't you talk to the chief right now? I'm on my way to his office, and we can speak to him together."

"I'm afraid I can't right now. I teach a night class at NYU twice a week, and I have no time. And I don't want to rush my conversation with the chief."

"You schedule your conversation with the chief, and tomorrow morning, I'll schedule one too, about you and how you overstep your duties here and meddle in police business," Hunter said, motioning to Cameron to keep walking. "Good night, *Doctor* Schechter," he added, using her patronizing tone.

Cameron and Hunter left her standing at the top of the stairs, watching them descend. Hunter glared up at her and gave her a mock salute as they continued down the winding stairs.

"Don't let her bother you," he said to Cameron. "I'll take care of her. And between you and me, the chief isn't really fond of her either. He complimented her appearance once, and she called him a misogynist. He looked like he wanted to punch her in the face." He laughed. "Instead, he told her that if he were truly a misogynist, he'd fire her ass for calling him a misogynist and that she would do well to remember who she was speaking to. She likes to poke the bear, and one of these days, the bear will tire of being poked and that will be the end of Dr. Schechter."

CHAPTER 19

After class ended, Dr. Adrianne Schechter answered questions from students and then went on her way. She always walked home after class unless the weather was inclement, in which case she would call an Uber. She enjoyed the chilly air as she walked away from the school, thinking about the consultant, Cameron Cooper, hired to profile a serial killer. It angered Adrianne that Detective Finnegan had selected an outside advisor when she was right down the hallway. But she still had a responsibility to the job she'd agreed to do. That included dealing with a consultant who presented the potential to put an officer in harm's way.

Adrianne specialized in police and public safety psychology and recognized the signs when an officer was in trouble, and Cameron Cooper didn't behave in a way that she judged reasonable. She would have to be delicate when she spoke to the chief in the morning, something that wasn't easy for her. She preferred to be direct when she spoke to people and not sugar-coat her words, but if she approached the chief sounding pushy or angry, she might find herself out of a job she enjoyed.

And there was Detective Hunter Finnegan. He'd never liked her, she speculated. However, he displayed a particular interest in Cameron Cooper, and his admiration for her was apparent. She recognized Hunter's growing affection for the doctor, and the way he came to her defense so swiftly earlier spoke volumes. He was falling for a woman she was certain hid deep emotional scars. Hunter would talk to the chief after she did and make her appear jealous, like a vengeful interloper with ill intentions when she was merely doing her job—warning Dwyer she suspected someone in his department was not mentally sound.

Adrianne reached into her coat pocket to warm her hands, and her fingers grazed the Taser Pulse she'd bought for protection. Jolted out of her thoughts, she glanced around, fearful that a killer was following her. She discreetly pulled the Taser out of her pocket, checked the cartridge, and turned the safety switch to on.

Life had changed dramatically in the last several weeks as a serial killer held her neighborhood hostage, with no one knowing when and who would be his next victim. As a police psychologist, her job was to help all department personnel through critical incidents. Her normally quiet days of evaluations mixed with an occasional mandatory meeting with an officer after an altercation or a gun firing had ended. For the past few weeks, she'd maintained a full schedule of personnel who needed to talk about their concerns and fears now that someone was targeting them. Some officers felt inadequate in their abilities to protect others or themselves. Some suffered survivor's guilt, and some felt enraged by the killer's audacity. Those who were acquainted with the victims, worked with them, and were friends with them grieved with her. They came into her office crying, trying to make sense of the senseless.

Of the three victims, Adrianne had met the two police officers, Jennie Saunders and Linda Birch. She wasn't close to the two women. She'd only met them because she'd evaluated them over the years. She remembered them as dedicated police officers who did the work because they enjoyed being a positive influence in their communities. They enjoyed helping people and were eager in their pursuit of a career with the NYPD.

She'd run into Linda Birch the afternoon before she died and casually asked how things were, too distracted by the death of Officer Jennifer Saunders to give Linda her full attention. She'd only half-listened when the younger woman went on about her boyfriend's birthday and how he made her "really, really happy." As someone who was paid to listen, she felt she'd failed that day. She wondered what would have happened if she'd paid more attention and stopped to talk to Linda in depth. What if she'd genuinely cared about the answer to her question and taken a few minutes to chat? Would Linda still be alive? Would those few minutes have made a difference in Linda's destiny? She shook her head, deciding the thought a ridiculous and futile musing and not the way a trained psychologist should think.

She didn't know Amy Larsen, the administrative aide at another precinct. However, ever since Amy died the same way as Jennie Saunders and Linda Birch, Adrianne had felt sure they were dealing with a serial killer. The death of the three women had resulted in increased patrols and a heightened sense of her surroundings.

Navigating the streets on autopilot, Adrianne made lefts and rights without thought as she walked home. One last left turn, and she arrived on her quiet, brownstone-lined street. Many houses displayed freshly planted mums in flower boxes on the street level windows. The windows on her own home exhibited a mix of the fall flower in deep purple and yellow in window boxes her husband had built himself. Her townhouse stood halfway down the block, on a street built with cobblestone more than a century ago. Those cobblestones enchanted her. She would often sit by her window gazing out at them, imagining they were newly laid, and horses traveled on them instead of cars. She thought about the family who had lived in her house then and who may have sat at that window before her.

One day, she supposed, *I'll go down to town hall, view the city records, and read about the family who lived here before me, where they came from, and if children once ran through this house, filling it with life and laughter.*

She spied the man walking toward her dressed all in black, eating an ice cream cone. They met almost directly in front of the gate at the front of her house. Adrianne's hand gripped the Taser in her pocket, but the man didn't lunge at her, wield a knife in her direction, or even say anything to her. He nodded as their eyes met and kept eating his ice cream. She let out a held breath and shook her head at herself, then smiled at how she'd almost stunned some poor guy eating ice cream! How would she explain that one to the chief?

I thought he was going to stab me with his ice cream cone, so I let him have it! He would've found it hilarious, she mused.

The ground floor entrance to her brownstone sat tucked beneath the steep front steps that led to the double door entry of the house. A hundred years ago, the gated entry would have been the servants' entrance, but today it served as Adrianne's preferred way into her home. The doorway led her to the kitchen and dining room, which were always her first stop. At the bottom of three short stone steps, an old iron gate painted black and original to the house protected the small, cave-like vestibule. A single light bulb hung from the ceiling, and a short, wooden bench left by the previous owners sat against the wall. On rainy days, she'd stowed her umbrella and wellies next to the bench but stopped when a family of mice took up residence in her right boot. The mice and the boots ended up in the garbage. To the left, a wooden interior door with a small window opened into the house.

Adrianne unlocked the gate and stepped inside the vestibule. The compact space was dark as she hit the light switch. When the bulb didn't flicker on, she flipped the switch up and down once more to no avail. *The bulb must've burned out*, she thought. She turned around to close the gate behind her, gasping suddenly when she saw a figure standing in the doorway. Before Adrianne could react, the person stepped closer and plunged a knife into her abdomen. The man with the ice cream had stabbed her.

She sank onto the wooden bench as the stranger held onto her, knife still in place, their eyes locked together. She freed her Taser from her coat pocket, squeezed the trigger, and grimaced as Ice Cream Man convulsed in front of her and dropped to the floor, thrashing.

It would be instant death if she pulled the blade out, so she kept the knife steady with her left hand as her right hand controlled the Taser. She needed her phone from the purse at her feet. She would have to let go of either the Taser or the knife. As Adrianne leaned down toward her purse, she pressed the fixed electrodes of the Taser to her assailant's leg, sending a fresh wave of electricity through him and paralyzing him anew, hoping it would be enough to let her grab her phone.

Dropping the Taser, she fumbled in the dark for her purse, fighting off dizziness and trying not to pass out. Her hand touched the leather bag, and she heaved it up onto her lap. The knife twisted in her gut, and a warmth spread over her as her blood seeped from the jagged opening. Running out of time, she tried to remain still as she searched for her phone. She dialed 911 just as the man on the floor struggled to a standing position. Dropping the phone on her lap, she scrabbled for the Taser, but it fell out of reach.

When the faint voice of the 911 operator emanated from her cell, she screamed, "Help me! He's stabbed me. Please help me..." Her words turned to sobs as she held onto the knife, knowing her husband would find her sitting on the little wooden bench drenched in blood.

The stranger staggered, grabbing for the knife, still shaken from being stunned twice.

Adrianne knew the moment he yanked the knife from her body she would bleed out. She looked up, and to her astonishment, her assailant's beard hung from the left side of his face.

"You," she whispered. "Why?"

He ripped the knife from her hand and her body.

As the world grew darker, she thought, *I know you*.

CHAPTER 20

THE BUZZING ALARM AWOKE Cameron from a deep sleep. Bleary-eyed, she checked the time and headed to the bathroom for a steamy shower. After she finished dressing, she walked through her apartment searching for her phone. She found it dead on the kitchen counter next to her purse. She plugged the phone in to charge, filled her Keurig, and as she waited for the water to heat, grabbed a yogurt and fresh fruit from the fridge and stirred them together. The cell phone flickered on, and she tapped in her code. Four voice mails and five text messages chimed for attention.

What the heck, she thought as she continued to make her coffee.

Cameron perched on a counter stool, listening to the first message. Hunter had called, asking her to call him as soon as she got the message. The timestamp read 1:12 a.m. The next three were also from Hunter, each one more urgent than the last.

The last message startled her as his voice shouted, "Cam. Where are you? I'm getting worried that you haven't called me back. Call me ASAP."

The text messages were all from him. She recalled the night before, trying to figure out what could be so urgent. They had eaten dinner at an Italian restaurant Hunter recommended. The food was delicious, the wine too plentiful, and the kiss...amazing. Images of the previous evening flooded her mind as she tapped call and waited for Hunter to answer. *I guess he couldn't wait to talk after last night,* she flattered herself.

Hunter answered, "My God, Cameron. Where have you been? Are you okay?"

"I'm fine," she said happily. "I just got your messages. Last night was—"

"I've got bad news. Adrianne Schechter is dead—stabbed. I'm still at the scene. I'll text you the address. Meet me here."

"Stabbed," she repeated. "Do you mean Stealth?"

"Her cause of death would indicate so. I'll fill you in when you get here."

Cameron gulped her yogurt and coffee before rushing out the door.

The address Hunter had texted her turned out to be Adrianne's home address. When Cameron arrived, the street was swarming with cops. Cruisers stopped traffic from entering the block. Cameron hurried past the grim faces of the officers with a flash of her credentials. Police tape cordoned off a stately brownstone like a line drawn with a yellow sharpie. Rechargeable lighting units with telescoping heads aimed at the brownstone's vestibule glared brightly even in the morning light.

She spotted Hunter and hurried to him. "I can't believe this, Hunter. I'm in shock."

"Damn it, Cameron! I was worried sick about you all night. I imagined a double homicide. I was ready to go to your place and break the door down." He grabbed her and held her tight.

"My phone died, and I didn't realize it until this morning," she said, pushing back from him so she could see his face. "I told you I shouldn't have drunk that wine last night. I came in, threw my stuff on the counter, went straight to bed, and was out cold all night. I'm sorry I worried you. Fill me in on what I missed."

"Dr. Schechter dialed 911 before she died. The operator heard her pleading for help. She said, 'He stabbed me.' When the patrol officers got here, they weren't sure exactly where the call had come from, so they knocked on a few doors until they came to this house. Schechter's husband wasn't aware if Adrianne had come home from teaching. They searched the house…didn't find her. Then they checked here," Hunter said, motioning to the entrance under the front steps. "Her husband opened the gate and found her."

"Can I take a closer look?"

"Sure, come on."

Hunter lifted the yellow tape for them to duck under.

Cameron approached the vestibule expecting to see Adrianne's lifeless body on the floor but saw only a pool of blood. "The coroner took her already?" she asked.

"Yeah, about an hour ago."

"Where was she found?"

"Sitting on the bench. Her body was propped up, leaning into the corner. He took her shoes, but nothing else seems to be missing. Money was in her wallet, her jewelry intact. Her cell phone was on her lap. We found a Taser on the ground. Her husband said she kept it for protection. She'd fired it, so if she got the guy, we might find some DNA evidence on the barbs."

"And the cause of death?"

"Single stab wound to the gut."

"Shit, this is unbelievable. Anything else found?"

"The forensic team found hair on the floor that was too short to be Adrianne's and not the right color to be her husband's. Hopefully, something will come from that."

"What about the camera next to the door?"

"Schechter's husband played the video for us. The guy held his gloved hand up in front of his face as he approached and then pushed the camera toward the house, away from himself. We only have a partial of his face, but a partial is more than we had before.

As Cameron stood absorbing the crime scene and making mental notes, a chill ran through her and what seemed like a fuzzy recollection of a dream teased her mind. She shook the sensation off as she turned back to Hunter. "You look beat. Did you get any sleep last night?"

"A couple hours before I got the call."

"What are you going to do now?"

"I'm going home to shower quickly and have more coffee. I'll meet you back at the station."

An electric energy besieged the precinct as personnel reeled in the aftermath of another colleague's death. Anger crossed some faces as tears and numbness defined others. Voices rose in fury and disbelief. Phones rang non-stop as concerned citizens called to ask for information and offer tips.

Cameron was busy tacking Adrianne Schechter's photo and stats to the whiteboard in the back office when she saw Hunter arrive. She watched him through the window as he took off his coat and hung it on the back of his chair. He looked exhausted. She moved to the doorway and gently said, "Hey. Feeling any better?"

"No. Not really. If anything, I'm angrier and more frustrated." He slumped into his chair and began sifting through the stack of messages on his desk.

She slowly approached his desk, glancing around the squad room to see if anyone was looking their way. When she got closer to him, she noticed a red, splotchy spot below his jawline. "What happened to your neck?"

"Oh, nothing," Hunter said, touching the spot in question. "I was rushing and cut myself shaving."

"Might be time for a new razor."

"What about you? What's that mark?" Hunter asked, nodding at a raw spot near Cam's collarbone.

"I think I have fricking bed bugs. I have a bunch of these marks on me. Or my neighbor's nasty dog has fleas, and I got them in the elevator. I'll call the company with the beagle that sniffs out bugs to come over to my place and have a look. In the meantime, I'm washing my bedsheets and blanket in hot water, and I'm throwing away the mattress cover. Shoot."

"What?"

"I just remembered I bought a new mattress cover. It works like a giant bag for the mattress. They're the best if you're worried about bed bugs, you know? But I'll never get it on by myself. I'll ask the super to help me."

"I can help you," Hunter offered.

"Thanks, but you have more important things to do here."

"I have time after work. I'll stop by later, on my way home, and give you a hand."

"If you're sure you won't be too tired."

"Never too tired to help a friend with a bug problem."

"Thanks, I appreciate it. I tacked Dr. Schechter's information to the whiteboard. Her death is so...surreal. She was just here yesterday, albeit glaring at me, but she was alive and well, and now...she's gone. Did her husband hear anything?"

"No. Albert Schechter had fallen asleep watching television. He woke up when the police rang the bell investigating the 911 call," Hunter said, motioning for Cam to take a seat. "He didn't know if she'd returned from teaching. The patrol officers helped him search the house and the yard. When they didn't find her, they searched the last possible place—the street level entrance. And there she was...."

"And there she was," Cameron repeated. "And then what?"

"He freaked out. The two officers had to drag him off her to see if they could help her, but it was too late. She was dead. The coroner said even if they were standing right there when it happened, they wouldn't have been able to save her. The knife sliced right through the artery. A surgeon wouldn't have been able to save her at that point," he said, rubbing his face with his hands. "I need more coffee. Do you want some?"

"I have a fresh mug, thanks," Cameron said, studying Hunter. She detected the stress in his expression. "We'll find this guy, Hunter. He'll mess up sooner or later. They always do."

"Yeah, I'm voting for sooner," he said, standing. "And when we do find him, the son-of-a-bitch will be sorry he was ever born."

Cameron remained at the desk as he walked away, leaving an unobstructed view of the whiteboard she'd methodically fussed over. Through the office window, she spotted the newly pinned photograph of Adrianne Shechter staring back at her, seemingly with great disapproval.

CHAPTER 21

A WEEK HAD PASSED since Stealth spied an old enemy while watching the news.

It was sweet to follow her home, but this hunter would never kill an animal in its den. Some places allowed hunts to take place during the hibernation season. Stealth had never understood the point. To slaughter an animal while it slept destroyed the challenge and thrill, sullying the hunt.

I need her to see me and to understand that I won, Stealth thought. *I wouldn't even do it if she were awake. In her home, she has nowhere to run, no chance to escape, and that's no fun. A good hunt means the prey can outwit the predator, even fight back and escape. She'll be on her guard, so stalking her won't be so easy this time. She won't walk around by herself after dark, but the overly confident ones tempt fate. She's entirely too confident, borderline cocky. Maybe she wants to catch me all by herself and be a hero, or perhaps she'll try to prove something to her colleagues or herself. Or me. The only thing she'll show me is that she bleeds just like everyone else.*

I will make sure she understands that with her gone, I will have earned my freedom forever. Killing her will be difficult but not impossible. Once she's gone, I will have the power. I will be in control.

CHAPTER 22

THE ONLY CRIME SCENE Cameron hadn't visited on her two-day trek was the first one she'd investigated with Hunter and Levine. The alley where Medina Montan had died seven long weeks ago had haunted her ever since with a strange sensation of déjà vu. Seven weeks. Seven weeks of dead ends. Seven weeks and another woman, Adrianne Schechter, was dead. She left the police station early to ensure enough daylight to walk the alley. The cool air of late November chilled her face as she walked.

When she reached her destination, her stomach clenched as her instincts sent out a warning. She unbuttoned her coat and rested a hand on the Glock in its holster. On full alert, she pushed the sensation of dread aside and proceeded. Slices of late afternoon sunlight pierced the alley, giving it a black and golden-striped effect. The pungent smell of garbage filled the air, and it occurred to Cam that the odor of trash surrounded Medina Montan before she died. She hesitated for a moment, uncertain about why she felt compelled to search the alley and what she was looking for. Her heart beat a rapid warning signal to her brain.

Markings on the ground and a faint stain of blood were still visible where an unlucky passerby found Medina dead. Eventually, as Mother Nature did her cleaning with rain and snow, any evidence that a woman had died tragically on that spot would disappear.

Questions tugged at the back of her brain. *Why would Medina walk into a dark alley with a man? Did he drag her? Was she lured?* She meandered back toward the sidewalk, scrutinizing the ground as she went.

Many people had come and gone through the alley on that day alone, herself included. Nothing in the report suggested the attacker had dragged Medina. As Cameron studied the area carefully, she found no sign that she was forcibly taken, and photos from the scene showed no indication of an abduction.

More questions clouded her thoughts. *So she willingly walked into a dark alley with a stranger? Was he handsome, and she wanted to hook up? Was he a fast talker, a real charmer? Did he tell her someone needed help back here?*

A loud crash from behind caused Cameron to jump and swing around in alarm. A fat, orange cat had jumped up onto a garbage can and tipped it over, causing the clatter. She tripped and almost fell trying to back away. Taking a few deep breaths to calm herself down, she laughed at herself. Her heart raced, and with it, her thoughts. She was no longer able to deny the question that taunted her. *Did she know him?*

More and more, the evidence convinced her that all the women knew their attacker. There were no signs of a struggle at the crime scenes, and yet some victims were cops—women who were able to defend themselves. But if their attacker was an acquaintance, someone they were comfortable with, then they would be off guard.

There had to be someone in the NYPD these women had in common. *A commanding officer? No, not all of them were cops. A lover? Possibly. A rejected suitor? Another employee?*

It was her best working theory, given the similarities of the women. They were all employed by the department, so it would make sense that the killer was an employee of the department but not necessarily a cop. But all the women were from different stations, and Amy Larsen had called 911 and given a description, not a name, of her attacker. It was possible that in the dark, panic-stricken, she didn't recognize him. Could the killer have worked for all the precincts over the years? Who would most likely move around frequently? Not a cop. They didn't move around often. Someone on temporary assignments like a tech guy? Someone who would travel from station to station to work on computers, security cameras, or building maintenance?

Dusk consumed the alley as a shiver ran through Cameron. The cat that had startled her sat glaring in a corner, and when their eyes met, it let out a long hiss.

A now-familiar voice spoke. *"You shouldn't be here."*

Cam swung around, searching for the source. It was only her and the fat cat. She quickly stepped out of the alley and onto the bustling sidewalk, where she took deep breaths of the fresh night air. She hailed an approaching taxi.

The visit to the alley and the ominous warning had made her anxious. Was her mind playing tricks on her or trying to warn her? Why shouldn't she be there? And yet, she felt satisfied that she was on the right track to catch a killer.

CHAPTER 23

On her way home, Cameron called Hunter. When the call went to voice mail, she left a message asking him to call her back. While she waited to hear from him, she ran into the Japanese restaurant around the corner from her building and picked up some sushi rolls for dinner. She considered going to the police station to check on him, but her hungry and tired body needed a break.

Once in her apartment, she stripped off her work clothes, leaving them thrown over a chair, and pulled on a pair of yoga tights and an oversized sweatshirt. It felt good to walk around in her bare feet as she wandered from the bedroom, through the living room, and into the kitchen. She put the sushi in the fridge, grabbed a bottle of Merlot off the counter, opened it and, knowing better, poured a healthy glassful for herself. Walking back into the living room, she turned on instrumental music for meditation, took a long sip of wine, and set her glass on the pecan and iron coffee table centered in front of a navy sofa.

Cameron practiced yoga as a way of relieving tension and warding off migraines. The poses were great stress relievers, and they had the added benefit of clearing her mind. Whenever she found herself stymied on a case, she would do yoga to increase the blood flowing to her brain for a fresh perspective.

Just as she lengthened her legs into a full downward dog, her cell phone chimed.

"Hello?"

"Hey, Cameron. I got your message. What's up?"

"Hi, Hunter. Listen, I'm sure you're exhausted. You don't have to stop by tonight. The super is a pleasant guy and won't mind helping me with the mattress."

"I'm fine. I'm meeting the chief right now, so I'll stop by on my way home. Okay?"

"Yep. See you then."

Twenty minutes later, Cameron finished her yoga routine. She called down to the doorman and told him she expected Hunter Finnegan shortly, to send him right up. She swallowed a large mouthful of the wine, stretched out on the sofa, and relaxed, waiting for Hunter. The music playing softly in the background, she closed her eyes, drew in a deep breath, and slowly released it, sinking farther into the soft, down-filled cushions of the sofa. She thought about Hunter. Just as it had been seven weeks since Medina Montan was murdered, it had been seven weeks since she met Hunter. Seven weeks of a growing attraction. Seven weeks of flirtatious moments and knowing glances. It was easy to be attracted to him physically. The man was gorgeous. Handsome, tall, lean, and muscular. He was her idea of sexy. It was even easier to be attracted to him on a deeper level though. He was passionate, dedicated, honest, and kind, with a quick sense of humor. Even his tidiness and periodic brooding were appealing to her. Last night, they had finally had their first date. Even though it wasn't technically a date, it had ended like a real date with a real kiss. She'd been falling in love with him since day one and the way he kissed her had been confirmation that he felt the same. As she reminisced about the previous night, sleep overcame her tired body, but her mind still whirled around the case and Hunter.

She dreamed in fragmented sequences between alleyways and a smiling Hunter. Cam found herself wrapped in Hunter's arms, holding him close as he whispered in her ear. She couldn't make out what he said, and when she gazed up at him, he had no face and held a gleaming knife. Screaming, she punched and kicked the faceless man and ran away. She found herself in an alley. A fat cat perched on a can hissed as she tried to run faster.

One leg suddenly became shorter than the other, hindering her efforts. The faceless man pursued her, getting closer and closer. She tried to scream again, but no sound escaped her. She reached the end of the alley. Trapped, she climbed up on garbage cans to jump over the wall, but they fell over, banging together. The banging reverberated, hurting her ears, and she covered them with her hands. The faceless man reached her, his knife held high. She grabbed his arm, struggling with him as a sense of doom filled her and tears streamed down her face.

Bolting upright on the couch, Cameron prepared to fight for her life. Her heart pounded and she panted as if she'd run a race. Knocks on the door startled her, and she realized it was the banging in her dream.

"Cameron? It's Hunter. Are you okay? Answer me!"

She got up, still shaky from her nightmare, and opened the door for him.

"Cameron, are you okay? I could hear you. It sounded like you were struggling. What's going on?" He searched her face with his intense green eyes and then glanced around the apartment, scrutinizing everything in his sight. He brushed her hair away from her face. "You're all sweaty."

"Bad dream," she said, shaking her head. "I'm fine, really. I dozed off and had a nightmare."

"Come on now, sit." He walked her to the couch and then went into the kitchen.

Cameron obediently sat, taking deep breaths and trying to calm herself.

Hunter returned with a glass of ice water, handing it to her.

The cold water hit the spot as she drank the full glass before taking another breath.

Hunter sat down next to her as if she were a butterfly he didn't want to startle. He studied her, his trained eyes searching her for clues. "Better?" he asked.

"Yes, thanks for the water." She laughed a little. "Wow, that was some nightmare. Have you ever had a dream that takes over your entire body? Your mind and body react like you're actually in trouble?"

"What was the dream about?"

"Just your typical dream. A faceless man chased me, and I came to a dead end. He had me trapped, and I fought with him. Then I woke up to you knocking on the door."

"Uh-huh," he said, squinting as he looked at her. "Do you have these dreams often?"

"Detective Finnegan, are you attempting to analyze *me*?" she said, squinting back at him. "I've never had this dream before, that I can remember, and I can assure you it's only a reflection of my being in an alley today and a fat cat surprising me."

"In an alley? And a fat cat? Did it chase you?" he said, relaxing somewhat.

"No, it knocked over a garbage can and startled me. Nothing else. Okay? Satisfied?"

He looked her over again and shook his head, his lips pursed in a tight grin. He wasn't satisfied but willing to drop the subject for the time being. "What's all this?" he asked, nodding at the yoga mat and blocks Cameron had left on the floor.

"I was doing a little yoga earlier to de-stress."

"Ah, I know what you mean. Don't tell anyone I told you this, but I have a soaking tub with jets at my place. I like to end my week with a soak and a scotch," Hunter said with a wink. "So, where's the bug bed?"

"I think it's bed bug."

"Is it?"

"Follow me, please," she said, shaking her head.

Cameron led Hunter into the bedroom where she'd already stripped-down the king-size mattress.

"Whoa. No wonder you can't get this thing in the bag by yourself. I'll stand the mattress up on one side while you slip the bag over the top."

Hunter held the oversized mattress on end as Cam wrestled with the mattress protector. She pulled the cover on, and they eased the mattress back onto the bed frame. Cam zipped the protector up and stood back to regard their handy work.

"We make a talented team in more ways than one, don't we?" she said, somewhat impressed that they had stuffed the huge mattress inside the bag.

"Yes, we have conquered the bug bed," he said, laughing.

"Yeah, ha ha. But seriously, thanks again. Can I get you something? I don't have much, but I have tap water or wine." She shrugged. "Oh, and coffee and orange juice!"

"Sure." He chuckled a little. Glancing past her at the glass of wine on the coffee table, he added, "If you're having wine, I'll join you. I could use it. The chief ripped into me earlier about the 'appearance of little progress' in the case."

"He's a tough old bastard, isn't he?"

"Yeah, sometimes, I guess. Mostly he's okay. I have a lot of respect for him. He's worked hard and smart to get where he is today."

Cameron handed Hunter a crystal wine glass more than half full of the Merlot she'd opened earlier, then sat down on the opposite end of the couch from him and took a sip from her own glass. She said, "I searched the alley where Officer Montan died. I found no sign of struggle, no indication the killer dragged Medina. It was as if she simply walked into the alley with her attacker. I had to ask myself, why would she do that? The more I process the information we have, the more I think Medina knew her attacker. I think all the victims knew their attacker." She studied Hunter's face as he pondered the likelihood of the women knowing the man who would kill them. "I still believe the killer works for the police department."

He gazed at her with narrowed eyes, frowning, as he listened.

"I'm not saying he's a cop," she added quickly. "I'm saying he might be someone who works for the department in a different capacity. Someone who has reason to travel from station to station, like a tech guy." His expression softened, and she resisted the urge to add that Stealth could still be another cop. "We should consider people who do maintenance for the city like air conditioning and heating. There are a lot of private contractors who come in and out, fixing things."

He sat back and closed his eyes, considering her suggestion. "First thing in the morning, I'll have Barone and Murphy check out who's been coming and going the last few months. The chief's assistant keeps a log of who's done work." He seemed satisfied for the moment. "Excellent work, *Doctor* Cooper. However, I don't approve of you going into alleys by yourself, especially at night. It's dangerous. Next time you want to visit a crime scene, I want to go with you."

"I think you have more important things to do, *Detective* Finnegan, than babysit me. Do I need to remind you I worked for the FBI and still carry a gun?"

"No, no, you don't." He smirked and leaned back against the couch, sinking into the down cushions. "I still don't want you taking unnecessary chances. You never know what can happen or who you'll meet in an alley."

"Hey, do you like sushi rolls?" Cameron asked as she sprang from the couch. "I picked some up on my way home, and now I'm starving."

"I do, but I should probably finish my wine and get going."

"Don't be silly. I have plenty. I couldn't decide what I was in the mood for, so I ordered two different entrées. Come on, we can taste test and see which one we like better—the tuna avocado or the shrimp cucumber roll."

"Sure, why not? I am a little hungry myself."

"I'm not much of a cook," Cameron said as she headed toward the open kitchen in her apartment. "Thank God there are so many restaurants around here that offer takeout, or I'd starve." She opened the fridge, pulled out two containers, and placed them on the breakfast bar separating the living room from the kitchen. "Bring the wine glasses over here. We can eat at the counter."

Hunter rose from the couch and brought the two glasses over as Cameron placed plates, napkins, and chopsticks on the countertop.

"Chopsticks or a fork?" she asked.

"Chopsticks," Hunter said as he sat on one of the two barstools in front of the island. "This looks pretty good. What's the name of the restaurant?"

"Look See. They're right next to Antoine's around the corner. Here, help yourself," Cameron said, handing Hunter chopsticks.

"To the demise of the bed bug," he said, clinking his glass to hers.

She giggled. "I'll drink to that."

He poked a roll with his chopstick. "I enjoyed last night."

Blushing, Cam answered, "Me too." Memories from the evening before flipped through her mind.

"The, uh, food at Savo's is great, isn't it?"

"Oh, yeah, delicious. I was stuffed." She smiled, feeling like a teenage girl talking to her crush.

"And the wine..."

She laughed. "Oh, yes, the wine. Too much wine."

"And the rainstorm out of nowhere."

"My favorite part of the night." She visualized them walking to his car when the rain poured down. They had taken cover in a tight doorway, their bodies in close proximity. He'd leaned into her, she'd turned her face up to his, and they had kissed. Slow and sensual. Goosebumps covered her arms at the mental image.

"Mine too." He glanced at her. "I'd like to do it again."

She nodded. "That would be lovely."

They broke out in huge smiles, giggling in unison.

"You're okay?" he asked, still smiling. "Since...we're working together?"

"I don't care," she said, surprising him. "If I were a cop also, it wouldn't matter, right? The fact that we're working on the same case shouldn't stop us. This case will be over soon. And to be honest, Hunter, I haven't felt this way about anyone in a long time."

"I feel the same," he said, studying her. "I guess it's okay then if I tell you how damn beautiful you are?"

"If you want to embarrass me, yes."

"You are," he said, leaning over to her and pressing his lips to hers. "You really are."

They devoured the food, voted the tuna avocado roll as the clear winner of the taste test, and moved to the couch to relax. Cam put her feet up on the sofa and sipped her wine, enjoying herself immensely.

Hunter relaxed, taking her foot in his big hands to massage it. "My God, Cameron! What happened to the bottom of your foot?"

His reaction surprised her. Between the wine and the kiss, she'd forgotten about her feet and how she let no one see them. They told a story she didn't care to share. "Nothing, just some scarring," she said, tucking her feet under her.

"Why didn't you tell me about this? Especially after you saw the photos, why didn't you tell me?" His voice rose slightly.

"I don't know what you're talking about. Please stop shouting. You're making my head throb." She groaned a little.

"Cameron, look at me," he demanded, appearing horrified. "These scars—how did you get them?" He grabbed both of her feet, examining them, tracing each scar with the tip of his finger.

She pulled her feet from his hands. "You're overreacting. It happened a long time ago. I don't like to talk about it," she said, hoping he would stop.

He didn't. He moved up next to her and took her hand in his. His eyes were wide and fearful.

Anxiety washed over Cam's body, touching every nerve, leaving her skin tingling. "Hunter, you're scaring me and giving me a headache. Please *stop*."

"No, I'm sorry. You need to tell me how you got those scars and why you didn't mention them before."

"Why are you so concerned about some scars on my feet, and what photos are you talking about?" Queasiness crept through her.

"I'm talking about the photos from the crime scenes, the ones of the women's feet."

"I didn't see any pictures of feet when I went through the files," she said.

"You were looking at the picture of Jennie Saunders's foot when you became ill your first week on the job. It was on top of the pile. I know that's what you were looking at when I walked in." He examined her face with those keen eyes that missed nothing. "Do you remember?"

"No," she said, shaking her head.

"Cameron, listen to me, okay? Stealth stabbed each woman once in the abdomen, cutting through her aorta and killing her. Afterwards, he took off her shoes and cut the bottoms of her feet. Each woman had an identical pattern of cut marks on her soles." He paused before continuing. "The scars on your feet match that pattern." He moved closer to her, rubbing her back, and being as gentle as if she were a newborn. "How long have you had those scars?" he asked in a soft voice.

"Twelve years," she said, fighting the urge to vomit in front of him once again.

"What happened?" he asked again.

"I was with the FBI. We were investigating a...serial killer."

Hunter remembered the story Agent Alexander had told him. The time to confess had arrived. "I know about the kidnapping, how you escaped and saved another woman at the same time."

"Wha— How do you know?" Cam asked, irritated. *He checked up on me!*

"I had some concerns, so I called Jeff Alexander. He only gave me a brief sketch of the details. He didn't want to tell me anything, but I pressured him. I promise you he had your back the whole time." His eyes searched hers.

Cameron saw his worried expression and decided it wasn't the time to pick a fight.

"He mentioned nothing about the scars on your feet. Did Jonette do this to you?"

"No." She'd suppressed the memories for so long that she hesitated to delve into them. The kidnapping was one of the scariest and darkest events in her life, and that was saying a lot. She drew her knees to her chest, wrapping her arms around them, squeezing them into her body, and took a deep breath before continuing. "When Jonette kidnapped me, he took me to an abandoned plantation home determined to teach me a lesson for interfering with his 'work,' so he tortured me. I didn't break down the way he wanted me to, so he changed tactics and kidnapped a co-ed named Lisa Allen. He tortured her in front of me until she passed out, and then he did the same to me. When I came to, it was dark, and he was gone. He left us tied up in the cellar, and we were surrounded by the scratching and squeaking of mice and rats everywhere. I was terrified."

She took a deep breath and wiped away a tear running down her cheek. "We freed ourselves and were working on escaping the house when Jonette came back. We didn't see him come in through another door. It was us against him, and Lisa and I knew either we escaped alive or he did. We attacked him. If it had been one on one, he would've won, but since there were two of us, we overtook him. When we had him on the ground, we had our chance to run, so I motioned to Lisa to go. She grabbed a fire poker and smashed the window. We jumped from the window onto the grass and the shattered glass below. I was dazed for a moment until Lisa screamed, 'run.' I got up and bolted. I was so scared, I never felt the glass shards ripping into my bare feet."

Hunter's eyes were moist. He pulled her into a tight hug and held her for a moment, then whispered in her ear, "I'm so sorry."

Tears welled in her eyes.

"Jesus!" he said, pulling back. "You know what this means, right? This blows our theory about a jilted lover or a contractor at the police station."

"What blows the theory?"

"We thought the cuts on the feet were a calling card, and the missing shoes, trophies. But now I think the killer is looking for you. I think he checks the bottoms of his victims' feet for the scars, your scars, and when they aren't there, he puts them there. I think Jonette has returned."

"What? That's insane, Hunter! Why would you say that to me?" she said, annoyed, or in denial. And then the pieces came together in her mind. She jumped from the couch with the realization that the Stealth Stalker wasn't just seeking a particular type of woman, He was looking for a specific woman—her. Stealth was Jonette, and he'd returned to fulfill his promise. A promise to hunt and kill her.

Her body shook at the understanding that women had died because someone was looking for her, trying to kill her, hunting her. The thought of Jonette being Stealth became too much all at once. Her anger welled inside of her, suffocating her, and she couldn't breathe.

Hunter stood in slow motion, watching her. He reached out a hand, one of his perfect, long-fingered hands, hands a pianist would envy. He was talking. She saw his mouth moving, but his voice seemed far away, and the words were indecipherable. He held her shoulders, looking at her eye to eye.

What is he saying?

Hunter shook her. "Breathe! Breathe!"

She gasped a breath of air and sobbed it out all at once. As she was about to crumble to the floor, he caught her and drew her into him close, the warmth of him on her cheek. She pushed him away, her fury evident in her eyes. A maniac had killed innocent women in his hunt for her.

"One thing bothers me," Hunter said as he wrapped her in a blanket. "All our vics were brunette, and you're blonde. It doesn't add up."

Cameron blinked at him and his naivety. "Hunter, I dye my hair. When Jonette knew me, my hair *was* brown."

Hunter stroked the side of Cam's head, closed his eyes, and shook his head.

"What?" she asked.

"There was something about the victims that bothered me. They all looked similar, but they also looked familiar. I just realized why. They resemble you." He held her in a comforting hug. "I'll be right back. I'm going into the other room to make a phone call. Okay?"

She slowly nodded and watched him walk through the door.

In her mind, the same words repeated. *I'm going to die! I'm going to die!*

Then, a child's voice whispered, *"We'll be fine. He can't kill us without killing himself."*

Cam's eyes searched the room for the child, but she was alone.

CHAPTER 24

AFTER A FITFUL NIGHT of sleep peppered with frightful dreams and voices whispering to her, Cameron awoke. She sat up cautiously, testing her strength. Seeming okay, she stood and took baby steps toward the bathroom. The sound of running water startled her. She turned to run for her gun when she remembered Hunter had insisted upon sleeping on the couch the night before. He didn't want to leave her alone under the circumstances. She realized he must be in the shower.

Cam walked through the living room, a sense of something out of place nagging her. She started the coffee and checked the fridge for anything edible. No such luck. Then she noticed the small dinette in the corner held fresh bagels, cream cheese, and juice. She was dumbstruck.

What time did Hunter get up and how was I that out of it that I didn't hear him?

She surveyed the rest of the apartment and realized what was wrong. Nothing was out of place. Her shoes weren't on the floor. Her jacket, usually thrown on a chair, hung on a hook by the door. The wine bottle and glasses from the night before were put away. The place was clean.

Did Hunter clean my apartment?

She sat at the table and looked around at her spruced-up place. It looked good tidy. Yet, she was uncomfortable about the entire thing. Was the apartment so bad that he'd felt compelled to clean it? She may not be the neatest person in the world, but she wasn't a hoarder, and the place wasn't unbearable.

A little OCD, Jason? She gasped at the subconscious Freudian slip. *Holy shit! Where did that come from? A little OCD, Hunter! Hunter! God, that's horrible. Where on earth did that come from?!*

She heard Hunter coming out of the bathroom and hopped off the couch to check herself in the mirror that hung on the wall by the door. Under-eye bags, check. Matted hair, check. Looking scary, check. She ran her fingers through her hair and splashed cold water from the kitchen sink on her face, knowing it wouldn't do much good. She thought about how she looked right then and how her apartment looked most of the time—messy. *Geez, I wonder if Hunter thinks I'm a big mess?*

He came into the living room, rolling his shirt sleeves up as he walked, and Cam recognized the concern in his eyes.

"Good morning. How are you feeling this morning?" he said.

"Morning. So far, I'm okay. No headache, and I found this wonderful spread here," she said, nodding to the food. "I made coffee. Would you like some?"

She stood, but he was one step ahead of her, saying, "I'll get it."

He opened the cabinet that held the coffee mugs and pulled out her favorite. He filled it nearly to the brim and then to her amazement, he opened the fridge, pulled out a small container of light cream, and poured some into the mug. He brought it to her and sat down in the chair next to her.

"I hope the cream you poured into my coffee wasn't something you just found in there." She sniffed her coffee and eyed it for the telltale sign of curdled milk.

"No. I just bought it at the bagel place. You don't cook much, do you?" He had that little smirk on his face again.

She couldn't help but smile back. "No, I don't. It's usually just me, so why bother?"

He got up chuckling to himself, opened the knife drawer, and pulled out a long, serrated knife. It startled Cam to see it, and then she remembered the bagels on the table. The sight of the knife brought back the events of the previous evening. It had seemed like a terrible dream to her, but now she knew it had all happened. The smile faded from her lips as it all came back to her in waves, crashing and ebbing in her subconscious, the pieces coming together again.

Her memory from the night before was foggy. Everything had unfolded during a stress-induced migraine. She looked at Hunter, tears brimming her eyes and, as if he read her mind, he rushed to her side.

"I...I just remembered about last night," she said, withdrawing from him. "Could it be? Is he looking for me? After all these years?" The questions were thoughts escaping from her mind. She wasn't expecting any real answers from him.

Hunter sat next to her and grabbed one hand as reassurance.

She let him hold her hand, hoping he would say it wasn't true, that a psychopath wasn't hunting her and killing women who looked like her.

"Cam, we will do everything possible to protect you." He watched her closely as he spoke. "He doesn't know you changed your hair, or he'd be going after blondes. So, you're still hidden from him. We put out an APB for Jonette last night, and Barone distributed the police sketch of him. It was already on the morning news today." He paused for a moment, avoiding eye contact. "I have to point out the obvious here, Cam. He knows you're in New York City, and he's here too. This guy has been off the radar for over ten years and now, out of the blue, he shows up where you are. You haven't even been living here that long. You've changed your name and your hair. How did he find you so quickly and so easily?"

Yes, how did he? And once more, she heard a child's warning hushed in her ear. *"He's the enemy."*

Cam pulled her hand from his and stood. Was her subconscious trying to tell her Hunter was the enemy? She needed to do something productive to keep her imagination in check, so she went to the large wardrobe in the corner of her living room and opened the doors wide. Kneeling in front of it, she pulled open the large drawer at the bottom, took a deep breath, and extracted a file she hadn't looked at in years. Written across the front of it in large, black print she recognized as her own handwriting were three letters: JJJ. It was her personal file she'd kept on Jason Julius Jonette. It was time to open it and delve into the psychopath's head again—a time she'd feared would come and had dreaded for over a decade.

She sat down on the couch, placed the file on the coffee table, and stared at it, willing it to combust, but there it sat, unburnt. She ran her fingers over the smooth cardboard file that contained her work, her theories regarding the J-Bird and what made him tick. It had been years since she'd sealed this file, hoping she would never have to open it again. She'd forgotten that it sat hidden in her apartment in a dark corner where she never cast her eyes. But Jonette, or someone pretending to be him, had forced her hand by giving him new life through death—the death of innocent women who had died because they resembled her. Her body trembled, and she squeezed her eyes closed, trying to erase the thought from her mind. She startled and almost slid off when Hunter sat next to her on the couch, but as always, he caught her and held her steady.

"What's that?"

"It's my file on Jonette. I haven't looked at it in years, but I think it's time. Hopefully, this will be the last time I need to."

"I'll stay and help you," Hunter offered.

"No. You go, and I'll work from here today. If I come across anything pertinent, I'll call you immediately. I promise."

"I want to put a cop on your door—"

"No. No cops on my door. I'm a trained agent, remember? He would never come here, to where I live, and try to hurt me. Besides, I'm still hidden from him, remember? The blonde hair?" She pointed to her head, then glimpsed herself in the mirror and realized her dark roots betrayed her.

Seeing the concerned look on Hunter's face, she said, "I promise I'll double lock the door and I won't open it for anybody."

His expression was dark and serious. "Where's your gun?"

"In its lockbox in my closet where it is always."

"Go get it, load it, and make sure you have it near you at all times. I'm serious. Cam, this guy will not give up. He's figured out you're here, and it's only a matter of time before he figures out the rest."

"I will, I promise."

"Now," he said, crossing his arms in front of him.

She retrieved her gun, showed him it was loaded, and placed it on the table next to the JJJ file. "Happy?" she asked.

"I'm concerned about you. You've grown on me, you know? I don't want anything to happen to you," he said, nudging her with his arm.

She looked up at him, gazing into those serious green eyes. He'd grown on her too, and she didn't want him to leave. Their love for each other had been steadily growing, and she felt as if it had suddenly bloomed. She touched his arm and said, "I'll make you a bagel to go. Can you come back later?"

"Yes, absolutely." He followed her to the table.

She cut two bagels and slathered them with cream cheese, wrapped one in a napkin for Hunter, and put one on a plate for herself. "Here you go. When you come back later, can you bring me the file I left in the office on Stealth Stalker? I want to make some comparisons."

"Sure. Remember, if you need anything at all, call me. Okay?" Hunter hugged her unexpectedly and whispered in her ear, "Be safe."

"I will. Promise."

After Hunter left, Cam sat down on the floor between the couch and the coffee table with her bagel and coffee. She stared at the JJJ file. It still hadn't caught fire. *Oh well, here goes nothing.* She opened it up to the artist's sketch of Jonette, and her breath caught. It had been so long since she'd looked at the evil bastard, it startled her. One by one, she flipped through the pages as she ate her bagel. He'd marked none of their bodies. Never drawn blood. The more she read through her reports, the more she thought Stealth Stalker was a copycat and not Jason Jonette.

How would a copycat know about my scars? She deliberated. *How would Jonette know about my scars? Only the doctor and nurses in the hospital and*

FBI agents on the case knew about my injuries. There were evidence photos, but the FBI never made them public. He would've needed access to the hospital records or the FBI records to see them. I never saw the evidence photos of the current victim's feet with cut marks matching my scars even though Hunter insisted I did.

Something wasn't right.

CHAPTER 25

The profile Cameron was building of the killer led her back to the same conclusion time and time again. Stealth Stalker had a compulsion toward neatness and order. Each victim suffered one stab wound and their bodies were left in the same position. Their hands were neatly folded over the wound every time, with not even a hair out of place, the shoes removed, socks or hosiery removed, shoes taken. Medina Montan was the only victim whose clothes were touched, and even though he'd sliced the clothes up, he put the pieces back together on her body. It wasn't a typical move for Stealth. She had to question if Medina's murder had been committed by the same killer or a copycat of a copycat. She concluded the killer had obsessive-compulsive disorder, access to police stations, and possibly knew his victims.

Cameron had two terrible thoughts running through her head ever since Hunter had cleaned her apartment and found the knife drawer on his first try, and she'd unconsciously thought of him as Jason. And there was that annoying little voice that kept saying, *"He's the enemy."*

Who's the enemy? Is my subconscious trying to warn me?

The next morning, she called Jeff Alexander. It was her turn to investigate what she'd gotten herself into. Detective Hunter Finnegan had checked on her, and it was only fair she check on him. She didn't expect to find anything except maybe a speeding ticket, but even that seemed doubtful. Hunter was so upstanding and so kind, she suspected he'd done nothing wrong in his entire life.

"Alexander," he answered on the first ring.

"Hi, Jeff. It's Cameron Cooper. How are you?"

"Cameron! What a surprise. Hey, it's great to hear from you. I'm fine. How's New York treating you?" The smile was evident in his voice.

"I like New York. Living here suits me, and I like that I don't need a car here. Are you busy? Do you have a few minutes to chat?"

"Sure, I have a few minutes, although I have a feeling I know what this about."

"Hunter Finnegan told me about your conversation, and don't worry, I'm not angry. He swore to me up and down that you had my back the entire time. And he also explained that you only told him pertinent information. I trust you, Jeff. I know you would never gossip or divulge too much. The question is, how much do you trust me?"

"I trust you with my life, Cam," he said somberly.

"That's what I wanted to hear. I have a favor to ask, and I believe you owe me," Cam said the last part slowly and lowered her voice, inferring she was serious about her request.

"Okay. If I can help, I will."

She caught the hesitation in his voice. "It's my turn. I want information this time."

"Info on what?"

"I want the back story on Hunter Finnegan. You filled him in about me, and now I want some info on him. Is there any reason I shouldn't trust him? Are there any red flags on him?" She waited as Jeff contemplated what he would say.

"You want me to tell you what I know about him personally? It's not much, Cam. We went to college together. We both studied criminal justice. He's a good guy. He never got into any trouble, and he bailed me out a couple of times."

"I want more," she said.

"More? Like what?"

She could almost feel him squirming through the phone. "I want you to turn on your FBI issued computer, type his name in, and tell me what pops up."

"Cam, what's up? Why are you asking me to break the rules for you? If you want me to help you, then you have to give me a good reason."

Jeff was right, she was asking him to break the rules. But she wasn't sure why. Was she just being childish and checking on Hunter because he'd checked on her, or was it because she'd had a nightmare?

"He's the enemy."

A shiver ran through her and her pulse quickened, thinking about the voice she kept hearing. Jeff was waiting for an answer, and it needed to be convincing.

"I have a lot of questions and no answers. It's a gut feeling." It was all she had, and she held her breath as she waited for Jeff to respond. Had he said that to her, she would have laughed out loud, but Jeff wasn't her. He was nicer.

"A gut feeling? Seriously? Is that all you have? You want me to risk my job for a gut feeling?" His voice rose with each question.

"Look, Jeff, it may not be a good reason, but you owe me, don't you? What if I'm the one you should worry about? You discussed a Fed case with a cop. You discussed me with a cop I happen to be working with. I could make life difficult for you." She hated herself for stooping so low, but she needed answers.

"Yeah, you could make my life difficult, but you won't. I know you too well, Cam. You can huff and puff all you like, but you'd never follow through because I did nothing wrong. That being said, I will help you because we *are* friends. Not because you threatened me. Understood?"

"Yes. And thank you. And I'm sorry." She meant it. She should never have gone there, not with Jeff.

His fingers tapped on a keyboard and his breathing was loud. He sounded a little angry, but he would forgive her. Eventually. And then he said one word under his breath, but Cam caught it, from 900 miles away. "Shit."

She held her breath, waiting for Jeff Alexander to tell her what he'd found. When he didn't respond, she prompted, "What is it, Jeff? What does it say?"

"You won't like this, and neither do I. There's a sealed file on Hunter. That's not good."

"Open it," she said.

"Open it?" He sounded incredulous. "You know what could happen if I open this without authority? I could get fired. He could find out! Did you think about that? What if he finds out I opened his sealed file?"

"What year is it from?"

"1993."

"Open it. It's old. The probability that anyone will notice is extremely low. And if someone does, I'll take full responsibility. I'll say I did it." She took a deep breath and regained her composure. She needed the information as an investigating officer. It was strictly professional now, not personal.

"God! Cameron, if you get me fired, I'll never forgive you, and you'll foot the bills for my kids' college educations. Got it?"

"Got it. Now open it." She couldn't take it anymore.

His fingers tapped once more, his breathing even more pronounced. "Did you know he was married?"

"Yes, he mentioned he's a widower. Why? Does it have something to do with the file?"

"Uh, yeah." He said nothing else.

"Care to elaborate?" She was losing her patience.

"Okay, it's not that bad. Let's start with the fact that they exonerated Hunter and work back, okay?"

"Okay," she said reluctantly. "Hunter's innocent of whatever is in the file."

"It says that he was a person of interest in connection with the death of his wife." Jeff stopped and took a deep breath. "Did he mention to you how she died?"

"No, I assumed an accident or an illness. What happened?"

"Cameron, I don't want to upset you. Just remember the police cleared him. Okay?"

"Okay," she agreed, but mentally she prepared for the worst.

"Elizabeth Finnegan was strangled."

Nothing could have prepared her for those words.

"You okay?" Jeff asked. "Cameron? Say something."

Strangled? It was the worst word in the English language. It conjured up Jason Jonette, and all his victims positioned like sleeping dolls. One by one, she recalled their faces, lifeless, perfect in death. *Strangled*. The word itself practically strangled her.

"My God, strangled?" *What did Jeff tell me to remember? He told me just a minute ago. Remember... Remember... Hunter was innocent. That's it—she was strangled, and he was innocent.* She inhaled as her thoughts cleared. "What else does it say? Who found her?"

"This isn't Jonette, Cam. Hunter found her. It says here they surmised she interrupted a robbery. Someone strangled her with their hands. The bruising on her neck was so severe the coroner could measure the size of the hands that choked her. That's how they cleared Hunter—his hands were larger than the perp's. They arrested him under suspicion because he was the only one seen going into the apartment. Neighbors testified it had been quiet until Hunter yelled for help. When they ran in, he was kneeling over her body. Police found no sign of forced entry. Neighbors also testified they had heard the couple arguing early that morning." Jeff was reading snippets of the report to her.

"If he's innocent, why seal the record?" Cam asked.

Silence came over the line as Jeff Alexander pondered the question. "The only thing I can come up with is that he was a young cop, newlywed, now devastated and falsely accused. Maybe they took pity on him, didn't want the accusation held against him even after they cleared him. He was already a decorated cop with excellent evaluations when this happened. In a special notes section, it says a street gang killed his partner in front of him six months prior." Jeff paused for a moment. "They closed the case and made the charges against him go away the only way they could. They couldn't take it back, so they sealed it."

A tear rolled down her cheek, the stress of the last twenty-four hours taking a toll. "How old was he when all of this happened?"

"It says twenty-four. Poor kid. I had no idea," Jeff said with sadness in his voice.

Cam felt terrible. She tried to remember why she'd called in the first place. *Stupid gut feeling. I should've known better. He was hiding something, just not what I thought he was hiding.* She thanked Jeff and got off the phone, embarrassed she'd thought poorly of Hunter and put Jeff on the spot over her wild suspicions. And how would she hide from Hunter that she knew what happened to his young wife?

CHAPTER 26

A LL WEEK, DETECTIVE RHONDA Saintil had had an uneasy feeling that someone was watching her. Saintil and every other brunette in the area were taking extra precautions, never walking alone after dark, and some had even changed their hair color.

Saintil didn't always have the luxury of waiting for someone to walk with, and taking a cab home every day wasn't practical. She needed to get back by 5:35 every day, or there would be consequences. And now, as the sun set earlier every night, she would leave work in the dark soon.

She always carried her service revolver with her, but as added protection, she now carried a four-inch pocketknife. She wasn't sure how the killer got so physically close to his victims with no apparent struggle, but if he was sneaking up on them, as was the theory, taking time to reach for a gun might mean her death while a knife in hand was a weapon ready to go.

Rhonda watched the clock as she finished her paperwork. It had been a rough week with the death of Adrianne Schechter. Heightened security tactics were instated, but she knew it wasn't enough. The secure measures would only challenge the killer, make it more interesting for him.

She straightened her desk and left the daily paperwork on Hunter's desk. He was at a weekly meeting of a joint task force established to capture the Stealth Stalker Killer and would find her reports when he got back. They were still waiting on forensic evidence from Adrianne Schechter's Taser. One electrode had DNA on its barb.

He must've been too stunned by Adrianne's attack to grab the Taser before he ran, she thought, somewhat amused by the pun. The potential DNA evidence was the first break they'd had.

Standing at Hunter's desk, she peered through the window of the small office where he and the doctor worked. She studied the whiteboard with the map and photos of the victims taped to it. She wasn't sure what to make of Dr. Cooper, who seemed nice enough, but there was no way she would get into a deep conversation, or any conversation, with a shrink. There was too much she didn't want to reveal about herself. And wasn't that what shrinks did? Get into your head to look around in all the dark corners?

No thanks. I've kept my secrets this long, and I don't plan on blowing it now. She'd consciously decided to steer clear of Cameron Cooper ever since her arrival in September.

The longing looks between Cameron and Hunter, the secrets, the touches that lingered, hadn't escaped her. They obviously had a thing for one another, but it was no concern of hers. What they did in their free time was their business just like her personal life was her business. As long as they could keep their professional and private worlds separate and it had no impact on her, she didn't care what they did.

Rhonda grabbed her coat and backpack and headed for the door. The night air surprised her. It was cold even for New York in early December, and she quickly buttoned up her coat, pulling the collar up and stuffing her hands in her pockets. Her fingers grazed the knife, and she pulled back from it. She'd forgotten about it and could have seriously cut herself in her haste to warm her hands. With caution, she wrapped her hand around the handle of the knife and checked for anyone suspicious-looking as she walked closer to the street than the buildings because it seemed safer to her.

No need to tempt fate or anyone else.

The clock on a bank across the street caught her eye. Eighteen minutes past five. She picked up her pace, racing against time as she power-walked her way home to get there before 5:35. She thought about her kids, her son, Nick, and her daughter, Alexa. They were the reason she worked so hard and why she had to get home on time. Without her there, they would be sitting ducks.

Crossing streets and turning corners like the lifer she was, she hurried home. She knew these streets as if she'd built them herself. She'd been born and raised in the city, and now she was raising her kids in the same neighborhood where she grew up.

Checking the time again, Rhonda decided to cut through the block using the passageway between the buildings. Approaching the narrow lane, she peered down the length of it. She could see the street on the other side, and as far as she could tell, there was no one around. Wrapping her hand around the handle of the knife, she quietly proceeded.

Halfway down the alley, a stack of old wooden crates she'd passed hundreds of times suddenly felt like they were about to spring to life and devour her. They seemed so ominous in the dark. She considered pulling out her gun but decided the idea was ridiculous. She told herself that she was just being paranoid and to keep moving, which she did. The boxes didn't jump her, and a psychopath didn't attack her. As she reached the street at the end of the passage, she took a deep breath and had to laugh at herself for being so dramatic.

Rhonda opened the door to her apartment building and took the steps two at a time to get to her fourth-floor apartment faster. As she put the key in her door, she could hear the familiar sound of footsteps starting up the stairs. She looked at her watch. Five-thirty-five, just in time.

CHAPTER 27

Two days of working from home were more than Cameron could handle even with Hunter bringing her dinner nightly. She wanted to be back in the precinct with the hustle and bustle of law enforcement around her. Spending the entire day in the gray office where she could see and hear other people proved cathartic. She'd gone over each file word by word and decided to call it a night. When she'd come back from lunch, the floor had been quiet. Many officers had gone to a memorial mass held for their fallen comrades. Not being religious, she'd opted to stay behind and work.

A low hum replaced the quietness as the officers returned to work after the mass. Loud voices, phones ringing, and a general atmosphere of chaos had come back with them.

She gathered the files up, putting everything back in the order Hunter had them. His records were organized and meticulous. He color-coded, alphabetized, and put them in order by date. She remembered her first day here and Hunter's cross reaction when someone had carelessly put a folder in the wrong place. He expected to find them how he left them, and if he didn't, he became visibly irritated.

As she grabbed the handle of the door, the sight of Hunter and Rhonda through the window stopped her cold. They both looked very intense sitting at his desk, and a sense came over her that she didn't want them to see her. Hunter tapped his long fingers on his lip. It was his tell. He had something serious on his mind and was trying to formulate the right way to begin the discussion. Rhonda looked stoic and uncomfortable as she sat, back straight and stiff, on the edge of her chair. He started talking, and she gave her usual one-word answers, an expression of annoyance on her face.

Hunter leaned in on his desk, closing the distance between them, and said something that sent Rhonda Saintil into a fit. She stood up, wagging her finger in his face. With her eyebrows furrowed, it looked like she was speaking hatefully to him. It shocked Cameron to watch. She couldn't imagine what Hunter had said to elicit such a response, and she wished she could hear the conversation.

As Rhonda reached down to grab her bag, her eyes locked with Cam's. She'd caught Cam watching through the window. Embarrassed, Cam opened the door, pretending she wasn't spying but just opening the door as Rhonda spotted her. Their eyes stayed locked as Rhonda stood, then the officer glanced at Hunter and back to Cam.

"You should be careful about who you play with, Doc. Sometimes danger is closer than we realize," she snapped at Cam, her words dripping with anger. And with that, Rhonda turned and stomped away.

Cam opened her mouth to ask Hunter what had happened, but he abruptly got up and grabbed his coat and walked away, following the same path as Rhonda.

What the heck? What did Rhonda mean by danger is closer than we realize? Was she being dramatic because Hunter angered her, or was she sending me a warning?

Cameron followed Hunter, but his long strides kept her from catching up to him. She called to him, but he seemed not to hear her. She'd never seen this side of him, so angry and pensive. By the time she exited the building, he'd already rounded the corner.

Still clutching the folders in her hands, Cam trekked back into the police station and back up to Hunter's desk. His filing cabinet, which he always kept locked, was not, and she pulled the giant drawer open. She flipped through the files until she found the one marked "Stealth Stalker" and replaced the folders she'd been reading. As she closed the drawer, a file labeled "Unsolved Cases" caught her eye. It contained several yellow folders and one red. She looked around. Some officers chatted on the other side of the room. She pulled the red folder out of the drawer and opened it. It was the file on Hunter's wife and in it, she found newspaper clippings about her murder and notes in Hunter's handwriting. Clipped to a yellowing piece of paper was a picture of the young Elizabeth Finnegan. She was attractive with dark, shoulder-length hair, high cheekbones emphasizing her slim face, and even in this black-and-white photo, it was apparent she had very light-colored eyes. Something about the picture set Cameron on edge. As she studied the image, she looked up to think about what bothered her and glimpsed her work on the whiteboard. Her eyes darted from photo to photo. The eyes of the dead looked back at her, and it occurred to her that young Elizabeth had the same physical characteristics as the women whose pictures hung on the board. Her hands trembled as she looked through the folder.

It's just a coincidence, she told herself, but that felt like a lie. Cam didn't believe in coincidences. She believed, however, that under the right circumstance, anyone was capable of murder.

"You can take it. Go ahead, take it, but be careful. He's the enemy," the now-familiar voice of a girl whispered to her, perhaps her subconscious warning her. In futility, she looked over her shoulder, searching for the child.

Her head throbbed as she shoved the folder into her bag. She looked around once more for the child. *Am I losing it?* She headed for the stairs, where she ran into Detective Murphy on her way down.

"Hey, Doc. How's it going?" he said in his usual jovial style.

"Fine, just fine," she said, out of breath from racing down the stairs.

"Hey, everything all right? You look a little spooked or something."

Spooked is a good word. I'm definitely spooked. "I'm good. Just in a hurry," she lied.

"If you need anything, give me a call. Good night." He started back up the steps with a wave.

"Thanks, Detective. Good night." Nauseous waves rippled over her.

CHAPTER 28

On her way home from work, Cameron couldn't get Hunter and Rhonda out of her mind. She'd never seen either of them in a heated argument, and the way they had spoken to each other was unsettling. The cab pulled up in front of her building, and even though her gut ached, she told the driver to continue to another address, Hunter's building. Out of curiosity, she'd looked up his address before she left the station house, not really with the intent of going there, but now she felt compelled to see where he lived.

As she went over in her mind what she knew about him, she couldn't help but make mental check marks against Stealth's attributes. Hunter was immaculate, bordering on obsessive, from the files he kept, to the way he'd straightened her apartment, to the pristine condition of his shoes. Stealth was compulsive, leaving each victim in the same position and nothing out of place at each crime scene. Check. Hunter had worked in the police department for nearly twenty-five years and could easily have known the victims. The killer, she believed, worked within the police department and had crossed paths with all the victims. Check. Hunter's deceased wife looked strikingly similar to the dead women. Stealth had a type. Check.

The killer was a white male with a black beard. Hunter didn't have a beard, but was that enough to cross him off the list of suspects?

And there was the child's voice. *"He's the enemy."* Was it her subconscious trying to warn her, or was she losing her mind and hearing voices?

The cab stopped in front of Hunter's building, and she looked out the window at the modern steel and glass structure speckled with lit windows. Neat little bushes pruned into perfect squares lined the front of the building at the sidewalk, and a black awning with silver scrollwork covered the walkway at the front entrance. A tall man in a black uniform and white gloves rushed to the taxi to open her door. The sight of him surprised Cam. She hadn't expected a tough cop like Hunter to live in a building with a doorman. But the rest of the building corresponded with what she would expect, pristine with tight lines and well taken care of.

"Good evening, ma'am," the doorman said politely. "Are you visiting Ninety-Nine tonight?"

She paid the cabbie and accepted the doorman's extended hand to help her out of the cab. "Yes, I am."

"Who are you here to see?"

She didn't want to tell him, but she wasn't getting by him, so she conceded. "Hunter Finnegan."

"Detective Finnegan didn't tell me he was expecting anyone this evening. I'll announce you." Cameron detected a slight Russian accent.

He held open one of the oversized glass doors for her, and she walked into a beautiful lobby featuring brilliant white marble floors and walls. Enormous glass and steel chandeliers hung from the high ceiling and behind the reception desk, embedded into the marble wall, was a shiny steel 99. It was as if she'd walked into daylight from the dark city outside.

"Do you have to announce me?" she asked, still not confident in her unannounced visit. "I wanted to surprise Detective Finnegan."

He looked at her as if waiting for further explanation.

"I'm his...friend," she said, forcing a smile. "I...just wanted to surprise him."

"I'm sorry, ma'am. It's our policy that we announce all guests upon arrival. Whom should I say is calling?"

"Cameron Cooper."

With that, he picked up his phone and called Hunter's apartment.

An uneasy feeling spread through her, and she fought the urge to grab the phone out of his hands, hang it up, and run like an unhinged person from the building. But she'd given her name, her real name. It was too late. *Damn it!*

"Good evening, Detective Finnegan, this is Erik. Ms. Cameron Cooper is in reception." He listened for a moment and then concluded, "Yes, sir. Good evening."

Erik hung up the phone and nodded at her. "Detective Finnegan is waiting for you." He walked over to the elevator and pressed the call button for Cam, then stood with her waiting for the car to arrive. When the steel doors slid open, he pressed a hand to the door and motioned for her to enter. She walked meekly into the elevator and, as she turned to face him, he leaned in and pressed the nine button. "He's in 919. Good evening, Ms. Cooper." And with that, the doors slid closed.

The mirrored interior of the elevator multiplied Cam's reflection over and over. Mesmerized by the effect, she thought, *And here are the many faces of Cameron Cooper.*

The doors opened to a well-lit foyer. A large, shiny 9 hung on the wall across from the elevator, two modern club chairs in charcoal gray leather sat on either side, and a beautiful glass sculpture of the Chrysler Building, about four feet tall, sat between them. She stepped out of the elevator, onto a deep pile carpet. The place had the air of an upscale hotel. A small sign on the wall indicated that apartments 910-920 were to the right.

She started down the hallway, growing more anxious with each step. Why had she come here again? Oh right, falling in love, possibly with a serial killer. Need more info. She took deep breaths to relax and hoped Hunter wouldn't be angry that she'd showed up uninvited.

Before she could knock on the door, it opened, an affable Hunter on the other side.

"Cam! What a great surprise. Come here."

Before she could say a word, he pulled her into him, gently kissed her, and hugged her warmly. His arms enveloped her and embraced her to him even closer, their bodies pressed together. Her own hands reached around his broad back and skimmed his muscles. She didn't want him to let go. Relief replaced anxiety at the unexpected greeting. She'd thought he would be cross at her dropping in, but he was quite the opposite, and now the thought of Hunter as a lover overtook the idea of him as a killer. Seeing the way he looked at her made her ashamed that she'd thought he could ever hurt anyone. And yet, she needed to be sure.

"Wow," she said as he pulled back. "That's the best hello I've ever gotten."

"Really?" he said with a smug undertone. "Maybe you should surprise me more often." That boyish grin once again crossed his lips.

"Maybe I will," she said, mentally noting his scent, a clean, fresh citrus and sandalwood, and how toned his body felt.

"Come on in and explain to me why you're out alone? I would've come to your place." He stepped behind her and slid her coat off her shoulders and down her arms, skimming her with his fingers as he did.

Goosebumps prickled her skin. "Yeah, about that. I apologize for dropping in uninvited. I hope I'm not intruding."

"No, you could never intrude. I guess I haven't been clear about my feelings if you think you could," he said, brushing a stray hair from her face. "Any time I get to spend with you is time I enjoy."

She blew out a breath she wasn't aware she'd been holding. "I feel the same way. I guess I'm just overly cautious about personal relationships. And, you know, you haven't invited me here. I thought maybe you didn't want me here."

"What? I haven't invited you here because I don't want you leaving by yourself to go home. I'm afraid for you." He closed the gap between them and ran his hands down her arms until their fingers entwined. "You're always welcome here."

"So how about the nickel tour?" She may have felt bad for thinking he could be complicit in murder, but she still wanted to see everything. A little more insight into him personally and how he lived had value since, with every passing day, she fell faster and faster for him.

"Okay. It won't be a very long tour, but if you play your cards right, at the end, you may just get a special bonus." He took her by the hand. "Entrez" he said, sweeping an arm in front of him. "We shall start our tour here in the living room. Note the masculine-like furniture, because I, of course, am extremely masculine and what else would a macho, tough guy like me have but masculine furniture?"

"Very nice," she said, enjoying the playful side of Hunter. "And very masculine."

"This way, madam," he said, leading her toward a hallway. He passed one door on the left and opened another door at the end of the hall. "Behind Door Number One, we have the powder room."

She glanced in and nodded. "Uh-huh. So it is."

Across the hall stood another door. He grinned as he let his fingers linger on its brass handle. "This is the pièce de résistance," he said in an awful attempt at a French accent as he swung the door open.

He stepped aside so Cam could pass him on her way into the darkness. He flicked the switch and two lamps on either side of a king-size bed turned on. It was a sizeable bedroom, nicely decorated, and unsurprisingly neat. A gray down comforter lay neatly folded at the end of the bed and four plump pillows leaned against an iron and wood headboard. On the wall over the bed hung an iron sculpture of a sailboat matching the steely gray of the headboard. The two side tables also matched, as did a chest of drawers on the opposite wall. In the corner, an overstuffed chair sat with rolled arms in a plaid fabric.

"Manly, no?"

"Yes, yes. Manly," she said, rolling her eyes.

Across from the bed were two doors. He opened one, revealing a huge bathroom with a spacious walk-in shower, complete with body sprays and a rain shower, a whirlpool tub, and a double vanity with a stone countertop.

"Impressive," Cam said. "Is this the standard bathroom or an upgrade?" She was sort of kidding, but sort of not. How did a cop afford all this?

"This is my gift to me," he said, smiling broadly. "When I get home after a hard day of crime-solving, I need this oasis to calm my mind. Can I show the lady how the jets massage away the worries of the day?" He looked at her with that boyish grin once more.

Her skin tingling, she replied, "The lady would like to continue with the tour, please."

"Very well, we can always circle back to take a closer look at the amenities of Chez Finnegan." He stepped back into the bedroom and opened the next door.

A ceiling light automatically flicked on when the door opened and a walk-in-closet any clothes hog would envy lit up. There were shelves and drawers and individual slanted sections for shoes and hanging space for short and long clothes, all in mahogany wood. Men's clothes hung perfectly in a row, shoes that looked new were lined up, ties had special hooks as did belts—it looked like a small, fine men's boutique.

She gaped at the luxuriousness of Hunter's closet. *No wonder he cleaned up around my place. He's a neat freak!* With that thought, she careened back to reality and why she'd visited in the first place—to snoop and make mental notes. "Nice. Very nice," she said, trying to sound unimpressed.

"Really, that's it? My last—" He laughed a little and then kept going. "This way, madam."

"Your last what?"

He shook his head. "The last, uh, woman who saw that closet nearly fainted. It usually gets more of a reaction."

"Is that so? I guess I'm just not so shallow that a closet can make me swoon." *The last woman blah, blah, blah. Ugh!* She felt heat rising in her face. Hunter's smug grin made her realize the little green monster of jealousy sitting on her shoulder was apparent to him and she'd reacted in a way that had pleased him none the less. Time to move on. "Next on tour?"

"Right this way," he said, motioning to the hall. "Straight away into the living room, we will find the next room on our tour."

"What about this door on the right?" she said as he walked past the only door left unopened. "What's behind Door Number Three?"

"That's the den."

"The den? I believe you left that room off the tour. Hiding something from me?"

"Hmm, you've found me out. It's really my lair," Hunter said with a glare and then burst out laughing. "I never go in there. I think it's haunted. Just kidding. It's just a dusty old room that I don't use. Nothing to see." He continued down the hall and then, spreading his arms out and turning a circle, said, "You've already seen the living room." He walked through a wide archway into the next room. "This is the dining room. And through that door is the kitchen, something I know you aren't familiar with. It's a room where people cook and prepare food...to eat."

"Really? People do that? Isn't that what takeout is for?" Cam mocked him back.

"Make yourself comfortable while I see if there's any takeout lying around."

She liked it when he teased her. The flirting made her smile and feel happy. She wandered around Hunter's meticulous living room. There wasn't a lot to see, just two leather couches, the marble fireplace, two end tables, and a bookshelf in the corner. She picked up a wedding photo of a pretty, youthful woman with shoulder-length, dark hair and studied it. She recognized the bride from the picture in the file she'd taken. Elizabeth Finnegan, Hunter's wife. Suddenly she remembered her conversation with Jeff Alexander, and a pang of guilt struck her. She should come clean to Hunter that she'd called Jeff and pressured him to open the sealed file. That would be an awkward conversation, so she decided to save it for another day.

She put the frame down and relaxed on the couch to wait for Hunter. He pushed through the swinging kitchen door carrying a tray and placed it on the glass table in front of her. Arranged on the tray was a bottle of wine, two glasses, and a cutting board with warm brie and sliced French bread.

"You just had this lying around?"

"What? I like brie. And a handsome man like myself needs to be prepared in case a beautiful woman just drops in," he said, leaning in.

She thought he was about to kiss her again, but he didn't. "Uh-huh. Okay, handsome, let's see a little less talk and a little more wine flowing."

He poured the dark Merlot into a glass and handed it to her. "I'll start dinner since I'm sure you haven't eaten a proper meal today." He looked at her intently, and she stared back innocently. "Yep. That's what I figured." He stood and headed back to the kitchen.

Cam helped herself to the cheese and bread, impressed by how delicious it tasted. She realized that, except for the extreme tidiness, Hunter was perfect, and she felt awful again for considering him as a match for Stealth.

Hunter came back into the living room and sat next to Cam. He held up his glass. "To life and love and the time to enjoy both."

They clinked glasses and sipped the wine.

He met her gaze and said, "You are always welcome here. I *really* like you, Dr. Cameron Cooper." A slight smile graced his handsome face. "The last several weeks working with you and getting to know you have been...great." He laughed uneasily at his awkwardness and lack of a better word, then put a hand to his face and covered his eyes, sighing. "That didn't come out the way I wanted it to."

Cam took his hand in hers. "I like you too, very handsome Detective Hunter Finnegan." This time, she leaned in and kissed him.

"I wasn't sure if we should proceed this way," he said, shifting on the couch to face her, "since we work so closely together. But I can't help myself. You are so beautiful and smart, and I can't get you out of my mind. Ever since the first day you stood at my desk."

Cam remembered the day. It seemed like years ago now. Their relationship had grown and changed. And now they were at the cusp of an intimate connection like she'd never felt before in her life. They had clicked so easily, so naturally. It relieved her to hear that he was falling for her just as she was for him.

A dinging came from the kitchen. "That's dinner," Hunter said and stood. "I'll be back in a minute."

"I'm going to the powder room." Cam went into the bathroom, peed, washed her hands, and finger fluffed her hair.

Opening the bathroom door, she came back into the hall but paused where Door Number Three stood in front of her, closed tight, teasing her, beckoning her to turn its curved brass handle and open it. She wandered past, examining the dark brown-stained mahogany door, more and more curious about the secrets it hid. Hunter wasn't back in the living room yet, so she carefully backed up, watching the kitchen door, and stopped next to Door Number Three.

Cautiously resting her fingertips on its cool metal handle, she slipped her hand around it, never taking her eyes off the kitchen door, and pressed the handle down. The door pulled from its frame, revealing the inky room behind it. She deftly slid her left hand up the wall, searching for a light switch, and flipped it up. Four high-hats in the ceiling flicked on, illuminating the contents of the room. She quietly took a few steps into the room to look around. At first, she only noticed the furniture. An ornate desk and chair with a few pictures in frames on it, a couch that looked dated with matching tables on either side, across from it a sofa table pushed up against the wall, and next to it a large glass curio case that must have been eight feet tall stood in the corner. The contents of the glass case stopped her cold. A young black bear stood upright on its hind legs, mouth askew, so it appeared to be almost smiling. There was a small, stuffed sparrow perched on its paw. Then she noticed the rest of the décor in the room. In front of the couch lay a dark brown bearskin rug. Mounted on the wall above it were two deer heads with ten points each. Stuffed wildlife posed on the tables. A raccoon crouched in fear. Two ducks worked as bookends. A fox stood peering out from beneath the sofa table. Her heart pounded as her eyes met the marble eyes of each woodland creature.

As she looked from one grotesquely arranged animal to another, her eyes stopped at a pair of raccoons posed upright in the center of the sofa table, facing one another with their little arms outstretched, acting as the support stand for a six-inch hunting knife! She gasped and stepped back, almost falling over a stuffed bobcat sitting just next to the doorway.

Hunter called out from the kitchen that dinner was ready, and she quickly turned off the light and closed the door behind her, then headed back to the living room, her heart beating a little faster. She took a big gulp of her wine and tried to breathe deeply, remembering why she'd come here in the first place: the fight with Rhonda Saintil and the remarkable similarities between Hunter, Stealth, and Jonette.

Hunter pushed through the kitchen door carrying two ceramic bowls, one with fresh pasta in a meat sauce and the other containing fresh Italian bread. "Bring the wine and glasses over here. We'll eat in the dining room," he said.

Cameron obligingly picked up the bottle and their glasses, taking another gulp in the process, and brought them into the dining room. "That was fast."

"Fresh pasta only takes a few minutes to cook. Don't worry, I can teach you a few things. You're all flushed. Thinking about the jetted tub?" He smiled.

"Or it could be the wine." *Or the collection of dead animals in the next room. Oh, and how about that knife you have there? You know, it looks like the type our serial killer might use.* "This is a swanky place you have here. I didn't realize how well New York City cops lived," she said, watching Hunter more closely now, examining his every mannerism, dissecting his every word.

"This was my wife's condo. It's probably worth ten times what she bought it for all those years ago. I could never afford to buy this place today, but I'm happy to have it."

"Oh." She guessed that made some sense. "I came over here for a reason," she said, trying to distract Hunter.

"To have your way with me?"

She tried to smile at his attempt at foreplay. "No, sorry."

He dished out the food and poured more wine as she tried to find the words.

"I wanted to ask what happened earlier. The argument with Rhonda? I overheard you, though I didn't mean to eavesdrop. I saw the two of you looking kind of intense and then arguing. Remember? She told me I should be careful about who I played with and left abruptly. And then you left. I called out to you, but you didn't seem to hear me."

"Oh, that. It's nothing I want to talk about right now," he said, his smile fading.

"I'm a superb listener. Perhaps I can help," she offered.

"I was concerned about Rhonda and asked if she would like an escort home, but she didn't appreciate my concern. She got angry and accused me of..." He took a sip of wine. "...impropriety, we'll say. Now let's eat before it gets cold."

"What do you mean impropriety? What did she accuse you of?"

"I don't want to talk about it now. Can I get you anything else?"

"No, thanks. This looks delicious. You're truly a man full of surprises." A happy and flirtatious man one moment, angry and brooding the next. She sat there watching him devour his pasta as if she weren't in the room, and she knew she had to get out of there. And then the voice of the child she couldn't see, only hear, whispered to her, *"He likes to kill things."*

CHAPTER 29

Cameron escaped from Hunter's apartment with some argument. She'd told him the wine had brought on a migraine and she needed to get home to take her medicine. He'd weakly suggested taking her himself, but she insisted she would be fine and that she would go straight home, from his door to hers.

Once in the taxi, she called Detective Glen Levine. "Detective Levine, it's Cameron Cooper. I need to speak with you. It's urgent."

"Hello, Dr. Cooper. I'm listening. How can I help you?"

"I need to speak to you in person. Can you meet me?"

"Can it wait until tomor—"

"No," she said impatiently. Her nerves were on fire. Everything and everyone, from the marble eyes of the dead animals, to the present smell of vomit in the back seat of the dirty cab, to Levine trying to push her off was irritating her. "I need to speak to you now. And I need to see you in person. I'll come to you. What's the address?"

"I'm having dinner at Mosconi's. Do you know it?"

"Yes. I'll be there in ten." She disconnected the call and told the cabbie to take her to Mosconi's.

She needed another perspective on her thoughts. She had to be wrong. She couldn't be falling in love with a killer. There was so much circumstantial evidence, and she needed Levine to tell her she was mistaken, that she had no business consulting because she no longer knew what she was doing. That would be acceptable. It would be okay to be wrong because it would mean she was free to love Hunter and start her life over. She could go into private practice. Or teach. Or paint. It didn't matter as long as she and Hunter were together.

The cab pulled up in front of the restaurant and as she got out, the aroma of garlic wafted in the air, reminding her she never ate her dinner at Hunter's.

Cam spotted Levine's clean-shaven head right away. She waited until he looked her way and they made eye contact, then she nodded to the bar. He excused himself from his party and casually came her way. They grabbed a corner booth in the bar area, and she leaned in close to Levine.

"So, what's this all about, Doc?" Levine asked.

"I need to ask you something, and I want you to keep an open mind, okay?"

"Sure." His face was tight and his demeanor cool.

"Did Hunter know any of the victims?" she asked, hoping he hadn't.

"Yeah, probably all of them. Why do you ask?"

All? She grew uncomfortable. "How? Did he work at other stations?"

"Hunter's been around for a long time. You meet people. It's fair to say he dated a lot of women over the last twenty years."

"Are you saying he didn't just know them, he dated them? All of them?"

"No, not all of them. Three out of five. Everyone knew Dr. Schechter. And Amy Larsen liked to set him up on blind dates once in a while. She liked playing match-maker. Don't misunderstand, Doc, he's not some kind of serial dater. He was just lonely after... Hey, wait a minute! You don't think he has something to do with those women being murdered, do you?" His eyes flickered with anger as he pointed one perfectly manicured finger at her.

"I'm just trying to work something out that's been bothering me," Cam said, trying to assuage him.

"What? What's bothering the all-knowing Dr. Cooper?"

"I don't appreciate the sarcasm. Can you just hear me out?" she said, stiffening her back.

"Fine, let's hear it. Make it quick though. My dinner is getting cold while I'm listening to this garbage."

"My profile of the killer is someone meticulous, probably obsessive, like Hunter," she started.

"Hunter is a little excessively neat, but I wouldn't label him obsessive, okay?"

"No, it's not okay. The victim profile is women between thirty-five and forty-five, average height of five-seven, light eyes, and brunette hair. Did you know his wife?"

"No, I never met his wife. She died before I met Hunter. What does she have to do with any of this?"

"His wife was five-six, brunette, and if she were still alive, she would be forty-three years old. Are you aware how she died?"

"Yeah, somebody murdered the poor girl. However, she wasn't stabbed. An intruder strangled her, and the court exonerated Hunter. The killer had used his bare hands, which left bruises on his wife's neck that didn't match Hunter's hand size. Therefore, he didn't do it." Levine slapped a hand on the table and sat back, staring at Cam, challenging her like a defense attorney facing an unworthy opponent. "You're wasting my time and besides that, I thought you and Hunter had something going on, that you cared for each other or something. I'm a detective, remember? I see the way the two of you look and act around one another. Where is this coming from?"

"It isn't uncommon for serial killers to start out killing when they're young. They start with small things like insects and work their way up to small animals. One day, the neighbor can't find her cat. They constantly crave the next thrill, the next kill. They work up to bigger, stronger animals for more of a challenge, until they decide on the biggest challenge there is—another human being."

"Yeah? So what? Hunter, ironically, doesn't like to hunt."

"He has a trophy room."

"What do you mean? Like football trophies?"

"A *trophy* room. Dead stuffed animals everywhere!"

"No, he doesn't. I've known that man for nearly twenty years, and not once has he ever mentioned going hunting," Levine said, shaking his shiny, bald head from side to side.

"Oh, yes, he does," she hissed back at him. "I saw it. I was in his apartment tonight. I asked for the tour, and he skipped one door. He told me it was a dusty old room that he never used. When he went into the kitchen, curiosity got the better of me and I took a peek. My God! There were deer heads, a stuffed fox, and a bear in a glass case! The topper, two poor little raccoons holding a six-inch hunting knife! I almost fell over when I saw them. Are you still willing to sit there and tell me I'm wrong?"

Levine sat there staring at her, eyes narrowed and scowling. He was considering her words, not fighting her, not disagreeing with her, not telling her she'd lost her mind.

"Look, I'm not sure what to think. I don't want to believe that Hunter is capable of hurting anyone. I...I care for him very much." She chose her next words carefully. "The other night, he was angry with Adrianne Schechter. We ran into her on our way to dinner. She said she would have a talk with Chief Dwyer first thing in the morning about me. She seemed to feel I was unfit for the job. Anyway, he told me not to worry, that he would take care of her. He said he wouldn't stand for anyone treating someone on his team unprofessionally and that one day the bear would tire of being poked and that would be the end of Dr. Schechter. And then she was murdered." She waited for a response and then prompted Levine, "Tell me I'm wrong. Tell me I'm crazy."

He leaned into her and, in a low tone, said, "Now you think Hunter killed Dr. Schechter? You're wrong, and you're crazy." He stood up and straightened his jacket to walk away.

"There's one more thing," she said.

Levine stopped, glancing over his shoulder at her. "The thing with my feet."

"What about your feet?" he said, turning toward her.

"I have scars on the bottoms of my feet. Hunter said they match the cuts on the victim's feet. He said I saw the pictures, but I didn't. I would've remembered something so personal to myself."

"The victim's soles were sliced up. Hunter and I discussed the possibility that this guy is your J-Bird, the psycho that you and the FBI let get away. Or a copycat. Or a disciple of his. How would anyone outside of the people who worked on the J-Bird case with you know about the scars on your feet?"

"Hunter knew."

"No, he didn't. He told me he was shocked when he saw your feet that night."

"I met Hunter for the first time three months before I started working on this case. A mutual friend of ours recommended me to him. I stopped into the station to introduce myself. Hunter was sort of abrupt with me. Anyway, he offered to walk me out, and as we were going down the stairs, one of my sandals flew off. Hunter ran down the stairs and brought it back to me. I sat down on the step to put it back on and he had a clear view of the bottom of my foot." She hadn't thought about that day until right then. She was so embarrassed and in such a rush to put her sandal back on that she did the one thing she never did—she exposed the bottom of her foot and with it the scars of her past.

"If he was abrupt with you, as you said, then there's a good chance he wasn't even paying attention when you put the shoe back on. Not to mention our guy has a beard. Last I checked, Hunter is clean-shaven and has been since I've known him." Levine stared at her before adding, "You know, if Dr. Schechter thought you were unstable, maybe you're the one we should be concerned about." With that, he turned and walked away.

Cam had hoped hearing Levine tell her she was wrong would be enough to convince her she was falling for the right guy. But it wasn't. He'd brought up a good point about the beard, but anyone could buy a fake beard to disguise themselves, and in the dark, who could tell the difference? His words weren't convincing or soothing. The conversation just made her more anxious.

She went back to her apartment and pored over her notes. The killer was compulsively neat, had a type of woman he preferred, and most likely knew his victims. The photo of Hunter's wife kept coming to mind. She easily fit into the group of women killed. Her murder was never solved, and Hunter was the one who had found her. Now he lived in her upscale condo, which he could never afford on his own.

Levine had corroborated Hunter's story about the victims' feet being cut, but she never saw those pictures even though he'd said she did. *Is he an associate of the J-Bird? Are they working together to torture me all these years later? Jonette would never approach me directly. I'd recognize him in a second. But if they were working together, Hunter could watch me while Jonette killed.*

Her mind reeled at the thought of Hunter being a killer. And then she remembered how he seemed to know where everything was in her apartment, as if he'd been there before, and how he'd cleaned the place up. Even on days when Hunter wasn't around, things seemed to inexplicably get tidied up. Clothes she left on the floor were hanging the next morning, and shoes were put back in the closet. A shiver ran through her. She thought she'd been sleepwalking, but what if something much worse was happening? What if he was watching her even at night? The thought of someone standing over her as she slept made her feel sick. She couldn't help but think she should sleep with her gun, though she wasn't sure what made her even consider Hunter as a suspect.

"He's the enemy. He likes to kill things." The voice of a child was the reason. As a field agent, she'd learned to trust her gut. It was usually dead-on, the subconscious, a first alert warning system built into the brain that we ignore or reason away. But she'd learned to pay attention to hers, and right now, that voice was trying to tell her something. Yet, she felt safe with Hunter.

She also considered how he hadn't come clean about knowing most, if not all the victims, even after she'd suggested the victims and killer were acquainted. He could have argued that theory away by saying he was friends with them and it wasn't unusual for police personnel to know each other.

Cam felt ashamed for considering Hunter as complicit in the Stealth killings. Was her fear of human intimacy turning him into a monster as an excuse not to get too close, not to fall in love? She had to figure out definitively if Hunter was guilty, and there was only one way to prove it. She needed the knife the raccoons held in their tiny paws.

CHAPTER 30

Hunter sat alone in his dining room shoving pasta into his mouth, frustrated by how the day had turned out. The chief had been all over him about not solving the most significant case of his career. He'd argued with Rhonda Saintil, and now, when the day had turned around with a great evening with Cameron, he'd blown it by letting her leave. It didn't escape him that her mood had changed dramatically between the time he went into the kitchen and when he came out with the food, but he was so caught up in his own thoughts that he didn't question why.

He'd forgotten about the chief and his argument with Rhonda when Cameron showed up on his doorstep. He'd needed her at that moment, a distraction from an awful day. When Cameron brought the argument up at dinner, he'd plummeted back into a foul mood. He'd shut down and didn't want to talk about it, and really, it was personal and he couldn't discuss it anyway. When Cameron said the wine brought on a migraine and needed to leave, he'd let her.

He felt terrible for not insisting on taking her home or, at the very least, for not asking her to stay. He picked up his phone and called her. No answer. He texted her: *U ok?* and cleaned up the table while he waited for her to respond. She didn't answer him, so he tried her home phone, thinking she may have turned the cell phone off when she got home. No answer at home either.

He sat in front of the TV, trying to distract himself, but it didn't help. He worried about her safety. A serial killer waited out there, and Hunter was sure Cameron was his target.

Damn it! Why did I let her leave here alone?

He threw on his jacket and headed for the door. Just as he hailed a cab, Cameron answered his text. "I'm home. Going to bed. See you tomorrow."

He let out a sigh of relief and texted her back, "Sorry about tonight. We'll talk in the morning. Good night."

Hunter went back up to his apartment and poured himself a scotch. Sitting alone in the darkness of his living room, Cameron's familiar scent of coconut and vanilla fresh on his mind, he wished she hadn't gone. He thought about the first time he'd met her. That fateful step in the stairwell when her sandal had flown off and he retrieved it, handing it back to her, and how she'd blushed. The moment she'd blushed was when he'd begun to fall for her.

They had worked closely together for the last several weeks, sometimes late into the evening, pursuing a killer. Sometimes they hadn't even discussed the case. She'd told him about Georgia, and he'd promised to take her to a Yankee game. They had slowly gotten to know one another, their mutual attraction growing stronger until they finally had their moment in the rain. He could see them sharing a future together. He was falling hard and fast. When she was around, he was happier than he'd been in a long time and when she wasn't, he couldn't get his mind off her. And now he'd let her go out alone into the darkness where a killer waited because he couldn't get over a crappy day.

My God! I am such an ass.

But that killer gave him a reason to call her, to ask for her help, to meet her again and see if it was all real...the sweaty palms, the amped-up heart, the twinge in the pit of his stomach.

He considered getting up and going over to her place to check on her, but it was late and he didn't want to wake her, especially if she wasn't feeling well. He decided he would check on her first thing in the morning and apologize for his behavior. Turning the television on for distraction, he dozed off on the couch, his sleep wrought with nightmares.

CHAPTER 31

NEARLY 11:00, IT WAS time for Diane Downing.

Stealth sat on a supple leather couch and pressed the red "on" button of the remote control. The television sprang to life just as Diane appeared on camera.

Perfect timing! She's more beautiful than usual this evening, if that's even possible.

Her auburn hair was pulled back in a chignon, bringing her incredible facial features to the forefront. She wore a deep emerald-green silk blouse that complemented her coloring perfectly.

As soon as I'm free of my girl, I will find Diane and make her mine. We can live in a little cottage, perhaps in the mountains where no one can disturb us.

Diane started with breaking news about a bomb threat at a local school.

What is wrong with people? Threatening and targeting children. Honestly, it's quite pathetic. Fortunately, it was a false alarm.

She continued with various other news stories: a water main break in Midtown, a robbery at a local store culminating with the owner chasing the robber away with a machete, and another politician texting naked pictures of himself to his intern.

Jeez, what a pervert, and that is who people elect to office.

A police artist's sketch appeared in a box next to Diane's pretty face.

What's that? Is that supposed to be me? I'm better looking than that.

Stealth pressed the volume button on the remote.

"Chief Michael Dwyer has released this artist's sketch of a person of interest in the deaths of female police personnel over the last several weeks. One victim described the serial killer police refer to as the Stealth Stalker to a 911 operator as she lay dying. Amy Larsen, the killer's third victim, informed the operator that her assailant was a white male with a black beard and dark clothing. Police are asking if you see anyone who fits this description and is acting suspiciously to call 911 immediately. They advise against approaching anyone you don't know and to be alert at all times as to your surroundings. The Stealth Stalker has murdered five women to date, and this case is obviously a top priority for New York police."

The news continued, but there was no need to keep watching, even for Diane. Stealth listened only to news worthy of time spent in front of a television—the update about the Stealth Stalker.

Soon I will be a mystery. The consummate unsolved crime. Eventually, the deaths of those women will become cold cases, and with time, the majority will forget about me as they fixate on the latest celebrity misbehaving. Once I've taken care of my girl, I will disappear, hopefully with Diane, and if the itch returns, I'll deal with it then.

CHAPTER 32

The next morning, Hunter and Levine attended an early morning meeting with the police commissioner. Afterward, they stood on the sidewalk with their coffees, talking about the case.

"Hunter, I have something I need to tell you," Levine started. "Last night when I was out to dinner…"

"Hey, Hunter, how are you?" Detective Gina Rossi interrupted.

"Gina, good. How are you?" Hunter countered.

"Good."

"This is Glen Levine. Glen, Gina Rossi. Gina is a detective at the third precinct. Glen is part of my team," Hunter said, introducing the detectives.

Levine extended a hand. "It's nice to meet you."

"You too," Rossi said. "Hey, I heard Dr. Cooper has been helping you with the Stealth Stalker. How's she doing?"

"Dr. Cooper is an impressive addition to our team. She's been a huge help," Hunter answered.

"I'd almost feel sorry for Stealth if he came across her. Damn, that woman is a maniac," Rossi said, chuckling.

Hunter and Levine exchanged looks. "What do you mean?" Hunter asked.

"Dr. Cooper's kick-ass southern self comes out when her adrenaline is running on high. Do you know what I mean?"

"No. I'm not sure that we do," Levine said.

Rossi looked surprised. "Didn't you hear how our serial rapist died? Doc wrapped a lamp cord around his neck and killed him. She was all southern drawl right after she used the base of the lamp to smash his face in just for good measure."

Rossi's account stunned the two men.

"We heard you caught the guy, he resisted arrest and died at the scene, but beyond that, I didn't get the details," Hunter said.

"Let me tell you. We were called to an apartment building about an intruder and screaming coming from one of the units. The description matched the rapist, so we went in full force and Doc was with us. When we got to the apartment where the screams were reported coming from, we kicked the door in," Rossi explained. "As soon as we entered, we discovered the victim's body, assumed the guy ran, and split up, hoping the guy was still in the building. We left Doc alone with the body as we searched. But the rapist was hiding in the apartment. He attacked her, she pulled her gun, he knocked it away. They fought, he threw her down, and she hit her head on a table, causing a gash in her forehead. When she got up, she somehow wrapped a lamp cord around his neck and choked him to death. When I asked what happened, she said, 'He attacked me, and I killed him. I killed the animal.' Her southern drawl was in full force. And then she made a funny comment, something about 'no one kills my girl except me.' I asked what she meant, and she looked right through me, went to the bathroom, and washed up."

Rossi continued, "After she washed up and calmed down, she complained of a migraine. She said it all happened so fast, and she couldn't remember what happened after he cracked her head on the table. She looked pretty banged up, and the place was a mess, so we knew they fought, but the fine details were gone. It was like she blocked it from her memory."

Hunter was speechless.

Dismayed, Levine said, "Hunter, did you know about this?"

"No. Gina, why didn't you tell me when I called and asked about her?"

"I figured you had the details about how she caught our guy, and that's why you wanted her on your team. You asked if I'd recommend her, and I said absolutely. I still do. That guy might still be out there if it weren't for Doc." Gina looked at her phone. "I gotta go. It was good seeing you, Hunter. I'm sure you guys will catch that asshole killer any day now—especially with the doc on your team. Tell her I said 'hello.' "

Hunter and Levine stood there absorbing what they had just been told, shocked that the woman they were working with was capable of such a feat.

"Cameron is in good shape, but that's unbelievable," Levine said.

"Yeah, that must've been some rush of adrenaline. That guy was what—six-one?"

"Six-three."

"Maybe she just got lucky."

"You got it *bad*, don't you?"

"Is it that obvious?" Hunter asked, somewhat embarrassed.

"Oh, yeah. I've known you for how many years now? I've never seen you like this with a woman. Your entire demeanor changes when she's around. She cares about you too," Levine said, deciding not to tell Hunter about his encounter with Cameron the previous night after all.

CHAPTER 33

Having spent most of the night locked in her bathroom, Detective Rhonda Saintil had plenty of time to contemplate her conversation with Hunter Finnegan. She'd been so angry with him, not just for keeping her late but for prying into her personal life, that she'd refused to listen to his words. When he asked her to sit down for a moment, she realized it would be a personal discussion and she shut down. She had no interest in whatever he wanted to discuss and would volunteer no information to him.

Lying on the cold tile floor gave her a fresh perspective. Hunter's concern was justified. He was only offering his help, not being nosy. She'd thought about it all night long. Rhonda had gotten herself and her children into a dangerous situation. As she raised her tired, bruised, and swollen body from the floor, she decided the time had arrived to do something before a tragedy occurred. She would take Hunter up on his offer for help and protection. She showered, standing under the water jets for a long time, allowing the steaming water to soothe her sore body and give her strength anew to do what she knew she had to do.

Rhonda listened at the door before opening it and peeked around, confirming it was safe to come out. The bedroom was empty, so she quickly grabbed her clothes and ran back to the bathroom, locking the door. She hurried to dress and then once again opened the door, peering into the hallway. Sneaking into her children's bedroom, she woke them and told them they were playing a game to see who could get ready for school the fastest and the quietest. They had to pretend that Daddy was a sleeping bear, and they didn't want to wake the bear. After helping them dress, the three tiptoed through the living room where her husband lay sleeping on the couch.

Once they were securely on the sidewalk outside, she gave them each a high five and told them they could be super spies since they snuck out like pros. The children laughed at their mom acting so silly. As a reward, she took them to the corner diner and let them order whatever they wanted for breakfast, including donuts.

After Rhonda had the kids safely in school, she hurried to get to work. On her way, she phoned her parents. Her father answered, and she asked him if the offer for her and her kids to move in with them was still on the table. The news overjoyed her father, and he told her he was proud of her and thankful that she'd found the courage to leave the bastard. She explained to him that she needed them to pick the children up from school that day, and her father told her that day, and every day, he would be happy to pick his grandchildren up.

With the logistics of where she would go with her kids off her list of things to do that morning, she thought about the next step she needed to take, talking to Hunter. She had to apologize for her behavior and accept his offer for help. Running late, she took the shortcut that the night before had seemed so scary, smiling to herself at how dramatic she was. She went over in her mind what she would say to Hunter and the plan for the rest of her and her children's lives.

Consumed in thought and excited about her decision for a fresh start, she never saw the figure camouflaged by the boxes. He grabbed her from behind, pushing her to the wall. She slammed an elbow into his face and twisted around, seizing her assailant's right arm as she moved. Had he been right-handed, she would have had him on the ground in seconds. Instead, he stabbed her in the side. Pain shot through her body like a lightning bolt. She looked at her attacker with disbelief as she grabbed onto the other arm.

This can't be happening, she thought as her knees weakened.

Slowly she slid down the wall, his eyes following her. There was something familiar about those eyes, as if she'd looked into them before.

Images of her children clouded her mind, and it was all she needed to fight harder. She'd undoubtedly survived worse than this over the last ten years. She wouldn't allow him to get away, and she wouldn't die at his hands. She couldn't let him pull the knife out even though he'd missed his target and struck her off-center. The blade could have pierced an organ.

He studied her as she knelt in the dirty street, held up by the building and clinging to his arm. He leaned in close to her, her brown eyes wide, and he whispered darkly, "You're not her."

Locking eyes with her attacker, Rhonda slipped her right hand into her pocket and grasped the wood grip of her own knife. She envisioned how it would go down in her head and then acted. With a loud grunt, she pulled the knife from her pocket and drove it deep into her assailant's leg. He let out a scream and flailed backward, letting go of his own blade and grabbing onto the one protruding from his thigh. Rhonda pushed herself up using the building for support, held the knife steady, and stumbled out to the sidewalk.

A woman screamed as Rhonda crumbled to the ground, passing out from the pain, her vision darkening. She took deep breaths, fighting her way back to consciousness, and realized people surrounded her. A woman held her hand as a man talked to the 911 operator, and someone else placed a folded scarf under her head. She was safe, and help was on the way.

A man announced he was a nurse and to move aside, but when she opened her eyes to look at her Samaritan, she saw Stealth.

"No," she cried out, alerting everyone around her.

It was too late. Her attacker grabbed the knife from her side and limped away. A young man yelled at Stealth as a woman put pressure on the wound.

Detective Rhonda Saintil lay on the frigid concrete, surrounded by strangers trying to save her life, fighting the darkness as it consumed her.

CHAPTER 34

Chaos consumed the precinct over the news that there had been another attack. Detectives Finnegan and Levine grabbed their jackets and ran for the door. Murphy and Barone followed, along with half the people in the building. Word was a dozen people had witnessed the attacker, who looked wounded, fleeing on foot. Police dogs were en route, and officers had already begun scouring the area.

Finnegan, Murphy, and Barone climbed in as Levine threw the blue light on top of his car and then pulled out with screeching tires. This was the closest they had ever been to catching the Stealth Stalker, and there wasn't a second to spare. When they arrived at the scene, paramedics were loading someone into the back of an ambulance and officers were questioning bystanders.

Hunter spotted the lieutenant in charge and rushed over to him. "Sanchez, catch me up."

"I've got bad news, Detective. The victim is one of ours. More precisely, she's one of yours." Lieutenant Miguel Sanchez nodded to the ambulance.

Hunter suddenly realized he hadn't heard from Cameron that morning and he panicked. His eyes darted to the ambulance where paramedics worked on someone. He whispered, "Cameron."

"The victim is Detective Rhonda Saintil. She's from your precinct, right?"

"Saintil?" Hunter said, shocked. In all the excitement, he hadn't noticed she was missing.

"Oh, my God. No, no," he mumbled, relieved it wasn't Cameron but angry that yet again someone close to him had fallen victim to a maniac.

"The good news is that she's still alive," Sanchez said.

"What? She's still alive? I have to get over there." Hunter ran to the ambulance and jumped into the back before the paramedics could stop him. "I'm Detective Finnegan. That's Detective Saintil, and I'm riding with you."

The medic tending to Saintil nodded in agreement and kept working on her. The other medic slammed the doors to the ambulance closed and, with sirens blaring, they raced to the hospital.

Hunter studied Saintil. She was pale and her eyes were closed. The medic had started an IV and kept a firm hand over the wound in her side.

"How is she? Will she be okay?" Hunter asked, taking Rhonda's hand in his own and rubbing it gently.

"She took a knife in the side and lost a lot of blood. She needs to get to surgery ASAP. The surgical team is waiting and so far, she's been a lucky lady. Hopefully, that luck holds out."

When they arrived at the hospital, staff rushed Saintil to an operating room and led Hunter to a private waiting room. Her husband would arrive any minute, and Hunter couldn't bear the thought of looking into his eyes, knowing that if he'd caught this son-of-a-bitch, she wouldn't be fighting for her life right now.

He paced back and forth in the small beige room, desperate for Saintil to survive. The scenario conjured up his wife and his first partner, Thomas Riley, all over again. He'd been helpless to save them, and now he'd failed Rhonda Saintil.

Levine rushed into the room, his face flushed with sweat beading on his forehead. "How is she? Have you heard anything?" he asked, trying to catch his breath.

"No. They just took her into surgery. It'll probably be awhile. Has anyone called her husband?"

"Dwyer is handling it personally. He was headed to their apartment and should be there now," Levine said, wiping his face with a handkerchief. "This is just unreal. I mean, Saintil? Of all people? I can't believe this."

"What did you find out at the scene?" Hunter asked, relieved to have Levine with him and distracting him from his thoughts and clenching stomach.

"She hurt the bastard. And we have a description."

"What do you mean, she hurt him? How?"

"One witness said the man who pulled the knife out of her was bleeding and limping. We found a bloody knife in the alley along with more blood on the ground and blood splatter on the building. Forensics is over there now taking samples."

"And the description?"

Levine pulled out a small note pad from his breast pocket. He flipped through it and found the page he needed. "Assailant is a white male. Approximately forty to forty-five, dressed all in black. He has a beard and mustache. Witnesses are being transported to the station to sit down with the sketch artist."

"The ground search is still in progress?"

"Yes. With air support." The usually cool Levine looked tense. "This is the break we've been waiting for. This guy has broken his protocol by going out in the early morning. All the other attacks happened at night. I think he's getting restless. And that restlessness has caused him to make a mistake, a huge mistake."

"I agree," Hunter said. "By this afternoon, we'll have a sketch to show the public. Someone out there knows who this guy is, and it will only be a matter of time. When Sanchez said the victim was one of mine, I immediately thought of Cameron. I felt sick. My gut tells me it's her he's after. But there's something else, something I just can't put my finger on."

CHAPTER 35

Hunter called Cameron again to no avail. Now, with Rhonda in surgery, he couldn't wait any longer for Cam to call him back or show up. He would go out of his mind, so he decided to go to her apartment and check on her himself.

"Take me to Cameron's place," he said to Levine. "I have a bad feeling and I need to check on her now."

The drive to Cameron's seemed to take forever when it was only a quick ten minutes. Hunter tapped his fingers on the armrest as Levine weaved in and out of traffic. When they got to Cameron's building, Levine screeched to a stop at the front doors, two tires on the sidewalk. The doorman started to yell, but then he saw the guns and gold medallions hanging on the two men's belts and the blue light on Levine's dash and quickly held the door open, asking if he could help.

Hunter and Levine hurried past him with no acknowledgment and headed straight to the elevator. Pressing the call button several times, Hunter's anxiety grew as Levine stood coolly by, skeptical that Cameron faced any real danger. The elevator arrived, and they watched in silence as the floor numbers lit up as they passed each one, Hunter becoming even more stressed. Just as the elevator doors opened, his worse fears were realized by the loud screams coming from Cameron's apartment.

The detectives instinctively drew their guns and positioned themselves outside the door.

"Cameron! It's Hunter! I'm coming in!" With one swift kick from Hunter's leg, the door to her apartment flew open.

She screamed again, "Help me!" And the two men rushed to her bedroom, ready to shoot.

The scene shocked them when they entered. Cameron stood shaking in the center of the room, crying, her nightshirt soaked in blood and her hands red. Hunter scooped her up and carried her out to the living room, where he placed her on the couch and then frantically searched for the source of all the blood. Levine, on full alert, searched the bedroom, bathroom, and walk-in closet for an intruder. When he found no one, he inspected the rest of the apartment with no luck. He grabbed some kitchen towels and threw them to Hunter as he checked the windows, which were all locked. Hunter yelled to him to call 911, and Levine did as ordered.

Hunter spoke in soothing tones to Cameron, who panted and appeared dazed. When he finally found the wound and applied pressure, Cameron struck out at him and screamed.

"Don't touch me! You did this to me, you son of a bitch! Get away. Get away!" she shrieked, crying and hysterical, hitting Hunter like he was a demon.

Hunter could see the terror in her eyes and tried to hold her arms down as she clawed and hit him again.

Levine intervened, wrapping his arms around her upper body and pinning her arms down as Hunter put pressure on the wound.

She twisted around to look at Levine. "Let me go. He did this. He tried to kill me! Can't you see what's happening here? He tried to kill me, and now he's come to finish me off." Cameron kicked and shrieked as the two men wrestled with her, trying to help her.

Uniformed cops arrived and assisted in holding her down. It took four men to contain Cameron as she thrashed and screamed accusations at Hunter that he was Stealth and the person who had attacked and tried to kill her. By the time the paramedics got there, she was subdued, weakened from the blood loss and her violent reaction to Hunter.

The paramedics worked on her as they swiftly loaded her into the ambulance.

When Hunter moved to climb into the ambulance, Levine grabbed his arm to stop him. "You should ride with me."

Hunter tugged his arm away from Levine. "I'm riding with her."

"No, you're not, Detective," Levine said as he raised his gun, pointing it at Hunter.

"What the hell are you doing? Put your gun away, *Detective*."

"Just back away from the ambulance, and there will be no problems, okay? You and I need to have a little talk. The paramedics will take care of Cameron."

One of the uniformed cops noticed what was happening and approached, hand on his gun. "Guys? What's happening here? Everything okay?"

The paramedic stuck his head out of the ambulance. "We need to go." He slammed the door closed and the ambulance took off, leaving Hunter and Levine in a standoff.

Hunter shook his head and scoffed, "What the hell are you doing?"

The uniformed cop had his gun drawn now, not sure who to point it at. Another officer approached cautiously.

"You don't seriously think I did this, do you?"

"The doc was pretty emphatic that you did. What would you think if you were me?"

Hunter shouted, "What would I think? What would I *think*?!" Fighting the urge to punch him in the face, he continued yelling at Levine, "I'll tell you what I would think! I would think I've known you for the past seventeen years and that I know you well enough to know you weren't capable of such a thing! That's what *I* would think!"

Cool and level as ever, Levine replied, "Let's go back to the station and talk calmly about it."

"Why? Why are you doing this? I need to get to the hospital. I need to see if she's okay! What if it were your wife? Wouldn't you want to be there?"

"She came to me last night with the theory that you were Stealth."

Hunter turned with a jerk. "What? Why? Why would she say that?" His eyes were wide with shock.

"She said you matched her profile. Let me ask you something. Do you hunt? Like deer and other assorted animals?"

"No, I don't hunt. What the hell does that have to do with any of this?"

"Do you have a trophy room in your apartment?"

"Yeah, I do," Hunter answered, watching Levine. "Why do you ask?"

"If you don't hunt, how do you explain the trophy room?"

"It's not mine. My wife liked to hunt. The room is her old office. I never go in there. It's where I...found her. It's still too painful even after all this time." He stood silent as his mind wandered around thoughts of his late wife. "Who told you about the office?"

"Cam told me. She said she saw it last night. It was the clincher in a list of reasons why she surmised you were our guy."

"So that's why she was screaming at me? She thinks I'm a murderer? She thinks I tried to kill her? And what do you think?"

"Where were you last night?" Levine held the gun steady.

"Home. Cameron stopped by. I made a little dinner. I didn't leave until this morning when I met you at the commissioner's. You can check with my doorman. Ask him to show you the building's surveillance video—it covers all exits to the building. You'll see I didn't do this."

Levine stood still, studying Hunter and gripping his gun. Hunter knew Levine very well and how his mind worked. He was clearly trying to decide if Hunter was lying and manipulating him.

"So, you didn't do it?" Levine finally asked.

"No, of course I didn't do it. I...love her. Don't you understand that?" Hunter himself hadn't understood how much until right then, when he said the words aloud.

"I think our guy—or possibly a copycat—is still out there," Levine said, lowering his gun. After so many years on the job, he recognized when someone lied to him.

The two officers let out audible sighs of relief and lowered their guns. The older one approached Levine. "What just happened here?"

"I doubted my friend for a moment. It could've been tragic, but I trust him when he says he's innocent. However"—Levine looked at Hunter—"the doc said she saw a knife in your trophy room. Something about a raccoon holding it. I'll need that knife just to do my due diligence."

"Fine, take the knife, search the apartment. I don't care. I have nothing to hide. Glen, please take me to the hospital now?" Hunter said.

"Okay. Hop in my truck. Let's go." Hunter turned and walked toward Levine's truck as Levine moved toward the cops and whispered, "Get the knife and get it to forensics and get the security video of his building. Make sure it corroborates his story. And make sure you have a proper search warrant." Levine may have trusted his instincts, but he relied heavily on facts and needed proof to back it up. As he turned to walk toward his truck, he shouted over his shoulder, "Thanks for your help, officers. Get back upstairs and watch the apartment until forensics arrives."

Hunter looked at his old friend as they drove to the hospital, exhausted from the morning's events. The answers he devised only left him with more questions. A killer had spent weeks targeting women who resembled Cam, cutting their feet to match Cam's scars, leaving Hunter to conclude that the J-Bird had found her.

"It's got to be the J-Bird," Hunter said, checking Levine's face for his reaction.

"It doesn't fit his previous routines. He has never struck in broad daylight and never twice in one day. And the J-Bird was a strangler," Levine said.

"Then maybe a disciple of his? In any event, he's getting desperate. He knows we have DNA evidence, and it's only a matter of time until we can put it through the system. If he has a record, we'll have him. He can sense that he's running out of time. I don't even know if Cameron has family we should be contacting."

Levine pulled into the ER parking garage. The two men hurried into the ER and straight to the head of the line at the desk. Flashing his badge, Hunter told the nurse behind the counter they were there on a case and needed to check on the female stabbing victim brought in earlier. The nurse nodded her head and pressed a button, unlocking the door and letting them into the inner corridors of the ER.

Aimee Torres, a regular ER nurse, spotted the two men. "Detectives, can I help you?"

"Yeah, we need an update on the stabbing victim brought in earlier," Hunter said.

"Which one? We have two, don't we?" Aimee asked, looking through charts on her computer.

"The one brought in fifteen minutes ago. Cameron Cooper." Hunter caught a look from Levine. "And the other one, Detective Rhonda Saintil. I need reports on both. Please."

Hunter was anxious and barely able to control himself. After waiting impatiently for the nurse to tell him something from the computer she was looking at, he prompted, "Nurse? Can you speed it up a little?"

"I'm looking as fast as the computer will allow me," Nurse Torres said without looking up. "I have nothing to report yet. It looks like Cameron Cooper is being prepped for surgery, and Rhonda Saintil is still in surgery. Why don't you two sit over there, grab a cup of coffee, and I'll see what I can find out, okay?"

"Yes. That's fine. Thank you, nurse. We'll wait over there," Levine said as he led Hunter by the elbow over to the chairs. "Sit," he said to Hunter. "I'll get the coffee."

Hunter sat down, raking his long fingers through his hair. *How did this happen?*

Levine handed him a hot cup of black coffee and sat down in the chair next to him. "We'll find who did this. And the doc and Saintil will be fine. We're in one of the best damn hospitals in the world, right?" He patted Hunter on a shoulder.

"Yeah, right," Hunter said, wishing he believed him. Even if Cameron came out of this okay, somebody had tried to kill her, somebody who would try again. It all seemed so disconcerting, as if the obvious answer dangled in front of his face just out of reach.

Levine stood up next to him as he checked a text message from Barone. "Barone wants us to come back to Cameron's apartment. He said the scene doesn't add up. What's that about?"

"I guess we'll find out. I'll check with the nurse on Cam and Rhonda's progress, and then we can go."

"By the way, I did know," Levine said with a small grin.

"Know what?" Hunter snapped.

"That you were in love with the doc."

CHAPTER 36

AFTER THE DOCTOR TOLD Hunter he could see her for just a few minutes, he slipped quietly into Rhonda Saintil's hospital room. He stood next to her bed and grimaced at her condition. She had tubes, IVs, and wires attached to her in every direction. Bruises covered her arms, her lips appeared dry and cracked, and her hair was a tangled mess around her pale face.

This is what it looks like being close to death. She must have put up a helluva fight, he thought.

Hunter lightly ran his fingers down her arm and grasped her hand. He stood there for a moment with his eyes closed and said a silent prayer that his friend would be all right. When he opened his eyes again, Rhonda was looking up at him.

He smiled and leaned down to her, still holding her hand, and kissed the top of her head. "You're a survivor," he whispered to her.

Rhonda tried to speak but only made a croaking sound.

Hunter offered some water with a straw, and she sipped it. He then pressed the button for the nurse. "We have to alert the nurse you're awake, right?" he said, smiling at Rhonda and grasping her hand once more.

The nurse, a toned and lean woman with beautiful red hair and a quick smile, hurried in. As soon as she saw Rhonda's open eyes, she spoke to her directly. "Well now, look who's awake. I'm your nurse, Kathleen." She raised the bed slightly and then turned to the blinking and humming monitors next to the bedside, checking each one. "It looks like you're doing fine, Rhonda. Do you remember what happened?" The pretty redhead leaned over Rhonda, stroking an arm as she spoke to her.

Rhonda slowly shook her head no, she didn't remember.

"That's okay. It's expected. Sometimes when we suffer a trauma, our brain protects us by blocking it out. It may come back to you. It may not. But for now, I'll tell you, okay?" Kathleen spoke in low tones to Rhonda, and Hunter walked around to the other side of the bed so he wouldn't miss anything. "A man assaulted you on the street, stabbed you in the side with what appears to be a large knife. You've had surgery to close the wound, and right now you're in the medical intensive care unit. Do you understand so far?"

Rhonda nodded yes as Kathleen reached for the water glass and offered her another sip.

"You're doing very well." She continued to speak as she took Rhonda's temperature and pulse. "Ah, you have no fever. Excellent. Pulse is steady. Oxygen levels are good. How do you feel? Any pronounced pain anywhere?"

"I don't think so," Rhonda said in a hoarse whisper. "My mouth is just very dry."

"That's normal after surgery. You can have another sip of water in a little while. We'll let the anesthesia wear off a little more, and then we can reevaluate how you're feeling. Okay? Questions?"

Rhonda turned toward Hunter. "Did you catch him? Was it Stealth?"

"Not yet, and yes, we're sure it was Stealth. But we're closing in, and now"—he looked down at Rhonda and grasped her hand—"because of you, we have a more detailed description of who we're looking for. I need you to remember." He looked at her intently. "It's crucial."

Rhonda nodded again. Her eyes searched his and then slowly closed.

He knew she would do her best to remember, but for now, she needed to rest and heal. Hunter followed the nurse out of the room and stopped her in the hallway. "Excuse me, Nurse?"

"Yes, Detective?" she said, not looking up from her computer.

"I was wondering about the marks on Detective Saintil, the bruising on her arms and the marks on her upper chest. Are they from the attack?"

"No, those marks are older. Some of the ones on her chest are scars, and some are fresh." Kathleen stopped what she was doing and gave Hunter a look like she wanted to say something but was prohibited. "She also has severe bruising on her back and legs," she added, again with a look that made Hunter's stomach clench.

"What do you suppose caused those marks?" Hunter asked, though he'd already surmised the answer.

"Well, Detective, I can't discuss a patient's health issues with you unless they give permission. However, since this is a police investigation, I will tell you that a cigarette might make marks like those. The bruising could happen if someone were in a fight. But the bruising on Rhonda is a mixture of older and newer contusions."

"So, you believe someone beat her?"

"The patient presents with several contusions not related to her attack and stabbing this morning," Kathleen said, nodding up and down as she spoke, telling Hunter that yes, that was her diagnosis.

Hunter was aware she couldn't come right out and say it, but as a cop, he recognized abuse when he saw it, and he now had substantial evidence to back up what he suspected Detective Rhonda Saintil had been hiding for so long. Her husband was physically assaulting her regularly.

"Have you seen Detective Saintil's husband around lately?" Hunter asked.

"Not in a while," Kathleen said, raising her eyebrows. "Does Rhonda have any children?"

"Yes, two." Hunter became more concerned now that he had the evidence to support his suspicions.

"If I were you, Detective, I would send someone to that house right away to check on those kids. I'm not saying anything is going on there. Just a friendly check from some friendly cops, that's all."

Hunter knew she was right. He needed to get someone over there pronto. Rhonda had been doing her best to protect those kids, and now with her in the hospital, her abuser's rage would focus on them. He quickly called Murphy and filled him in on what he believed Saintil had been going through. He told him to grab a uniformed cop and get over to her apartment right away, check out the situation, and then report back immediately.

It was the reason they had argued. Hunter had always thought it was strange that he'd never met Rhonda's husband and she'd always had an excuse. He was sick. He worked odd hours. He was visiting relatives. How could he have been so dense? The long sleeves and shirts buttoned up to her chin even on the hottest day, the way she would wince if you grabbed her by the arm and how, when 5:00 rolled around, she watched the clock like it would explode. She needed to get home to protect her kids.

He'd finally put it all together and tried to broach the subject tactfully, but she would have none of it. He'd offered to help, but she'd said there was nothing to help. He'd offered protection, a place to stay with her kids, but she'd said it wasn't necessary. He'd offered discretion, and she'd told him to mind his own business.

Just outside the doors of the MICU, Hunter saw Chief Michael Dwyer and his aide talking with a doctor. The chief had announced a press conference and wanted to speak to him before he spoke to the press. They needed to handle it cautiously. Hunter was confident that the Stealth Stalker would watch to learn what new information they had, and they couldn't give away too much information just yet. He didn't want this guy to disappear overnight.

CHAPTER 37

Hunter and Levine went back to Cameron's apartment to see what had Barone so baffled. The nurse told Hunter she would call when Cameron was out of surgery and since they could get back to the hospital in mere minutes, he decided it would be better to be busy than to sit in the hospital corridor with nothing to focus on besides Cameron's attack and how she was now fighting for her life.

The two men rode the elevator in silence as they both tried to solve the case in their heads. It had gone on too long now with little progress and the entire department—the entire city—was on edge. When the elevator doors opened, Hunter and Levine found two uniformed cops guarding the entrance to Cameron's apartment.

Hunter nodded to them as he approached. "Officers, is Detective Barone still inside?" he asked.

"Yes, Detective," a young cop with a baby face answered. "He told us to wait here until forensics arrives."

"They haven't gotten here yet? Why the hell not?" Hunter stopped, realizing the young cops wouldn't have a clue why. "Sorry, guys, it's not your fault. It's been a helluva day."

Hunter and Levine walked into the apartment, the bloody towels still on the couch where they had left them as they struggled with Cameron. Hunter's entire body tensed.

"Barone? Are you still in here?" Hunter called out, not wanting to go back into the bedroom.

"Yeah, Boss," Barone said as he walked out of the bedroom. "How are Rhonda and Doc doing?"

"Rhonda is in recovery, doing well. Cameron is still in surgery. What have you found here?"

"Come on in and see for yourself."

Hunter and Levine followed Barone back into the bedroom where Barone had been taking photos and marking evidence. The three men stood for a moment taking in the scene: a bed covered in blood, a floor covered in blood, bloody footprints. It was a typical crime scene as far as Hunter could tell. There was nothing extraordinary about it except that all the blood belonged to someone he cared for.

"Okay, I give. Why are you so confused?" Hunter asked, a little irritated.

"Look, Boss," Barone said as he lifted the blanket and sheet on the bed with a gloved hand. "What would make sense to me is that he attacked Doc in bed. See, the blood is all over the top sheet and the bottom sheet. So I figured he stabbed her as she slept. There's only one problem—no holes."

"What do you mean, no holes?" Levine said, crouching down to look at the blood pattern on the floor.

"There are no holes in the blanket or the sheets. You'd think he stabbed her through the sheet, right? But there are no holes in any of the bed linens."

"She didn't have them pulled over her," Levine offered.

"So, what? She got stabbed and then pulled the sheet up?" Barone was getting agitated. "There's no splatter, which means the sheet covered her when it happened. And check out the footprints. It's like she looked at herself in the mirror as she was bleeding or at least standing in front of it, but there's no pooling. So she got out of bed, walked over to the mirror and then over here, and stood in the middle of the room where there is pooling? But the footprints look like she walked away from the mirror, over to the bed, and then away from the bed, over to here. It just doesn't add up. What the hell happened here?"

Hunter needed time alone without all of Barone's talking. "Do me a favor," he said to Barone. "Go outside and see if you can spot the forensics guys. Maybe they're lost."

"Okay, Boss. I'll be right back." Barone walked out, talking to himself about bloody footprints to nowhere.

Hunter approached the over-sized mirror and squatted down, inspecting the footprints nearest to it. Barone was right, something was off. The prints near the mirror faced away from it as if Cameron had had her back to the mirror, like she'd walked out of the mirror and into the room. When he tried to stand up, Hunter lost his balance and caught himself by putting one of his hands flat on the mirror. As he stood, he pushed off the mirror, which clicked and popped away from the wall. He looked at Levine, and the two men turned toward it. Hunter drew it away from the wall. It wasn't just a mirror. It was a door.

"What is it? A safe in the wall?" Levine asked.

Hunter stepped back and drew his gun as a light flicked on.

Levine automatically pulled his weapon when he saw Hunter's reaction. "What is it?" he whispered.

Hunter cautiously took a few steps forward and motioned for Levine to follow. The mirror was a door to another apartment. The two men looked around in awe as they searched for any sign of movement.

"Police! Is there anyone here?" Hunter called out.

From where they entered, Hunter and Levine stood in a living room with two couches, side tables, sliding doors to a balcony, and straight ahead, a galley kitchen with a breakfast bar. A trail of bloody footprints on the white carpet ran through the apartment from another room and into Cameron's bedroom. He motioned to Levine to check behind the breakfast bar. He crept around one side and Levine around the other.

"Hello?" Hunter called out again.

They listened outside a closed door for any noises before Hunter tried the doorknob. He pushed the door open and instinctively flipped the light switch. More footprints led through a bedroom from another room. His gut grew tighter.

He looked at Levine as if to say, "What the hell?"

Levine shrugged his shoulders.

They made their way across the room, revolvers raised, and Levine opened the first door, revealing a walk-in closet. On the right side hung a collection of men's suits, all black with black shoes neatly lined up on the floor beneath. On the left side, they found newspaper clippings of each one of their victims tacked to the wall, and on the floor below each picture, a pair of women's shoes.

"Son-of-a-bitch! Those aren't Cameron's footprints, they're Stealth's. He's been living right next door to Cameron this entire time! And probably stalking her even as she slept!" Hunter exclaimed.

"But why not just kill her? Why kill all these look-a-likes?" Levine asked as he looked at the photos of the women.

"He likes to play games." Hunter nudged a pair of shoes, which were diminutive compared to his own, with his foot. "He's on the small side by the looks of these suits and shoes."

The two men moved on to the bathroom. Hunter flipped on the lights and gasped, shocked by what he saw.

"Holy shit!" Levine said as he looked over Hunter's shoulder.

The two men stood there stunned, not knowing what to make of what they were seeing until Detective Barone broke the silence.

"Boss? Boss! You in here?" Barone shouted.

"Yeah. We're in the bedroom. Be careful you don't disturb anything as you walk through the apartment."

Hunter and Levine looked over their shoulders at Barone as he entered the bedroom.

"What the hell is this place?" Barone said.

The detectives stood gawking into the bathroom. From what they had just found in there, Hunter feared he knew the answer.

CHAPTER 38

THE PATIENT IN RECOVERY Room Three struggled to open his eyes and focus on the surroundings. He didn't recognize where he was or remember how he'd gotten there. A strange woman stood in front of a computer screen and an annoying beeping chirped in his buzzing ears. He stirred, alerting the woman in the room that he was awake, and she approached him.

"Hi there. I'm Carrie, your post-op nurse. You're in Hudson East Hospital, and you're doing just fine. Once the anesthesia wears off, we'll bring you to the medical intensive care unit and put you in a private room, probably in a half hour. Do you have any questions?"

He could barely keep his eyes open, never mind speak. He stared at her, dazed. He had a lot of questions. *Why am I in the hospital? What happened, and did someone operate on me?*

Too weak to voice his thoughts, he closed his eyes and blocked them out. He would figure it out later. Right now, he just wanted to sleep.

When he woke again, he found himself in a sterile white room with a glass wall looking out onto a busy nurses' station, though a curtain obstructed part of his view. The same beeping sound from earlier chirped in his ear. An IV was stuck in his arm, and when he tried to sit up, he found his left leg immobilized and numb. Weakness and nausea gripped his body. The events of the day were foggy as bits and pieces flashed in his memory, but nothing seemed to make sense.

He found the control for the bed and pressed the button to raise his head. As the bed inched into a sitting position, he could see his surroundings better. A nurse at the desk outside noticed the bed moving and hurried into the room.

"Hi. I'm glad to see you're awake. My name is George, and I'm your nurse this afternoon," he said as he checked the monitors next to the bed. "How are you feeling?"

"What happened? Why am I here?"

"You suffered a serious knife wound to the thigh. It nicked the femoral artery. If the police hadn't found you when they did, you would've bled out. You've had surgery to close the wound, and it went very well. I'm just going to check the dressing on your leg."

George slipped on a pair of latex gloves, gently pulled the blanket and sheet away from the injured leg, and peeled the tape holding down large gauze bandages away from the patient's skin. He lifted the bandage, exposing a six-inch incision in the leg that had been closed with the intricate knotting of black thread. It appeared red and puffy and dried blood was intertwined with the stitches. The sight of it made the patient gag.

"Hey, you okay?" George asked.

"I need some water."

George went to the sink, filled a pink plastic pitcher with water, and brought it over to the bedside table. He filled a cup and put a straw in it, offering a sip.

"Better?" George asked.

"Yes. Can you cover that up, please?" the patient asked, nodding at the wound.

"Of course. It looks good. There's no oozing. It's swollen and red, but that's expected with an injury like this. Do you remember how it happened?"

He shook his head. He needed to get out of there. "When can I go home?"

George gave him a tight smile. "Probably not for at least a few days. The surgeon will be in to speak to you in a little while. In the meantime, I'll get you some food. If you need me, just press this button," he said, pointing to a button on the side panel of the bed. "I'll be back in a few minutes." He finished tucking the blanket around him and left.

The patient looked at the door, expecting to find a cop, but no one stood guard. What had happened slowly came back to him. He'd been hunting when everything went wrong.

He'd followed her, learned her routine, and canvassed the area for the perfect place to take her down. He hid in the pathway between two buildings she frequently used to get to and from work. It had a lot of debris, including a stack of boxes and pallets that created the perfect blind. He chose an early morning hunt, confident he had her this time and wanting the sun shining on her face when she realized what was happening.

He hid behind the boxes and, as she hurried past, he silently stepped out behind her and grabbed her arm. She fought back and swung around, and he drove his knife into her. They locked eyes, and at that moment, he realized he'd failed again. She wasn't the one. This one was a worthy adversary, though. She did something no one else had done in a long time. She struck back, stabbing him in the leg.

It slowly came back to him. The pain of her knife slicing into him had sent him reeling backward. He mustered the strength to pull the blade free of his leg, but it was too late. She'd made it to the sidewalk. He needed his knife back, so he garnered his strength, hobbled out to where a crowd had gathered around her, lied that he was a nurse offering help, snatched his knife out of her, and staggered away as fast as his wounded leg would allow.

He didn't recall when the police found him or how he'd arrived at the hospital.

I must've passed out on my way home. Where's my knife? I need it. It's the only thing they need to tie me to my prey.

He spotted the TV hanging on the wall across from him. He needed to see the news and learn what the police had reported. That would help him figure out his next move.

As he reached for the remote, searing pain in his head caused him to recoil.

He lay back and closed his eyes, trying to breathe through the pain. When he opened his eyes, the bright light of the room burned through to his brain, causing the pain to flare up again. He closed his eyes and kept his breathing steady and deep.

The machine that regulated his pain medicine made a whirring sound and then a click. The drug traveled through his veins, leaving numbness in its wake. Sweet relief. He needed to get out of there before they discovered his identity, but the drugs took over, leaving him tranquil and drowsy. Unable to fight it, he slept.

CHAPTER 39

As he stood looking into the bathroom, Levine couldn't believe his eyes. On the floor lay a pile of blood-stained clothes. On the counter, a Styrofoam head sat knocked on its side, a short brunette wig tossed next to it, and what looked like a beard and mustache next to that. Bloody handprints covered the head and the counter, and a knife drenched in dried blood rested in the sink.

"What the hell?" Levine said as he tried to make sense of what he saw.

Hunter was way ahead of him. The pieces were coming together in his head—the footprints, the suits, and now the wig with matching beard and mustache. "My God," he said as he turned from the scene and walked back into the bedroom. He ran his fingers through his hair, surveying the mess in front of him. Nothing made sense to him, and yet somehow, it all made sense.

"What are you thinking, Hunter?" Levine asked. "Was this guy living next door to Cameron, wearing a disguise and killing look-a-likes?"

"I'm not sure. His footprints are all over the place in here and go into her apartment!" he said, gesturing with outstretched arms to the surrounding room. "A secret apartment attached to *her* apartment! God!" Hunter rubbed his face and shook his head from side to side. *How could it be?*

"It looks like when Saintil cut him, he came back here to end the charade. Grabbed Cameron and tried to kill her, but she got away. Ran back to her place, and that's when we found her."

"Possibly... Barone! Get forensics in here, pronto. I want you to oversee everything personally. Take pictures on your phone now, before they arrive. Make sure they bag everything properly. And when they're done going over the place, I want you to go over it one more time. Call Murphy and tell him to get over here to help you."

"Okay, Boss."

"And find out who owns or rents this apartment. Check if the building has surveillance equipment."

Barone texted Murphy. "Boss, this is insane! Was this guy living right next door to her? With a secret door to her place? It seems really fucking brazen!"

"I won't speculate until we have some facts. But we're about to catch this guy."

Hunter's phone buzzed with a text message. "It's Dwyer. Let's go, Levine."

"Where are we going?"

"We're going to the hospital. To talk to the one person who can answer all our questions."

On the way to the hospital, Hunter silently reviewed the facts. Cameron was a criminal psychologist and a former FBI agent recommended to him by his friend, Jeff Alexander. She didn't just show up offering to help. She'd previously tangled with a serial killer who had gotten away. Soon after their first meeting, the killings started. She surmised the killer had access to the department and even accused him of being culpable. Her apartment had a secret door into the apartment next door where they found what he was sure was the weapon used in five murders.

Could it be Jonette or a Jonette copycat? Someone Jonette groomed to do his dirty work for him, and torturing Cameron was just a bonus? Maybe Jonette always wore a disguise? Was it something worse?

The questions were endless, and it concerned Hunter that he had no answers, at least none he liked.

When Hunter and Levine got to the hospital, they hurried directly to Cameron's room where they found her sleeping. Hunter looked at her through the glass wall of the intensive care unit. She looked so vulnerable, he yearned to hold her in his arms and tell her it would all be okay, but he wasn't sure himself that it would be. He walked over to the nurses' station and caught the attention of a man sitting at a computer.

"Hi. I'm Detective Finnegan, and this is Detective Levine. We're here to check on Cameron Cooper. How's she doing?"

"Hey, I'm George, her nurse. Her surgery went very well. She did lose a lot of blood and needed a transfusion. She's weak but was awake for a little while."

"Can we talk to her?" Hunter asked.

"You can, but there's something I have to tell you before you go in there." George hesitated, studying each man's face. "We had to call for a psych evaluation."

Every muscle in Hunter's body tightened.

"Why?" Levine asked when Hunter didn't.

"When she first awoke, she seemed a little mixed up. Her voice sounded childlike, and she asked for her mommy." George had a sad expression on his face as he delivered the unpleasant news.

"We all want our mothers when we're in the hospital. It doesn't seem that strange for someone who's been through what she has today," Levine said, trying to get George to reveal more.

"True, but..." George took a deep breath. "When I brought her some food a little while ago, I called her Cameron, and she told me that wasn't her name. She told me her name was Angel. Since I have a photocopy of her ID, I was sure her name was Cameron. So I fished around a little. I asked her for her birthday to verify my records. She told me she didn't know when her birthday was."

Something in Hunter's mind snapped to attention. It couldn't be. He was aware Cameron had changed her name at least once, and it was possible she'd changed it multiple times, and because of everything that had happened, it confused her now.

"That's interesting," Levine said, clearly trying to play it cool. "Is it common for assault patients who nearly died, had surgery, and are still under the influence of anesthesia and pain meds to show confusion?"

"Well, yes, sometimes, but not to this extent. At least not that I'm aware. And I *don't* appreciate the sarcasm, detective. I've worked here a long time and I know the difference between mild confusion and a patient in distress."

"Was the doctor in to see her yet?" Hunter asked.

"No. I'm still waiting for her to come down. Cameron is resting so the doctor will probably wait a couple more hours before she tries to talk to her," George said as he watched Cameron through the glass wall. "In the meantime, we're watching her closely."

"Thanks for your help," Hunter said, struggling with what to do next.

He slipped into her room as Levine stayed in the hallway texting. He stood at the foot of the bed watching her sleep. Her skin was so pale, and she looked like a child lying in the hospital bed surrounded by humming monitors. He wanted to climb into bed with her and protect her, but he wasn't sure from whom or what she needed protection.

Cameron stirred, and Hunter moved closer to her. He gently picked up her hand, stroking the back of it with his thumb. He brushed the hair from her forehead and lightly kissed her. Her eyes fluttered open just as he pressed his lips to her skin.

"Hunter? No! Please don't hurt me, please?" Cameron's eyes were wide and fearful. "Someone help me, help me," she called, her voice weak. She pulled her hand from his and tried to move away from him to no avail.

"What? I would never hurt you," Hunter said, pulling away, startled by her reaction. "I'm here to help you."

"No, no, no," Cameron cried. "Go away! I know who you are. What you are! Please stop."

Levine and George both heard the commotion concurrently and hurried into Cameron's room.

"What's wrong?" George asked, rushing to Cameron's side. "Are you in pain?"

"Please help me. This man...he tried to kill me. Call the police." Cameron grabbed onto George's hands, trying to pull him closer to her for protection.

George looked at Hunter and Levine, not knowing what to make of the situation. "You two should leave the room."

"Nurse...George," Hunter said. "I promise you I didn't hurt her. I'm here to find out what happened to her. To see what she remembers."

Levine tapped Hunter on the shoulder and nodded toward the door. It was better for Cameron to remain calm, so he followed Levine out the door and over to the nurses' station. The two men watched from there as George and Cameron exchanged words, George looking at them from time to time. He nodded as she spoke, fluffed a pillow behind her head, gave her a sip of water and, on his way out the door, the two men heard him comment that he would be right back.

"I told her I was calling security. And I am."

"You know we're police detectives, right?" Levine said, eyebrows raised and mouth tight.

"Yes, sir, I do. But my patient is very uncomfortable with one of you and has accused you of hurting her, a statement I have a responsibility to take seriously," he said as he pressed an emergency button alerting security. "It would be best for everyone if the two of you just waited patiently for security to arrive so we can straighten this out."

"This is ridiculous!" Hunter said, his voice rising. "I didn't hurt her. I'm here to find out who did!"

"Anger will not help the situation," George said, backing a step away from the much larger Hunter.

"What? Now *you're* afraid of me? Give me a break!"

Levine, cool as always, tapped Hunter on the shoulder. "Come on, let's take a seat over there where Cameron can't see us and George can do his job. I'll call Chief Dwyer, who's still here somewhere, and we can get this all straightened out."

"Sounds good to me," George said, folding his arms over his chest. "And I'll go sit with Ms. Cooper until we straighten it out."

Four security guards came around the corner just then, led by Paul Van Whellan, a rather large, very serious-looking man, and the only one armed with a gun. The other three, all dressed in the same uniform of a tan shirt and brown pants, carried stun guns.

"What's the situation?" Van Whellan asked.

"My patient became very distraught when that man"—George pointed at Hunter—"entered her room. She said he tried to hurt her."

Van Whellan looked Hunter up and down. "Did you see anything happen?"

"No. Someone stabbed my patient and left her for dead. She said he was the one that did it."

The other security guards moved instinctively around Hunter, surrounding him. Though they didn't have guns, they could easily overtake him.

"Look," Levine said, stepping toward Paul Van Whellan, "I can expl—"

"Who are you, sir?" Van Whellan placed a meaty hand on the grip of his gun.

"I'm Detective Glen Levine," Levine said, showing his badge. "This is my partner, Detective Hunter Finnegan. We're here investigating two crimes that occurred this morning, both stabbings. The first victim was Detective Rhonda Saintil, who is right across the hall here, and the other is the woman in that room, Dr. Cameron Cooper. We suspect there's a connection to the Stealth Stalker killings. Our chief is in the hospital. If you can find him, he'll verify our story."

Van Whellan nodded to one of the other security guards. "Go find the police chief. Ask him to come here pronto. And you," he said, pointing to the other one, "stand outside the patient's door until we have this settled. As for you, Detectives, I'm sure you won't mind coming with me to the waiting room just at the end of the hall while we clear this up, will you?"

"No problem," Levine answered before Hunter objected.

"I'll go wait with Ms. Cooper while you all figure this out," George said.

Cameron watched through the glass wall as the men spoke and then went their separate ways. Scared, she tried to calm herself to no avail. Her memory was fuzzy. She couldn't actually remember who had attacked her or why she blamed Hunter. She remembered waking up in horrible pain, pulling back the sheets and finding herself and the bed soaked in blood. Hunter appeared first in her room when she'd screamed. It had to be him. He was there, in her apartment. Wasn't he?

"I'll stay right here with you," George said, pulling a chair next to her bed. "Security is investigating, and the police chief is in the building. Close your eyes. You need to sleep. I promise I won't leave."

Exhausted, Cam tried to fight the need to sleep, afraid Hunter would come back, but it was useless. She decided George would keep her safe. She closed her eyes and drifted off for a moment. Just opening her eyes once more, she whispered to George, "Where's my chocolate milk?"

CHAPTER 40

She opened her eyes to a strange, dimly lit room, and it scared her just a little. Grown-ups were outside a window doing stuff. One lady talked on the phone while another one sat at a desk reading. She looked around for her mom, but she was all alone.

She was in a bed, in a room with a whole wall made of glass. Most of the lights were off, but it wasn't too dark because the light got in from where the grown-ups worked. A bunch of machines next to her bed made humming noises like, "hmmm." A skinny tube held by tape was stuck in her arm, and her eyes followed it to a bag hanging from a pole. She held up her hand to check out a funny plastic thing snapped onto her finger. Other wires coming from the machines were taped to her chest. The machines had a lot of blinking lights and lines that moved. There was even a little heart that kept blinking on and off, on and off. She didn't know what they did, but they were fun to watch. A pink chair sat in the corner, and a TV hung on the wall.

A man came in with lots of food. "Hi, Cameron. My name is George."

"My name is Angel."

He stopped what he was doing and looked at her. "Angel, right, my mistake. Angel, can you tell me when is your birthday?"

"I don't know. I want Mommy. She knows when my birthday is."

He looked at her funny again, then held her hand. "You'll be just fine. I'll look for your mom in a minute."

I hope everybody here isn't as weird as this guy.

He pushed a button that made the bed move.

Angel liked it—it was kinda fun. She wanted to play with it but was afraid he would yell at her and put her in the closet, so she didn't touch the button. Then he pulled a table right over the top of the bed in front of her.

"Whoa, that's cool!" Angel liked the bed table a lot and wished she had one just like it in her room at home.

George put a tray with food on it and told her she should eat, but it didn't look very good. There was some brown stuff and some white stuff. It looked gross. She smelled something bad coming from some black liquid in a cup. She asked him if he had peanut butter and jelly and chocolate milk instead, and he looked at her weird again.

Maybe he's never had chocolate milk! Everybody's had chocolate milk. *What's wrong with this guy?*

George said, "I'll get some chocolate milk when I look for your mom." He held her wrist and looked at his watch. He asked her a bunch of questions like what day was it, what city were we in, and who was president.

Angel stared blankly at him, wondering why he asked her those things. How should she know who was president? She was only six! And why was he asking her those questions? He's the grownup. He should have the answers instead of asking a kid.

"For a grownup, you're kinda dumb," she said, "'Specially if you don't know what day it is."

She wasn't so sure he would find her mom or some chocolate milk. She pointed to the TV hanging on the wall and asked him if she could watch it, and he said sure, but he needed to call someone to turn it on. *This guy can't even turn on a TV!* If she could reach it, she would turn it on herself. But every time she moved too much, it hurt a lot. She was too scared to look and see why it hurt, so she just tried not to move. She wondered how he knew her friend, Cammy. And why did he think she was her? Maybe she was here too. *Oh, no, maybe Cammy got hurt too.* She wished he would hurry up and find Mommy. *Maybe I got here because Monster Kurt hurt Cammy and me, and maybe he hurt Mommy too. She said he'd never hurt us again.*

She hoped Mommy was okay.

I guess I'll just lie here until George comes back with Mommy and some chocolate milk. I'm really tired anyway, so I'll just watch the lights blink, blink, blink...

CHAPTER 41

Cleared by the chief as "definitely not suspects in the stabbing of Dr. Cameron Cooper," Hunter Finnegan and Glen Levine sat across from each other at a table in the hospital cafeteria. Hunter mindlessly fidgeted with a spoon, and Levine sat back, observing.

When he couldn't take it anymore, Levine leaned into the table and spoke first. "I'm going back up. Cameron won't speak to you, but she trusted me enough to come to me last night. I'll see what she remembers."

Hunter considered it and agreed. Levine, with his levelheaded approach, would keep things calm and not upset her.

Levine headed back to Cameron's room, going over in his mind what he would say, the questions he needed answered, and prayed that Cameron wouldn't only remember but offer a reasonable explanation about the apartment adjoining hers.

He approached her room with caution, watching her through the window. She was alone, and George had left his post.

"Cameron," he said, standing in the doorway. "Is it okay if I come in?"

"Are you alone?"

"Yes, just me."

"What happened? Is Hunter in custody?" Cameron asked.

Levine looked into her eyes to make sure he recognized the person talking to him. He moved a chair near the bed to sit down next to her. "No, he's not. He didn't hurt you. You may have imagined he did, but we have enough evidence to prove he didn't." He spoke softly. "But you assumed that already, didn't you?"

"I told you my educated opinion last night, and you wouldn't listen. Now look at me!" Tears rimmed her eyes. "If you hadn't dismissed me, I wouldn't be here right now with a six-inch opening in me."

"Why *did* you come to me last night? Why not go straight to the chief? Hmm? Is it because you trust me and my judgment, because I know Hunter better than anyone else?" He offered her a white cup half-filled with water. "Because you hoped I would dismiss you, stand up for Hunter, and that's what you really wanted all along?"

"I told you I saw the knife! And I have this. . .this nagging feeling, that's all. It's all so...confusing. And I'm tired," she said, looking away. "I don't know. I'm not sure."

"I asked him about the knife and the trophy room. The trophies be-longed to his wife. He doesn't go in there because that's where he found her when she died. Makes sense, doesn't it?" he said, his voice smooth. "Just to make sure, I pulled up the records on her death, which confirmed he found her in that room and her obituary stated she was an avid hunter. I also asked Hunter for the knife, and it's being tested right now for human DNA. He let us take whatever we wanted. All he wanted to do was get here to be with you. He's opened his entire apartment to us. If he were guilty of any crime, would he allow us to do that?"

"I guess," she said. "But why was Hunter in my apartment this morning? I woke up covered in blood, and he just happened to be there?"

"I was there too, remember? We'd just come from checking on Saintil, who is across the hall from you recovering from surgery. Hunter wasn't able to get in touch with you. He called and texted you all morning from the moment we found out about Rhonda. He was worried, so as soon as we finished here, we rushed straight to your place. You screamed for help, Hunter busted down the door, and we found you in your bedroom. He was with me all morning. I promise you that is the truth."

Cameron craned her neck, trying to see through the glass walls of the intensive care unit to where Rhonda was recovering. "What happened to Detective Saintil? Is she okay?"

"Stealth attacked her early this morning. She's a tough one. She hurt her attacker and staggered to the sidewalk where witnesses helped her. The doctor said she should make a full recovery. Eyewitnesses saw the guy who did it, and we have an excellent idea now of what he looks like. And he looks nothing like Hunter. In fact, look, I have a composite sketch the police artist just uploaded." He held up his phone to show Cameron the sketch.

She gasped. "My God, it's Jonette."

Levine shook his head. "We suspect it's someone who wants us to believe it is. Dresses like him, same facial hair. His method is a little different, but just as effective." He gave Cameron a moment to process his words and then asked, "Do you remember anything from this morning?"

"Not really," she said, trying to recall her morning. "The last thing I remember was going to bed last night. I get migraines, and the one last night was worse than ever, so I went to bed early...around eight. Glen, please, what's happened to me?" A tear escaped and trickled down her cheek.

Levine grabbed a tissue and caught it, dabbing her cheek. He needed to be gentle with this woman who had already been through so much. He noticed her body trembling through the thin hospital sheet and blanket and squeezed her hand.

"It's okay. Everything is okay. You're okay. You'll be just fine," he said. "You trust me, right?"

She nodded slowly. "I want to trust you, but I'm...not sure. It's frightening to get attacked and not remember how it happened."

Levine continued, "We're still sorting out exactly what happened to you this morning. All I can say for sure is that you have a terrible wound. Hunter and I found you in your apartment, bloody, and we rushed you here immediately. You had surgery, and from what I understand, it was a success. With a little rehab, you should be fine physically." He offered her some more water. "Did anyone come to your apartment this morning?"

Cameron slowly shook her head no.

"Cameron," Levine continued carefully, "have you met your next-door neighbor?"

"I own the apartment next door. I planned on using it as an office, but after I renovated, I decided not to. I might sub-let. The apartment should be empty. Is someone living there?"

Levine perceived her reading his expression and managed not to react. He kept his eyes soft and a slight smile on his face. The last thing he wanted to do was upset Cameron. He needed to proceed with extreme caution and not pressure her too much.

"There appears to be someone using the apartment. Barone is trying to get hold of building security video to see who's been coming and going."

"Why are you asking about a neighbor? Do you think one of my neighbors attacked me?"

"That's what we're trying to figure out. You have no memory of how you were cut?"

"I told you no. I don't remember anything after going to bed last night." Tears flowed freely, wetting her cheeks.

Levine pulled a few more tissues from the box, handing them to her. He considered his next question. "I need to ask you something, and I understand that the answer is confidential, and I promise not to divulge anything you tell me to anyone else without your permission, okay?"

Cameron nodded.

"Have you ever gone by another name besides Cameron Cooper?"

She looked at him with wide eyes. "Yes."

"Can you tell me more?" Levine asked gently.

"After Jonette, I changed my name because I was afraid he'd come after me."

"Why would he come after you?"

"Because..." Cameron took a deep breath and let it out. She closed her eyes and finished, "He said he would."

"When did he say that?"

"He kidnapped a college girl and me and held us captive in an old house. We freed ourselves by jumping through a window. He screamed to me as we ran across the front lawn that he'd never stop looking for me, and when he found me, he would kill me."

Hunter appeared at the door. "Jeff didn't mention that, and neither did you when I told you I had suspicions that Jonette committed the murders here. Why?"

"You promised to wait downstairs for me," Levine said, rising from the chair.

"I couldn't take it anymore. Cameron, please, can I come in? I promise you I'll stay over here in the corner. I would never hurt you. I want to help you."

"I guess," she said uncertainly. "You can come in, but Glen has to stay."

"Thank you," Hunter said, entering the room but staying close to the door. "Jonette said he would never stop looking for you?"

"I didn't tell anyone that part. I wanted to forget it, pretend he never said it and live my life without fear of him around every corner. That's when I changed my name. I assumed with an alias, he'd never find me."

"What was your name?" Hunter asked.

"Cameron Chadwick."

"Are there any other names you've gone by? Do you have a middle name?"

"My full name is Angela Cameron Chadwick. My mother called me Angela, well, mostly Angel, when I was a child. But she stopped using Angela when I started a new school and switched to Cameron."

"Why?" Hunter asked.

"Why are you asking me these questions? Someone attacked me. I almost died, and instead of searching for the person who did this to me, you're giving me the third degree. Why? Why can't you just leave me alone?" she demanded, agitated just as she'd been earlier in her apartment when she accused Hunter of attacking her. She covered her face with her hands and moaned.

"It's okay. I'm sorry. We're just trying to get some basic information," Levine said, trying to soothe her. He wasn't ready to reveal that she'd told the nurse her name was Angel. It may have been nothing more than confusion from the anesthesia.

"I'm exhausted," she said, pulling the blanket up over her chest. "Can we continue this later? I just need to close my eyes."

"Yes, we can finish later. And hopefully, we'll have more answers for you later. You rest and don't be afraid. There's a uniformed cop guarding you. You couldn't be any safer right now," Hunter said.

"Just one more thing, Cam. Do you ever lose track of time?" Levine asked, watching her closely. "You close your eyes and when you open them again, it's hours later and you're not sure how the time passed?"

"No, never."

"Okay, good. We'll check on you in the morning. Sleep tight," Levine said.

"Thanks," Cameron said and closed her eyes.

"Oh, and take care of that leg," Levine added.

Levine walked out of the room ahead of Hunter, who stood for a moment watching her before he quietly left the room.

CHAPTER 42

Hunter stood at the nurses' station watching Cameron sleep as he waited for George to reappear. Other nurses and a doctor milled about, but he didn't want to speak to any of them. He didn't want to re-explain the day's events to anyone, and since George was already aware of the situation, he waited. Exhausted from the day, he considered escaping to the visitors' lounge just at the end of the hall but decided if he sat down for even a moment, he would fall asleep. He wasn't ready to sleep yet. He had too many questions. He took out the small notebook he carried with him everywhere and jotted down the facts from the day. Then he wrote down the questions that beleaguered his mind, hoping that if he put them down on paper, he would get them out of his head. He'd calmed down when he noticed Cameron stirring.

At first, Hunter watched, unmoving. She sat up and looked around, and even though their eyes met for just a moment, it seemed as if she didn't notice him. He observed as she lifted the blanket and stared down at her wounded leg. Then she picked up the remote for the bed and raised the head up to a sitting position. She took a sip from the white plastic cup on the table and then pushed the tray to the side. Cameron pulled the blankets off herself, swung her good leg over the edge of the bed, and then moved her other leg with both hands.

Hunter bolted for her door. "Hey, what are you doing there?" he said as he rushed into the room. "You're in no condition to get out of bed yet. You'll tear out all your stitches."

She looked up at him, eyes wide and brows furrowed deeply as he moved her legs back onto the bed and replaced the blanket.

"How dare you! Get your fucking hands off me," she said. "You can't keep me here. You can't force me to stay if I don't want to!"

Hunter stepped back, startled. Cameron had never spoken to him like that before, and her voice was not her own, but husky with a slight southern twang.

"Who the hell are you?" she demanded.

"It's me, Hunter. You're in the hospital," he answered, confused by Cameron's reaction. "Don't you remember? We talked about what happened earlier."

"I have no idea what you're talking about. This is the first time I've ever laid eyes on you. Where's the nurse? And I hope to God *you* are not my doctor."

Hunter looked over his shoulder, hoping to see George or anyone at this point who could help him, but the nurses' station was strangely empty. "I'm not your doctor. I'm a friend. Someone assaulted you earlier today, and you had surgery to repair a serious injury. Do you remember any of that?"

Cameron glanced down at the blanket covering her and touched where the bandaging bulged through. "No, I don't. If you aren't my doctor, then where is he? I want to speak to him immediately. It's outrageous that there's no hospital personnel here to tend to me." She looked Hunter up and down. "And you are no friend of mine. Do you know why? Because I have no friends. I find people to be incredibly annoying. So what are you doing here?"

Hunter realized he needed to play it cool until George came back. He also understood he wasn't speaking to Cameron Cooper and needed to act fast.

"I'm an administrator with the hospital. We need some basic information from you for our files so we can send billing information to your insurance company." Hunter walked over to the computer workstation and pretended to type. "Let's start with your name."

Cameron rolled her eyes. "I don't have any insurance. I'll pay the hospital in cash. Which is one more reason why I need to leave here as soon as possible. I can't afford some astronomical bill."

"The doctor will need your name to write out prescriptions for antibiotics and pain management. Besides, it's hospital policy to fill out all forms in full."

They looked at one another, Cameron untrusting and Hunter hopeful she would give the name he was familiar with. When she spoke, however, the words hit Hunter like solid blocks slamming into his skull.

"Fine," she said. "My name is Jason Jonette."

Hunter's mouth dropped. *I'm imagining things*, he thought. There was no way Cameron Cooper just told him her name was Jason Jonette. He gripped the computer workstation with both hands to steady himself and stared at the woman he'd so quickly fallen for. Was she in there, somewhere?

Just as Hunter braced himself to tell her she wasn't Jason Jonette, George reappeared. He let out an audible sigh at the sight of the nurse.

"Look who's sitting up and looking much better already!" George said. "How are you feeling, Angel? Better? I know it's late, but when I saw you were up, I grabbed your food tray. You must be starving by now."

Cameron looked at George, then at Hunter and back to George. A scowl darkened her face. She folded her arms across her chest, leaned back against the bed, and looked George up and down. "Please tell me you're not my doctor," she said.

"No, I'm George, your nurse. We talked earlier, remember? You asked me for some chocolate milk and peanut butter and jelly. And here they are," he said, producing a tall glass of chocolate milk like a magician producing a rabbit from a hat. He swung the table around in front of Cameron and placed the glass and plate on it. He beamed at Cameron, expecting delight at the sight of the ice-cold milk with a bright pink bendy straw protruding from it, but when he looked at Cameron, she rolled her eyes and glared at him. "What's wrong? Oh, I know you were expecting your mom. I'm sorry, Sweetie. I haven't found her yet, but I won't give up." George turned and winked at Hunter. "The specialist is on her way down now."

"Do I look like a five-year-old to you? You moron! I don't want chocolate milk, and my mother is dead. If you want to get me a drink, make it a bourbon and get the hell out of here."

Stunned, George gaped at Cameron, and since he didn't have a quick response, he walked out of the room.

Hunter walked out right behind him. "What the hell is happening?" he asked. "She just told me her name is Jason Jonette, for God's sake!"

"I'm not sure. I've dealt with schizophrenia before, but this is different. She may still be in shock from the attack. I'll page Dr. Franzen again."

Hunter's mind reeled. His inner voice shouted at him that everything that had just happened was real. Cameron had just told him her name was Jason Jonette. Observing her through the glass, the urge to bolt overcame him. He hurried toward the visitors' lounge, but when he got there, he kept on going, through the doors, past Levine and Chief Dwyer, and down the stairs. He needed to get out of the hospital.

Chilly December air hit him in the face as he pushed through the hospital doors. The smell of the city erased the hospital odor and the bold sounds around him replaced the dull hum that had seemed to follow him all day. He took in deep breaths, trying to calm himself. Just down the street, Hunter caught sight of a church with a small grotto to the side of its entrance. He rushed toward it and just as he got behind the stone wall of the chamber, he sank to his knees and the events of the day flashed in his mind. The secret apartment, the bloody knife, the wig and the beard, and Cameron's injury—a knife wound to her thigh. It was the same wound Rhonda Saintil had inflicted on her attacker. When she claimed her name was Jason Jonette, the pieces came together for him. It all suddenly made sense.

Hunter screamed, slamming a fist into the soft grass. The pain and anger of his realization was too much for him. All of it—it was all Cameron. He stayed there for a minute, on his hands and knees, breathing heavily, his body weak and suddenly exhausted.

The same message played over and over in his mind, torturing him.

Cameron Cooper is the Stealth Stalker!

CHAPTER 43

Nothing would be the same again. The woman Hunter cared so much for was a psychopath. A murderer. He sat back on his heels and wiped his face with his hands, angry, defeated, and more alone than ever.

A statue of Mary, the Virgin Mother, was tucked in a niche above him, her arms reaching out to him with a soft smile on her lips. He'd fallen right at her feet. He pressed his back to the stone wall of the grotto, eyeing the statue illuminated by the soft glow of candles. The searing anger that consumed him quelled. Rows of candles surrounded her, some burning brightly and some waiting for the faithful to bring them to life with the flick of a flame. His Catholic upbringing kicked in as he studied the beautiful face of the sculpture. He pulled a lighting stick from the box, held it over a flame until it flared, and lit a candle. Genuflecting at Mary's feet, he gazed up at her. Hunter bowed his head, taking deep breaths of the chilly air. He covered his face with his hands and said aloud, "Help me, please."

The serenity of the grotto took hold of him as he looked up once more at the tranquil face of Mary. He stood and touched her cheek. He'd needed the stress release of letting go of his composure to reason clearly again.

As the pieces came together in his mind, he tried to hold it together. This wasn't the end of the case, but the beginning of his worst nightmares coming true. He would deal with this nightmare just as he had in the past. He'd lived through the murders of his partner and his wife, and he would survive whatever happened with Cameron. It wasn't the path he wanted or would have chosen, but he would get through it all.

Hunter regained his self-control, nodded at Mary, whispered a thank you, and headed back to the hospital determined to confront Cameron.

The elevator doors slid open, and Hunter stepped out to find the police officer he'd left at Cameron's door and two hospital security guards with guns drawn. Inside her room, Levine and Murphy also had their weapons drawn. George, and a man with a video camera, cowered as Cameron tightly gripped a woman in a white coat.

Hunter rushed to the doorway and into the room. "Detective Levine, what's going on here?" he said.

Levine's eyes stayed trained on Cameron and the woman she had her arm clamped around. "Detective Finnegan, nice of you to join us. Dr. Cooper and Dr. Franzen were just getting acquainted with one another when things went a little south."

Cameron had a needle in her hand, holding it pressed against the smaller woman's neck.

"Dr. Franzen." Hunter met her eyes and nodded. "I'm Detective Finnegan. Cameron, why are you holding Dr. Franzen against her will?"

"Are you talking to me?" Cameron's speech was inflected with a deep southern drawl. "I told you my name is Jason, not Cameron. And this bitch tried to stick me with this needle. Now I want to leave, and you're going to make that happen. Get me a clear path out of here, or she's going down."

"Dr. Franzen, what's in the syringe?" Hunter asked.

"It's just a sedative. Cameron was getting agitated, and I wanted to calm her down. That's when she grabbed me."

"What is wrong with you people? Why do you keep referring to me as she? I'm a man. My name is Jason Jonette."

"Dr. Franzen, would it do any harm to show Jason his reflection in a mirror?"

"It's hard to say. It could force her to face reality or drive the patient into a deeper psychosis." Dr. Franzen paused, seeming to weigh the pros and cons. "Go ahead, Detective, get a mirror."

Hunter nodded to George, who hurried out for the mirror. Then he turned to Cameron and said, "Jason, let's try an experiment. It'll help you get out of here faster. Okay?"

"What kind of experiment? Are you going to trick me so you can stick me with some other drug? Huh?" Cameron tightened her grip on Dr. Franzen and shook her a little.

Dr. Franzen responded, "Jason, we're not trying to trick you. We're trying to help you. Please try to understand that. No one here is trying to hurt you. We're all on your side."

"I don't believe you," Cameron hissed into Dr. Franzen's ear, pressing the needle into her skin and causing a tiny prick of blood to form.

"This is a hospital. We heal people here. You have a serious injury, and the doctors saved your life this morning. Do you remember that?" Dr. Franzen asked.

"All I remember is asking to leave and you showing up with this needle."

George appeared with the mirror and handed it over to Hunter. Levine and Murphy were still standing with guns pointed at Cameron. Hunter motioned for them to relax their positions and lower their weapons.

"Jason, I want you to look in this mirror and tell me what you see." Hunter moved closer to Cameron and Dr. Franzen, holding the mirror in front of them. He watched Cameron's expression to see her reaction.

Cameron looked at herself, then at Dr. Franzen, and then back at herself again. She moved her head and watched as the person in the mirror followed in unison. She opened and closed her mouth, closed one eye, and loosened her grip on Dr. Franzen to touch her face. "This is some kind of trick. That is not me! That's that, that..."

"What? Jason, what do you see?" Hunter asked.

"That's the bitch I've been hunting. What have you done? How have you done this?" Cameron let go of Dr. Franzen and, dropping the needle, grabbed the mirror from Hunter's hands. She examined herself, touching the face in the mirror and then touching her own. Her body shook as her face reddened. "How did you do this?" she screamed and threw the mirror at Hunter.

It shattered into pieces as it hit the wall. Levine and Murphy once again took a position to shoot.

Rage overcame her as she clenched her hands into fists and her face contorted into that of a monster. "You did this," she said, looking at Hunter. "Somehow, you rigged that mirror so I would think I was looking at that bitch. You can't stop me from killing her. No one can."

Grabbing the needle, she lunged at Hunter. He overpowered her, wrapping his arms tightly around her as she kicked her feet violently. George ran to get a fresh needle as Levine and Franzen helped subdue a screaming Cameron. The three wrestled her to the bed and restrained her hands and feet. Her leg oozed blood as stitches popped.

She continued to scream repeatedly, "I'll kill her. I'll kill all of you!"

George reappeared with the sedative, and Dr. Franzen quickly administered it. "Call the surgeon," she said to George. "We need to get this leg sewn back up."

Cameron relaxed as the drug took effect. Her eyes rolled shut and then opened again. She was sweaty and breathing hard from her struggle. She closed her eyes for a few seconds, and when she opened them again, she appeared much calmer. Focusing on Hunter, she reached for him and whispered before losing consciousness, "Hello, my love. I'm so happy you're here."

"Can anyone tell me what the hell just happened here?" Murphy said, still holding a tight grip on his gun.

"You can put your gun away, Detective. She's sedated. George, can you make sure the restraints are secure?" Hunter said, taking charge.

"Everyone out," Dr. Franzen commanded. "Cameron needs her rest, and she will be under close observation. I will need to approve any visitors."

Everyone except George filed from the room.

"Dr. Franzen, right?" Hunter said, stopping her by the nurses' desk. "This is an ongoing police investigation, and she's a key figure in that investigation. You can't limit us. If we need to speak to her, we will."

"Detective Finnegan, *right*?" Dr. Franzen said with a note of sarcasm. "Cameron Cooper is my patient now, and I can tell you from what I just experienced that her injured leg is the least of her problems. We need to be very careful about how we proceed with her."

"How can we be sure she's not faking?" Levine interjected.

Franzen answered indignantly, "Faking? Faking what? Another personality? Why would she do that?"

"To get away with murder," Levine said, giving Hunter a look of disdain.

"If she's faking, we'll be able to tell, but not until we've fully examined her. She'll go under an extensive psychiatric screening that should answer all your questions."

"She's a psychologist herself. With all her extensive training, she knows how to beat the system. She'll be able to fake her way right out of this hospital and right out of jail," Levine said, trying not to let his anger overcome his professionalism.

"I assure you, Detective, no one is that good." Dr. Franzen hurried back into Cameron's room, closing the door behind her.

Hunter felt Levine staring him down but wasn't ready to engage him. Without making eye contact, he said, "We'll continue this first thing in the morning. I need some sleep." And with that, Hunter Finnegan walked away from a very tense Glen Levine.

CHAPTER 44

CAMERON AWOKE GROGGY AND confused. At first unsure where she was, she soon remembered—the hospital. She had a leg injury and had undergone surgery to close the wound. She looked around her sparsely furnished room. It contained one chair, a corner cabinet, and monitors next to her bed. On the other side of a glass partition, people worked at the nurses' station. She raised her hands to rub her face but restraints held them back.

What the hell? She wiggled in the bed to sit up and found both of her ankles also restrained. *What the hell is going on here?* "Nurse. Nurse!" she yelled to the people at the desk.

An older woman popped her head up, looking at her over a computer screen. She spoke to the other person as she stood, taking her time coming into the room.

"Good morning," she said. "I'm Grace, the head nurse on this floor. Can you tell me what your name is?" she said as she slowly raised the bed, bringing Cam to a sitting position.

"I'm Cameron Cooper. Don't you have a chart on me?" She knew something was very wrong.

"Yes, I do," Grace said as she poured water into a plastic cup and offered her some through a straw.

The water quenched her dry throat and her robust thirst, the result of a drug-induced sleep.

"Why am I restrained, Grace?" Cam hoped Grace would say she'd had an adverse reaction to a medication they had given her and almost hurt herself.

Grace smiled as her fingertips gently touched the inside of Cam's wrist, and she took her pulse. Then she checked her temperature.

"Grace? The restraints?"

"Cameron, you had a rough night. The restraints are there for your own protection and the staff's protection. Do you remember anything from last night?"

"Last night? The last thing I remember is speaking to Hunt...Detectives Finnegan and Levine. I needed to rest, so they left so I could get some sleep. Why do you ask?"

"The doctor will explain everything to you. In the meantime, you must be hungry. I'll get you some breakfast."

"Wait a minute. What about the restraints? Aren't you going to take them off?"

"I'm sorry, Cameron, I'm not authorized. When Dr. Franzen gets here, she'll decide if they can come off. Just relax and try not to think about it. I'll be right back."

Not authorized? Her mind raced, and the worst-case scenarios flooded her thoughts. *Did I hurt someone on staff? Why can't I remember anything about last night? Especially if I had a rough night, as Grace said.*

Cam took in her surroundings. She occupied a different room from the previous night, but she didn't remember being moved. An IV in her arm led to a bag of fluid and an unopened piggyback bag, probably some kind of drug. The restraints alarmed her, and the fact that Grace wouldn't remove them even now that she was awake made them even more disturbing.

Then she noticed the police officer outside her door. Cam hadn't noticed him when Grace first came in. Hunter had said something about a cop outside her door, but for her protection. She had the uneasy feeling that now he was there for everyone else's welfare.

That can't be, though. I'm not dangerous. I wouldn't hurt anyone.

She closed her eyes, trying to remember what had happened in the last twenty-four hours. Cam had lied to Levine when she said she never lost time. In truth, some days were a blur and it seemed like she missed everything. Not just from the previous week, but from the last several months. Ever since she'd left Georgia, she would close her eyes for just a moment and when she opened them again, it would be hours later. Sometimes she wasn't even in the same place as when she'd closed them. She would close her eyes sitting on her couch and open them lying in bed. She'd self-diagnosed with sleepwalking and considered seeing a colleague, but instead tried relaxation techniques and other self-help treatments.

Maybe I'm worse off than I realized.

Grace came back in carrying a tray and placed it on the table next to her. She lowered the bed and pulled up a chair next to it, then offered Cam some coffee through a straw.

"Coffee through a straw?" she said.

"You don't want it?"

She wanted it, so she took a sip. "It's lukewarm. Can you heat it up a little?"

"I don't want you to burn your mouth." Her voice was soothing and low as if she were trying hard to keep her calm.

This isn't good. "Have you seen Detective Finnegan this morning?" Cam asked, taking another sip of tepid coffee.

"No, I haven't. Would you like some toast or cereal?" Grace took the cover off the food tray to reveal a plate of toast and eggs, a bowl of Special K, a small carton of milk, and three plastic spoons.

Ravenous, her stomach gurgled at the smell of the food. "I'll have some toast with the jam on it, please. These restraints aren't necessary. If you would just remove one, I'll feed myself."

Grace opened a small packet of strawberry jam and spread it on the toast with one spoon. She offered it to Cam, and she took a bite. The crisp toast and jam tasted like the sweetest thing she'd ever had. By the time they finished their little Mama and baby show, Cam had eaten everything on the tray. She finished the last of the coffee, which was now cold, and asked to use the bathroom. Grace smiled that little smile and said she'd be right back. It surprised Cam when she returned with a bedpan.

"Seriously? You want me to use that?" Grace was pissing her off.

"I'm sorry, Cameron. It's hospital policy. Until Dr. Franzen arrives and clears you, you need to remain restrained." Grace pulled the curtain around the bed to give Cam privacy, and then she slipped the pan under her. It surprised Cam that the thin hospital gown was her only attire.

"What did I do? Please, you've got to tell me. I've been racking my brain ever since I woke up shackled to the bed, trying to figure out what I did. I can't remember anything."

"Dr. Franzen will explain everything to you. I'll get you a toothbrush and a bowl so you can brush your teeth."

Grace stepped into the bathroom, turning the water on—the oldest trick in the world, running water to get someone to pee faster. And it worked. She came back after a discreet minute or two, carrying a small basin and a cup of water. She placed them on the table where the tray had been, carefully lifted Cam, and slid the pan out. As she lifted her, Cam got a glimpse of her leg and noticed the new bandages.

"I don't remember having my dressing changed. Was my wound oozing?"

"You pulled some stitches, and the wound bled again. The surgeon needed to re-close it. He put on a different dressing to prevent it from happening again."

I pulled the stitches? The surgeon came to see me? Why can't I remember?
"I don't remember any of that. How did I pull the stitches?"

"You became upset last night and tried to get up, opening the wound," Grace said carefully.

"What upset me, Grace?"

"I wasn't there, Cameron. That's all the information I received from the nurse who cared for you last night."

The doctor in Cam took over. She had little insight into her condition, and Grace seemed unwilling to share more. Her mind whirled with multiple scenarios that ended with her potentially restrained. And the faster her mind spun, the faster her heart beat.

Levine had asked her about the wound on her leg and a possible next-door neighbor. She had no memory of being stabbed, and no one should live next door. She had no memory of the night before either, but apparently there was a lot to remember. Grace said she'd reopened a surgical closure because something upset her.

I must have been thrashing to do that.

The food tray caught her eye. *Three plastic spoons. Three plastic spoons. Why were there three plastic spoons?* Something about them bothered her. Then it hit her. *Three plastic spoons! No knife, no fork, just spoons! I'm in the psych ward!*

Her heart and her mind collided in an internal explosion, and she bolted upright, her arms pulling against the restraints.

Grace swirled around from the patient portal to face her.

Cam shouted, "I'm in the psych ward. Why? Tell me now. You tell me now!"

"Calm down, Cameron. Calm down or I'll..." she trailed off as she pressed Cam's shoulder back against the pillow.

"Or you'll *what*?" Cam followed Grace's eyes as she glanced at the IV bags hanging on the stand. The piggyback bag hanging next to her must contain a sedative. Cam took deep breaths and tried to calm herself out of fear that Grace would use it. The last thing she wanted was to go to sleep, maybe ever again. She needed to calm down and talk to Hunter. He would tell her the truth.

"I'm calm. I'm calm," Cam said, trying to convince her. "No need to do anything hasty. Okay?"

Grace looked at her with concern and then seemed satisfied that Cam had calmed herself. A woman in a white coat walked in just as Grace coated a toothbrush with a minty paste.

"Dr. Franzen. Good morning. Cameron is doing well this morning and is eager to speak to you. Cameron, this is Dr. Franzen."

Dr. Franzen was petite with dirty blonde hair hanging to her shoulders. She had her hands pushed deep into the pockets of her clinical coat, uncomfortable with Cam. She walked over to the edge of the bed and looked at her with no expression.

"Hello. Are you Cameron Cooper?"

"Yes, I am. Didn't you meet me last night?"

"Do you remember meeting me last night?" Dr. Franzen asked.

Cam looked at Grace, who wasn't pleased with her, and back to Dr. Franzen. "No, I don't. Grace told me we met last night." She noticed the woman's neck looked bruised and had a small cut.

"I met someone last night, but it wasn't Cameron Cooper. Last night I met a little girl named Angel, and I met someone else."

Hunter walked into the room, interrupting her.

"Hunter! Thank God! I'm so happy to see you. You've got to help me. They have me restrained! Can you believe it? Please come here and undo these for me," Cam said, trying her best to raise her hands and show him the buckles around her wrists.

Hunter stood next to Dr. Franzen, just out of reach. "Cameron? Is that you?" he asked.

"Of course it's me. Who else would it be?" *Oh, no.* Her mind threw up a red flag.

He stepped closer to the bed, examining her. His eyes were bloodshot, and his hands clenched into fists. He released a heavy sigh, a sign of his relief. He moved as if to take her hand, but then pulled away. His head dropped, and he stepped back again. He rubbed his face with both hands, opened his eyes, but it wasn't relief or joy she saw. It was anger.

"What's wrong?" Cam asked him.

He shook his head and reached for the notepad and pen in his jacket pocket. "Where were you yesterday?"

"You saw me yesterday. And last night, right?"

"Do you recall last night?" His brow furrowed.

"No, but the nurse told me you were here late."

"I was here late, very late. I stayed and watched you sleep. I wanted to be here in case you needed me."

"Thank you," she said. "Can you please come closer? I need a hug."

Hunter looked at Dr. Franzen and then back at Cam.

"Hunter, please ask them to take off the restraints."

He looked over his shoulder at Dr. Franzen. "Can you take them off now? She's back to herself again."

Dr. Franzen was unmoved.

"I promise I'll stay here with her, and I will be responsible for anything that happens."

"It's not that simple, Detective. The hospital has rules for everyone's safety, including Cameron's. What if I take off the restraints, and we have another episode like last night?"

"Then I'll handle the situation."

Dr. Franzen hesitated. "Fine, but only the hands. Not the feet, and only as long as you're in the room, otherwise she'll remain restrained. My colleague, Dr. Heisser, will join us in a moment. Nurse, please tell us when you finish here. Detective, I would like to speak to you in the hall please."

Hunter didn't look at Cam again. He told Grace he would be right back and left the room.

As Grace pulled the curtain once more and Hunter disappeared from sight, a twinge of anxiety washed over Cam. Grace couldn't move fast enough. She wanted Hunter back in the room but had to be patient to prove she had control. Grace wouldn't remove the restraints while they were alone. Cam would have to wait for the doctors and Hunter to come back.

By the time Grace finished and drew back the curtain, a small group had gathered outside the door. One by one, they filed into Cam's hospital room. First, Hunter, who looked as though he wanted to hit something or someone, then Dr. Franzen, a man she assumed was Dr. Heisser, another younger man carrying a video camera, and Detective Levine.

"Normally, we would do this in an office setting, but given your condition, Cameron, we'll have to make do here," Dr. Franzen stated. "This is Dr. Reid Heisser. He's a psychiatrist on staff at St. Christina's. And this is my assistant, Edward Yong."

They both said a cordial hello, but the expression on Levine's face struck a chord with Cam. He frowned at her, his sharp blue eyes narrowed. He seemed angry. Furious. The way he stared at her was upsetting.

"Let's get started," Dr. Franzen said as Edward Yong turned on his video camera. "We'll be taping this meeting, okay?"

Cam nodded her consent.

"Cameron, do you remember being taken to the hospital yesterday?"

"No, not really. I remember waking up here. Not here in this room, but in another room."

"Do you remember a nurse named George?"

"Yes. He's very kind."

"Do you remember asking George for a glass of chocolate milk and a peanut butter and jelly sandwich?"

"No." *Did I?*

"Do you remember telling George you wanted your mommy?"

"No. Of course not. My mother's dead. I would never ask for her. George misunderstood."

"Cameron, when George asked for your name, you told him it was Angel."

I told someone my name was Angel? "I must have been confused. The attack and surgery exhausted me. Angel was a childhood nickname. Everyone called me that. It must've just slipped out when I was vulnerable."

"Are you familiar with a man named Jason Jonette?" Dr. Franzen continued.

"Yes."

"When was the last time you encountered him?"

"Over ten years ago."

"Did anyone else meet Jason Jonette, or were you the only one?"

"No, he kidnapped a college girl at the same time. Why? Does this have something to do with me being attacked? Did Jonette do it?" She looked at Hunter for a sign, but he remained stoic.

"No, Jonette didn't attack you. Your injury is the result of an attack, though. You work with Rhonda Saintil, correct?"

"Yes."

"Are you aware that she was attacked yesterday as well?"

"Yes. Is she all right?" Once again, her eyes examined Hunter.

"Detective Saintil will recover from her injury. However, when she was assaulted, she managed to injure her attacker by stabbing them in the leg. Very similar to the wound you have. In fact, identical to your wound," Franzen said, looking over at Dr. Heisser.

Cam instinctively ran her hand over her leg. *What are the odds I'd have the same wound as Rhonda's attacker?*

Dr. Heisser stepped forward and sat on the edge of the bed. He was a handsome man with dark chocolate brown eyes and light brown hair, fortyish and in good shape. He spoke in a mild tone. "Cameron, last night you became very distraught when Dr. Franzen was speaking to you. Do you recall?"

"No."

"You were acting strange. Your speech and mannerisms changed, and you claimed you had another name."

"Were you there also?" Cam asked.

"No. Edward was there and videotaped your meeting with Dr. Franzen. I'd like to show you that videotape now, but I have to warn you, it won't be easy to watch. When you spoke to Dr. Franzen last night, you told her your name was Jason Jonette."

Wait, what?

"You also told Detective Finnegan the same thing. When Dr. Franzen began examining you, asking you a series of questions, you became extremely agitated. She needed to calm you down, and when she tried to sedate you, you grabbed the needle from her hand and threatened to stick her with it if she didn't let you leave the hospital."

"That's impossible," Cam said angrily. She wanted to slap this fool for telling such an outlandish story, but she had to keep it together. "Dr. Franzen must be mistaken," she said, glaring at her. "You're aware that I'm a doctor? A well-respected doctor, an expert in my field?"

"Yes, I am aware. I'm also aware that you experienced catastrophic assaults not only during your time with the FBI, but when you were a child." His tone was soft, almost soothing, if it weren't for the words he spoke. "You and I both understand that the mind, as complex as it is, can trigger its own safety net. Sometimes that safety net manifests itself in the form of another awareness, a person within the person, someone who can cope with what is happening when it's too much for us."

"Are you suggesting I have a split personality?"

"It goes beyond that. Would you like to watch the video from last night?"

She didn't want to, but she had to. If what Dr. Heisser stated was true, she was in serious trouble. The only way to prove him wrong and save herself was to view the video. She nodded.

"Edward, please bring the DVD over."

Edward reached into his pocket and pulled out a jewel case with a DVD inside and handed it to Dr. Heisser, who put the DVD into the player attached to the TV. He hit "play" and looked at Cam. "If it becomes too much for you, tell me to stop and I'll turn it off."

Cam glanced over at Hunter, who looked down at the ground.

The video started. She watched herself sitting in bed as Dr. Franzen asked her questions. Cam had to admit she had an odd expression on her face. She listened to her response in shock. A deep voice dripping with disdain and a southern twang came out of her mouth. She spewed hatred at Dr. Franzen and turned irate. Cam barely kept her mouth from hanging open as she watched someone who looked like her violently grab Dr. Franzen and threaten her with a needle. It was surreal to watch. *This can't be happening.*

She froze in astonishment, and then the woman in the video who looked like her said the words, "My name is Jason Jonette." Her head swooned. Unable to watch any longer, she signaled Dr. Heisser to turn it off. She struggled to process what she'd just watched.

Dr. Heisser turned off the monitor and stood observing her, as did everyone else in the room. Cam felt as though she were suffocating. She tried to breathe in, but terror had a grip on her body. She wasn't in control, physically nor mentally. Her body shuddered and when she finally sucked some air in, it gushed back out in a sob. She became hysterical. Tears streamed down her face, dripping onto the crisp white hospital sheet.

"What's happening?" Cam screamed. "Why are you doing this to me? *That* did not happen," she said, pointing at the television.

Dr. Franzen motioned for everyone to clear the room as Dr. Heisser tried to calm her.

"Hunter, no! Please don't leave me here with them. Please, Hunter. You can't believe them! It's a lie, please. You know me. You know this isn't the truth."

He hesitated for a moment before hurrying out of the room.

Cam sat helplessly watching as he passed the glass wall separating her from the rest of the world. "Noooo..." she screamed as sobs continued to rack her body.

Dr. Heisser handed her a tissue, then the entire box, and then he stared at her as if waiting for something to happen.

"What?" she snapped, blowing her nose and wiping her face. "That wasn't real. I'm not sure what the hell is going on here, but someone manufactured that nonsense to make me look schizophrenic."

He said nothing, did nothing, just continued staring at her.

"Are you just going to stand there gawking at me?"

"This hospital is far too reputable to 'manufacture' a video like the one we just watched. The video and your portrayal were real. You *do* understand that, right?"

"None of that ever happened!"

"Are you absolutely sure?" His tone remained soothing as he searched for clues about her mental health in her facial expressions, her words, and the way her body reacted.

She wasn't sure. She didn't remember a lot about the night before, but why would she ever claim her name was Jason Jonette? It was absurd, a disturbing revelation that wasn't true.

As she contemplated everything unfolding and Dr. Heisser observed her, Chief Michael Dwyer appeared, his body filling the doorway. The expression on his face was one of contempt directed at Cam and it made her fearful. He'd either watched the video or someone had told him about it. He took one step into her room and motioned for a uniformed cop to follow.

"Cameron Cooper," he started, "you are under arrest for the murders of Jennifer Saunders, Linda Birch, Amy Larsen, Adrianne Schechter, Medina Montan, and the attempted murder of Rhonda Saintil. Officer Bronson will read you your rights and I will make sure you spend the rest of your life in jail with hell to follow."

CHAPTER 45

Hunter wandered along the promenade, trying to clear his head and make sense of everything that had happened in the last twenty-four hours. He stopped and leaned his arms on the steel railing, looking out at the black satin water mirroring the skyline. He watched the water's gentle motion, and it brought comfort to him, soothing his raw nerves and calming his senses. The water always had a hypnotizing effect on him.

Life would never be the same. Everyone around him would demand Cameron's arrest. They would turn to him to slap the cuffs on her, and they would want it done as quickly as possible. No one would care that she might be sick. She was a cop killer, an unforgivable crime, no matter her state of mind. People would claim she'd faked her illness and was cognizant of her actions the whole time. It would be tough to prove that she had any mental disorder. Even the best doctors would find it difficult to provide solid, irreproachable evidence she was genuinely ill. And even if the leading experts in the human psyche testified that she wasn't in control of her actions, the police community would never accept it.

Hunter wasn't even sure he accepted it. When he'd realized it was a serial killer striking police personnel, he'd wanted to see the person responsible for his colleagues' deaths get the maximum penalty. Now that he knew that person was most likely Cameron, he wasn't sure what to think. He'd fallen in love with her, and his first instinct was to protect her, but somewhere inside of her hid a murderer. Or even worse, only a killer existed and the woman he loved was merely an illusion. The two couldn't be separated. They would either survive or die as one.

What if she's faking? The question had snuck into Hunter's mind, and it startled him. It was the question he tried to avoid beyond everything else, but his conscience wouldn't let him bury it any longer. What if? What if she was just a killer who liked to play games? What better cover up than to come into the police station and present herself as an expert, ready and willing to help solve the crime? She could keep abreast of the leads they had, the information they had gathered, and be forewarned if they were getting too close to finding her. It would give her the opportunity to throw them off her trail, place suspicion on someone else. What if, when Rhonda stabbed her, she'd come up with the elaborate scheme of multiple personalities because there was no way to explain her injury? And who better to fake such an illness than an expert in psychology?

He ran his hands through his hair and shook his head. The more he considered it, the more plausible it seemed. As the expert "profiler," she could steer them in any direction, creating the perfect serial killer to cover her tracks. She spoke, and he listened. Had she used his attraction toward her to her advantage? How could he be so stupid?

Hunter was no longer sure what was real. Confused and frustrated, he felt angry. There had to be a way to get her to reveal her true self. He needed the truth. Either she was mentally ill, or she was the perfect psychopath.

As he stood watching the water, he sensed he wasn't alone. He turned around to see Levine sitting on the bench behind him, watching him. Levine was the last person he needed in his face just then, but inevitably, the two would face off. Hunter didn't have the energy to do it at that point. He let out a heavy sigh, dropped his head down, and closed his eyes, praying that Levine would just leave him alone.

Levine didn't budge.

"Hunter," he said. "How are you doing?"

Hunter raised his head and looked at Levine to see if it was his friend who sat there or his lead detective. Reluctant, he walked over and sat down next to Levine. "Who's asking?"

Levine smiled and put his hand on Hunter's shoulder. "I am." He gave Hunter a tight squeeze.

Hunter's eyes moistened. "Not well."

"What can I do to help you?"

"I'm not sure there's anything to do," Hunter said, shaking his head. "This whole damn situation is impossible. The evidence points at Cameron committing these crimes, whether or not she knows it. There's no getting around that, is there? And when the forensic reports come back on the knife and the DNA samples from Rhonda's crime scene and the apartment next to Cameron's, I'm fairly certain what the conclusions will be."

Levine considered it. "Hunter, there's still a slight chance that she's innocent. Barone and Murphy are working overtime to check every fact. They're going over every inch of that apartment to see if they can find evidence of someone else playing a part in all this. You may be right. Someone could be setting her up."

"Come on, Glen, after what you witnessed in her hospital room? She told us her name was Jason Jonette, for God's sake! And then she asked for her mommy. My only worry at this point is that she's..." Hunter caught himself before he let the rest of the sentence fall out of his mouth.

"She's what?" Levine asked, studying Hunter.

Hunter leaned forward with his elbows on his knees, closed his eyes, and raked his long fingers through his hair. He didn't want to say the words aloud. He didn't want to admit that Cameron could be a cold-blooded killer.

"Hunter, you can tell me. I'm here as your friend. Whatever you confide in me will stay right here between us. What is it you're worried about?"

Hunter looked over his shoulder at his longtime friend. He trusted Levine, but he didn't trust himself to get the words out without falling apart. He took a deep breath and let it go. "I'm worried she's not sick." He sat back and looked Levine in the eyes. "I'm worried we were just pieces in her game. She kept us close to stay ahead." His voice trembled, and he swallowed hard. Cameron had trapped him on the thin line between hate and love.

"I fell in love with this woman. I haven't been so happy in a long time. On the one hand, I see the woman I love, and she's sick and she needs me. I don't want to turn my back on her. I want to help her. Maybe there's a cure and hope for her, for us. But the cop in me, that guy, he sees what everyone else sees: a manipulative, cunning psycho who murdered in cold blood. I'm not sure which one she is or if that's even a question. She could be both, and I can't separate the woman I love from the murderous bitch we met last night. What makes me even more furious is the idea that the woman I love *is* a murderous bitch, a disciple of Jonette, and they have always worked together."

Levine put his hand back on Hunter's shoulder and squeezed. "If that's the case, then we'll figure out a way to prove it. Do you want to know what I think?"

"Yeah."

"You may be on to something. She might be just some twisted freak who gets off on killing women who look like her. We're just aware of the people she's killed here. She could've been working with Jonette in Georgia, fooling the FBI. There might be a whole slew of missing women, and no one put their cases together because they weren't looking for the right connections. We need to take a photo of Cameron, put it into the missing persons bank, run facial recognition, and see how many women out there are missing and look like her. She...they could've been doing this for years."

Hunter was incredulous at Levine's words. He hadn't expected him to turn on Cameron that way. He stood up and took a few steps away from his friend, his heart pounding in his ears. Anger built from the center of his body, and his hands clenched into fists. It was one thing for him to say the words that Cameron might be guilty, but to hear Levine say it? It was too much.

"What the hell are you talking about? Did you see how scared she was? How upset? No one could fake that! No one is that good. I know that because I've been a goddamn detective for seventeen years and I can tell when someone is lying to me because I am fucking good at my job. I thought you were good at your job, too, but maybe that's where I've been wrong!" Hunter shouted the words at Levine and wanted to take out all his anger with one good punch to Levine's smug, ugly lying face.

"Are you sure? You're the one who just said it's possible she's faking. I'm just saying I agree," Levine said, shrugging.

"Fuck you. You don't know her the way I do. She would never have knowingly hurt those women."

"She didn't just hurt them. That bitch killed them—brutally murdered our friends and colleagues. Women who were daughters, wives, and mothers. How many children are out there who no longer have their moms? Suffering because of psycho Cameron?" Levine stood and faced Hunter toe to toe.

Hunter recoiled his arm and sent a fist right for Levine's chin, but Levine saw it coming and grabbed his arm, stopping Hunter just inches from his face.

"What are you doing? Huh? You going to hit me? Why, Hunter, huh? Why do you want to hit me? I'm not the person you should be angry at."

"Because you have no idea what the fuck you're talking about. I know it in my heart and soul that Cameron did not knowingly commit those murders. She's desperately ill and needs help."

Levine released Hunter's arm and put a hand on each one of his shoulders. "Well then, what are you doing trying to mess up my beautiful face? You answered your own question—'what if she's faking?' If you say you know in your heart and soul that she's sick, that she has multiple personalities or something, then I believe you, but the fact remains, sick or not, she's a killer and there will be consequences. You need to prepare yourself for what will happen next."

The anger drained from Hunter's body, and he embraced Levine, knowing what he'd just done.

Levine stepped back and continued. "Look, Hunter, five women are dead. That's a fact. The chief and everyone else in the department want blood. Cameron's blood. If you stand by Cameron, it may cost you everything—your friends and your job. I agree that all the evidence will point to her, and under normal circumstances, it would be a closed case ending with Cameron going to prison for the rest of her life. You see that, right?"

"Yeah, I do."

"Good. At least you're not completely unreasonable. But these aren't normal circumstances. It seems as if Cameron had some kind of mental break. But that doesn't make it any better. Even if they declare her incompetent, she's still guilty of murder. She may not end up in Bedford Hills, but she won't walk either. The court will remand her to a psychiatric hospital. I'm not sure which outcome is worse."

Hunter knew Levine was right. Cameron was going to prison. It was just a matter of where and when.

"If you feel she needs help, then you should go back to that hospital and see to it she gets it. If that were my wife up there, I wouldn't leave her side until the best doctors in the world came to help her. Now you go do the same for the woman you love."

"Thank you, Glen, for helping me work this through. I'm sorry I lost it there."

"When I left the hospital, the doctor had given Cameron a sedative to help her sleep. Take a breather, research what you can do to help her. You should also distance yourself from her. It won't do her any good if you're fired for sympathizing with a murderer. And you don't want to look complicit."

"Complicit!" Hunter's anger swelled again.

"Don't freak out. I understand you had nothing to do with the killings, but that doesn't mean everyone else will see it that way. Remember, they're out for blood, and the more blood, the better."

Hunter heeded Levine's words. If he attempted to help Cameron in any way, he would have to be careful. First, he needed the doctor's prognosis on her condition, and then he would figure out what to do next.

"I appreciate you listening. And I agree with everything you just said. Thanks again. I'm lucky to have a friend like you."

"Hunter, my friend, I've always got your back."

CHAPTER 46

THE ENTIRE PRECINCT WAS talking about the killer who had ingratiated herself into their lives, won their trust, and worked side by side with them during the day as she picked them off one by one at night. It was unreal to think about how many times she'd sat among them discussing the case and hypothesizing while sipping coffee and chatting like she was one of them. A comrade, a friend, a confidant, all the while spinning a web around them as she planned her next attack and chose her next victim.

Hunter heard the whispers, felt the stares, and was aware people stopped talking as he walked past or entered a room. He assumed they thought he was an idiot, or worse, that he was complicit. He kept his back straight, head held high, and the poker face of a veteran cop. Never let them know what you're thinking—that's what Thomas Riley had taught him.

He needed facts, and today he would get them. Today he would learn "for a fact" if Cameron had committed the crimes charged against her. Today, he would receive the DNA reports on Adrianne Schechter's Taser, Rhonda Saintil's knife, and the knife found in the apartment adjoining Cameron's. Today, he would have all his questions answered, or at least the easily answered questions, and then he would plan what to do next.

When he arrived at his desk, he found a case folder waiting for him. Inside were the answers Hunter needed, but not necessarily what he wanted. He opened the file, knowing it was the point of no return. He reviewed the reports, the DNA evidence, and the pictures from the crime scenes, and it all pointed in one direction and one direction only.

The police commissioner summoned all the detectives involved in the case, Hunter and Levine included, to meet in the conference room with Chief Dwyer at 1:00 p.m. Hunter gathered his files and reports from his team and tried to act normal. Murphy and Barone had done their due diligence. They had checked, double-checked, and checked once more that their findings were accurate. They wouldn't give the killer any loopholes to crawl through and out of jail.

Hunter was presenting their findings to the group of detectives gathered that day, the men and women who had worked overtime to catch a killer and would now want that killer to pay dearly. He would have to stand before the chief and all his colleagues and present the indisputable evidence that the woman he'd fallen in love with was a murderer.

He stood just outside the door of the conference room and listened to the conversations taking place. The anger was palpable. Hunter took a deep breath and entered the room as all eyes turned to him. It should have been a celebratory moment. They had caught a serial killer, but for Hunter, it was humiliating as his fellow detectives shot him looks and shook their heads.

Three hours later, Hunter sat and watched his friends and colleagues file out of the room, some giving him a nod, some a look of disdain, and one "good job, Detective," which came from Levine. Hunter was defeated and exhausted. It had been a grueling three hours going over the hard evidence, all of which pointed to Cameron as a serial killer, and now Hunter still had the worst part of the day ahead of him. He had to tell Cameron.

"I can't imagine how hard that must've been for you," Levine said, approaching the table in front of the room where Hunter sat. "You did an impressive job, and you were as professional as always."

"Thanks," Hunter said as he gathered his folders into a small box. "I have to be honest, I feel like shit."

"I'm sure you do. I don't envy the position you're in, but you did the right thing. Some of the others might still question you, but Murphy and Barone have your back." Levine waited for Hunter to meet his eyes, then added, "And so do I. Don't forget that, Hunter. I'm always here for my partner."

"Thanks, I appreciate it," Hunter said, rising to shake Levine's hand. "You're a great friend, Glen."

"Let's get something to eat, my treat."

Hunter shook his head. "I need to go to the hospital and explain all of this to Cameron. I need to see her reaction, look into her eyes, read her body language. My gut may say she's innocent, but let's face it, I'm biased and I'm compromised. I need to back up my instincts with facts. That's how I've always worked, and I won't change now. Everything here, in this box, proves her guilt to everyone who just left this room, but it can also prove her innocence."

By the time Hunter got to the hospital, it was late afternoon and the sun hung low on the horizon. He rode up the elevator, going over in his mind what he would say to Cameron. When the doors opened, he was met by Grace, the head nurse of the floor taking care of Cameron. She was a middle-aged woman with short, stylishly cut gray hair who had an air of authority about her. Her years of experience on this floor were obvious in the way she spoke and handled her patients. The younger nurses had concern about caring for an accused killer, so Grace had taken over. It was easier to do it herself than to have an already stressed staff pushed any further.

"Detective Finnegan," she said, giving him the once over. "Here to see Cameron Cooper?"

"Yes, I am," Hunter said. "How is she today?"

"She's been apprehensive most of the day. She's been waiting for you. The longer she waits, the more anxious she becomes."

"What makes you say that?"

"She's been asking about you all day. Sometimes it doesn't take a detective," Grace said, smiling at Hunter. "I take it you don't have good news?"

"No, not really. Is it okay if I talk to her?"

"Sure," she said, and the two walked together toward Cameron's room. "I can tell she's made some progress."

"Really? In what way," Hunter asked, afraid to get too hopeful too soon.

"She hasn't had any migraines since she's been on this floor. And the alter known as Jason Jonette has not appeared." They had stopped just outside Cameron's door. "And her leg is healing very well. The physical therapist has been in to see her and had her up and walking. She seemed to enjoy getting out of bed."

"I'm sure she did. Handcuffed to a bed all the time can't be comfortable."

"Hunter? Hunter, is that you?" Cameron called out from her room. "Please come in. I've been waiting for you all day. Hunter?"

Grace gave Hunter a brief squeeze on his arm and a smile. "If you need me, Detective, I'll be right here," she said, patting the spot she'd just squeezed.

"Thank you. I appreciate your help." Hunter took a deep breath and entered Cameron's room.

She was sitting up in the bed, the television on but no sound and the curtains open, revealing the blinking lights of the dark city outside.

"Hunter! Where have you been all day? I've been waiting for you. I was afraid...I would never see you again," she said, looking down at her blanket, unconsciously smoothing it with her hands. The chains of her handcuffs followed her movements like shiny snakes tethered to her.

"Hi, Cam. How are you feeling?"

"Good, thanks, but where were you?"

"I...I had meetings all day at the station. That's why I'm here. I have some information to go over with you. Your lawyer is meeting us here."

"Look at me, will you?" she said, raising her hands, chains dangling from her wrists. "The chief did this. He came in here with a cop and told me I was under arrest for murder! And then he handcuffed me to the bed! I didn't hurt anyone. You believe me, don't you? I've never hurt anyone, and if Rhonda Saintil said I did, then she's lying. She hasn't liked me since day one. I'm not a killer."

Hunter studied her face. She was angry, and all indications were that he was talking to the woman he knew as Cameron Cooper. "We should wait for your attorney. I'll be right back."

"No, don't leave! I've waited all day for you. Please, talk to me. Tell me what's going on. Tell me why Dwyer has done this."

Just as Hunter was about to walk out, a tall, trim, weathered-looking man in his sixties walked in, black leather briefcase in hand and a black cashmere coat folded over his other arm. "Good afternoon, I'm Andrew Westmoreland," he said, looking back and forth from Cameron to Hunter.

"I'm Detective Hunter Finnegan," Hunter said, extending his hand to Westmorland.

He was an elegant-looking man with a full head of white hair neatly trimmed close to his head, small, oval wire glasses sat on his nose, and a silver mustache framed perfect white teeth when he smiled.

"It's a pleasure to meet you. And you must be Cameron Cooper," he said, walking over to Cameron and shaking her hand. "I've been going over your case, Ms. Cooper. It's very interesting, indeed."

"Doctor," Cameron said, sitting up a little straighter in bed.

"I beg your pardon?"

"I'm Dr. Cooper, not Miss."

"I apologize, Dr. Cooper." Westmoreland placed his briefcase on a chair and draped his coat over the back. "Would it be all right if we kept it less formal? Please call me Andrew, and may I call you Cameron?"

"That depends. Who are you?" Cameron asked, looking the stranger up and down.

"I'm your attorney. I'm here to counsel you and to defend you in court if it comes to that."

"I didn't hire an attorney, so who hired you?"

Andrew gave Hunter a quick side glance and then stepped closer to Cameron. "An anonymous benefactor hired me. I'm assuming someone who cares deeply about getting justice for you," he said. "I advise you not to speak to anyone without my being present, and that includes Detective Finnegan."

"Hunter's my friend. I can tell him anything. And the only reason I haven't asked you to leave, Andrew, is because I recognize your name and I'm aware you're the best attorney in the city. Hell, maybe even in the country. But I can't afford you, so you might want to think twice about staying."

"Don't worry about legal fees. The only thing I want you to concentrate on is getting well. Now let's listen to what Detective Finnegan has to say."

This was it, the moment Hunter had been dreading, the moment he would lay out at Cameron's feet the reasons Dwyer had handcuffed her to the bed. "Cameron, I don't have to be here today, and this is very difficult for me. I could've sent Levine. Hell, I probably should have, but I wanted to be the one to tell you what the department's findings were. Do you remember I asked you about the apartment next to yours?"

Cameron nodded.

"A secret door adjoins the apartment next door to yours. Detectives thoroughly searched it for DNA and other evidence. In it, we found seven men's suits, seven pairs of men's shoes, and various other men's clothing items, all of which appear to be your size."

Cameron scoffed at this comment, and Andrew motioned to her to calm down.

"The DNA samples gathered from those items are a match to you. There were also photographs of the women murdered taped to the closet wall along with their stolen shoes. Your fingerprints are the only fingerprints on the photos."

"What? This is absurd! Hunter, would you listen to yourself? That can't be true."

"It's okay, Cameron," Andrew said. "Let the detective finish, please."

Hunter swallowed hard. The next one was the big one. He read directly from the report. "Investigators found a brunette wig with a matching beard and mustache in the bathroom. DNA matched that of Cameron Cooper. Officers also found a bloody knife in the basin. The fingerprints on the knife are those of Cameron Cooper and Rhonda Saintil. Blood on the knife matches Detective Saintil's blood, and the knife also had trace amounts of blood from two other victims."

Cameron sat staring at Hunter, her face flushed. Her jaw tightened and she gripped the blanket in tight fists.

"Test results from the blood samples collected at the scene of Rhonda Saintil's attack and where she counterattacked her assailant by stabbing him or her in the leg, concluded the blood belonged to Rhonda Saintil and Cameron Cooper. The blood found on the knife Detective Saintil used to stab her attacker is that of Cameron Cooper.

"And finally, the DNA evidence found on the Taser barbs used by Dr. Adrianne Schechter to defend herself against her killer matches Cameron Cooper." Hunter remembered the bed bug story, and anger welled inside him. It was clear to him now that the marks on Cameron's skin were a result of being Tasered by Adrianne.

There it was, all the proof in the world that a jury would need to convict Cameron of multiple murders and send her to jail for the rest of her life.

Hunter closed the file and looked at Cameron. She sat back in the bed, tears streaming down her face. He wasn't sure if she was angry or hurt.

"The handcuffs will remain on at all times until New York City Corrections officers transfer you from the hospital to jail to await trial."

"Thank you, Detective. Please make sure a copy of your findings is on my desk by first thing tomorrow morning."

"This copy is for you," Hunter said, handing the folder to Andrew.

"Hunter, how could you? You of all people? I expected you to have my back. I thought you would help me, protect me, but it seems like you've already convicted me." Cameron stared at Hunter, waiting for a response.

"I'm just here to state the facts that the New York Police Department's investigation has discovered. We still need to interview your doctors before we decide how to proceed. I can assure you, Cameron, that I am only seeking the truth and will see justice fairly served."

"Thank you, Detective," Andrew interjected. "If you'll excuse us now, I'd like to speak to my client in private."

"Cameron, I'm only doing my job. I'll be back tomorrow. I hope you have a good night's sleep. Andrew...good luck."

Hunter left Cameron with the best criminal lawyer money could buy, the lawyer he'd hired for her.

CHAPTER 47

Dr. Reid Heisser stood at the nurses' station, watching the woman in the bed on the other side of a glass wall wrestle with her restraints until it looked like she might cry. He walked over to the door, said something to the police officer standing guard, and entered the room.

"Hello," he said.

"Hi," the woman said, looking down at the blankets covering her. She sat in the bed, legs straight out in front of her. She appeared childlike, averting her eyes, her hair messy and unbrushed, and a light blue hospital gown hung limply around her slight frame.

"I'm Dr. Heisser. Do you remember me?"

"No."

"Do you mind if I sit down and ask you a few questions?"

"No." She pouted a little.

"Is there something wrong?" he asked.

She nodded her head up and down.

"Do you want to tell me?"

"Why are my hands tied up?" she asked in a small voice.

"So you won't hurt yourself or someone else." He waited for a response, but she said nothing as her lower lip quivered. "Would you like me to take them off?"

She nodded again.

"Okay. Let's make a deal. I'll take off the handcuffs, but you have to answer all my questions truthfully. Deal?"

"Deal," she said, not looking up.

Dr. Heisser put down his notebook, walked over to the cop, and asked him to open the handcuffs. The police officer complied and unlocked just the ones on her wrists, then returned to his post. Dr. Heisser sat down on the chair next to Cameron's bed.

"What about my feet?" she asked.

"Let's see how things go first, okay?"

"Okay," she said, not sure what he meant by "how things go."

"Let's start with names. I already told you, I'm Dr. Heisser. What's your name?"

"Angel."

"Angel. That's a beautiful name. How old are you, Angel?"

"Six. How old are you?"

Amused at the question thrown back at him, he answered, "I'm forty-eight. Angel, can you tell me where we are?"

"In the hospital. I hurt my leg."

"How did you hurt your leg?"

She shrugged. "George told me I got hurt. He didn't know a lot. He doesn't seem very smart," she said, whispering the last part.

Dr. Heisser smiled again. "Angel, do you know someone named Cameron?"

"Yes. She's my friend. I whisper secrets to her."

"Is she a nice person? Do you like Cameron?"

"Yes. She's very nice. She helps people like police officers do. But sometimes she needs my help."

"Why does she need your help?" Dr. Heisser asked, leaning in a little closer to see her eyes as she spoke.

"Sometimes, the bad man comes and tries to hurt her, and she needs me to help save her. And when she's scared, I talk to her."

"Who is the bad man? What's his name?"

"He told me not to tell you or else he'll hurt me. He thinks he can send me away forever, but Cameron won't let that happen. He thinks he can hurt both of us, but he's dumb. He can't hurt us without hurting himself and he won't do that because he's a bully. Bullies are always afraid of getting hurt. And that's why they're bullies! Mommy told me that!" She put her hands on her hips and nodded once. "If anyone will go away, it's him, just like the last bully who hurt us. Mommy sent him away forever."

Dr. Heisser scribbled, "Mommy?" in his notebook. Who was she? Another identity? Cameron's real mother? "Who was the bully that hurt you?"

"Mommy called him Kurt and Cammy called him Daddy, but I called him Monster, and he was mean. He used to hit us!" she said, her eyes wide. "We would hide in the closet, and I told Cammy to close her eyes, and I would protect her from the monster."

"What happened to Monster?" Heisser asked, writing it down.

"One day, Cammy was crying and calling me. She was in the closet, and Mommy was screaming. I didn't make any noise, but he found me. He grabbed me and yanked me out! I saw Mommy lying on the floor. She looked dead. I was soooo scared he would make me dead too, but Mommy called him. Kurt! Kurt!" she said, imitating Mommy. "He dropped me on the floor and then there was the biggest, loudest noise ever. And then it happened again. I covered my face and squeezed my eyes closed. Mommy picked me up and ran outside and said it was okay. She said Daddy was gone forever and would never hurt us again."

"Do you remember what happened next?"

"Mommy rocked me. She smelled good. Like Mommy. And that's all I remember about the day Kurt Monster went away." She folded her arms for effect and sat back in the bed.

"Angel, who is the bad man you were talking about before?"

"I can't tell you," she whispered.

"It's okay, Angel, I promise. No one can hurt you here. If you tell me about him, maybe I can make him go away."

"His name's Jason. He's a really bad man."

"Do you talk to Jason?"

"Sometimes, when he's being bad or trying to hurt Cammy, I yell at him and tell him to leave us alone."

"Does Cameron talk to him?"

"No. I don't think she can hear him."

"Why can't she hear him?"

"I don't know," Angel said, shrugging.

"Can Jason hear Cameron?"

"I don't know. Ask him," she said, rolling her eyes. "I'm tired, and I don't want to talk about this anymore."

"I understand you're tired, sweetie," Dr. Heisser said, patting her hand. "But the more you can tell me about Jason, the more I can help you and Cameron get rid of him for good. Okay?"

"Okay, but I don't want to do this anymore."

"Just a few more questions, I promise. You said Jason is bad and tries to hurt Cammy. What does he do that's bad?"

"He hurts people. He has a big knife, and he hurts them with it."

"You can see him do this?"

"No, but I can hear him do it. He thinks about it all the time."

"How does he try to hurt Cammy?"

"Ugh! Don't you get it?" Angel said, slapping a hand to her forehead. "He wants to hurt Cammy. He wants her to go away forever so he can be in charge, but he can't see her. He sees other girls he thinks are her, and he hurts them with his knife, but then he gets mad because it's not Cammy."

"Angel, how long have you known Jason?"

"Not very long."

"Do you remember the first time Jason spoke to you?"

"Yes. Cammy saw a dead lady in a room. Somebody hit her the same way Monster used to hit us, and she died."

"Do you remember when that happened?"

"No, but it was hot in the room. And the birds made a lot of noises outside."

Dr. Heisser jotted down the information in his notebook.

"Can you tell me how many girls Jason has hurt?"

"A bunch."

"More than two?"

She nodded.

"More than five?"

"I don't know, maybe."

"Is there anyone else who talks to you or Cameron?"

"Sometimes Charlotte, but she doesn't talk to me. She's a snob," Angel said, scrunching her face and sticking her tongue out.

Heisser wrote, "Charlotte." "Can Cammy hear you? Does she talk to you?"

"She hasn't talked to me in a long time. Only when we hid in the closet. But I think she can hear me when I talk to her. I want to watch TV."

"Okay, Angel, I'll let you rest. Thank you for talking with me. You've helped me a lot. I'd like to talk to you another day. Would that be okay with you?"

"Maybe," she said, shrugging.

"What if I bring you chocolate milk and a cookie? Then can we talk more?" Heisser asked.

"Let's see 'em." Angel grinned.

CHAPTER 48

"Gentleman, please come in and have a seat," Donna Franzen said to Hunter and Levine. "I'm sure you're eager to review our findings, and I'm sure you have many questions."

Hunter and Levine followed Dr. Franzen into her office, where Dr. Reid Heisser sat at a small round table in the corner, reading a file marked "Cooper, Cameron."

"Good morning, detectives," Dr. Heisser said, standing and shaking hands with both men. "I hope Dr. Franzen and I can be of some help to you today."

"Yes, so do we," Hunter said, sitting down across from Heisser.

Levine took the chair between them, and Dr. Franzen sat across from him.

"Where would you like to begin, Detective Finnegan?" Dr. Franzen asked.

Hunter gave Levine a quick look and opened his notebook, where he'd scribbled question after question. Levine followed suit, opening a leather-bound notepad and revealing numbered questions neatly written.

"First off, I need to remind you both that this is an ongoing investigation into the murders of five people and the attempted murder of a sixth person. We will notify the DA's office of any pertinent information discovered today and the DA may call you as witnesses at any trial that takes place. Understood?" Hunter asked, fidgeting with his pen.

"Understood," Heisser responded.

"We both understand," Franzen added. "And the two of you need to remember that as Cameron Cooper's doctors, we're obligated to protect our patient's privacy. The only reason we can speak to you today is because she has given us her permission, against her attorney's advice. We'll answer your questions to the best of our ability and knowledge, but mental illness is not an exact science. The mind is very complicated. We base our findings on experience and years of research that can sometimes be subjective. There is no physical proof to examine, such as when you fracture a bone. When a bone breaks, you can see the break in an x-ray, but when the mind fractures, there is no solid physical proof. It's a very complicated and drawn-out process assessing cases like Cameron's. It may take months or years of therapy to conclude if she allegedly committed crimes and why she may have done so."

"Yes," Heisser stated, nodding in agreement with what Franzen had just said.

"We just need confirmation that she consciously killed those women in cold blood or if she had no control and no memory as she states," Levine said, getting straight to the point. "Do you believe she has multiple personalities?"

Franzen glanced quickly at Dr. Heisser, since it was his area of expertise and caring for violent mentally ill people was what he did every day.

"We've diagnosed Cameron with dissociative identity disorder or DID. We don't use the term multiple personalities anymore. I've been visiting Cameron every day this week at varying times of the day," Heisser began. "And after extensive conversations with her, I've diagnosed four separate identities so far."

"Four!" Hunter interrupted. "What do you mean four?"

"And what do you mean 'so far'?" Levine asked, writing the information on his notepad.

"DID happens when there is a splintering of a personality, and two or more identities or 'alters' have control over a person's behavior. When one alternate takes over from another, it's called 'switching.' The alters can have different ages, races, and genders and can even be animals. There have been cases where patients present with twenty or more identities. There have also been cases where patients had over 100 separate identities," Franzen explained. "The dissociation means that one identity has no memory of what the other identities think, feel, or do when they switch. DID is a coping mechanism where the person needs to escape from a situation that is too traumatic, violent, or stressful for them to handle so an alter takes control."

"So, there could be more alters who are just as violent as Jason?" Levine asked, not sure he bought any of it.

Franzen and Heisser glanced at one another.

"We don't know," Franzen answered.

"This is what we've learned," Heisser said, picking up his file and reading from it. "There is Cameron Cooper, also known as Angela Cameron Chadwick. She's the primary identity, but over this past week, I have met three other identities or 'alters.' The first alter is Angel, a six-year-old girl who has been around for a very long time and is Cameron's protector. She keeps all of Cameron's worst memories. Angel appeared when Cameron was a child and suffered physical abuse by a parent. Cameron knows her stepfather abused her, but she has no memories of him beating her or her mother or of the night when her mother shot him to death. But Angel does.

"When Cameron becomes stressed or anxious, Angel whispers to her. Sometimes they're words of comfort and sometimes warnings. Then there is Charlotte Montgomery. She's tough to distinguish from Cameron Cooper, but if you pay attention, you can tell when you're speaking to her. She's in control of herself. She speaks softly and purposely, considering what she will say before she says it, whereas Cameron Cooper answers quickly and off the top of her head. Her posture differs from Cameron's. She sits up, back straight, head raised, hands folded in her lap. Charlotte Montgomery comes from a wealthy family with two loving parents who adore her and a picture-perfect childhood. She was even a debutante," Heisser said, looking over his glasses for the group's reaction.

The two detectives hung on his every word and Levine wrote quickly, trying to keep up.

"She's unaware of the other alters, unlike Angel, who is fully aware of them."

Hunter recalled Cameron vomiting at the office, the interview with Charlie Saunders, her encounter with Dr. Schechter, and realized he'd met Charlotte Montgomery.

"What about when she claimed her name was Jason Jonette?" Levine had grown impatient.

"Yes, Jason Jonette. That's a complicated alter," Heisser said, his brows furrowing as he looked at his notes. He dropped the file in front of him on the table and looked at the two men, considering what he would say. "The alter known as Jason Jonette is, as you know, incredibly violent. Cameron has no memory of what happens when Jason has taken command. He's egotistical and selfish and sees himself as the consummate hunter. He maintains that his only purpose in life is to kill. This alter, I can only assume, resulted from Cameron Cooper's near-death experience with the real Jason Jonette."

"You've lost me," Hunter said, rubbing his hands over his face. "Jason Jonette tried to kill Cameron, so she became him?"

"Let me explain," Heisser said. "People who suffer from dissociative identity disorder have many symptoms, including sleepwalking, amnesia, headaches, anxiety, time loss, and...attempted suicide. In fact, 70% of people with DID will try to commit suicide. When Cameron escaped from Jonette over ten years ago, he swore he would hunt her and kill her. People with this disorder can suffer from posttraumatic stress. On some level, the pressure and anxiety of living with the threat that Jonette would kill her became too much for her, and she became depressed and suicidal, but for Cameron, suicide would never be a choice. Her personality fractured again, creating the alter Jason Jonette, who is all too willing to kill her. He is a very strong alter and deems that if he can kill her, he will be the dominant identity.

"Now remember, I've only been observing Cameron for a week, but based on what I've learned this past week, it seems the alter known as Jason Jonette was trying to kill her but since he couldn't see her, he killed women who looked like her. The question is, why did she develop the alter that calls himself Jason Jonette?"

"The real question is, are you as deranged as she is?" Levine said. "Forgive my bluntness, but what you just said makes no sense. Does it, Hunter?"

Hunter had no answer. Cameron suffered from headaches, and sometimes she had no explanation as to why she didn't answer her phone for hours or would show up late at the precinct and pass it off as having lost track of time. She could be anxious and impatient. He questioned if any of it was real. "How easy would it be for someone to fake all of this?" he asked, dreading the answer.

"Oh, it would be very difficult," Heisser answered with Franzen nodding in agreement. "If someone wanted to fake having DID, he or she would have to be methodical in their actions, speech, what they did all day and how, where, and why they did what they did all day. Not just for themselves but for each identity they claim to have. Eventually, they would make a mistake, especially if they're under the scrutiny of a doctor trained in human behavior."

"Is there any way to tell for sure?" Levine asked.

"We'll hypnotize her. Patients with dissociative identity disorder are typically treated with hypnotherapy, and the alters respond very well to it. We'll also perform brain imaging, which sometimes verifies identity switching."

"Gentlemen, this is not a simple process. Remember, it could take months or years to diagnose her," Dr. Franzen added.

"What caused this to happen in the first place?" Hunter asked, more defeated than ever.

"It was most likely the abuse she suffered as a child. I'm sure that's when her personality initially fractured. She prayed to her 'angel' to protect her. And then, the alter called Angel took over and Cameron no longer remembered what happened when her stepfather beat her. That kind of trauma had a damaging psychological impact on her and then seeing her mother shoot her stepfather to death…it's a wonder she can function as highly as she has all her life," Heisser explained. "Regarding when the other identities manifested, it's hard to say. Only extensive therapy and time will provide answers."

"Is there a cure for this disorder, or will she be like this for the rest of her life?" Hunter asked, hoping for just a little good news.

"No, sadly, there is no cure, no pills to take. We can provide Cameron with long-term therapy and manage her anxiety and headaches with medicine, but there are no traditional drugs to treat her disorder. Our long-term goal is to purge the alters and unite them into one personality, Cameron Cooper. We're hopeful that someday, she'll function within the normal confines of society. It's my recommendation that if she makes enough improvement and is discharged, she never returns to law enforcement in any capacity. Any other questions, Detectives?" Franzen asked, checking the time.

"In your opinion, is she responsible for the murders committed?" Levine asked, blunt as always.

Heisser and Franzen answered concurrently, "No."

"Cameron Cooper is not responsible. Her alter, Jason Jonette, committed those crimes. Cameron Cooper has no memory of what happened and never will. She wasn't in control of her body when Jason took over and allegedly committed murder. It may have been her body, but it wasn't her conscious mind," Dr. Franzen said. "Cameron Cooper is not the person who committed murder."

CHAPTER 49

It was a beautiful, sunny day, as Hunter and Cameron walked through the park. They were smiling at one another, holding hands, and she carried a single white tulip in her free hand. She saw children on the playground laughing. Cam had never been so happy. Hunter unexpectedly embraced her, lifting her off her feet and swinging her around. As he put her down, he pulled her close to him and said, "Marry me."

Stunned and thrilled all at once, she said, "What?"

He laughed, then repeated, "Marry me, you beautiful, crazy serial killer, you."

Now she was just stunned. "What?" she said again.

He released her and pointed to a park bench a few feet away. Rhonda Saintil sat there in a white sundress, smiling at Hunter, but when she looked at Cam, her dress turned a deep crimson red as blood oozed from her. She grabbed her stomach with both hands, trying to stop the blood, but it only got worse. She fell to her knees and cried out to Hunter for help. He rushed to her, but it was too late. She lay dead on the soft green grass.

The children surrounded her and cried out in loud shrieking howls, pointing at Cam and screaming, "You killed Mommy."

The children closed in on her now and grabbed her clothes and hair, crying that they needed their mommy. Cam looked for Hunter to help her, but he and Rhonda were sitting on the bench together and she had on a wedding dress stained red. They looked at her and kissed, and then he picked her up and carried her away, once again lifeless. He stared at Cam and said, "Look what you've done."

She shouted, "I'm innocent," but the children wailed over her and Hunter didn't hear her. He disappeared, and Cam stumbled alone in the woods.

A shadowy figure stood next to a tree, and she backed away from the danger. She ran the other way, but her feet grew too heavy to lift and the stranger was catching up to her. She tried to scream, but no sound came from her as she frantically looked for Hunter, but all she saw was the danger. He was right in front of her, but a black hoodie concealed his face. He dragged it back, revealing her worst nightmare—Jason Jonette. She hit him and scratched him, but he laughed at her and took her hands in his. She watched in horror as her hands melded into his and became one. Now she wore the black hoodie.

"No, no," she cried, looking down at her hand and the jagged knife that dripped with blood.

Hunter's voice called her from behind.

She turned and found him holding out his heart in his hand as blood dripped from between his fingers. "Why? Why did you kill me?" he asked.

She screamed, and he vanished.

Now, alone in a dark closet and terrified, she heard her mother's frightened voice trying to protect her, but it was useless. The monster was coming, and she was helpless to his rage. Her body shook. She pulled a coat over her and closed her eyes, pretending to be invisible, but the monster knew she hid there, and he grabbed her by her hair and yanked her from her hiding spot. She saw her mother sprawled out on the living room rug, unconscious, bruised, and bleeding, and she screamed and squeezed her eyes closed so she wouldn't have to see her.

Hunter's voice once again called her, "Cameron. Cameron!"

She opened her eyes with a start, her heart pounding, her hair sticking to her sweaty face.

Hunter held her hand and brushed the hair from her cheek. "Hey, it's okay. Nightmare?"

Her body trembled as she attempted to throw her arms around Hunter's neck, but the handcuffs yanked them back to the sides of the bed. For a moment, she forgot her dream and forgot that she was in the psych ward and under constant scrutiny. She forgot she faced murder charges.

Instead of Cam embracing Hunter, he hugged her and whispered in her ear, "It's okay. I'm here and you're safe now." He opened the handcuffs and rubbed her wrists. After ten days, she still wasn't accustomed to them. Hunter took her hands in his, "You want to talk about your dream?"

"It was just a bad one. All the awful stuff in my head collided and merged," she said, taking a sip from the water he offered her. "Some part was happy, but I don't remember now."

Hunter moved to the restraints on her feet, as Dr. Franzen had said Cam only needed to wear them at night when the staff was light. He opened each one and then sat on a chair next to the bed. He looked like he wanted to say something, but he just didn't have the words.

"Is something wrong, Hunter?"

He smiled and averted his eyes from hers.

Hmm, not a good sign.

"Cameron, you're getting transferred this afternoon," he said, finally meeting her eyes.

She was afraid to ask where. *Are they sending me to prison? Probably solitary to keep me safe from the guards and the prisoners.* "Oh," was all she mustered to say.

"You aren't going to prison. It's not that bad," Hunter said, but it was obvious he didn't believe his own words. "Your attorney, the DA, and the judge met along with Dr. Franzen and Dr. Heisser, Levine, myself...and the chief. They showed the judge the video of your first night here, and he's declared you unfit to stand trial by reason of...insanity." Dwyer had almost gone insane over the verdict. "You're being remanded to St. Christina's.

You know, on the water by the fields. It will be a...uh...permanent situation."

"What? No, Hunter, they can't. I won't go. Where's my lawyer? I want to speak to Andrew. I demand a trial! Get me Andrew. This can't happen. Not Christina's." She swung her legs off the bed and stood in front of him, grabbing his hands and pulling at him. She needed him to understand the severity of the situation. She preferred prison to St. Christina's. She'd never been there but horrible rumors about it had circulated for years.

"You have no choice. The judge declared you mentally unfit to withstand trial. They'll help you get well there," he said, standing and looking over his shoulder at the nurses' station. "You'll have rehab for your leg and...and you'll get help."

"I've heard what they do to people there. They use 'secret experimental' therapies not approved by the government. They see the prisoners there as lab rats because most of them have committed violent crimes and they don't deserve the same treatment as other prisoners. The inmates at St. Christina's are insane and incurable, right? So it's no loss to society to do a little experimenting on them." She tried to limp away from him, but he held tight to her elbow.

He glanced again at the nurses' station and gave a thumbs-up to the on-call nurse, who noticed the movement in her room. "Cameron, you need to calm down, and you need to sit down. You know what will happen if the nurse thinks you're having an episode," he whispered the last word. "And Christina's is not that way at all. The city and state wouldn't allow it. You're letting your imagination get the best of you."

"Do you think I'm insane?"

He stared at her, expressionless.

"Wow. I guess you do."

"I don't think you're insane. I'm still processing everything that has happened."

"They diagnosed me with dissociative identity disorder," Cam said, slumping down onto a beige hospital chair, the cold vinyl covering a shock to her naked behind. "And when can I get some underwear back?" she shouted, tucking her hospital gown under her.

"Yeah, Dr. Franzen and Dr. Heisser tried to explain it to Levine and me," he said, ignoring her underwear comment.

"In lay terms, it means multiple personalities. Dr. Heisser will try to confirm it today after he hypnotizes me."

"What will happen?"

"I've never been hypnotized before, and if Dr. Heisser hypnotizes me and he's able to prompt other personalities to speak to him, then I guess I'll have to accept that I've got problems, serious problems. From what I've been told for the past week, only Angel has been around, asking for Mommy."

"Yes, we had a pleasant chat last night," Hunter said, amused.

"What does that mean?" Now he was just annoying her.

"Nothing. I just like seeing that side of you."

"Don't you understand, Hunter? These aren't 'sides' of me. These are manifestations of my subconscious brought on by a shitty childhood. If what Dr. Heisser and Dr. Franzen say is true, these 'personalities' are entirely separate from my conscious being. That's why I have no memory of what happens when they take over. I have no control. I didn't kill those women...not me in my right mind, anyway. I need to stop this from happening so I can try to live a somewhat normal life even if it's in a psychiatric hospital, but *not* St. C's."

"I'm sorry about St. Christina's. There's nothing I can do about it. That decision is made. Your lawyer argued for someplace up-state, but the judge wouldn't listen since Dr. Heisser works there and he asked to have you remanded there. He wants to help you."

"I guess I don't get a say in it since I'm the prisoner," she said, defeated.

"I'm trying to understand. Tell me how I can help you."

"You've been helping me by not turning on me, by supporting me. I can't say I'd do the same if our positions were reversed. After all, I accused you of being the killer. I even talked to Levine about it. How ironic is that? Me accusing someone else of being a killer?"

"Levine mentioned it. The trophy room was my wife's office. The trophies belonged to her."

"I'm so sorry, Hunter. I knew in my heart you weren't the killer, but logically it all sort of pointed at you. Ironically, every time I looked in the mirror, the killer looked back."

"Dr. Franzen said this may have started from a trauma when you were young. Is that what you meant by a shitty childhood?"

"Yeah, remember the little girl I told you about whose stepfather beat her and her mother? The mother shot and killed him?"

"Yes, I do." Hunter bowed his head.

"That was me," she whispered. "I used to hide in the closet and pretend to be invisible. My mother always got the worst of it. Occasionally, when she was too weak to fight back or unconscious, he'd come after me. I'm lucky I don't remember most of it. From what I've been told, Angel keeps those memories for me.

"I've been analyzing this a lot. Aside from the horrific truth that my mind and body allegedly went on a killing spree, the craziest part of all this is that I was actually trying to kill myself. Sure, it's not really me, but I have an alter that tried to kill me. And then there's Angel. She speaks to me sometimes. She's my protector, always warning me and whispering in my ear. I thought I was hallucinating her voice, but she's there all the time, in my head. She kept telling me, 'he's the enemy.' I assumed she was referring to you, but now I understand she meant the other identity. Dr. Heisser said Angel can hear...him."

Hunter silently listened to her ramble.

She could only imagine what he was thinking. She knew he realized how serious it was, and while she was grateful for his love and support, she felt as if she'd trapped him somehow.

"Hunter, this will be a lengthy process. If I really have DID, then there are no drugs, no pills to take to make it go away. Considering the crimes I've been charged with, it could be years, maybe never, before I'm deemed well enough to go back into society. You're not obligated to stand by me. I don't want you to ruin your career, or your life, for me. I want you to move on, okay?"

He looked past her out the window to the horizon. It was a beautiful, cloudless day in New York City. He seemed so serene sitting there, the morning sun shining on his handsome face. It wasn't necessary for him to respond, so she stood to go back to bed. She would have to be in bed, shackled, before Dr. Franzen came for her anyway. As she started, he slipped his hand into hers, the warmth from him a reminder of their nights together.

"No," he said.

She stopped, frozen. *No? No, what?*

"You aren't getting rid of me that easily." He took her hand and kissed the back before standing close to her. "I love you, Cameron, and I will see this thing through to wherever it takes us, no matter how long it takes." He pulled her closer for one tender kiss.

She wanted to melt into him. How could he stand by her? The force would ostracize him and even punish him for not turning on her. She wouldn't allow him to do it.

"Hunter, it's okay. I appreciate you standing by me, but you don't want the reputation as the cop with the serial killer girlfriend. And if they take me to St. Christina's, they may not allow you to even visit me. The things that they say I've done...they'll put me in maximum security. They've concluded I have no control over myself, and even I have to admit, it doesn't look like I do." The shock of self-awareness of her own crimes, even though she had no memory of committing them, was debilitating, and she needed to lie down.

She climbed into the bed, and Hunter sat next to her on the edge, intertwining his fingers with hers. It exhausted her constantly going over the crimes charged against her and why. She had the answer to what she'd done, but not the why. The question as to why and how she committed such heinous acts was a constant in her subconscious thoughts that haunted her day and night. Had she become the very thing she swore to bring down, an evil preying on the innocent?

"You need to condemn me publicly. If you don't, you'll lose your job and everything that you've worked so hard for. Even if you're not fired, you'll lose the respect of your colleagues. I'm right. It's okay, I promise."

Hunter sat playing with her fingers entwined with his own and kept his eyes down. He examined her hands, the hands he'd held so often as they strolled through the city, the hands that had held his face so lovingly, the hands that had blood on them from five murders. Hunter didn't want to admit she was right, but she was right. He took a deep breath and looked up at her with those beautiful green eyes that had mesmerized her the first time they met.

"After my wife died, I doubted I would fall in love again, but you brought hope back into my life." His eyes moistened. "I'm not capable of saying goodbye to you."

"I feel the same way, and that's why I have to let you go. We have no future. You said it yourself—it will be a permanent situation. I wish you all the love in the world that you deserve. So let's not say goodbye, let's just say see you later." Cam leaned in, kissed him gently on his lips, and held out her wrists for him to restrain them again.

Hunter took in a deep breath and, shaking his head, he placed a handcuff on each wrist. He moved closer to her and embraced her, squeezing her against his body as he stroked the back of her head with one hand. When he let go, his eyes were wet, and she touched his handsome face one last time.

"See you later, Detective Hunter Finnegan."

"See you later, Dr. Cameron Cooper."

He squeezed her hands, stood, and walked toward the door.

"Hunter? Don't forget, you have to denounce me. Just like any other case you've solved. The bad guy was caught and is being punished to the fullest extent of the law."

Hunter nodded, took one last look at Cam, and hurried away.

She made sure he'd left before she caught her breath, buried her face in her pillow, and cried.

CHAPTER 50

Before the press conference, Dwyer called Hunter into his office and told him to take a seat. Hunter had been dreading the moment he would have to answer to the chief, but it was inevitable.

"I'm hearing rumors, Hunter, rumors about you and our serial killer," the chief said. "Would you like to clear the air about those rumors?"

The chief sat back in his chair and looked uncharacteristically relaxed, his face expressionless, his hands folded on his round belly. Hunter had prepared, though. He'd expected his relationship with Cameron would be a topic of discussion at some point, and Levine had helped him prep for this conversation.

"I'll discuss anything you'd like regarding the case, but first you'll have to tell me what rumors you're referring to since I prefer dealing only with facts. I don't pay attention to or give rumors any credence." It was a dangerous verbal slap on the chief's hand, but Hunter had done nothing wrong and wouldn't let Dwyer treat him as the enemy.

Chief Dwyer leaned onto his desk with both elbows, lowered his head, and narrowed his eyes, his infamous look of intimidation. Then he chuckled before he started in the low voice he reserved for when he was pissed, "Don't fuck with me, Hunter. You know what I'm talking about. You were sleeping with the enemy. Holding hands and prancing around town with a serial killer."

"Is there a question you'd like to ask me, sir?" Hunter took a page out of Saintil's book, remaining stoic. He wouldn't let this guy intimidate him, even if he was his boss.

"Yeah, there are a few questions," Dwyer said, smirking at Hunter's audacity. "Were you and Cameron Stealth romantically involved while she killed our own people?"

"Yes, I was in a relationship with Cameron Cooper." The chief shook his head at Hunter's admission, but then Hunter continued, "But she's not a serial killer."

Michael Dwyer's eyes looked as if they might pop right out of his head as he slammed one meaty hand down, stood up, and leaned on the desk, face turning deep red. Now he was angry. "Whose hands plunged a knife into five of our colleagues' guts? Whose fingerprints were found on the knife that killed our friends? Whose blood was found at the scene where Detective Saintil counter-struck her attacker, our serial killer?"

Hunter took his time and reflected before he answered. He examined the chief's face, noticing the deep red it had turned, the eyebrows furrowed in anger, the vein bulging near his temple. *Perhaps it'll blow, and I won't have to answer.* "The answer to all your questions is Cameron Cooper. However, her doctors agree that she wasn't responsible for the deaths of our friends and colleagues. She's sick with a psychological disorder. She has no memory of attacking anyone." Hunter thought for sure Dwyer was about to jump over his desk and wring his neck.

"Prove it," Dwyer said in a low, menacing voice.

"Did you read Detective Saintil's statement regarding the person who attacked her?"

"Yes."

"She stated that her attacker was a lefty. The doctors also testified to the judge that the alternative personality known as Jason Jonette is left-handed. Cameron is right-handed. Furthermore, under hypnosis, Dr. Heisser communicated with the alter, Jason Jonette, who admitted to killing those women. Dr. Heisser swore, under oath, that Cameron Cooper was not faking her disorder. She's just as much a victim as everyone else."

"A victim, huh? A victim that's still alive, unlike the actual victims." Dwyer sat back down in his chair. "Cameron Cooper is getting away with murder. What I want to know now is how deep in are you?"

"I don't understand."

"There are rumblings in the department that you may be complicit. How do you carry on an intimate relationship with someone, clueless she's a killer? Are you so in love with this woman that you protected a murderer?"

"I was the one who discovered the apartment adjoining Cameron's. I was the one who was there when she announced her name was Jason Jonette. My team gathered the evidence resulting in Cameron's arrest. I've done nothing to obstruct justice. I've worked day and night to get justice for those who died at the hands of Stealth. Your question is out of line and insulting." Hunter was the one getting angry now. He wouldn't allow the chief to intimidate him, and he wouldn't betray Cameron.

"And yes, I'm in love with her, which makes this entire situation painful and difficult for me, but I'm acting with nothing but professionalism. I've put my badge before my personal feelings. The woman I love is incarcerated in one of the most dangerous psychiatric hospitals in the country, and there is nothing I can do about it. And I lied to her about it. I told her it wasn't so bad. I can't even visit her. Imagine what that would be like if it were someone you loved."

Michael Dwyer listened, really listened, to Hunter's words. He sat back, satisfied that Hunter wasn't complicit, especially since, as he'd said, the judge had sent Cameron to a psych hospital, a place probably worse than any prison.

"This is how this will play out," Dwyer started. "You will be at the press conference. In fact, you will be the one briefing the press. You will only give the facts of the case. There will be no personal interjection of any kind. You will not admit to having a private relationship with Cameron Cooper.

You will explain that she is unfit to stand trial and is incarcerated at St. Christina's State Hospital for the Criminally Insane. If, at any point, you even hint that Cameron was not responsible for her actions, I will not just fire you, I will make your life a living hell. Do we understand each other?"

"Yes, sir." Hunter had no choice, he had to do what the chief demanded, and he had to do it for Cameron.

Forcing Hunter to stand before the press and name Cameron as the Stealth Stalker was the chief's way of punishing him, a power move to remind Hunter who was in charge and that he was lucky not to be facing charges of his own. The time had come to face his punishment. Hunter had prepared a statement, and he intended to read it and turn the podium back over to the chief. He wouldn't take questions from the reporters waiting for him to speak.

Thirty minutes later, Chief Michael Dwyer stood before the reporters gathered at his request, opened his arms wide, smiled smugly, and announced, "It's a beautiful day in New York City. We have caught a serial killer, justice is served, and the perpetrator is imprisoned for the rest of her life."

Camera shutters clicked, murmurs erupted, and hands flew into the air as reporters who had waited patiently for the press conference to start all tried to get their questions answered first.

Chief Dwyer held his hand to them in a stopping motion. "I spoke to Mayor Wallace this morning, and he expressed that his office, the city council, and the people of New York are indebted to the New York Police Department for ending this nightmare before anyone else suffered at the hands of this cold-blooded killer. I'm sure you have a lot of questions, so I will turn the podium over to my lead detective, Detective Hunter Finnegan, who, with his team and the special teams assigned to this case throughout the precinct, has worked tirelessly around the clock to solve this horrendous crime spree and bring a killer to justice."

Dwyer stepped to the side to give Hunter room to step up to the podium, and as Hunter passed him, Dwyer whispered, "Remember what we discussed, Detective."

Hunter stepped up to the microphone. "Good afternoon, I am Detective Hunter Finnegan. After months of investigating, we have caught the serial killer known as the Stealth Stalker. Thanks to the evidence our detectives gathered, eyewitness accounts, and the survival of the last victim, we arrested and charged Dr. Cameron Cooper in the deaths of Jennifer Saunders, Linda Birch, Amy Larsen, Medina Montan, and Adrianne Schechter, and the attempted murder and assault on Rhonda Saintil.

"After consulting with the District Attorney, Dr. Cooper's attorney, and experts in psychiatry, a judge has deemed Dr. Cooper unfit to stand trial. As of this afternoon, Cameron Cooper is remanded to St. Christina's State Hospital for the Criminally Insane, where she will remain indefinitely or until doctors diagnose her well enough to stand trial.

"We, the brothers and sisters of the NYPD, send our deepest condolences to the families of our fallen comrades. We hope that the arrest and incarceration of Cameron Cooper can bring closure to the families and rest to the souls of the fallen. I want to thank everyone involved in solving this case and bringing a killer to justice."

Hunter turned to walk away as Chief Dwyer stepped in front of him, blocking his way.

"Well said," Dwyer said, grabbing Hunter's hand and shaking it in a show of accord for the press. "I should make you field their questions, but since you look like shit, I'll have a heart and let you go. Just remember that what we discussed today has no expiration date. You will always maintain Cameron's guilt."

Hunter walked away from the reporters shouting questions, the chief and his intimidation tactics, and his colleagues now satisfied that he was the cop they had always known him to be. Dwyer would handle the press, his coworkers would move on to the next case, and he would once again have to adjust to losing an important person in his life, for now anyway.

He headed straight home, poured himself a scotch, and stood looking out over the city he loved as the sun set on it. He reflected on everything that had happened from the first time he'd met Cameron. She made him feel self-conscious and nervous, something tough to accomplish. He could see her face blush as he handed her shoe to her when she slipped on the stairs, those blue eyes that seemed to study every inch of his face, and if he closed his eyes, he was sure he smelled vanilla and coconut.

He hadn't been aware then how much she'd been through in life. The abuse as a child, seeing her mother shoot her stepfather to death, being kidnapped by a psychopath, and living with the threat he would be back to kill her. The daily stress of a job that constantly reminded her that the world was an ugly place, all of it silently chipped away at her psyche until it all became too much.

She was smart, fierce, and gentle. She was everything to him: a friend, lover, confidante. He was no longer alone in a city where loneliness was practically an epidemic. Everything they had built together had come crashing down, but then again, it hadn't been built on a strong foundation.

Hunter thought about Chief Dwyer and his threats, his conversation with Levine about how he needed to distance himself from Cameron, and his last conversation with Cameron, in which she'd told him in no uncertain terms he needed to walk away. They were all, in their own way, looking out for him, reminding him he still had a future where he would need a job and the support of family and friends.

When Hunter had walked out of the hospital, a dull ache pulled in his chest. It had hurt his heart to say goodbye to her. He couldn't do it, he wouldn't do it, and now he realized that his job as a detective was the answer. The job that everyone kept reminding him was so important, that job that would give him access to St. Christina's and to Cameron. He would use his position as a detective to keep Cameron in his life, even if it meant keeping it a secret from everyone. To support her and stand by her was the right thing to do. One day he would see her well and free again. It didn't matter to him how long it took, how many obstacles were in the way, or what others whispered. Their love for each other was strong enough to withstand the wait.

Hunter raised his glass as the last moment of sunlight faded and the city turned into a sparkling gem with the flicker of a million lights and made a toast, "See you soon, Cameron Cooper."

EPILOGUE

St. Christina the Astonishing was the patron saint of millers, psychiatrists, and...the insane. The nightmare that swallowed Cameron was fittingly called St. Christina's State Hospital, a maximum security forensic mental hospital. She'd heard rumors, but some were too scary to think true. Now she discovered firsthand what happened behind the walls and bars of St. Christina's.

She'd been assigned to the tenth floor, which offered standard amenities such as individual rooms with steel doors locked tight overnight; bars on the windows, inside and outside just for good measure; and armed guards who knocked you on your ass first and asked questions later. The impenetrable cell doors were unlocked first thing in the morning, and patients roamed the floor because, after all, it was a hospital and not a prison. A creamy white paint set the walls apart from the light blue linoleum flooring, which ran throughout the entire unit, and the sickening odor of bleach mixed with urine permeated the air. Shatter-proof glass enclosed the nurses' station. Guards watched every move via closed-circuit cameras mounted in every corner, and the employees wore personal alarm buttons.

While the entire building was maximum security, there were different levels of security, and Cameron was remanded to the highest security unit for three months. After that time, the doctors would evaluate her and determine if she was eligible for transfer to another floor not as severe. Just two weeks shy of her three months, an incident occurred involving a sadistic aide who wanted to meet her alters, and sadly, Jason happily obliged. The aide didn't die, thankfully, but she spent quite some time in an ICU recovering. It pushed back Cam's evaluation another three months and put her under even closer scrutiny since an employee had been involved.

Cameron had therapy three times a week with Dr. Heisser and physical therapy for her leg once a week. Heisser and the physical therapist were the only people she had actual conversations with for three months. When PT ended, it was just Heisser. Then one day, a miracle happened. After six months, they finally moved her to the ninth floor, still maximum security but for the less violent. And she had a visitor.

"Hello there." Hunter Finnegan stood before her in the cafeteria with a bouquet of tulips, her favorite.

"Hunter," she exclaimed. "How did you do this? How did you get in here?"

"I've stayed in contact with Dr. Heisser," he said, motioning for her to sit. "He arranged the visit today. He said if it went well, we could make visits a regular occurrence. He's optimistic it will help with your...recovery."

Hunter was still uncomfortable talking about her condition. He was sweet to visit her even after she'd told him to stay away. And Dr. Heisser was right, his visits helped. Her depression lifted now that she had something to look forward to. Seeing his handsome face and talking to him was the best medicine. That first visit turned into a second one, and after a few months, Hunter visited her bi-monthly. Every other Saturday, at 3:00 p.m. sharp, he arrived smiling and happy to see her.

Someone is happy to see me.

After a year at St. Christina's, Cameron had learned a lot: never (ever) make eye contact, stay in your own room as much as possible, be the last one for dinner (the kitchen staff always saved her a plate), mind your own business, and never give up hope.

Hunter had taught her to never accept defeat. He was determined to see her healthy and free someday. He saw possibility where she saw none. He had hope when she felt despair. He would give her strength to work harder and take back her sanity.

During their last visit, Hunter did something Cameron had never expected—he offered her a job. She would work within the constraints of St. C's, but she would use her expertise as a criminal psychologist to investigate a case. She had a chance to give back, make amends for the misery she'd caused, and she would contribute something positive to the city she'd devastated.

And she would work with Hunter.

Cameron Cooper's fractured mind left her imprisoned in a concrete and steel monster with no hope of freedom ever being offered to her. Hunter Finnegan stood on the other side of those walls, chipping away until he found a way in. He wouldn't rest until he took Cameron's hand and brought her into the light, healed and whole. In the meantime, there was a serial killer to catch.

The Chelsea Choker wanted to play, and Cameron Cooper knew all the tricks.

Acknowledgments

Thank you to my husband, Kevin, for being my very first reader and having the courage to tell me what you didn't like as well as what you did like. And for being my biggest supporter and champion.

Thank you to my life-long friend Lillian for the thorough critique and recommendations on improving my book and professional feedback on too many covers. And thanks to Thomas for taking the time to read my book and answering all of my questions honestly.

Thank you to Tom, Lisa, Mary, Bob, and Susan for keeping my secret and being the most supportive (and fun) group of neighbors ever! And for all of your positive support and enthusiasm.

Thank you to Dave Chesson of Kindlepreneur for all of your hard work and advice that you offer to writers like me. You are my go-to source for anything about writing a book.

And always, thank you to my children, Colin, Kirsten & Kyle. Without your encouragement and support, none of this would be possible.

C.S. Dodds is the pen name of Christine Dodds. She has loved books for as long as she can remember. When she was a small child, her mother took her to the library weekly where she would renew the same book over and over – *And To Think That I Saw It On Mulberry Street* by Sr. Seuss. Looking back, it's unclear why her mother didn't just buy her the book. Eventually, her sister would purchase the book for her - when she graduated from college!

A lover of psychological thrillers and suspense, writing her own book has been a long-time dream of Christine's. Over the years, she has started and stopped writing several books, always caving to that inner voice of doubt. Until one day, she followed her dreams, and wrote a book. *Fractured*, her debut novel, is that book.

Christine was born in the West Village of New York City and currently resides in New Jersey. She is married to a man who was her first-grade crush. They have three children, who they are very proud of, and who certainly make life interesting.

Did you enjoy reading *Fractured?* If so, please send Christine an email at christine@csdodds.com She would love to hear from you.

Reviews are the lifeblood of authors. Please consider leaving a review at:

https://www.amazon.com/author/c.s.-dodds

https://www.goodreads.com/author/show/22653778.C_S_Dodds

Check out Christine's website to get updates about new releases and to join her mailing list at: www.csdodds.com

On the following pages, please enjoy a short excerpt from the next book in the Cameron Cooper series, *Justice & Redemption: The Chelsea Choker.*

JUSTICE & REDEMPTION
The Chelsea Choker

I'M ON A MISSION tonight to do the bidding of my mentor, my champion, my hero, the only person in the world who understands me and listens. He has taught me everything I know—patience, skill, persistence, and the most important factor—no remorse.

Jay knew me before we even met. He knew my loneliness, my desperate need for attention and love, my yearning to belong somewhere, to someone. He had appeared when I was at my lowest. Homeless, living on the street, afraid every night, and hungry.

It was a simple gesture. He'd asked if I wanted to join him for dinner at a diner around the corner from where I hid in the shadows. I'm not even sure how he saw me. I'd thought I had done an expert job camouflaging myself from the strangers who passed by every day, but he'd looked right into my eyes as I peeked through the cardboard box I called home.

Hungry and stretching my dollars, I'd agreed to go because I knew he could do nothing to me in such a public place. Besides, we were about the same size, and I thought I would be a good match for him if he got any ideas. I heard people on the streets sometimes did favors for others for money or food or just a human touch. I wouldn't go there. Prostitute myself out of need. I was on the street because I sought my independence. I wanted to be in control of myself, not constantly doing what others told me to do. So, I went with him, but I made sure the terms were clear.

"Just dinner, right?"

"Yes, just dinner. And conversation, is that okay?" he had asked.

"I guess it depends on what you want to talk about. I don't answer questions I don't want to, got it?"

"Agreed," he'd said.

We'd gone around the corner to the diner, where we sat in a corner booth. Jay hung his jacket on a hook on a post separating the stalls, and there we sat, looking one another over.

"My name is Jay. What's yours?"

"Max." I don't know why I'd told him the truth. I looked around. There were enough people in the diner that I'd felt safe if this guy was a perv.

"Hello, Max. It's very nice to meet you. Would you like to hang your jacket up?" He'd motioned to where his own black jacket was hanging.

"No, I'm good. I'll just put it here." I'd nodded to the red vinyl seat next to me as I wiggled my arms free of my jacket sleeves.

The waitress had come over with two glasses of ice water, tossed two straws on the table, and handed a menu to each of us. She didn't seem to notice I wasn't exactly the cleanest looking person in the place. "You need a minute?"

"Yes, thank you," Jay had answered.

He'd opened his menu and looked it over. I opened mine and pretended to read it, but I was looking at him. There was nothing special about the guy—middle-aged, white guy, gray in his hair and beard—his beard sprinkled with more grey than his head, small black-framed glasses that sat right at the bridge of his nose, which was straight and proportionate to his face. Just your average guy. He dressed well, probably had money, and had a soft southern drawl when he spoke. I couldn't figure out what was happening. Was he just a friendly guy doing his good deed for the week, or was there something more dangerous happening and I just couldn't see it yet?

"What looks good to you, Max?" Jay had put down his menu, slid the paper off a straw, and placed it in a glass, taking a sip.

I did the same. Picked up a straw, stripped it of its paper wrapper, plopped it in the other glass, and took a long, steady drink. I was thirsty and the icy water felt good going down my throat.

I'd asked, "Is there a limit?"

"What do you mean?"

"To how much I can spend?"

Jay had laughed a little. "That's very considerate of you, Max, and no, no limit. Order whatever you like."

The waitress came back just then.

"Are you ready, or do you need a few more minutes?"

"I believe we are ready. Right, Max?"

I'd nodded my head yes.

"I'll have the turkey dinner special and a cup of coffee. Max?"

"I'll have the cheeseburger deluxe with regular fries and a coke."

The waitress took our menus and trotted off.

He'd sat there looking at me with a grin on his face. I have to admit it was a little creepy, but I was used to creepy. People called me creepy.

"Would you mind telling me about yourself, Max? Where are you from? How did you end up living in a box on the street?"

"I don't know," I'd said, shrugging my shoulders.

"You don't know what? Where you're from or how you ended up homeless?"

I didn't want to answer a bunch of questions. For all I knew, he was a cop or a private detective sent by my crazy father to find me. That thought had made me smile. My father couldn't give a shit where I was—he would never spend money to find me.

"I choose to live on the street. It makes for good people watching."

"It must get scary sometimes, not to mention cold and... lonely."

"I have plenty of friends. The homeless are their own community—we look out for each other." I'd lied. I didn't talk to anyone, make eye contact with anyone, or accept anything from anyone unless they dropped it at my feet. Like this one time, this guy was going around handing out socks and baggies filled with toiletries to all the vagrants. When he got to me, he'd squatted down in front of me and tried to start a conversation. I didn't even look up. He gave up and left the stuff on the ground next to me. When he was out of sight, I grabbed the baggy and socks and put them in my secret hiding spot.

"How long have you been here in the city?"

"Long enough. How long have you lived here?" Let's see how he likes a million questions—I'm full of them.

The waitress had come back with our drinks and dropped another straw on the table for my coke. That one I didn't open. I'd save it for another day, another use. Jay took his coffee black, which hadn't surprised me. His slim physique made me think he didn't enjoy sweets, so no sugar in his coffee.

"I just moved here recently from the south. My work has brought me here rather unexpectedly."

"What do you do?" I didn't care what this asshole did, but if I asked the questions, I was in control of the conversation.

He'd sat looking at me for a few seconds, which made me uncomfortable, and then he answered.

"I'm an appraiser."

"What do you appraise?"

"I can appraise almost anything, but I work mostly in the fine arts. Paintings and sculptures."

"Oh." My disinterest had oozed from every pore.

The waitress slipped our plates in front of us and asked if we needed anything else. Jay answered no, and she moved on to the next table. I was starving, but I didn't let him see it. I'd inspected my burger—lifted the bun, took off the tomato and lettuce, added some ketchup, put the bun top back on, and cut it in half. I'd taken my time taking that first incredible delicious bite, the juice and grease from the meat running down my chin, the gooey cheese mixing in with the bread and the burger in my mouth—it was heaven. And it was all I could do not to moan as I'd washed it all down with a slurp of my soda. *My God, this might be the best damn burger I've ever had,* I remembered thinking.

"How's your food?" he'd asked. "Any good?"

"It's okay," I'd said with a mouth full of ketchup and perfectly cooked French fries, as only diners seem to know how to do—crunchy on the outside and tender on the inside. I'd looked around, feigning boredom with the whole scene, but really, I'd been excited to be having my first hot meal since I couldn't remember when.

He'd seemed amused as he ate his own dinner. I'd noticed how he cut his meat, put some stuffing on top, a little cranberry sauce, and finally stabbed a green bean with his fork before stabbing the entire pile and eating it. The perfect bite. He did that with every bite until he finished the last morsel.

Conversation was sparse while we ate. Jay tried once more to get me to spill my guts, but I would share nothing personal with him. I still couldn't tell if he was some kind of freak or not. Now I realize how lucky I was that night.

The waitress came back and asked if we wanted dessert.

"Chocolate cake," I'd said. She nodded her head as she wrote. "To go. And a tuna sandwich," I added. I'd glanced quickly at Jay to see his reaction. There was nothing, not even a blink.

"And you, hon? Refresh your coffee or something else?" She nodded her head in Jay's direction.

"Yes, a little more coffee, please. But no dessert."

I'd wanted to get out of there, but I wanted that chocolate cake, so I sat fidgeting, waiting for the cake. I slipped my jacket back on so I could make a fast exit when the waitress came back. This guy knew where I slept, and I needed to move somewhere else. It was easy to move when your home was already in a box.

The waitress returned, but only to refill his coffee, and she waddled off again. I couldn't help but notice her colossal ass. It was some behind she had. It seemed to move separately from the rest of her body as it jiggled and wiggled under her waitress uniform, contrary to the rest of her body. Momentarily, it had amused me, but then I'd sat impatiently, trying not to make eye contact with Jay, wishing the food would come already.

He sipped his coffee and peered over the rim at me. I'd felt his eyes on me, examining me, trying to pry into my brain.

"Thanks for dinner. It was good," I'd offered.

"Your welcome. And thank you for joining me. I don't enjoy eating alone; it was nice to have a sinner companion."

"What?"

"It's nice to have someone to eat dinner with."

Oh, dinner.

The waitress had returned with a brown bag. I'd stood, taking it from her hands, and looked at Jay. "Yea, it was cool. Well, bye." I headed for the door before he could say another word.

That was months ago, and since then, things have changed. Jay gave me projects to undertake at his command. The mission tonight was a soccer chick. I watched her play on the brightly lit field down by the piers. She's number seven and moves well. The muscles in her legs defined, her dirty blond hair pulled back in a ponytail, her face pink from exertion. Her team was winning thanks to a goal she just scored. My job was to swap my Poland Spring water bottle, that I held with the sleeve of my sweatshirt so as not to leave any fingerprints, with her identical bottle. Jay spiked the water in my bottle with a sedative.

Patience was the first thing Jay had taught me. I watched like any good fan as I inched closer and closer to Seven's gym bag which was thrown on the ground next to the field. Following the action of the game, I moved to either side of the bag. No one paid any attention. They were concentrating on the fast-paced game. Her team was in place to score again, and I got ready to swap the bottles. I stepped closer to her bag, and it happened. They scored. I threw my hands up in the air, pretending to cheer, and 'accidentally' dropped my bottle on top of her open bag. I bent over and picked up Seven's bottle instead. Standing up again, I clapped my hands for the team, taking a swig from it, just as if it were my own. It was too easy. I retreated from the area, keeping my head down to avoid any cameras, and found a place to wait for her near the exit.

The game ended, and I watched Seven head to the sidelines. She sat down on the turf next to her bag, took a quick sip from the bottle I dropped before replacing her cleats with a pair of flip flops. She chatted with her friends as they gathered their belongings and then she took a nice, long drink. The women walked casually toward the exit as the next game got underway. A few hung back to watch the game start, two others headed toward the porta-john as my intended walked toward the gate alone.

Seven exited onto the sidewalk, took a left, stopped for a moment as she finished the water, and threw the empty plastic bottle into the trash. I watched as she searched in her bag and pulled out her phone. She started down the sidewalk again as she checked her messages. I followed a few feet behind, knowing the drug in her water would hit her hard and fast, and it did. She swayed and staggered to the chain-link fence that surrounded the field. She dropped her phone and almost fell over trying to pick it up. No one else noticed the woman having a hard time standing. I stepped in quickly.

"Hi—are you okay? I'll get that." I bent over and picked up her phone.

She looked at me, her eyes half-closed, watery. Her chapped lips parted as her jaw slackened and she struggled to draw air. She leaned against the fence to keep herself upright, her body betraying her, morphing from solid muscle to a fluid mass.

"Here, let me help you." I took her arm around my neck and pulled her close. Her feet dragged along the cement. "Let's find someplace for you to sit." I helped her along the dimly lit sidewalk. Passerby's paid us no mind. People in cars passed us, clueless as to what was happening.

We came to the corner where there was a small park area at the end of the stadium. I steered her into it and over to some full bushes. She could barely stand as I eased her onto the ground and laid her on her back.

It was so easy. So much easier than Clara and Wayne, which was messy, even though I don't remember whacking at them. I do remember what it looked like when I was done, so much blood everywhere, on the floor, the couch, the ceiling... everywhere. And it was easier than my first with Jay.

The nerves were calm. The doubt eased. The guilt quieted. I knew what I was doing now as I slipped the silky blue ribbon around her neck, and how to do it efficiently, quickly, silently.

COMING SOON!

Follow Christine at www.csdodds.com for updates!

https://www.amazon.com/author/c.s.-dodds

https://www.goodreads.com/author/show/22653778.C_S_Dodds